FEATHER OF

MA'AT

Liminal Books

Liminal Books is an imprint of Between the Lines Publishing. The Liminal Books name and logo are trademarks of Between the Lines Publishing.

Copyright © 2023 by Lisa Llamrei

Cover design by Cherie Fox

Between the Lines Publishing
1769 Lexington Ave N, Ste 286
Roseville MN 55113
btwnthelines.com

First Published: September 2023

ISBN: (Paperback) 978-1-958901-56-4

ISBN: (Ebook) 978-1-958901-57-1

Library of Congress Control Number: 2023942123

FEATHER OF

MA'AT

Lisa Llamrei

This book is dedicated to:
Norma Thurston

My eighth-grade English teacher, and the first to take on the thankless task of teaching me the rules of creative writing.

Journey to the Duat
Part 1

I spin around to confront my assailant, but he is not there. I am not in my apartments. How he spirited me away, I do not know, but I shall not let it pass. I call for my bodyguard, but my voice is swallowed by the great chamber. No one answers.

A chill washes over me as I take in my surroundings. The ceiling is painted black with white stars, the walls with spells to help me pass through the gates of the Duat. The pillars are painted with my own image beside those of the gods. A sarcophagus dominates the room. Shaking my head, I step back. My breath is rapid, my heart pounds inside my chest. I cannot be here.

My arms are bare, as are my hands and fingers. And my neck. All of my jewelry, gone. I am dressed in a simple white linen shift. I look to the sarcophagus and laugh. I have been foolish. This is not real. It is a trick. One small step at a time, I approach the sarcophagus. The beaten gold is covered with more spells and my name. The doors are sealed. Someone is buried in it, but not I. He hasn't the fortitude to kill me and so seeks to drive me mad. My hand trembles as I break the seal. The man is quite capable of murder — he has done it before. Inside is another sarcophagus and inside that, another. He would not harm me. He could not. He loved me, once. When I finally reach the coffin, the first thing I see is my own name — Neferneferuaten Nefertiti.

I recoil as if burned and lean against the sarcophagus to keep from falling. It is a trick. A trick. I recall a sound like snapping wood and raise my hands to my neck. It should pain, but it does not. I run from the chamber, up the steps, through the next two chambers, which are full to the brim with my earthly goods. My passage out is blocked by a solid wall. I've been sealed in. I smash a palm against the plaster. Let me out. The plaster does not give. I beat both fists against the wall and cry, "I am not dead. I am not!" I keep hammering. No one answers. I lean my cheek against the cool surface. "Please," I beg, "help me."

My hands, which should be raw and bloodied by now, are whole and unblemished. This, more than anything else, tells me it is true, and I collapse on the floor. My body — surely, it is not my body, but my ba, my spirit — shivers.

A sob starts deep in my belly and erupts into a wail. I cannot die. Ankhesenpaaten, my only living child, still needs my protection. She and her husband are too young to rule on their own. I have failed her, just as I failed her sisters. The chill of the stone seeps into my bones. Bek. Longing for him tears at my heart. I yearn for oblivion.

No. I will not give in. I am Nefertiti, Queen of Kemet. I pull myself up onto my knees. I have been beset by a husband, by grief, by plague and even by the gods, and I have always prevailed. I will not be beaten now. He has taken my life, but he will not take my love. I have but one chance to reunite with Ankhesenpaaten, with Bek. I stand. I must go into the Duat and emerge victorious into the Field of Reeds.

Amenhotep III, Year 29

(ca. 1362 BCE)

I woke in the night with a need but unwilling to put aside the blankets and venture into the cold. Thus, I stayed until the need could no longer be ignored, at which time I roughly pushed aside the blankets, causing little Mutnedjmet to cry out.

Alerted by her child's cry, stepmother Tey caught me creeping to the edge of the camp. I jumped at the touch of her hand on my shoulder.

"What are you doing wandering about alone?"

"I have to pass water."

She sighed and pulled her blanket closer about her. "Don't think you're doing that here, you filthy animal. A child who has seen nine inundations should have more sense." She glanced back at her child, now soundly sleeping again. She removed a rushlight from beside the fire and set the end to glowing. "Here, I'll show you where you may relieve yourself."

I followed close behind her, not wanting to lose the dim glow of the torch. The sand was cold on my feet, the air even more so. My teeth chattered. The walk seemed endless, and finally I tugged on her blanket. "Why are we going so far?"

"So you do not soil our camp."

"I need to go now."

3

Tey whirled around and brought her face close to mine. Her breath smelled of onions and wine. "Do you wish to wake the whole camp?"

As I stood there shaking, both with cold and with fear, I felt the urine streaming down my legs. I shivered harder and cried, hoping Tey wouldn't notice my indiscretion.

She did, of course. "You disgust me," she said. Then she spun me around and left.

By the time I stopped crying and dried my tears enough to see, the dim glow from the fire ember was gone. With no moon, the only light came from the stars. I dropped to my knees, looking for footprints. Feeling for footprints. There were none. I kept looking, thinking there must be. Then I remembered Tey's blanket. With it dragging behind her, any footprints left in the powdery sand would be gone.

I turned around. Which way had we come from? I noticed a lack of stars at one end of the horizon. The river. That must be the river. We camped by the river. I headed toward the void.

After a time, I began to think something was wrong. Surely it had not been this far coming out. And as I neared the void, instead of staying flat, the dark patch rose out of the desert. I had been going in the wrong direction — toward the cliffs instead of the river. But that was good news. All I had to do was go back the other way, keeping the cliffs behind me.

Checking to make sure I was pointing precisely away from the cliffs, I started out. Soon, I tried running to keep warm. A sound stopped me dead. It was an animal sound; one I'd never heard before. A little like the cats at home, but bigger. Louder. I took a few more steps and heard it again. It was right in front of me, so I turned back toward the cliffs and started back.

I strained to listen but could hear nothing above the sound of my own heavy breathing and chattering teeth. I clamped my mouth shut. The roar came from one side.

It could outpace me with ease. It did not matter in which direction I walked; it could overtake me. My whole body shook, and tears flowed down my face. I bit my lip to keep myself quiet. Yet, perhaps, it would pass me by if it thought I was not worth the effort and find something bigger and more appetizing to hunt. I curled up in a ball, rocking back and forth, crying in silence, hoping if I buried myself in the sand, the thing chasing me wouldn't be able to find me.

I was startled by the touch of a hand on my shoulder. When I looked up, it was into the dark eyes of a young woman. She had straight, dark hair and wore a pleated dress of linen dyed blood red and covered in gold beads. Gold and carnelian jewelry adorned her arms, her fingers, her neck, her earlobes. Even her skin sparkled with a dusting of gold powder.

"Are you a queen?" I asked, rubbing my eyes with the back of my hand.

She smiled. "I am mightier than any queen."

"Where did you come from? I didn't see any boats here but ours," I said, shivering.

The woman held out a hand. "Time for questions later, young Nefertiti. Right now, we must get you warm."

I stood and took her hand. It seemed to radiate heat, and my shivering eased. "How do you know me?"

"I've been watching you. You are very important for the future of this land of Kemet."

"Me?" I did not see how this could be. Though my father's sister was the Great Royal Wife and beloved of the king, I myself was far from lines of succession. Being a girl, there was little other than queenship that could make me important to the country.

She nodded. "Yes. You."

Because I didn't think it polite to contradict her, I said nothing. As we walked, I noted that I could see her. At first, I thought the sun was beginning to rise, but looking around, I saw this wasn't so. It was as if the light came from the woman herself. Indeed, she illuminated a small sphere around her as well.

"Why do you glow like that?"

"Aren't you inquisitive."

I looked at my feet. "Sorry."

She looked down at me. "It was a compliment, not a criticism."

Never before had I been told that asking questions was a good thing. I decided to get another one in before she changed her mind. "What did you mean when you said I would be important for the future of Kemet?"

The woman waved her arm, and the scene transformed. Instead of an empty desert in the middle of the night, we were standing in the middle of a great city in full daylight. We stood in an avenue so broad a nobleman's house could have fit inside it with plenty of space left for foot traffic. The avenue was bisected by a grand bridge connecting a large palace and a smaller one. The top of the bridge was covered, yet in the middle was a window with a ledge. Anyone standing up there could surely see the whole of the city. I turned to see gleaming white walls of the palace enclosures and other buildings lining the sides of the avenue.

Not far from our position rose the largest temple pylons I had ever seen, and I could not resist drawing nearer. Blue and red flags snapped in the breeze at the top of flagpoles set into niches in the pylons. Between the flagpoles, colossal statues of a King stood sentinel. And a very odd king he was — with his sensual lips and rounded hips, he looked almost feminine. Above the statues, colorful relief portraits looked down on us. On both sides of the entranceway, he grabbed enemies by the hair, preparing to strike them. But as I approached, I realized they were not the same figure. The one on the right wore the traditional blue war crown and was surely a king. The one on the left wore a longer, more angular blue crown, and differed in one striking manner — she was female. The statues, likewise, might have been two different individuals.

I tried to speak but could manage no more than a whisper. "Is this place ruled by a woman-king?"

The woman shook her head and placed a hand on my shoulder. "If only it were."

I smiled. "This is the most beautiful city I've ever seen."

"Is it?" she asked. "Look more closely at the temple walls. At the roadway. They are new, yet already, they start to crumble. As if the city were thrown together in haste."

I looked more closely, and saw she was right. Grand though the city was, everywhere there were signs of decay. Cracked plaster. Loose and broken cobblestones.

"What happened?"

The woman crouched down so her face was level with mine. "Do you know what a debt is, Nefertiti?"

I nodded. "It's when someone gives you something or does something for you, and then you have to give them something in return."

"Very good. I have saved your life tonight. You must do something for me in return. Here, in this very spot, in this city that has not been built yet."

"What must I do?"

"That will become clear in time."

Since I wasn't being given a choice, I nodded. The city dissolved back into the dark desert sand. By now, light really was beginning to show above the line of the cliffs.

"Sleep now," she said. "Your father will find you in the morning."

I didn't remember lying down or closing my eyes, but when I opened them, I saw the figure of my father silhouetted against the bright sky. With him were our two boatmen. Gone was the cold air of the night, replaced by daytime's searing heat. My limbs were sticky, my sidelock of hair damp against my scalp.

Father placed a finger in front of his lips and then beckoned me. His other hand held his hunting bow. I shifted and found myself lying against a firm expanse of golden fur. Great clawed paws extended on either side of me.

As I rose and went to my father, the lioness rolled onto her belly. She shook her head and pushed herself up to her paws.

Father gestured for me to get behind him. He drew an arrow from the quiver on his back and readied his bow. The boatmen also held bows with arrows at their sides. They would defer to Father, let him make the kill, and prepare to act only if his arrow missed the mark and the animal attacked.

I peeked from behind Father's back. The lioness regarded him calmly with her dark eyes. Those eyes looked familiar, and not at all like cat eyes. I knew who the lioness was. As Father pulled the bowstring, I jumped against him.

The arrow flew off to the right, prompting one boatman to duck and cover, before it landed harmlessly in the sand. The lioness sat, calmly licking a paw.

Ay glared at me and raised a hand, ready to strike.

"She saved me, Father," I said. "I was lost, and she found me and kept me warm all night."

Father looked from me to the lioness, who by this time was on her feet. She walked to me and rubbed one temple against my forehead, then the other. I could see the boatmen readying their weapons and Father gesturing for them to hold back. When the lioness was done, she gave one last look to Father, flicked her tail at him, and bounded back out into the desert.

As she left, all three men fell to their knees and touched their foreheads to the ground. I did the same, without understanding why.

When the lioness was out of sight, Father stood and handed off his bow and quiver of arrows to one of the boatmen. The other went to retrieve the spent arrow. Father hoisted me onto his back and set off back for camp, with me giggling all the way.

When we returned, camp had already been struck, and so we boarded the skiff to take us back to the boat. When father handed me up onto the deck, the first person I saw was Tey. She stared, open-mouthed.

Father jumped up onto the deck, breathless. "You'll never guess where we found her," he said.

Tey fingered the necklace at her throat. "In the desert?"

Father tilted his head. "Naturally. She was with Sekhmet. The goddess protected her last night."

Tey's eyes widened. "You are mistaken. The desert sun produced a mirage."

The boat rocked as the boatmen climbed aboard.

"It did not," said Father. "When we found her, she was asleep with a great lioness."

Tey laughed a small, choked-sounding laugh.

"It's true, lady," said one of the boatmen. "We saw a lump on the sand, and when we got near — there she was, little Nefertiti, all curled up, sound asleep against the belly of the beast."

"That was no beast," said the other.

Father placed a hand on each of my shoulders. "Sekhmet saved her. She shall be sent to the temple of Ptah and Sekhmet in Mennefer."

I turned to look at him. He didn't mean to send me away?

When I turned back to Tey, her hands were shaking, her face in a grimace. "Why invest such resources in her? Surely you don't intend to enter her into a profession."

Father clapped her on the back. "There are worse things, but no. Sekhmet has marked Nefertiti. She has now claimed her twice — once as a baby, when she survived the plague that killed her mother, and again today." He raised an eyebrow. "With my brother-in-law's recent devotion to the goddess, this is a gift I dare not waste."

"But ..."

"Do you wish to anger a goddess? Do you wish to bring plague back here? Nefertiti has Sekhmet's favor — she would be spared — but what of Mutnedjmet?"

"You are right, as always," said Tey. "It shall be as you say." She gave me a quick, sidelong glance.

I understood two things in that moment: one, that my getting lost in the desert was not an accident, and two, that Tey was now afraid of me.

Amenhotep III, Year 32

(ca. 1359 BCE)

The throwing stick whirled through the air, momentarily silhouetted against the blue sky before missing the target by mere finger-widths and starting its downward trajectory to the ground.

Father stared, arms crossed. "Again."

His assistant threw another leather ball, and I another stick. This time, I missed by nearly a full cubit. Father signaled for his assistant to collect both targets and throwing sticks.

"You tire too easily." Father pinched my upper arm.

I pulled it back from him, stung.

"You lack muscle. We must build your strength."

"Why?"

"Well, so you can throw better, and longer. So you can handle a chariot better, and a sword."

"That, I understand," I said. "What I don't know is what good it does for a priestess to learn such things."

Father crossed his arms again and rocked back on his heels. "Sekhmet is a fierce goddess. She expects her ladies to be fierce." He stared past me, toward his returning assistant. "Thuy, go fetch a pitcher of beer."

As Thuy walked the short path back to the temple, I studied Father's face. "That is not it. At least, not all of it. None of the other priestesses-in-training are instructed in the arts of war."

At this, Father smiled. "Indulge me. I have no sons to whom to pass on my skills." He made a forced-casual shrug. "And, if the king should be impressed with you, that would not go amiss."

I froze, stunned. My mouth may, perhaps, have gaped open. "Surely, Father, you cannot mean ... the king is quite old ... older even than ..."

He turned to face me. "Yes, older even than your aged father — years older, don't forget. And you only lately come to womanhood. Yet, you have no cause to worry on that score. The king has already a great many wives and concubines. So long as you work hard, your skills, combined with your great beauty, will make you far too valuable to wither as a forgotten trophy in some back room of the women's quarters."

I sighed heavily, having not even been aware I'd been holding my breath until then.

"I do understand, however," continued Father, "that a Great Royal Wife has not yet been chosen for the Crown Prince."

I willed myself to keep staring at the ground. With the death of Djehutymose the previous year, that title now fell to the younger brother, Amenhotep, whom I remembered all too well.

The ball flew high, and I leaped to catch it. Too late — I was knocked down by one of the older boys. I picked myself up and noticed Princess Nebetah enter the courtyard, cradling something in her arms. I left the game to see what it was.

When I reached her, she shifted and I caught sight of black velvety ears and serpentine-green eyes. "It is my brother's kitten."

I glanced around. "Does he know you have it?"

Nebetah shook her head. "I found it in a corridor. I think it's sick."

I picked up the kitten and felt bones through the fur. It mewled. "It's certainly hungry. Let's go to the kitchens and see if we can find it some fish and a bowl of milk."

Before we could leave, Prince Amenhotep himself flew out into the courtyard, intent on joining the ball game. I turned to shield the kitten from his view, but instead succeeded in drawing his attention.

"What have you got?" He grabbed my shoulder and turned me around. "That is my kitten. You stole it."

I hugged the kitten tighter. "I did not steal it. I found it searching for food because you forgot to feed it."

Amenhotep grabbed the kitten and tried to wrest it from me. To avoid doing it harm, I let go. "Don't hurt it."

He smiled, but his eyes stayed hard. "You don't want me to hurt the cat."

Nebetah and I both shook our heads.

"Beg," he said.

Nebetah and I looked at each other. "Please," I said.

"On your knees."

We dropped to our knees. Nebetah cried. "Please don't hurt the kitten. I just wanted to play with it."

"So, it was you. I should have known," he said. "You're always touching my things." He threw the kitten to the ground and stomped on its back. "There. You can't have it."

The animal's screams pierced my ears. It tried to get up but could only scrabble with its forelegs. The hind legs lay useless, its back twisted.

In one motion, Nebetah rose to her feet and threw herself at her brother. Though he was a year older, he was not much bigger, and she knocked him to the ground. He grabbed a handful of her sidelock and tore out a chunk of it, leaving her scalp bleeding.

I took off running. Into the palace, over floors tiled blue like waves on the river, past green lily columns and painted waterfowl to the queen's apartments, and burst through the door to the sitting room, where the Great Royal Wife sat with her ladies. In my haste, I ran straight for her and grabbed her arm, ignoring all rules of proper behavior.

"Aunt," I said, "you must come quick. The prince has killed his kitten, and he is hurting Princess Nebetah."

Tiye pulled her arm away and rose out of her seat. She was not a tall woman, but as I was but a child, she loomed over me. I took in her downturned mouth and caught the glares of the other ladies, including Tey. I didn't even see the hand before it struck my cheek.

Tiye gestured to Tey. "Take her away and teach her some manners."

I dared not give voice to this memory or to any criticism of the prince. Instead, I raised my eyes and said, "Surely, that honor will go to one of his sisters, as is right by Ma'at." I believed Father would be unable to argue against such sound judgment, Ma'at being the sacred cosmic order, the way things have been since the beginning of time, that which keeps all of Kemet from descending into anarchy and chaos. I was wrong.

"The king himself broke tradition by marrying a commoner and making her his Great Royal Wife, and Ma'at has not been disturbed. He might be persuaded to do the same for his son. More, you at least are a niece of the current Great Royal Wife, which makes you a more likely candidate than Tiye herself was in her youth."

My major point of contention gone, I sought another. "The king did not have eligible sisters; the Crown Prince does." It was feeble — if Father was not bothered by the imminent destruction of Kemet and the Cosmos, I doubted anything less would dissuade him.

To my surprise, Father nodded and agreed with me. "True."

My heart soared. He would forget this folly and allow me to stay in the temple. And to stop practising with the cursed throwing stick.

"Which is why you must excel in order to be chosen."

This time, no force of will could keep me calm. "But you have already promised me to Sekhmet!"

He ignored my outburst, though the muscles in his jaw clenched. "That is to your advantage. The recent plagues have seen his majesty give her greater and greater honor in order to placate her. He may come to see having a trained priestess of Sekhmet for a daughter-in-law as additional protection."

Just then, Thuy returned, carrying a tray with a pitcher and two cups. Father filled both cups and handed one to me. I took it but did not drink.

"What grieves you, child?" he said. "Most girls would already be plotting how to set a trap for the prince's affections."

I briefly considered tipping my beer onto the desert sand and running back to the temple. Instead, I simply stared back at him.

Father clapped me on the shoulder and laughed. "This only proves how suited you are. Power should only ever be wielded by those who do not want it." He turned back toward the temple. "Come, you have worked hard enough on your throwing; it is time for your chariot lesson and then swimming."

I sipped at my beer as I followed Father. He was wrong about one thing — I *was* plotting. And he was not going to like the results.

Amenhotep III, Year 36

(ca. 1353 BCE)

The royal barge, with its flags of blue and white, pulled up to the high-water steps of the Temple of Sekhmet. As the eye painted on the bow drew past us, Mutnedjmet pulled on my sleeve, giggling and pointing. She had been told to act with decorum, yet her entire body trembled with excitement.

When the boards were laid out, I hooked a hand around Father's arm and boarded. I caught sight of Tey's glower and gave her a smile as we passed her.

The boat rocked as we stepped down onto the deck. Once Tey and Mutnedjmet had come aboard, a herald led us into the cabin. At the sight of the king and his Great Royal Wife lounging on cushions, we knelt on the deck and touched our foreheads to the planks.

"Rise," said the king's low, booming voice.

Father rose to his feet first and offered me a hand. I ignored it and gained my own footing.

"Surely, this is not the young Nefertiti who used to cause such mischief in the women's quarters," said the king. "You did not exaggerate when you spoke of her beauty, Ay."

Father inclined his head. "As you can see, it is no accomplishment of mine. My child is surely favored by the gods."

"Indeed."

15

I scanned the room as well as I was able while keeping my eyes respectfully lowered. The king reclined against the back wall of the cabin. His eye paint was smudged on one side, and his wig was slightly askew. To his right sat the Great Royal Wife, my father's sister, Tiye, resplendent in pristine white linen and flawlessly styled wig. To his left, a young man, long of face and gangly of limb, with a slight paunch protruding over the top of his white kilt. Though I had not seen him in many years, I had no difficulty recognizing the Crown Prince. He was bent over something I could not see well. Something moving within folds of linen. I hoped it was not something he intended to torture.

"Young lady."

I looked up at the king's words.

"Your esteemed father tells me you are well mannered, but I see no evidence of it."

My face burned hot and I lowered my eyes. "My deepest apologies, Majesty." Tiye frowned at me. I purposely did not look at Father as I was fighting back a smile. Though not orchestrated, my momentary lapse fit well into my plan.

Movement in front of the Crown Prince caught my eye. First one, then two chubby arms emerged from the linen folds. Pudgy fingers wiggled in the air. When the prince leaned over and put his hands out, I must have cried out because he stopped and stared at me, as did the others.

The king laughed. "Well, Ay, the young lady's inattention is your doing. You have kept her unmarried too long. She should have at least a couple of babes of her own by this time."

The prince scooped up the bundle. I tensed, but he merely brought the babe to his face and rubbed noses with it. He made a face and the child waved its arms.

"You are right, Majesty, of course," said Father. "But she has been claimed by the goddess." He shrugged. "What am I to do?"

Young Amenhotep saw me watching and gestured for me to come over for a better look.

I knelt by him. "It is the new princess, Beketaten?"

Amenhotep nodded. "Would you care to hold her?"

I held out my arms. Amenhotep placed the babe in them. I nestled her close to my chest and rocked her back and forth.

"You are good with her," he whispered.

Beketaten nestled against me, reaching with tiny fingers to clutch at the colored glass beads of my necklace. As I inhaled the new baby scent, I found myself smiling, and emotion clogged my throat.

"It seems," said the king, "the goddess may have to share her. She seems ready for other duties."

I looked up to see all assembled staring at me. I moved to give the child back to Amenhotep, but as I did so, she turned her head, open-mouthed to my breast.

Tiye clapped, and the wet nurse appeared to take Beketaten from me. Relieved, I handed her over.

The king invited us to take up cushions on the floor. As I did so, Father nodded to me, pleased. I waited for the opportunity to undo what I had unwittingly done. I didn't have long to wait, for I had barely left my impression upon the cushion when young Amenhotep invited me to walk on the deck. Father raised an eyebrow at me, his equivalent of a smile, as we made our way out. I vowed to ensure he did not keep smiling but knew I must do it discreetly, so he would not suspect it was deliberate.

Out in the open air, Amenhotep walked beside me, arms behind his back. A guard trailed us just out of earshot but kept us always in sight.

Amenhotep broke the silence. "I understand you trained as a priestess of Sekhmet."

"I have not yet completed my training," I said.

He nodded. "I had thought the training somewhat less rigorous, and less lengthy, for priestesses than it is for priests."

"For most, it is so. Given our position, though, my father felt I needed more learning than my counterparts."

"Such as?"

"Reading and writing, for one."

Amenhotep laughed. "Tell me, does Ay intend to sell your services as a scribe?"

I laughed as well. "Certainly not. His ambitions for me are decidedly higher." I glanced at him sideways to gauge his reaction to this insinuation. He seemed unsurprised.

"He and every other noble with an unmarried daughter who has seen at least twelve inundations."

I relaxed and smiled. "I see." Much competition was good news. Very good indeed.

"You don't look disappointed."

"In truth, I'm not." He stopped walking and turned to me. "I mean no insult. I simply have no wish to join the royal court."

"In other words, there is someone else you wish to marry."

I studied his face, wondering if he would find the existence of a rival to be a deterrent or a challenge. "Even were there not, I still would wish to remain in the service of Sekhmet."

Amenhotep walked close to the edge and looked out to shore. The waters were just beginning to rise, having already expanded the marshes. Ducks paddled amongst the reeds, giving me an idea, but Amenhotep spoke before I could.

"I take it your father does not know of your beloved?"

I joined him at the side of the barge. "I have not said that there is a beloved."

"Nor have you denied it," he said. "Tell me, Nefertiti, do you truly love your goddess so much?"

"It is not so much a matter of love." I told him the story of how Sekhmet had saved me from death that night in the desert long ago. "I owe her a great debt, and she intends to see I repay."

"So, you stay in her service against your will?"

I shook my head. "Not at all. The Temple of Sekhmet is where I belong. Nowhere else could I pursue such learning."

"Ah. So that is the attraction. What is your favorite course of study, besides reading and writing?"

"Languages. Besides Kemetic, I also speak and write Akkadian, Naharin, Assyrian, and Babylonian."

"Impressive. Of course, your family is from Naharin, so it must come easily for you."

I turned on him. "I had but one grandparent born in Naharin. The rest of my family is thoroughly Kemetic."

Amenhotep likewise turned and held up both hennaed palms. "This time it is I who meant no insult. You are a paragon of Kemetic culture." The corner of his mouth turned up.

He was teasing me.

"You know I have also trained for the priesthood," he said.

"Yes, I had heard. For the king's pet god."

Amenhotep's look darkened, and I cursed myself. This part of my plan depended on him feeling an attraction to me.

"The Aten gives light to the sun, to us, and to all people everywhere," he said. "Without him, plants would wither, and livestock die."

I paused to think. The Aten was the disc of the sun. He did not have a human aspect, as did the other gods, and he had no interest or effect in human affairs. Still, his contribution was vital. "I had not considered it before. I had always thought Amun-Ra's contribution of driving the solar ark the greater one, but you may be correct. Without light, the sun is without power."

Amenhotep smiled. At that moment, a commotion arose near the shore. A hawk diving for fish frightened a flock of ducks, which flew up in a frightful cacophony.

I sighed. "It has been too long since I have tasted fresh duck. And these so well fattened on the remains of the harvest."

"You would like me to catch some ducks for you?"

I shook my head. "No. I should like to catch some ducks for you."

Amenhotep laughed a full belly laugh. "I cannot turn down such an offer." He waved to the guard, now standing some distance from us.

We floated in a papyrus skiff, with a helmsman to guide us while we hunted. Two escorts rowed ahead of us in a second skiff, scouring ahead for crocodile and hippopotamus and working to flush out ducks for us.

Amenhotep stood in the front, throwing stick in hand. "Now you stand thus, with your left leg slightly ahead."

I studied his stance. His feet were a little too close together. He might have difficulty keeping his balance on the water.

"Remember to bend your knees," he continued, "so you can roll with the motion of the boat instead of toppling over the side." He raised his hand with the stick. "Hold the stick like this." He signaled to the men in the other boat. They threw an object into the water near the flock, and they responded by calling out and flying off.

Amenhotep drew back his arm and threw. He stumbled with the sudden motion of the boat caused by his shifting weight, but he recovered well. The stick missed by a finger-width. He scowled and insisted on repeating the entire performance a second time. His stick hit a wing, dropping the fowl to the water. Our escorts finished it off with a spear and retrieved the stick.

Amenhotep picked up another stick and handed it to me. "Now, you try."

I stood as he had demonstrated, feeling slightly wobbly, made a tentative motion with my throwing arm, and turned to him. "Have I got it right?"

He came up behind me and moved both of my arms into a better position. As he took his hand away, his fingers brushed the hair of my wig behind my ear and trailed down my neck. I tensed at the unwelcome contact and hoped he would not notice. He pulled away and signaled to our escorts.

As the ducks flew up, I shifted my stance, adjusted my aim, and threw. The duck dropped, dead.

Amenhotep leaned over the side of the boat. "Astonishing luck. You must try again, but do not be discouraged if it does not go as well. Duck hunting requires much practice and skill."

I waited for the duck to be retrieved and chose another stick. This time, when the duck rose into the air, one duck veered off to the side, away from its fellows. I pointed to it. "That one."

To keep the duck in my sights, I had to twist and throw from a different position. The result was the same. The stick met its mark and the duck fell, lifeless, to the water.

"You have done this before." Amenhotep wasn't smiling.

"When one's father is a military commander, one grows up with the military arts."

"Your father takes an unusual approach to the education of girl children."

"As he so often reminded me, he does not have any boy children to educate."

Amenhotep forced a smile. "Can you also handle a bow?"

"I can, but not so well as a throwing stick."

"Well, we will see who the more skilled hunter is." He waved to the escorts, asked them to come closer, and instructed them to keep the piles of ducks separate.

He pulled a bow from the edge of the skiff and handed it to me. I hefted it in one hand. It was too long for me, and heavy besides. I was accustomed to using equipment that outsized me, it having been constructed for men, but this was larger than I was used to, reaching from my foot to above the top of my head when slack.

I missed on my first attempt and again on my second. The third time, Amenhotep pointed out a duck for me to hit. It flew off too quickly, so I homed in on another and brought it down.

From there, we took it in turns, shifting now and then to sticks and then to bows. In the end, I killed seven ducks to his three, and mine all clean kills, before he tired of the game.

On the paddle back to the barge, we sat a distance apart. I tried to focus on the approaching barge but could not help glancing back at him. When I did, I found him studying me as if memorizing every minute feature of my person. I turned back but still felt his eyes on me.

On the barge, our families had moved out of the cabin and could be seen on deck. Father appeared to be standing casually by the edge, but every so often, his eyes darted sideways to our returning skiff. The Great Royal Wife took no such pains to hide her interest.

On approach, our escorts displayed the afternoon's haul. Tiye clapped her hands. As Amenhotep boarded, she embraced him and congratulated him on his hunting prowess. His voice was too low for me to hear his response, but Tiye spun her head to look at me, mouth agape.

As I boarded, Amenhotep bowed to Father. "I have had the pleasure of witnessing your daughter's skill both with throwing stick and bow. You must be a great teacher indeed."

I refused to meet Father's eyes. I had counted on Amenhotep taking the credit for himself.

Father cleared his throat. "Your praised is undeserved, for I had an exceptional pupil. You will find my daughter is well accomplished in many areas, though surely not so accomplished as your Highness."

Amenhotep glanced at me, something between eagerness and intensity in his eyes. As before, in the skiff, I found it disorienting. He nodded to Father and then retired to the cabin.

The king himself, and Tiye, turned away from me. Father followed suit. I was no longer worthy of consideration. I rushed, as if upset, past the assembly. Out of the corner of my eye, I saw Tey's smile of triumph. I was no longer an obstacle to her own daughter's advancement.

When I reached the rear of the barge, I threw myself against the outer wall of the cabin and smiled. My smile was so big and breathless that I covered my mouth for fear it would erupt into laughter, and I had to hide my face from the oarsmen in the stern.

I had won.

Once the feasting and celebrating was done, and we had parted company with the royal family, I slipped into the side entrance in the temple enclosure. I sped to my quarters, hoping to escape Father's wrath. A vain hope it was.

He entered my small room, one hand clenched into a fist. He drove it into the palm of his hand to emphasize his words as he paced. "I kept asking myself how you could possibly have been so stupid as to humiliate our Crown Prince and throw away any chance you ever had at becoming Great Royal Wife."

I bowed my head. "I am so sorry, Father. Pride is a particular failing of mine."

He stamped a foot. "Do not anger me further by lying. Your failings are many, but stupid you are not. You have done this deliberately." He advanced on me.

I backed up, but my knees buckled when I hit the bed, and I sat down. "No. I swear to you. I meant to allow him to win, but a madness came over me ..." His hand struck my face.

"You selfish, ungrateful girl." A blow to my stomach. "You spared no thought at all for me, or your stepmother, or your sister, that you could shame us like this."

A madness must truly have come over me at that point, for I stood to face him. "And you spared no thought for me. You would make a whore of me for the king's favor."

"You are a noblewoman. That is your purpose." He pushed me onto the cot and forced me to my side and then my front. He rested his weight on my back, pinning me to the cot, and rained blows on my posterior. Though I clenched my teeth and squeezed my eyelids, I could not stop the tears.

When at last he was spent, he knelt on the floor. "If it's whoredom you want, it will be arranged. Perhaps I can salvage something by getting a good price for you."

Amenhotep III, Year 37

(ca. 1354 BCE)

My trunks and jewel cases were packed with my belongings. I had renounced my plain white priestly garb in favor of green linens, the same shade as my eye makeup. I had chosen a new wig, fashioned after the styles of the south. It was shorter and lighter than the currently popular styles, layered with plaits that swung whenever I turned my head. I thought it better suited for the hotter climes I would be living in.

After my snub of the Crown Prince, Father had terminated my education. And while he did not make good on his promise to sell me as a whore, he did not much better by selling me as a concubine to a noble in Kush, who I was told paid an exorbitant price for me. I would see to his carnal needs and birth his bastards in a place where my father need never set eyes on me again. Father may have been able to destroy my happiness, but he would not hear that I cried over it.

The boat pushed away from the watersteps, and the boatman finessed it out into the current. As I watched the avenue of sphinxes and the temple pylons recede, a boat flying blue and white flags intercepted us. A herald called across. "Is this the Lady Nefertiti?"

"She is," said the boatman.

"Well, then, you'll have to turn around. I have orders here regarding her conduct from the king himself."

My shoulders sagged. This could not be good news.

Back at the temple, I walked the avenue of sphinxes and waited in the first courtyard while the herald delivered his message to the head priest. I had proven myself thoroughly unsuited for the position of Great Royal Wife, so a command from the king must be of an altogether different nature. I wandered through the columns, musing over this latest unwelcome twist of fate. Though becoming a concubine in far Kush meant living a life without status or will, at least the women's quarters would be small, and I would be unlikely to be forgotten. I might even be permitted to continue as a temple priestess. I would have children. Being taken by the king was a different matter. I remembered the far reaches of his vast women's quarters and the girls who arrived from all across the empire and beyond. Most, he saw once, satisfied himself with, and then left alone with no allies and no children. They were often each other's sole comfort.

The slap of sandals on stone alerted me to the presence of the priest, but I did not turn to greet him.

"Nefertiti, sweet."

I snapped my head around. "Renni."

He swallowed. "I have been permitted to bring you the news myself. You will not be traveling to Kush this day."

"I guessed."

"Instead, the king is negotiating a marriage contract for you with the Crown Prince."

I felt the color drain from my face. "That is not possible."

Renni took my hand in his. "I assure you; it is. If negotiations succeed, your father must pay the Kushite what he has lost. I understand he is demanding a price far above what he paid for you."

"He will get it," I said. "My father will pay anything for this marriage to happen."

"You should be grateful for that."

"And you?" I spat. "Are you grateful to be rid of me?"

"Temple life is not what the gods have planned for you. I am not what they have planned for you. You know this."

I titled my head in acknowledgement.

"I would think you'd be pleased to be the future Queen of Kemet."

"It is, I suppose, preferable to being a nobleman's trophy." I ran a finger down the smoothness of his scalp and drew nearer to him. "I will not be leaving today. We have some little time left."

He backed away. "No, we do not." He turned and sped away.

Chapter 5

Mutnedjmet tossed the throwing sticks. All four landed with the marked side up. She clapped and moved one of her pieces five squares and drooped when it landed on the water square.

"You don't have to move that one. Look here." I pointed to her piece sitting on square twenty-one. "If you move this one, you will land on the House of Happiness and also send my piece back to square fifteen."

She brightened and did as I advised. Then, she glanced up at me. "Why aren't you more excited?"

We had set up our senet game in the shade of a sycamore in a palace courtyard. The lush gardens were in full bloom. Red poppies, blue cornflowers, irises of many colors, and jasmine scented the air. Papyrus encircled a pond populated with white lotus flowers.

"I am very excited. I simply don't jump about like a child anymore." I tossed the sticks and took my turn. Amenhotep entered the courtyard. Alone. He started toward us.

She shuffled her bottom on the stool. "He's not very handsome, for a prince."

I kept my voice low. "He's not unpleasant to look at. Besides, there are other qualities more important than looks." Though what those were in Amenhotep's case, I had yet to discover.

"Easy for you to say," she mumbled, grabbing the throwing sticks.

"Good morning, beloved," said Amenhotep, "and young Lady Mutnedjmet. I see you are at leisure while the men decide your fate."

"My father thinks it best if I am out of the way," I said.

He rocked back on his heels, seemingly unsure of how to respond. "Might I have a private word with you?"

"Is that permitted during negotiations?"

"If I were not the Crown Prince, you and I would be drawing up the contract between ourselves."

"But you are."

"If you are not comfortable, your sister may stay here, and we will walk. We will not be out of her sight."

"Aw," said Mutnedjmet. "I was winning."

"It's fine, Nedji. His Highness and I will talk, and then we may resume our game. Just stay here." I rose.

She crossed her arms and pouted, looking far younger than her eight inundations. Amenhotep and I walked toward the pond, a couple of paces apart.

"We must speak before negotiations go any further. I want to know if you are acting of your own will. Do you wish to marry me and become the Great Royal Wife?"

I turned away.

Amenhotep sighed. "That is answer enough."

"I thought you would refuse me if I bested you at duck hunting."

"I see." He chuckled.

Surprised, I turned to face him.

"My apologies," he said, "but it was the duck hunting that made me want you. You have no idea how magnificent you are."

I took a deep breath to give myself time to formulate a response that would not betray my lack of reciprocation. "A king must put aside his own desires and do that which is best for Kemet. A Great Royal Wife must be a royal woman."

"You'll not remind me of my duties." His jaw clenched. "This has already been discussed, and it is not without precedence, as you well know. You, at least, are my cousin, whereas my mother had no royal ties whatsoever."

Amenhotep continued, "After our duck hunting excursion, I made some inquiries. It seems you are not only skilled in the military arts, but your teachers give you no end of praise. They say you have the mind of a man — as literate as the most highly trained scribe, fluent in foreign languages, well versed in history, mathematics, music, and medicine, among other subjects."

I bristled at being told I had the mind of a man, but even more so at the thought that he had been prying into my affairs. "Your spies are thorough. My father wished to conceal my achievements from you. He thought you would not want a woman who is more accomplished than you."

"Do not think for a moment that you are above me." He turned, and I could see his jaw working. After a time, he calmed enough to speak again. "I will admit, your skill with a throwing stick puts mine to shame, but as Crown Prince, no expense has been spared for my education, and I have an intellect that can only be seen as a gift from the gods."

I inclined my head and dissembled. "Of course, that is evident for all to see. My humble apologies."

Amenhotep sniffed. "Ay is more of a fool than he takes me for if he thinks I cannot see he wishes to wield power through you." He swept one arm across his chest. "He is nothing."

"If you know this and are not an admirer of my father, then why is it you wish to marry me?"

"I never said I did not admire his skills as a warrior and a commander. And a teacher," he said. "I fully intend to use those skills. It is his ambition that troubles me."

"Then why feed that ambition by taking me as Great Royal Wife?"

"Because the Aten wills it."

I am sure I must have gawped. Once, I had believed that all people were visited by gods as Sekhmet had once visited me, but some years prior, I had learned this was not the case. In fact, this was the very first time another had confided such to me. "The Aten speaks to you?"

"When I contemplate his beauty, he reveals his will," said Amenhotep. "The Aten is different from any other god. He is both male and female at once. Therefore, both are required to serve him. I have need of a woman worthy of that role and, until that day hunting in the marshes, I had given up hope of finding one. That day you were thrown into my path, I saw for the first time a female who approached being my equal. That you also possess such perfection of form is surely further sign of the Aten's favor."

My disappointment in learning that Amenhotep's relationship with his god was unlike that of mine with my goddess was tempered by the knowledge that I was free to choose. The thought of returning to the temple, and to Renni, brought back the manner of his dismissal of me. Amenhotep knew about Renni, or at least suspected. Had he told my father, and my father issued threats? Had Amenhotep himself issued threats? I dismissed the idea, as he had nothing to gain from it. Had he wished to force me into marriage, he could easily have done so without such elaborate machinations. The fact that he left the choice up to me made me inclined to accept, yet I did not wish to act with haste. He was not Renni, but royal marriages were seldom based on passion, and he did want me for my education and skills. That boded well for my continued ability to use them. "You have given me much to consider."

He took my hand in both of his. "I will not compel you to marry against your will, but my dearest hope is that you will consider becoming my Great Royal Wife. Together, we can bring glory to Kemet." He kissed my hennaed palm, his eyes never leaving mine, and then straightened.

On impulse, I kissed his cheek. I did not feel the sudden jolt I had with Renni.

He unclasped one of his necklaces, one of gold scarabs separated by gold beads. He moved behind me so as to clasp it around my neck. When I turned to face him, his eyes dropped to where the scarabs rested against my breasts. He returned his gaze to my face before speaking. "I can give you a little time to choose, but not much." He bowed to me and left the courtyard.

No, I did not desire him, but the warm glow he engendered, perhaps, could be fanned to a flame.

When I returned to Mutnedjmet, she was fairly bouncing on her stool. "You were right. He is charming. And he will be king. You are so lucky. What did he want to talk to about that couldn't wait until the wedding?"

I took my place across the senet board from her. "He has given me the chance to refuse him."

"He hasn't."

"He has."

"But you won't." Mutnedjmet narrowed her eyes. "Will you?"

"I have not yet decided," I said. "Now, is it my turn?"

The master of horse eyed me suspiciously.

"I assure you, I am well trained in horsemanship."

"That may be, Lady, but I do not have orders to allow you access to the chariots and the horses."

He flicked a glance at my bald head. I had adopted the style as a priestess-in-training and intended to keep it for its comfort. I supposed it was rather scandalous to appear this way in public, but wigs had a tendency to dislodge during a fast chariot run, and I intended to go very fast.

"Do you have orders barring me from them?"

He shifted from one foot to the other. "No."

"Ah. So, you have no specific orders one way or the other."

"Not in so many words, no."

"Well, then I am giving you an order now. I need the use of horses and a chariot for the next hour."

He bowed. "I can't do that, Lady."

"Do you know who I am? I am the betrothed of the Crown Prince."

"I do know, and that's the trouble, you see," he said. "If any harm were to come to you, it would not go well for whoever put you in harm's way, if you know what I mean."

I knew exactly what he meant. If anything were to go wrong during the ride, he would be severely punished. Yet, I needed this. The throwing stick practice, the archery, and the swimming had not calmed me as they usually did. My body was tense in a way that could only be calmed by the wind in my face and the reins in my hand.

"And how do you think it will go for you when I am queen and I remember the slight done to me today?"

"I would hope you'd justly reward a servant who honored his king's wishes under pressure and commend me for thinking of your safety, Lady."

My face burned, for I knew I had rightly been taken to task by an underling. "So, I shall. May I ask your name?"

"Ramose, Lady."

"Well, then, Ramose, how would it be if you watch me ready the chariot and horse, and if I can do that to your satisfaction, watch as I do a few small, slow circuits so you may judge my skill for yourself."

"And if I judge that you are not skilled enough to handle a chariot, you will leave?"

"Yes."

He thought for a moment. "Fine. Follow me."

He strode past the stables to the chariot shed. Upon inspection, I chose a lightweight model. No doubt, Ramose would think it a poor choice, others being stronger and more sturdy. But I had no need of sturdy — only fast. Ramose did not offer to help me attach the wheels or pull the chariot into the yard. No matter — those were chores Father had always made me do myself.

Leading me through the stables, Ramose stopped at the third and fourth stall. "How about these ones, Lady?"

I checked over the horses — stallions as high as the top of my head at the withers and well muscled. No doubt they had great stamina in battle. "I merely wish to ride a few circuits around the lake, not charge the enemy lines."

Ramose nearly smiled at that.

Reviewing the other stalls, I found a pair of smaller stallions, lean but still strong, and black as night. On seeing us, one did a little dance in his stall, eager to be out running. "These ones," I said.

Ramose leaned against the wall, watching while I bridled the horses, and collected the pads and leather girths. I led the horses to the yard myself and tucked my skirts into my sash before proceeding to harness the horses to the chariot. When finished, I invited Ramose to inspect my handiwork. While he was checking the tightness of the girths, I leaped aboard the chariot, snapped the reins, and shouted for the horses to run. As expected, they bolted, but I was prepared and held steady.

I kept the lake to my left. As I rounded the north end, the temple of Amun pulled into view, followed by the vast expanse of desert. To the south and east, the river glinted in the gaps between the palace buildings beyond the stables. The breeze skimmed my bare scalp and sent pleasant shivers down my neck. Soon, the rhythm of the run became predictable, and I could allow my thoughts to wander even as my hands and legs made the necessary adjustments. My previous exertions had helped me come to a decision. Marrying Amenhotep was not ideal, yet it was preferable to my other options at present. I needed the run simply to be sure my choice was sound.

With the world blurred around me and nothing to penetrate the sound of hooves and wind, I felt my ba lift. As I passed Ramose, still agape in the yard, I saw Amenhotep's face as I brought down duck after duck, his pride as he listed my scholarly accomplishments. I heard his voice when he said I was magnificent. He wanted me because of my knowledge and my skills, which meant I would be expected to use them. That I would be allowed to continue to enjoy driving the chariot was almost reason enough to marry him. That he was aware of my father's machinations and intended to thwart them sealed it. I would be out from under Father's thumb and allowed to continue my training. Yes, I had made the right choice. With this burden gone, I surrendered to the ride.

After several circuits, I noted Ramose had left the yard, gone to tend to the horses, I was certain. He would not sound the alarm for what I had done, for he would be blamed for failing to anticipate my ploy.

When at last my muscles ached and the horses were well lathered, I slowed them down and guided them back to the stables. On approach, I noticed a small figure seated against the stable wall.

"Nedji," I said as I dismounted.

She was already on her feet. "I have something to tell you."

"You came here looking for me?" I wondered if the entire palace knew I'd commandeered horses and a chariot and what would be the result if they did. "How did you know where to find me?"

"Easy," she said. "Whenever you want to think, you exercise, or you ride a chariot. I searched the archery range, and then the lake, and I saw you riding."

"Ah. You know me well." I unhooked the horses from the chariot. "First, I must see the horses are cared for." With Mutnedjmet following, I led the horses inside, found a stablehand, and instructed him to brush down the horses and dismantle and return the chariot.

"Come," I said to Mutnedjmet. "We can talk while we walk back to the palace."

She bit her lip. "I heard something."

I waited for her to continue. When she didn't, I prompted her. "What did you hear?"

She kicked the ground. "The Crown Prince talking with his mother in the courtyard."

"And how did you happen to hear a private conversation?"

"I didn't mean to. They thought they were alone. I was in the rushes, catching frogs."

"Frogs? You are too old for such silly pastimes."

"Do you want to know what they said or not?"

I sighed. "Fine. What did they say?"

"After scolding me like that, I don't think you deserve to know."

Stifling my urge to scold her again, I took a deep breath. "I am very sorry. I should have listened to you instead of reprimanding you."

Mutnedjmet considered my words for an interminable moment and then nodded. "The prince said he meant to have you no matter what, and if you refused his offer of Great Royal Wife, he would simply take you as a concubine and sire as many bastards as he could until you no longer pleased him."

I stopped walking. "You are lying."

"I'm not. Why would I?"

"Father has sent you to ensure that I accept Amenhotep's proposal. He does not want to see his hard work go to waste."

"Father doesn't even know the prince gave you a choice," she said. "Unless you told him."

I was not sure I believed her but decided that, in case she was telling me true, I should find out more. "Did the prince say anything else?"

"He said you were ..." She screwed up her face, searching for the correct word. "Reluctant. That you bested him at duck hunting on purpose to turn him away, but that only made him want to possess you even more, and ... that he thinks his talk of the Aten's will has persuaded you. And that making you think you had a choice would make you more pliable."

I felt as if the wind had been knocked out of me. Mutnedjmet might have deduced my true intentions with the duck hunt, but I had told no one of Amenhotep's words of the Aten, and she had been too far away to overhear that day. I found myself shivering uncontrollably.

"Neffie, are you okay?" Mutnedjmet's eyes were wide.

I closed my eyes, breathed deeply, and nodded.

"Did I do the wrong thing in telling you?" she asked. "I was afraid you'd refuse the prince and then end up worse off."

"You did right, Nedji. Thank you."

"You'll tell the prince you accept now."

I wanted to tell her not for anything. That I would kill myself first. Or him. Or take a chariot and run away. Far away, to Naharin, or even beyond, to the Hatti lands. There must be a way. But I said nothing. I simply turned away from her and started walking again toward the palace.

"No," said Mutnedjmet. "You can't."

Chapter 7

After bathing, I dressed in plain white linen and barricaded myself inside my guest quarters in the palace. I knelt to search my clothing trunk. At the bottom, I found my gilt statue of Sekhmet and placed her in the corner. She sat on her throne, her lioness face framed by long hair, and topped with the sun disc.

The tile floor was cold on my knees and my palms, and it comforted me. Though I could not predict when she would appear to me, I had found that the act of speaking with her brought her near, and even when she chose not to show herself, she still could place her wisdom in my heart.

This day, however, such was my distress that after only a short time prostrating myself on my knees, forehead touching the floor and arms outstretched, I heard the jingle of jewelry, and the slap of sandals on the floor. This time, there was also a faint whirring sound I had never associated with Sekhmet before.

I lifted my head from the floor and sat back on my knees. My small room had enlarged, and there she stood — my goddess, my patron — in all her golden glory, leaning against the wall. To her side, a green-skinned man in a skullcap sat at a potter's wheel, working a shapeless lump of clay. He could be none other than Sekhmet's husband, Ptah, the creator. Behind him, a woman stood with a hand on his shoulder. From the ostrich feather in her headdress, I recognized her as Ma'at, the cosmic balance. She looked at me with haunted eyes.

I stayed where I was and inclined my head toward Sekhmet. "You have heard of my dilemma?"

"I have seen your selfishness."

I looked up and met her eyes, shocked. I was not accustomed to such harsh words from her.

My goddess took a couple of steps toward me. "Have you forgotten the promise you made me?"

The one she extracted on pain of death, I thought, and then quashed it immediately, lest Sekhmet hear. Too late.

"Perhaps I should have left you to die."

"Forgive me, Goddess. I remember well my promise. I had not realized until now that my marriage to the Crown Prince was the means of fulfilling it. Is there not another way?"

"Rise, child. And gaze upon Ma'at."

I did so.

"Do you not see the sallowness of her complexion, the dark pits of her eyes?"

"I do."

"This is merely the beginning for her. In short time, she will grow weak, emaciated, as all of Kemet plunges into chaos."

"And it is young Amenhotep who will wreak this havoc?"

Sekhmet and Ma'at both nodded. Ptah remained focussed on his task.

"Then let me kill him and have done with it," I said.next

"That is your anger speaking," said Sekhmet. "You are not capable of killing. Not yet, at any rate."

My anger tripled at that. I clenched my jaw to avoid speaking in haste.

"Oh, that you have the strength and the cunning, I do not doubt. It is the will you lack, and that is all to the good. What would be the result should you murder Kemet's only legitimate heir?"

I thought of the invasions centuries ago, when the line of succession was lost and Kemet was broken apart. "Chaos," I said.

"Precisely," said Sekhmet. "It is your duty to prevent such, not cause it. You must rule by Amenhotep's side, so you can steer him always toward the good road. Toward Ma'at."

I sighed. "I wish with all my being it was not me who was charged with this task."

Sekhmet shrugged. "Then you should have been born in another place and time, for you are our best hope."

I contemplated her words. At that moment, I wished I had been born elsewhere. "How do I turn Amenhotep toward Ma'at?"

"By using the skills you already display and by honing those skills with each use. Satisfy him. Placate him. Make him trust you. Once he does, he will gladly hand you more and more responsibility, for he cares more for the title of *king* than the profession. Once you have gained that responsibility, use it judiciously."

I glanced at Ma'at. Her eyes were now downcast, and she was leaning on Ptah as he worked. Even her ostrich feather drooped. "And if I cannot sway him from his course?"

"Then you must minimize the effects of his folly and take charge of the next generation so that Amenhotep, the fourth of that name, will cause no lasting ripples on the river of eternity."

"The next generation?"

Sekhmet nodded. "Amenhotep is unduly influenced by his mother. Or, at the very least, is encouraged by her. You shall have the same power over the next Crown Prince. Use it."

I looked to Ptah. The clay on the wheel was taking shape. A small, rounded head on a pair of tiny shoulders now emerged from the lump. My breath caught in my throat.

I pointed at it. "Is that ..."

Sekhmet took me by the shoulders and steered me closer. "Yes. It is your child."

My feet drew nearer and I reached out a hand. Before my fingertips touched it, I thought better of this and drew back my hand, not wanting to mar the perfection of the tiny cheeks, the lotus bud lips.

Ptah looked up from his work and smiled at me. As I watched, the torso grew little by little with each revolution.

"Of course," said Sekhmet, "this child, and all of your others, will never receive the breath of life unless you marry the prince."

My child. My son. The next Crown Prince. And all of the others. I let out the breath I had been holding. I would have many children. The path laid out for me would not be without compensation. Tears blurred my vision.

Chapter 8

Amenhotep and I sat at tables at one end of the hall. The king sat at a table beside his son. Maya, high priest of Amun, sat on his other side. My aunt Tiye, the Great Royal Wife, had her table beside mine. Their daughters sat with Tiye, except for the infant Beketaten, who was with her nurse. Beside them, my family was seated at their own tables, lower than ours. Around the edges of the hall, all of the court — lesser wives, concubines, nobles, anyone of any importance — joined in the celebration of our marriage.

I tried not to stare at the king but could not help stealing glances. It had been some time since I'd last seen him this close, and he seemed to me much more aged. He chewed carefully, as if his mouth pained him, and I noticed that his food arrived already mashed or chopped very finely.

Drummers, harpers, and lute players kept time for a troupe of acrobats in the center of the hall. Naked dancing girls scattered themselves amongst the crowd, hoping for favors and, no doubt, the chance to do business later. Through it all, servants bustled between tables, refilling cups with wine and plates with food.

I had little appetite, myself. The myrrh and cinnamon perfume scenting my wig mingled with the perfumes of the other guests — henna, iris, frankincense, rose, cardamom, fragrant woods of all varieties — and that of the flower garlands worn by all. Combined with the stress of the previous few days, and the thought of what lay ahead that night, it was enough to make me feel quite nauseated. I longed to draw a deep breath but feared popping the netting of faience beads covering my gown.

Now that my new apartments were fully furnished and I had moved in, and now that we were holding our feast, there remained only one further duty to make the marriage valid. I kept stealing glances at Amenhotep, wondering if he was dreading it as much as I. He talked and laughed, occasionally throwing me a smile.

A pair of dancers, long and fair of limb, approached us. As they shimmied and undulated to the rhythm of the drums, the men banged cups on the table and hollered. When Tiye joined in, so did I. Both were casting glances at young Amenhotep. The taller one stopped in front of him, tilted her head ever so slightly, and looked up at him for the briefest moment; then her entire body erupted in a shimmy, hips knocking out a rhythm, arms swaying gracefully. Amenhotep howled and threw her a necklace of golden beads. She slipped her wrist through it without missing a beat.

I had the sudden thought that perhaps Amenhotep would choose a different companion this night, and I felt myself relax at the prospect. The dancer finished, and Amenhotep beckoned her forward. He took off one of his rings and tossed it to her. She curtsied and then danced away. I felt real hope that I would get a reprieve.

Tiye nudged me. "The entire hall can see you gawping."

I drew my gaze away from Amenhotep's dancers, ashamed of my lapse, and even more afraid Tiye would guess my thoughts.

"Jealousy will not serve you well."

"No, Aunt," I said.

"As the wife of the king, even the Great Royal Wife, you will be but one of many. If you wish to stay the first among wives, you'll not try to constrain him. You'll find, like most men, he responds better to flattery than criticism."

"Thank you, Aunt," I said. "Very good advice."

Tiye took a sip of beer and waved her hand. "I don't know why I'm bothering to help you. It should be my own Nebetah sitting here instead of you. It is she who carries the royal blood. But he does as he pleases, tradition be damned."

I refrained from pointing out that Tiye herself carried not a drop of royal blood.

Tiye put down her beer cup and nibbled a fig. She offered one to me.

"No, thank you, Aunt," I said.

She glanced at the profusion of mostly untouched dishes on my table. "Nerves are understandable, but you must eat. You're going to need your strength later."

"I have eaten some."

"More." She pushed a plate of beef at me.

"No, thank you. It's sweetened with figs."

"What is wrong with figs?"

"I don't like them."

"Since when?"

"I've never liked them, Aunt."

She narrowed her eyes. "Well, some roasted gazelle, then. It is savory, not sweet." She placed a bowl of it in my hands. "You need meat. It will help you conceive a son."

"Thank you, Aunt." I picked up a morsel and nibbled on it.

Tiye leaned in close and lowered her voice. "I could not prevent my son from choosing you but make no mistake — should you in any way fail in your duties to him, I will see that you are banished to Shedet, where you will never be seen or heard from again."

I considered saying I understood Shedet was quite beautiful but thought better of it. If I allowed her to intimidate me now, she would continue until she moved to the Blessed West. I looked straight ahead, lowered my own voice, and spoke with as little lip movement as possible. "If you could not prevent him from choosing me in the first place, I doubt you could make him cast me aside."

"Ah, but his heart is fickle. If you do not meet his expectations, he will soon lose interest." She tilted her head to her right. "You see that woman by the far column, the one with the terrible mole on her face?"

I saw the one she meant. "You are going to tell me she was once Amenhotep's beloved."

Tiye laughed. "Gods, no. She's as common as sand and twice as homely. She is, however, your new lady-in-waiting. Her name is Taheret."

As Great Royal Wife, it was Tiye's duty to oversee all the royal household. I had to accept this, but I was not required to like it. "I had thought to choose my own ladies, if I had need of them."

"You have need, trust me. Your greatest need as Great Royal Wife will be companionship. I chose her specifically for you because, of all the ladies here, she is least likely to turn my son's head."

Which meant also that she was least likely to be distracted by infatuation with her son. I would never be able to speak, or act, freely around this Taheret. Yet, I could not refuse her. "Thank you, Aunt. You are very kind."

Tiye waved her arm at Taheret, who immediately jumped up and came to us, followed by a young man. This man had a striking profile and square jaw. He was lean and sun-bronzed, with the flat belly and well-defined muscles Amenhotep lacked.

"Lady Nefertiti, may I present to you your new lady-in-waiting, Taheret, and her husband, Bek."

Taheret curtsied and Bek bowed.

Her husband. I was seized with the suspicion that Tiye had chosen Taheret not so she could spy on me, but so that I might be tempted into adultery by handsome Bek. Most likely both, I decided.

"Pleased to meet you both," I said.

They replied in kind. Bek's gaze lingered on me before dropping to the floor.

"Bek is the son of the chief sculptor, Men. As well as apprenticing with his father, he also works as assistant to our royal architect," said Tiye. "I am told he shows great promise."

"You flatter me, Majesty," said Bek.

"You are dismissed," said Tiye. "The lady shall call on Taheret tomorrow."

They both bowed and returned to their table.

While they walked, the atmosphere in the room changed. At first, I couldn't place it, but then I realized the music had stopped and the entertainers departed.

Maya, high priest of Amun, took the floor, hands raised. "The blessings of Amun, great god on the great throne, chief of the gods, lord of everlastingness, are upon us. Surely this union shall bring abundance, prosperity, and health to Kemet for millions and millions of years." He indicated to Amenhotep to rise. "Behold our Crown Prince, the hope of our generations, beloved of the Aten, the remote one, with millions under his care."

He indicated for me to rise next. I did so, willing myself not to tremble in front of so large a crowd.

"And behold his new wife, the Lady Nefertiti, beloved of Sekhmet, the one who presides over the country, the Lady of Vegetation, Generous One who protects the Double Land against the plague. So long as she is with us, the plague will not dare attack again."

Cheers resounded, for in late years, the plague had claimed too many. Evidently, I was the only one present who was not comforted by this proclamation. It left the possibility of my becoming a scapegoat should the plague return during my lifetime. Without moving my head, I glanced down at Tiye, wondering if she'd had a hand in this.

Maya continued. "May her womb bring forth many strong sons for Kemet. And may our next Crown Prince be started this night!"

The crowd roared. Cups hit tables. Drums sounded. Amenhotep held out his hand to me, and I took it. Together, we crossed through the center of the hall.

By the far column, Bek had his arm around Taheret's shoulders and bent to whisper in his ear. She smiled at him.

Once out of the hall, we turned toward our apartments. I turned my head to look at Amenhotep, but he kept staring straight ahead. He stopped at the door to my quarters. The guard stood aside to let us in.

"I had expected to go to your quarters," I said.

"I could hardly take you there," said Amenhotep. "I left instructions for the dancing girl to be sent there. She will be waiting for me."

"I see." I had been granted my reprieve after all. "Good night, then."

"It will be."

I sank onto the stool at my night table and removed my earrings, necklace, rings, and bracelets. I was about to remove my wig as well.

"Leave it on," said Amenhotep.

"Excuse me?" I hadn't realized he was still there.

"I prefer the wig. Now, take your clothes off."

"What about your dancing girl?"

"She'll wait. Right now, we have a duty to perform."

Sighing, I stood up. I kicked off my sandals and attempted to wriggle out of the bead net.

"You're taking too long." He grabbed the beadwork with both hands and pulled. Threads snapped, and beads clacked against the floor tiles in a torrent.

I pulled my dress, and the remnants of the netting, over my head.

"Turn around. Slowly."

I did.

I heard his breath escaping. "Exquisite."

When I turned back, Amenhotep had removed his sash and robe and was busy untying his kilt. It seemed to be giving him difficulty. I went to him and put my hands over his. "Let me." The knot was tight. I tried to dig my fingers into the fabric, but it wouldn't give. I pulled on the knot to bring it closer to me. By slipping one hand under the top of the kilt, I was able to work it a little better.

Amenhotep grabbed my buttocks, pulling me against him. I could feel his member hard against my pelvic bone. Both of my hands were trapped between us, and I wriggled to try and extricate them. Just as I managed to release them, Amenhotep lifted me off the floor and whispered, "Legs around my waist."

I did as commanded, grabbing him with both legs and arms. He shifted my weight until his manhood pressed against my womanhood, with only a very fine linen between us. A shiver shook my body, and a moan escaped my lips.

Amenhotep walked me over to my bed, and we fell together. I pushed his kilt up out of the way and drew him to me. I moaned again as he entered. My hips moved against his, matching his thrusts.

Amenhotep quickened his pace, emphasizing each thrust with a slap of his hand on the bed beside me.

My legs rose up, grasping him once again around the waist, guiding him toward that spot where I could feel him both inside and out.

"Tighter," he said, his pace unrelenting.

Startled, I opened my eyes.

"I said, hold tighter." His face contorted as if straining.

I squeezed with my thighs. His back arched, and his former rhythmic thrusting became erratic. He collapsed on top of me, panting. My passion still not sated, I wriggled against him, but he withdrew. After lying there a few moments, he rose from the bed and pulled his kilt off over his head.

"I owe your former suitor a debt of gratitude," he said, using his kilt to wipe himself clean. "He taught you well. Begetting heirs with you will be no tedious duty after all. Now lie there for a time so as not to lose any of my seed." He tossed the kilt aside, covered himself with only his robe, and left my quarters.

I threw a cushion at the door and lay back down. My mind was full of fury at having been treated like a receptacle, while my unsated body longed for his prompt return.

Journey to the Duat

Part 2

The chamber I am in, and the one next to it, are crowded with everything I will need once I reach the Field of Reeds: my chariots, my gaming boards, trunks full of clothing, and jewelry. Fine couches. I suppose I am expected to be grateful that at least Ay did not skimp on my funeral.

Under one of the couches, I spy my favorite jewelry trunk. I lift it onto the couch and open the lid. I pull out the pieces, one by one. The necklace of golden scarabs and lapis beads falls across my hand. I remember Akhenaten clasping it around my neck the day he purported to give me the freedom to choose. And later, much later, Bek removing it, his hot breath on my bare skin. Yes, this will do. Inside the trunk is a leather satchel. I put the necklace inside and add a few bracelets and some rings.

Since I cannot leave through the entrance, I sigh and turn back. Much as it pains me, I cannot undo that which has been done, and so I must fortify myself for the journey ahead. I retrace my steps back to the deepest part of the tomb. The descending passage is covered in spells. In my present form, I find the spells come easily. I remember them the moment I see them and can recall them instantly.

Inside the burial chamber is the false door — the portal through which I can pass. Once through, I find myself in a pillared hall. Lotus and papyrus columns lead the way from the tomb entrance, through the temple, and out into the open air.

I scrutinize the offering table near the entrance. It is fortunate that the table itself is carved with images of food in case the offerings should not be made, for it is nearly bare, holding only a few rotting figs and half a jug of wine. One last insult from Ay. I try to pick up a fig to throw it, but my hand passes through. My hand passes through the table as well. Outside the tomb, I am but a mist.

A figure brushes past me, and I turn. There are people here. I presume they are the priests performing their duties, but to me they are shadowy, unreal. It is they who seem insubstantial, not I.

As there is nothing more for me to do here, I walk out into the open air. The light outside is fading. As I turn, I can see the sun beginning to dip below the western horizon. I turn back to the east and start on the path to the river.

Waiting by the water steps, there is a boat — a small, wooden boat formed into the shape of a papyrus raft — on which stand four hooded figures. These are the three boatmen, together with the god who will lead me on my journey.

I hold out the satchel. One of the boatmen takes it, inspects the jewelry inside, nods, and passes it to his companions. When they have all approved, they move aside and allow me to board.

I sit in the one seat in the center of the deck. The fourth figure approaches and pushes back its hood. I gasp. Inside is a woman with dark eyes and straight, dark hair.

"Surprised to see me?" she says.

I freeze. Ordinarily, it is the sun god who accompanies the dead on their journey through the Duat. The change means that her interest in me has not yet ended, and that can bode either well or ill, depending on her mood. "You are not the one who is supposed to be here," I manage to say.

She sighs. "I thought it more appropriate for me to be your guide."

One of the boatmen pushes off with his pole. The boat floats along with the current a little way. As the sun disappears, a tributary opens up along the western bank. We follow its course.

Twelve hours of the night, and twelve gates to pass through before I can rise with the sun and go on to the blessed Field of Reeds. I close my eyes and hope the goddess's presence does not mean I have already been judged wanting.

Amenhotep IV, Year 1
(ca. 1353 BCE)

Sunlight glinted off the gold of the sacred barge as it plied the palace lake. The two Amenhoteps, father and son, stood atop the deck, recreating the voyage of the sun through the Duat.

I glanced at Tiye, thankfully seated too far away for whispered gibes. Two kings meant two Great Royal Wives, although I knew which of us would hold authority in the women's quarters and with the kings. But one need only look to the elder Amenhotep to know this situation would not endure for long. His degeneration had continued over the last several months. The pains in his mouth had prevented him from taking enough nourishment, and he was much withered, his limbs skeletal, his skin sagging where once there was firm flesh. He was also prone to fevers, infections, and periods of illness. It was a certainty he would soon be sailing with Ra to the glorious West.

Perhaps it was my condition, but even under the shade canopy, with slaves wielding ostrich-feather fans, I found the heat oppressive and wearying. Sweat pooled under my breasts, and between my belly and thighs. Even my son seemed subdued, only occasionally shifting his position or giving me a half-hearted kick. I shifted position to relieve pressure on my lower back.

"Shall I send for some wine for you?" asked Mutnedjmet, seated to my left.

I shook my head. "It is merely a slight discomfort. It shall pass."

"When the ceremonies are over, you must send for the masseur."

"Indeed, I shall, and follow it up with a dip in the lake."

To my right, Taheret joined in. "I do not understand why you insist on doing something as undignified as swimming."

"That is because you have not tried it," I said. "There is no better way to relax and cool a tired body."

"It is relaxing to do more work?" she said.

I did not respond. It was a conversation we had had many times. Taheret dared not disapprove of me openly and so limited herself to questioning why I would dream of doing such and such. Swimming, riding chariots, hunting. My wig, my clothes, my taste in jewelry. I suspected she was greatly influenced in this by my mother-in-law.

I spotted a familiar face jostle to the front of the crowd, and by Taheret's excited wriggle, I knew she had, too.

"My husband is the most loyal of subjects," she said. "And a most gifted architect. He will be a great servant to your husband for all his life and will build him many great monuments."

"We shall see," I said. "He is as yet untried."

The kings disembarked at the near side of the lake, in front of the assembled crowd. Now came the most fraught part of the Heb-Sed Festival. Both kings must race the Apis bull. Even from this distance, I could see the elder king's shaking as he donned the red crown of Upper Kemet. Tiye tensed. She moved as if to stand but stayed perched on the edge of her seat. The elder king must not be seen as weak. I wondered if, after thirty years together, I would be so solicitous of my own husband.

Both kings accepted a mace and scepter and set out. The bull ran beside them. The priests had first run it hard and given it a dose of poppy, before bringing it to the festival grounds. The purpose of the race was for the kings to prove they were capable of ruling the country, and it would not do for the bull to thunder past them.

At first, the two kings kept stride with each other, though out of deference to his father, the son ran at what was clearly a plodding pace for him. Even as the elder's steps slackened further, young Amenhotep stayed at his father's side until boredom took hold. Then he raced to the end of the course and circled back and around his father, all the while holding up both arms in expectation of adoration.

The crowd did not know how to respond. Both failing to applaud for the younger king and doing so at the expense of the elder were a serious breach of etiquette. There was a smattering of enthusiastic clapping and cheering, mostly from the younger attendees — those new to the court and eager to rise in position. It took no great foresight to know their fortunes depended on pleasing the younger king. The veterans at court — those who had long served the elder king — clapped with only half a heart, looking to each other or to the ground, not to the race.

By the time they had completed the fourth circuit, the old man — I felt shame at thinking of him as such, but such he was — was reduced to a shuffling step. At this point, Amenhotep the younger sprinted forward, completing the circuit in minutes. Many younger nobles whooped and hollered. Taheret joined in. She no doubt thought it a display of loyalty, but it did not endear her to me. Nor to her husband, I noted. Bek stood near enough for me to see him well. He remained silent, glared at her, and then looked to me in what seemed like apology.

The kings paused to exchange their red crowns for the white crowns of Lower Kemet. No doubt fearing the shift in loyalty provoked by his performance in the first set, Amenhotep the elder attempted a run. His feet fell heavily and then twisted with each other, and he froze. He dropped his scepter and clutched at his spine before crashing, face down, in the sand. An audible gasp erupted from the crowd. Amenhotep the younger turned his head. From where I sat, I could not see the expression on his face, but he made no move to go to his father.

Tiye and I both rose involuntarily, ready to go to his aid. We stared at each other, united for this one moment in our concern for our father-in-law and husband. When he moved and raised himself to his knees, we both sat down. As humiliating as it was to fall, it would be more humiliating still to accept help from two women, one in her middle years, the other heavy with child.

The crowd held their breath as their king attempted to rise to his feet. That his back and knees pained him was obvious in his movements. A few twitters came from the crowd. I could not identify the culprits. Young Amenhotep stood immobile, watching his father. Only after the elder made several unsuccessful attempts and fell again did he put down his mace and scepter and jog to his father's aid. He held out a hand, which his father accepted. He put an arm around his father's waist and took his weight for the remainder of the race, before dropping him gently back onto his throne.

The son remained standing and raised an arm for silence. Only when all murmuring subsided did he speak. "My divine father, Nebmaatre Amenhotep, Lord of the Two Lands, has ruled long and wise, and with the blessing of the Aten who watches over all of us, he will continue to do so for many years to come." This produced cheers. Amenhotep again raised his arm and waited for his moment. "And now I, Neferkhepure Waenre Amenhotep, Lord of the Two Lands, High Priest of Every Temple, shall continue to rule with the wisdom of my father." He gestured for me to join him. When I did, he continued. "Together with my Great Royal Wife, Neferneferuaten Nefertiti, who already carries within her the next Crown Prince, we shall long serve the Aten, the gods of the land, and the people."

Again, the divide between the young and the more mature was evident in the level of enthusiasm of response. I feared the new king enjoyed the popularity only of those who sought to curry favor, and whose loyalty would shift with the wind.

Chapter 10

When the pain woke me, I tried to ignore it and go back to sleep. The first time it had happened, I woke half the household in my excitement, sure the babe would soon be born but fearing it was still too early. Since then, the nightly pains had become a regular occurrence, every three or four nights, and it was now past my time. Yet, I had no reason to think this night was any different from all those before.

Just as I was growing sleepy again, another pain took my body. After the third time, I gave in, knowing sleep would not find me again. I slipped on a robe and sandals and woke Taheret, who had taken to sleeping on the floor in my chamber in the last month.

The two of us slipped out into a courtyard, trailed by two guards. The moon cast light enough for us to see. Taheret offered an arm, and I took it, leaning on her as I waddled.

"It will be tonight; I am certain," said Taheret.

Every time she said the same thing, and every time I responded the same way, yet I found it comforting. "I shall believe it when I am holding my son in my arms."

"You can believe it tonight. Look to the moon. It is at its fullest. This is the time babes are born."

"I pray to Sekhmet you are right. I grow weary of this burden."

We walked and walked. As each pain came and went, each one lesser than the last, my hope faded. The moon sank toward the west.

"Come, let us go back. I may return to sleep after all, this night."

As we passed through the door into the palace, I leaned against the wall, breathing heavily and rubbing my spine.

"Majesty?" said Taheret. "This is different from your other pains."

I shook my head. "It is not my belly that aches, it is my back."

Taheret straightened. "That is a sign. You recall Ipu said that the child was facing out and that when your time came, you would feel the pains in your back."

"Nonsense," I said. "It is simply the strain of carrying extra weight in front. Like a horse or an ass who develops a swayback in the last month."

Taheret ignored me. I heard her instructing a guard to fetch Ipu, the servant who had delivered Tiye's last few babes, along with those of my other ladies, and send her to the birthing pavilion.

"Stop," I said as he turned to go. "You will be disturbing her for naught. As you were."

The guard returned to his post.

"Do not listen to her Majesty. She is delirious with pain and knows not what she is saying."

Such impertinence. I was about to reprimand her when a spasm started in my lower back and radiated forward. My hand, resting on my swollen belly, felt the muscles contract. I turned my face to the wall but failed to stifle the cry. The guard turned and ran.

Taheret spoke to the remaining guard. "Help her Majesty to the birthing pavilion."

The guard looked unsure, and understandably so. It was forbidden for a commoner to touch me.

But Taheret was insistent. "Unless you wish to see your queen birth the Crown Prince here in the corridor, you will help her."

I saw the guard's face contort with fear. I expect the thought of witnessing childbed frightened him more than the fact of my personage. Whatever his motivation, I was grateful when he placed a firm arm around my waist, taking most of my rather considerable weight.

The birthing pavilion lay outside the palace walls, tucked against the outer enclosure. The way felt long, and, once, we had to stop while the pains took me. As we drew near, I caught the scent of lotus and convolvulus. Servants had been bringing fresh flowers here daily for some weeks now.

As we entered, the other ladies arrived. They ran around lighting lamps, fluffing the mattress, and piling fresh linens. Mutnedjmet ran to me, taking the guard's place. His relief was obvious as he fled.

"Do you wish to walk, Neffie?" asked Mutnedjmet.

I nodded. She led me on a circuit near the pavilion. I took care to stay near the enclosure wall, in case I needed support, for I feared leaning too heavily on Mutnedjmet, she being so slight. When a pain gripped me, I turned to face the wall, placing two hands on it, and moaned. Mutnedjmet placed a hand on my shoulder.

"Rub my back." She did. "Lower."

She moved her hand further down. "How's that?"

"Still lower." She finally hit the spot. "Don't be afraid to press hard. Use your fists."

By the time the pain subsided, Ipu had arrived, with her votive statue of Bes, god of childbirth, and a satchel. She led me back inside the pavilion and ordered me to lie down on the mattress. She squatted beside me.

"Knees up," she said.

I obeyed, and she lifted my robes. Placing one hand on my abdomen, she inserted two fingers inside me. I willed myself to relax so she could do her work. Once satisfied, she withdrew her fingers. Washing her hands in a bowl provided by one of the girls, she said, "The news is both good and bad. The way is opening, and the head is down, but there is still a long ways to go."

I rolled onto my side and tucked my knees to my chest; her ministrations having brought on another pain.

"Come down, placenta, come down." said Ipu to Bes. "I am Heru who conjures so that she who is giving birth becomes better than she was, as if she was already delivered. Look, Het-Heru will lay her hand on her with an amulet of health. I am Heru, who saves her." She repeated this three more times and then removed from her satchel a clay amulet of Bes and bound it to my forehead.

"Well, get up," she said.

The command startled me, and I raised my head.

"If you wish to birth your baby in less than two days' time, the best place to be is on your feet."

That roused me enough to work myself upright and to the edge of the mattress. With Taheret on one side, and Mutnedjmet on the other, I managed to stand.

"Go, and walk," said Ipu. Sit if you need a break, but do not lie down. Help your baby to drop."

Taheret protested. "But what if the child comes too quick and her Majesty has no time to return?"

"There is no danger of that for many hours yet," said Ipu.

"But ..." said Taheret.

Ipu put an arm around Taheret's shoulders, guiding her (and by extension, Mutnedjmet and myself as well) toward the entrance. "If that should happen, the two of you will squat with her under a sycamore, and I shall catch her baby where it lands. It would not be the first time."

So, Taheret and Mutnedjmet led me back out. Now, the Aten was rising, pouring his life-giving rays upon us. I muttered the prayer I had rehearsed many times already. "Come to me Het-Heru, my mistress, in my fine pavilion, in this happy hour with this pleasant north wind ..." My eyes strayed toward the east wall, beyond which lay the river, and beyond that, the eternal desert, the domain of Sekhmet. I prayed she would also be with me in my travail and see both my son and me safely through.

A thought struck me. "Has anyone informed my husband?"

"I sent word right away," said Mutnedjmet. "By now, he must be anxiously awaiting word of the new prince's arrival."

Taheret scowled, always desperate to prove her worth. Normally, I found it pitiable, but my present circumstance had wiped out what little patience I had. "Even now, you begrudge any kindness done for me by another — even my own sister. Your attitude does not endear you to me, and if it continues, you may go back to her Majesty and tell her of your failure."

I broke free of her arm and leaned against the enclosure wall. Mutnedjmet stood beside me, holding my shoulders while my body seized. Taheret stood aside, watching.

When the contraction faded, Taheret offered me her arm. "I know this is your pain talking, so I will not take offence."

It was my pain that caused me to say my thoughts aloud, but it was not what produced those thoughts in the first place. Cursing my lapse in discretion, I took the proffered arm, my silence allowing Taheret to believe her words.

The sun rose higher in the sky, nearing the zenith, and still I walked, always with two companions. They were not always the same companions — they changed shift as they grew weary — but I continued on, resting only occasionally, until my robes were drenched in sweat. The ladies removed my clothing, sponged me down with water, and gave me wine sweetened with honey to sip. At regular intervals, Ipu had me marched back into the pavilion for inspection and then marched outside again.

After one such inspection, she said I was to stay inside for now, and she ordered food brought to me. "It is to be a long effort, and you will need your strength."

By late afternoon, there was still no progress. Ipu bade me lie down again. "It is time to take steps," she said, and pulled a long, hooked instrument from her satchel. She cleaned it with natron and water and pushed some linen padding under me.

My eyes widened as she pressed a hand to my abdomen and moved the wicked looking thing toward my nether regions.

"Relax. I'm only going to break your waters. Labor usually speeds up after that."

"Usually?"

I could feel her hand moving inside me. "Childbed is tricky. It's never the same for any two women. But most of the time, this does the trick."

"And if it doesn't?"

Her hand jerked, and I felt a gush of warmth between my legs. She patted a knee. "Don't worry, this isn't my only trick."

I scrutinized her. Her face was relaxed, and she had no trouble meeting my eye. Nor did she hesitate when speaking. She was not worried. I decided I had no cause to be, either.

She ordered a girl to put fresh linen on the floor. When it was in place, she guided me to a standing position. Liquid streamed down my legs, in a torrent at first, and then slowed to a trickle, with an occasional gush when I shifted my weight. Ipu massaged my abdomen to hasten the process.

"Your baby is still facing forward. That may be why you are not progressing."

"Can he be turned?"

"Usually, they turn on their own during the birth."

That word again. Usually. "And if not?"

"Babies can be born this way, but in your case the head is not pressing in the right place. If breaking the waters does not help, we will have to persuade him to turn."

Should it come to that, I sincerely hoped my son did not inherit my resistance to persuasion. I grabbed Ipu by the shoulders as the pain engulfed me. She leaned into my body to support me. Once it was over, she smiled. "That was more like it." I sank back down on the mattress, while she scooped up the linen and showed me a clump of bright red. "Your womb is finally opening."

Seeing the relief evident on her face, I questioned my earlier assumption that she was not worried. Perhaps she was merely accomplished at hiding her emotions. As I was myself.

She called for padding and more linens and arranged them on the floor. "When the next pain comes, I want you on your hands and knees. It will be easier for you."

I did as I was told, but she'd lied about it being easier. While she kneaded the flesh on my lower back, I threw my head back and howled. Taheret was at my side, rubbing my shoulder and whispering in my ear that I was doing a fine job, and it wouldn't be much longer. I wanted to punch her.

Between the pains, I curled up on the linens, whimpering like a child. Tears streamed down my cheeks, and I made no effort to stop them. Each time the pain returned; it seemed I was less able to endure it.

After an interminable time, Ipu performed another examination. Then she sat back, hair and face slick with sweat. "Your womb is opening, but your baby has lost all the progress he has made. He has retreated back into the womb." She looked from Taheret to Mutnedjmet before settling on Mutnedjmet. "Go to the physician and have him make up some poppy." Mutnedjmet got up right away. "Tell him to make it strong," Ipu said to her retreating back.

"What now?" I asked.

"Now, we take a break," she said. "The poppy will help you sleep. You are too exhausted to go on like this. And, if you are lucky, when you wake, your baby will already be here." I noted the tension in her jaw, the creases in the corners of her eyes. Now, she was worried.

She and Taheret helped me back onto the mattress and made me comfortable. When the poppy arrived, it was bitter, but I swallowed it all. I just wanted it to stop. And it did.

I woke to probing hands. Someone had rolled me onto my back and pushed my knees up. Ipu smiled.

"It seems what your baby needed was for you to stop resisting."

"He is coming at last?"

"Not yet, but the way is finally open, and he is trying," she said. "Since you are awake, it would help for you to get back on your hands and knees."

I moaned.

Ipu raised a finger. "None of that now. That's what has made this take so long." She helped me to the floor.

My head ached, but my body felt stronger. When my middle contracted, Ipu worked her hands across it.

"We've just about got it. Next one." Another pain came and went. "That's it. Your baby has turned." She sat me on the mattress, called for the birthing bricks, and spread fresh linen on the floor between them. She ordered Taheret and Mutnedjmet to help me squat with one foot on each brick.

I felt a sudden urge for the privy. "I need the toilet," I said. "Now."

"No, you don't," said Ipu. "When the next pain comes, I want you to push. You two — support her."

My knees shook. Taheret and Mutnedjmet allowed me to lean on them. Ipu steadied my legs with her own body. "Push as if you were at the privy," she said.

I clenched my stomach muscles.

"You can do better than that," said Ipu.

I squeezed my eyes shut and groaned with the effort.

"Much better. A few more, and you'll be holding your baby."

A few more? I wasn't sure I could manage one, but I did. And another. After quite a few more attempts, I sagged. "I can't do this anymore."

"Yes, you can," said Taheret. "You're almost there."

Ipu nodded. "She's right." She took my hand and guided it between my legs. A hard, slippery, wet thing was lodged in there. "That's your baby's head. One more push and it will be out."

"Okay. One more," I said. "But only one." Next time, I pushed so hard Ipu asked me to ease up.

She massaged my aching membranes. "Slowly so you don't tear."

I couldn't stop. I felt the sting of tearing flesh, and still I could not ease up until the pressure was relieved. I looked down and saw a dark, slimy mass between my thighs.

Ipu slipped her hand in around my son's head, feeling all around. Then she reached in and gently pulled. When my body convulsed again, the baby slipped out into her hands. She jerked her chin toward Taheret. "Quick — remove the top layer of linens." Taheret did, rolling it up to conceal the blood and excrement.

I sat on the clean linen and reached out my arms for my son.

Ipu hesitated for a moment. "You have a very fine daughter," she said, offering me the child.

I could not speak. It is a son. It must be a son. Yet, I could plainly see it was not so. I took the child from Ipu and held her against my breast. She lay, sleeping.

Ipu massaged my abdomen and gave me a thorough inspection. "There is a tear, but it is not serious. It will take some stitches, but you will be fine."

I jiggled the child to rouse her, but she continued sleeping. I lifted an arm and let it go. It flopped back down. I filled with fear. "She is limp. She does not respond. What is wrong with her?"

"It is from the poppy, nothing more. It had the same effect on you."

"Are you sure?"

"Her color is good, and she is breathing well," said Ipu. "In a few weeks' time, you'll be wishing she would sleep so soundly. But for now, we must clean her and swaddle her before she catches a chill. And you are not quite finished yet."

Once it was over and we had both been washed, I lay with my new daughter on my bed in my own chambers. Ipu's words had proved correct — the babe wakened in good time and was now hungrily sucking. Soon, she would be sent to her wet nurse, but for now she was all mine. As her tiny jaw worked, I uncurled her fingers, admiring their perfection.

One of my ladies, Aset, sat on a cushion by my bed, stroking the babe's dark fuzz. "She is perfect, Highness."

"You will conceive soon; I am sure of it."

She smiled and then turned at the sound of a disturbance at my chamber door.

I braced myself. By now, my husband would know he did not have a son after all. I knew I would have to face his disappointment sooner or later, so I might as well get it done, but it was worse than I had feared. He was not alone.

Tiye floated into the room ahead of her son and the court physician. She looked down her nose at the baby and sneered. For her part, the babe released my nipple and yawned.

Amenhotep touched Aset's face and stroked her hair. Aset froze. As soon as Amenhotep removed his hand, she turned her head away. Her husband would welcome even less any such attention paid to her by the king.

"You had one duty to perform, and you have failed," said Tiye.

Still not knowing young Amenhotep's reaction to the news, I bit back a reminder that Tiye herself birthed several girls before giving her husband the much-needed son.

I focussed on the child so I would not have to see Amenhotep's face.

"Nonsense. She has performed beautifully," said Amenhotep.

Startled, I looked up at him.

He pushed ahead of Tiye. He was beaming. "We cannot continue our dynasty with only boys." He knelt beside my bed. With a tentative hand, he stroked the baby's head. "The Aten requires both male and female to make a whole. He has seen fit to send us a girl first. The next will be a boy. Or the next."

He took the baby in his arms and rocked back on his heels, cradling her in her swaddling clothes against him. "I have brought our physician here, so that he may say the proper prayers and bless the amulets to protect you both from the plague."

I shivered. The plague had returned this year, though not so bad as in previous years. "That is not necessary. I have been praying to Sekhmet and have made all the proper offerings."

"It is not enough," said Amenhotep. "Her power pales in comparison to that of the Aten."

I did not believe him but was happy to accept any protection given by any god who cared to offer it.

The physician prayed over a bracelet of tiny red carnelian discs and then tied it to the baby's arm. In a singsong voice, he praised the Aten and asked for his blessings, and his protection. "Your rising is beautiful, O living Aten, Lord of the eternity. You are radiant, beautiful, and gleaming; your love is great and powerful of rays. You are the mother and father of everything that you made; their eyes, when you rise, see because of you ..."

During his litany, Maya, head priest of Amun, entered my chamber. He waited for the physician to complete his prayers. "I have come to bless the new princess," he said.

Amenhotep kept his back to him. "You were not summoned."

Maya bowed. "An oversight, I am sure."

"No oversight. You may leave."

The man stood there, mouth agape.

Now, Amenhotep turned to face him but did not stand. "I said leave."

"You are turning down the protection of Amun?"

"I have no need of Amun. I have the Aten. You may go."

I touched his arm. "If Amun wishes to bless our child, surely we should let him."

Amenhotep pulled away from me and stood, with the baby still in his arms. "I shall forgive you this because you are just out of childbed. Maya, you may go now."

The old priest threw me one last look and then left. Tiye studied the babe. "She may grow to be quite comely; I suppose."

"She will be more than comely," said Amenhotep. "See how much she favors her mother. She shall be called Meritaten, for she is truly beloved of the Aten."

From the doorway, I could see the elder Amenhotep sitting up on his bed, watching me as I entered. I had prepared him wine and food that had been mashed to a paste so that he need not chew. I also brought him poppy, which he needed more and more as the days passed. As always, I braced myself on entering the sick room. The smell of decay, rot, and impending death hit like a wall once I passed the threshold. My stomach lurched as I passed over the rosette tiles and under the vulture goddess's images above. I closed my eyes and swallowed hard to keep from retching.

"I know the smell in here is deplorable, but it does not usually bother you so much," he said.

I smiled as I climbed the step to his inner chamber and placed the food and wine on his bedside table. "On the contrary, it always bothers me." I had to press the back of my hand against my mouth.

He indicated the chamber pot, already half-full with liquid excrement. I emptied all I had already eaten that day. When the heaving stopped, I stood, head bowed, humiliated that I had let him see my revulsion at so tender a time for him. "I apologize for my weakness."

"No need to apologize for giving me what I've been longing for."

"I do not know what you mean, Father." I did, of course, for I longed for it as well. Alas, though Meritaten was toddling around already, every time my hopes grew, they were quickly dashed. And, truth be told, young Amenhotep was spending so many nights with his ailing father that a conception at that time would have been miraculous. So, when my courses were delayed, I kept it to myself until I could be certain. I was now certain but hesitated to let him know. His father's condition continued to degenerate, and yet he lingered. He credited this entirely to his insistence on seeing the line of succession secured with a new Crown Prince, and I feared if he knew this could be in the offing, he might stop fighting the inevitable.

I admitted my motivation in this regard was entirely selfish, for I had grown quite fond of the old man. When he was lucid, he regaled me (and everyone within earshot) with tales of hunting expeditions and diplomatic missions. Most of the family had long since bored with his reminiscences, but I found them fascinating. I learned a great deal by asking why he made certain choices and not others, and what he wished he had done differently.

His rheumy eyes roved over my body. "I may be old and bedridden, but I am not dead yet. I still notice a young woman's curves, and yours have grown more pronounced as of late."

A warmth rose in my cheeks. "I did not wish to speak of it until I was sure."

A fit of coughing shook him. I went to rub his back and make him as comfortable as I could.

When the fit was over, he looked to me. "I am sure. My grandson will be born near the end of inundation, if I am not mistaken."

"Your timing is correct," I said, "but as for the other, I do not wish to give you false hope. This one could be another girl."

"It is a boy. I know it."

I shifted next to him and looked away. He placed a finger on my chin and turned my face back to his.

"Do not fret. You are young and clearly very fertile. If this child should be a girl, I would just have to stay here a little longer, for the next will surely be a boy. Or is it that you wish to rid yourself of the burden of caring for me?"

"Not at all, Father. I look forward to seeing you hold my son."

He turned serious. "I am glad it is you who holds my son. You are the best choice that boy ever made."

"Thank you, Father. I am also glad he chose me."

"I have no time for platitudes. I am dying."

I shook my head. "Not for a long—"

He waved a hand. "Whether tomorrow, or next month, or next year, it will happen. Soon."

I wanted to deny it again, but I knew he would not thank me for it. "I know."

"Have I ever told you of my negotiations with King Kadashman-Enlil of Babylon?"

I could recite it by heart. "I should love to hear about it." I seated myself on a chair by his bedside.

He smiled, and his eyes gazed upon something past the boundaries of his chamber walls. "During his father's reign, I took one of the then-prince's sisters to wife. But when Kadashman-Enlil himself came to the throne ..." Here, Amenhotep blew out his cheeks and shook his head. "He was a firebrand. First thing he did was increase the size of his army. Started making trouble with neighboring kings. I decided a renewal of our alliance was in order. I 'requested' that he send his sister for me to wife as well. Do you know what he wrote me?"

Yes, every word. Yet I leaned closer and said, "Tell me."

"He demanded to know if his sister was even still alive. As if she should die and I would send no word. The woman was a mistress of my household."

I shook my head in sympathy. "What did you do?"

"I wrote back and pointed out that he had never sent anyone to my court who actually knew his sister and could identify her. I mean, the man sent a donkey herder as a court delegate."

"Scandalous," I said.

"He saw reason. Even the king of far-off Babylon quakes at the name of the mighty King of Kemet." His breath rattled in his chest. "He agreed to send the girl, though he insisted I send a delegation to pick her up and asked for one of my daughters in exchange."

"As if a daughter of the King of Kemet would ever be given to a foreigner."

Amenhotep nodded and pointed at me. "Exactly what I told him. Then he demanded gold. A fine thing it is to give your daughter to acquire a nugget of gold from your neighbor."

"Did you send the gold?"

He winked. "Of course."

His bony hand wrapped itself around my wrist, and I was taken aback at the strength of his grip. "You must promise me to rule well."

"Of course, I will perform my duties to the best of my ability."

He tugged on my arm. "You must do better than that. Do not allow the priests of Amun to take over, but do not allow my son to upset the balance of Ma'at. You must keep Kemet from succumbing to the forces of chaos."

He did not want platitudes, so I spoke my mind. "It is not in my power to keep your son from doing anything he desires."

He let go of my wrist. "Have you not been paying attention? Did you think I have been telling you all about my kingship simply for the pleasure of my own voice?"

That's when I knew he was not the doddering fool everybody took him for. He had been instructing me, training me, and doing so in such a way that it went completely unremarked by anyone save himself. "Diplomacy first," I said, awed. "Negotiate while maintaining a position of strength and let him think he has won."

He nodded. "You are a natural. If I did not know better, I would have believed it was the first time you had ever heard that story."

For the first time, I felt hopeful about the task given me by Sekhmet so long ago and now again by my father-in-law.

Chapter 12

A hand shook me awake. I sat up and looked into the eyes of my husband. He held a lamp in one hand, the tiny flame casting dark shadows under his eyes. I blinked. It was unlike him to enter my chambers in the night, and I was unprepared.

"Let me send my ladies away," I said.

"They will pretend not to hear."

He set the lamp down on my night table and drew off his kilt. He was beyond ready. I knew well that with him at this point, there would be no gentle teasing or caresses, so I dutifully pushed my headrest out of the way, rolled onto my back and parted my legs. He was drawn forward by his member and entered me already thrusting. He grunted, and the bed slammed against the wall. I thought of my ladies, including my young sister, lying in the dark not daring to giggle.

I tried to match his rhythm, but it was erratic. After a time, I gave up, and simple raised my hips to him. He responded by increasing both his speed and strength. I all but felt my teeth rattle just as Amenhotep erupted in a jerking, shuddering, groaning climax. He collapsed on top of me, still convulsing in the aftermath. Even so, I felt him harden again.

"Let us remove ourselves to your chambers," I said. I hoped that now that he was partially sated, he would be less eager and I might, perhaps, derive some pleasure for myself. In a more private setting.

He pushed himself up to a sitting position. "Where is your maid Aset? Is she here?" He raised the lamp and searched the sleeping forms.

"Aset has a husband."

He shrugged. "She won't refuse a command from her king."

Indeed, she would not, but this was not a common request from a king, one that was not endorsed by the elder king. "Her husband could divorce her for it."

"Nonsense. He will be honored that the king thinks so highly of his wife."

I doubted the young man would be so pragmatic about it. I massaged Amenhotep's shoulders and brushed my lips against his neck. "I am with child again."

"I am relieved to hear it. I feared you were growing fat on sweetmeats, especially when you did not tell me."

"I wanted to be sure. We were disappointed so many times this past year."

"Now, go rouse Aset."

Dismayed that my distraction did not work, I snaked one hand down his thigh, and resigned myself to forgoing privacy. He grew even more rigid. "I can please you so much more than Aset can."

He kissed my neck. "Your jealousy excites me, but you need not fear. The prince in your womb will not be usurped. I want only her hands and her mouth. We can't have our servants giving themselves airs about raising the king's child."

"I can ..."

"Yes, I am well acquainted with all of your skills, but I must start building my own women's quarters. If she meets expectations, I will take her as a concubine. Her husband will be well compensated, of course."

Which meant, of course, that if she didn't meet expectations, she would be rejected by the king and possibly by her husband as well. I couldn't argue with his goal — the king was expected to maintain many wives and concubines to ensure the birth of many sons — but I could fault his methods.

"There are many unmarried women. All you need do is send out an edict. Every family in Kemet will be pleased to vie for the honor of sending one of their own daughters to be your concubine."

"Much has already passed between me and Aset. She gives me looks, wears provocative clothing, scents her hair with jasmine so that it wafts past me, inflaming me. She has been hoping for this."

I knew it was not true. I had seen Aset shrink from him whenever he was near, hoping he would not see her. I also knew she had heard this entire conversation, as had all my other ladies, and knew what awaited her. Nevertheless, to preserve the illusion of our privacy, I rose from my bed and tiptoed around the forms on the floor until I found Aset. I gently shook her and whispered, "I'm sorry," in her ear.

I lay down on the mat she vacated and did my best to pretend I did not hear. When she returned, she was crying. I went back to my own bed.

"She was truly abysmal. I had no choice but to take her completely."

After all of Aset's difficulty conceiving, I prayed this would not be the time she did. But at least she would not have to endure this again, and perhaps her husband would be understanding. "Then you will not be taking her as a concubine."

"Not for now, at least. I may try her again, to see how well she takes instruction. You have improved much with practice." He thought for a moment. "But I must take action now. I have inherited my father's women, but they are mostly old and withered. I'll have to send most of them to Shedet. No, all of them. I'll not sow my seed where my father sowed his."

I kept running through his words in my mind. "What do you mean 'have inherited'?"

"Did I not mention it? My Father passed over to the West this night."

"No! It cannot be. I was with him yesterday. He was having a good day."

"I assure you it is so. I was with him when he passed. He had one of his fits and could not breathe. I sent for the physician, but by the time he arrived, it was too late."

I allowed this to sink in. "You were with him in his death chamber ... and then you came straight here ... to me?"

"My father has just died. Do you begrudge me a little comfort?"

I patted his arm, conceding his grief. Yet, in my mind I kept hearing the agonizing shrieks of a dying kitten.

Chapter 13

Two colossal statues of the dead king rose above the ground, in front of the pylons flanking the entrance to his mortuary temple — so large, the heads of the tallest among us barely met the top of the pedestals on which they sat. He looked fit and serene, as he had not in his last days. His hands rested on his knees, his twin visages gazed east upon the river, and the rising sun priests brought the Wesir-King in his coffin through the temple entrance and loaded him onto the oxen sledge. A second sledge carried his canopic chest with the mummified remains of his innards. As the sledges moved out, the mourning women fell in behind them, tearing their hair, beating their bare breasts, and wailing their shrill, ululating cries. Behind them, the priests took their place, shaking sistrums and waving incense. I looked for the bull and calf, the birds, and other sacrifices, but they were not with the priests. Perhaps they would follow behind us.

Tiye stepped in next but was stopped by Amenhotep's hand on her shoulder. "I go first." He stepped in, taking me with him.

Tiye looked about to protest but fell in behind us with her daughters. I took a deep breath of the frankincense smoke, filling my lungs with memories of temple life, and then looked back to see Meritaten in the arms of her wet nurse. The child within rolled and kicked. The Aten watched from overhead, blessing us more than necessary with his warm breath, even under our sunshade. I thought how marvelous it would be if we could take the chariots and feel the cooling wind in our faces. It would be most disrespectful, but I felt the old king would understand, even if his wife and son did not. I almost laughed aloud at the thought of Tiye's face if we'd done that.

Amenhotep looked straight ahead, lost in thought. In spite of appearances to the contrary, he must have been feeling the burden of kingship, now that he must carry it alone. Even if he had hastened this inevitable outcome, the reality was surely greater than he had anticipated. I studied his face as best I could without letting him know I was doing so. If he bore any guilt for his father's death, he gave no sign.

A hawk circled close overhead. I wondered that it would approach so near. It began to tighten its circle and come down, and I saw that it had only appeared to be so close because it was so large; it had actually been very high up indeed. It whooshed down to earth, transforming into a human figure as it lit. Heru was also among us to see the old king welcomed into the Field of Reeds.

Amenhotep nudged me, and I realized I had been staring at what, to everyone else present, appeared to be empty space. Throughout the rest of the procession, I caught glimpses of billowing linen and green flesh, even tawny fur. From above, the hands of the Aten descended, holding out the ankh to the old king, but still remaining apart, aloof. I resisted the urge to turn and look at any of them directly. It was enough to know that Nebmaatre Amenhotep, Lord of the Two Lands, was being welcomed by the gods he had revered throughout his life.

We passed the entrance to the valley where most of my husband's ancestors, including my own grandparents, lay interred. We turned into the adjoining valley, in which Amenhotep, the third of that name, had constructed his tomb. The procession stopped at the tomb entrance, cut deep into the base of a cliff. The priest attached ropes to the coffin and prepared wooden rollers to move the king into his burial chamber. When they moved him into the entrance instead of standing him up outside, I grabbed Amenhotep's arm.

"Stop them. They have forgotten the Opening of the Mouth."

Amenhotep shook his head. "They are acting on my orders. My revered father is to have an Atenist burial, as was his wish. Instead of the old rituals, I shall enter the tomb once he is in his burial chamber and offer prayers to aid him in his journey to join the Father of us All."

My mouth went dry. "Without the Opening of the Mouth, he will not be able to speak in the afterlife. He will not be able to pass through into the Field of Reeds."

He merely contemplated the dark hole cut into the rock. "All of that is a lie. My father shall join the Aten disc, as I shall when it is my time."

Yes, perhaps they would. They were kings. As for the rest of us, without proper burial ... I could not bear to think of it.

The long wait was punctuated by murmurings and restless stares, and not only from the human attendees. The gods seemed equally perplexed. I dared not look directly at them, feeling guilty that I did not protest more, yet unsure what I could do in the moment to change Amenhotep's mind. After what seemed an interminable wait, the priests exited the tomb, and Amenhotep entered. Wesir, in his mummified form, went in, accompanied by his faithful wife, the goddess Aset, and their son, Heru. Sekhmet, Ptah, Het-Heru, and all the others followed. Save one. Only the Aten remained, reaching out with his hands but approaching no closer.

As we waited, I pictured the rites — first, the coffin would be purified with water poured from four different jars. Then, the mouth of the face on the coffin would be purified with natron, and the whole of it fumigated with incense before Amenhotep touched its mouth, the sacrifice of the bull and the presentation of the heart, the calf's foreleg — as if the force of my own will could replace that which Amenhotep had denied.

At once, I heard a horrific shrieking, as if living flesh were being flayed from bones. Never having attended a king's funeral before, I thought at first that it must be the mourning-women. I moved to reprimand them but found them to be silent. The shrieking continued, growing in intensity. My head pounded, and I covered my ears with my hands.

Tiye pulled one hand away from my ear. "What is wrong with you?"

I thought she must have gone deaf but then noticed that no one else was reacting to the sound. "My apologies. I am simply grief-stricken."

She frowned but did not admonish me further.

The screams were coming from inside the tomb, and were growing louder. The gods rushed from the entrance and flew off, raging. As they hurtled toward the crowd, Maya, high priest of Amun, flinched. Or did I imagine such? Could he really see them, as I could?

After a time, Amenhotep emerged into the daylight, arms raised. "The prayers to the gods successful. The king lives again."

Overhead, the Aten stretched his hand with the proffered ankh toward Amenhotep, giving no sign of having been moved by events. Inscrutable, unknowable.

In anticipation of Amenhotep's visit, I sent my serving women to sleep in a separate room. He had been coming to me nearly every night since his father's death, and I expected this day of the funeral he would have an extra level of tension to relieve.

He arrived shortly and wasted no time. Once he was sated, I dared ask what had been bothering me since we were at the tomb. "How went the prayers to all the gods inside the burial chamber?"

"To all the gods? Oh, no, I prayed only to the Aten."

I had known. He merely confirmed what I had suspected since the funeral. "I don't understand," I said. And I didn't. "Why would you deny your own father a chance at the afterlife?"

He rolled onto his side to face me. "The gods are a lie. They are stories meant to frighten children. Only the Aten exists."

This was folly. Was this what the old king had warned me about? "You are wrong," I said.

Amenhotep raised a hand and brought it down hard against my face. "I am the king," he hissed. "I am never wrong." He rose, gathered up his fallen kilt, and left.

The Duat

Gate 1

Part 1

The boat glides through the dark water, the boatman's pole making barely a ripple on the surface. Spanning the river and gradually growing nearer is the mountain of the west, cleft in two. The river passes between the two halves.

As we approach, a figure on either side lowers a barrier. A serpent surfaces from the water and coils itself around the barrier. They will block our passage unless I can name the gatekeeper correctly. I fear I will forget the contents of the Book after all, but I find it comes easily to mind.

"O Mistress of trembling, Chieftainess and Mistress of Destruction, the one who proclaims words which repel storms, the one who rescues the plundered one who has arrived. The name of its gatekeeper is 'Terror.'"

The serpent flicks its tongue as it retreats back into the depths. The other guardians remove the barrier. As the boat regains its forward momentum, I can see, fixed to the cliffs looming over us to each side, a head. The one to the right is a jackal, the other a ram. These heads serve to destroy those who are evil as they pass through the gate. I feel their eyes on me, even as I close mine and look down. I grip the seat with my hands and will my breathing to slow.

I hope the heads cannot see into my heart.

Amenhotep IV, Year 3

(ca. 1351 BCE)

Maya entered my audience chamber, bowing. The door remained open, with a guard watching to avoid any suggestion of impropriety. He uttered praises to me and heaped blessings on my new daughter, Meketaten.

I shifted in my seat, wishing he would get to the point. I still ached from the birth and longed for my bed and my baby.

"I am sure you asked to see me for a reason," I said, sounding curter than I had intended.

He nodded. "Are you aware that the king has seized some of the assets of the Temple of Amun and has removed all priests, including myself, from advisory positions?"

I knew this perfectly well. Amenhotep had told me, but I was not anxious to be used as a means of undermining him. "The king does not consult me on matters of state."

"Nevertheless, you do have his ear," said Maya. "He may listen to you."

"You have come to the wrong person," I said. "If you wish to prevail upon the king, you must speak with the viziers."

"The vizier of Upper Kemet has been removed from his position. His replacement is an untried schoolboy whose sole asset seems to be agreeing with the king in every matter."

His assessment of the new vizier, though unkind, struck me as accurate. I did not agree with Amenhotep's choice, but he did not ask my opinion. "It is the king's prerogative to effect any changes he wishes and to staff the government with those who will help, not hinder, his vision."

"This is a perturbation of Ma'at," said Maya. "We do things the way they have always been done, and that is what the gods expect of us, and this is Ma'at — cosmic order. But Ma'at is fragile, like a spider's web. Pull on one strand, and the whole becomes distorted. Even small changes can destroy the whole. The entire country will pay for what the king is doing. Witness the plagues that have resulted from his father's rejection of tradition in marrying a commoner."

"As my husband has done as well, you mean."

Maya sputtered and then bowed. "You are no commoner, Highness. You were born into the royal family, raised in the royal women's quarters."

"Only because my commoner father is brother to the commoner queen," I said. "I am not a close enough royal relation to satisfy your interpretation of Ma'at, and well we both know it, which raises the question of why you should bring your concerns to me."

"I beg your pardon, Highness, but you are the only one in a position to avert the oncoming catastrophe."

"I am not some silly child to be frightened by tales," I said. "I have studied history, and I know that the priests of Amun have not always been in a position of influence over the king. Five generations ago, a mere blink of the eye in Kemet's long history, the king's own ancestor bought the support of the priesthood in return for power." As a woman, she could not find support for her sole rule of Kemet any other way. Since that time, instead of receding to its former role, the priesthood of Amun had sought to increase its power with each successive generation, until it exerted more influence even than the viziers, who rightfully should wield power in the land. By the time my father-in-law had claimed the throne, the power of the Amun priesthood was second only to that of the king himself, and any further increase would surely be a usurpation of the kingship. I did not doubt Maya was aware of this already, which led me to suspect this was his goal.

"It is as you say," said Maya. "Hatshepsut sought our support in order to stay in power, but she was a great king who respected the ways of Ma'at. Despite her sex, she was the best choice for the throne at the time, and it was only right that we supported her."

Indeed, she was a great king. She enriched the coffers of Kemet a hundredfold and kept the nation well for her nephew until he came of age. "If that is so, you should not have needed bribery to do it. The king is simply returning Kemet to the Ma'at that existed before, when the priests knew their place."

In this, I was certain I was correct. This was not the perturbation of Ma'at about which Sekhmet had warned me.

"This is but the beginning," said Maya. "Once this is started, the king will pull us all further and further into chaos."

Chapter 15

Mutnedjmet, Taheret, and I sat on a blanket spread on the ground in a courtyard, watching Meritaten navigate the garden on her pudgy legs. Already, at two, she was leaving behind babyhood and becoming a child. At least, it seemed too soon to me. She caught sight of a frog hopping and decided to give chase. Each time she neared it, it hopped away before she could grasp it. After her third try, she ran faster, reached out sooner, and tripped over her own feet, landing face down in the soft earth.

When she rose, crying, I gathered her in my arms and brought her back to our blanket, rocking her softly.

"Such a shame," said Mutnedjmet. "She has your determination but her father's physical coordination."

"Hush," I said, but failed to hide a chuckle.

Taheret, too, smiled.

At that moment, the accused originator of Meritaten's lack of frog-catching abilities appeared, holding in his arms a number of papyrus scrolls. He fairly jogged over to us, a smile of what seemed to be triumph on his lips.

"Ah, here you are at last," he said. He looked at Mutnedjmet and Taheret and jerked his head, indicating that they should leave.

I moved to hand Meritaten over to Mutnedjmet, but Amenhotep stopped me. "Let the child stay." He knelt beside us as the women walked away and unrolled a scroll on the blanket. "Behold."

I shifted and put Meritaten down so I could see it better. She climbed onto her father's knee. He stroked her shaved head. On the papyrus was a red grid containing an architect's drawing of the walls and columns of a temple, but the building was unfinished. I glanced at Amenhotep. He wore a ridiculous smile, clearly expecting a grand exclamation from me, but I did not understand his excitement. "A new temple?" I ventured.

He exhaled sharply. "Not just a new temple — an entire new temple complex for the Aten."

"Of course. I look forward to seeing the plans when they are complete."

"They are complete."

I studied the papyrus. "Where is the roof on the sanctuary?"

"There is no roof, of course. We will worship the Aten while his beneficent light washes down upon us."

It sounded hot, uncomfortable, and positively draining for any lengthy ceremony. Over all the years I'd spent at Sekhmet's temple, the interior was always a blessed relief from the blazing heat of the sun. But I knew Amenhotep awaited a response that confirmed his brilliance. "How very innovative." Most Kemetians would not have considered that a compliment, but Amenhotep was not most Kemetians.

He pushed aside that scroll and opened another. This one was full of drawings of us. He was recognizable by his kingly crown, and the woman and children with him could be none other than me and our daughters. But these were unlike any drawings I had ever seen.

Meritaten stood on Amenhotep's knee and tugged on his earring. He grabbed her hand and kissed her chubby fingers. "These are some of the carvings proposed for the walls of the temple." He pointed to one where we stood in formal poses, offering our hands up to the Aten, whose rays held out life and blessings to us. "Here we are, worshipping the Aten." In another, he pointed to where we were seated, each with a child on our laps, the Aten shining down on us and offering life. "Here, we enjoy the blessings of the Aten."

"Instead of depicting us in an ideal way, you have chosen to portray us as we really are." This was intended only as an observation, but he took it as approval.

"Exactly. It is how the Aten fashioned us and how we should be seen by the people."

All of the figures in the drawings had slightly elongated heads, sagging bellies, and heavy thighs. He had not pictured us as we really were, but instead, we were all to be seen as he really was. But the oddities didn't stop there. "I am more than half your size in every image." This was unheard of. Artistic convention dictated that the king always appear larger than life, and the Great Royal Wife, if present at all, would appear no higher than his knee.

"Obviously. The Aten requires both of us, male and female, to be his representatives here on earth. This makes you the second most powerful person in Kemet, and you must be seen as such."

I frowned at him. His censure of the priests seemed natural, and necessary, but to publicly declare I was near his equal? True, Tiye had wielded considerable power, but it was of a more hidden nature. Was Maya correct? Was this the beginning of our submission to the forces of chaos?

"I mean it," he said. "When my father was still alive, I could not fully implement my vision for Kemet, but now I am free. I shall be truly the Aten's representative on earth, and you shall be my companion, charged with affairs of state. Anyone who has grievances must come to you first. Only if it is beyond your scope will you bring their concerns to me."

I gasped. The drawings did not merely represent an ideal but an intended reality. I glanced at Meritaten, who was now drowsing against her father's chest. If I were to be thrust into an active role, I would have little time to spend with my children. Yet, perhaps, it would benefit the girls to see their mother as one with power and respect. Yes, I could embrace this new function.

"Do not trouble yourself," said Amenhotep. "At first, you will tell everyone the same thing — that you will consult with the king and give it some thought — and I will instruct you on what is to be done. With time and training, you will be able to handle certain straightforward situations on your own."

Ah ... it was to be a sham, and illusion just like the drawings, after all. Or was it? I remembered the lessons taught to me by his own father: use diplomacy, negotiate, and let him think he has won. That, combined with the broad education bought for me by my father gave me cause to think I might excel in this new role.

Chapter 16

Amenhotep stood and spoke to the assembled guests. "As king, my highest duty is that of mediator between my people and the gods. In this, I am the keeper of Ma'at, the cosmic balance of the worlds. This day, I act in accordance with Ma'at in taking to wife my sister, daughter of both my mother and my father, blessed in the West. Though you have long known her as your princess, I now present her as a queen, my second-wife, Nebetah."

Amenhotep, it turned out, had many plans and never hesitated in implementing them. This one, I supposed, was inevitable. No matter how much he valued our daughters, after I gave birth to a third one, we were both forced to admit I may be unable to give him the son he needed.

Nebetah rose next to her brother, our husband. The crowd clapped and cheered. From Amenhotep's other side, I joined in. Tiye, beside her daughter, caught my eye and raised her wine cup. She could not prevent my marriage to her son, but in not producing a son of my own, I had paved the way for her to realize her own ambitions for her children. I let her believe it a moment longer.

Amenhotep raised his arms for silence and motioned me to stand beside him, which I did.

"This I have done together with the Great Royal Wife, my beloved, Mistress of the Two Lands, Nefer-Neferuaten-Nefertiti, mother of the princesses of Kemet, trusted counselor, priestess of Sekhmet, may she live forever."

As more applause erupted, I caught Tiye's eye and then turned from her. Neither she nor Nebetah had won, yet. I was still Great Royal Wife, and I was still young. I could still produce many sons for Kemet. Yet, I knew there was danger. My position depended entirely on the king's favor. Should Nebetah produce a son before me, she might yet replace me as Great Royal Wife. I had but three options if I did not wish to be relegated to a life of servitude in the women's quarters: give the king a son before Nebetah did, prevent Nebetah from conceiving, or make myself so invaluable to Amenhotep that he could not replace me.

The first option I dismissed altogether. If the gods had not yet heeded my prayers and offerings, I had no cause to think they would start doing so now. I could still hope, but the outcome was not within my control. The third option was the only one that would truly place me above all rivals. With care and skill, it could be accomplished without Amenhotep even being aware of the shift, at first. Yet, it would take time, and I was counting on the second option to buy me that time.

When the applause subsided, we sat back down. Amenhotep drew Nebetah onto his lap. He twined his fingers in her wig and nuzzled her neck. As the acrobats and dancers resumed their exertions, his hands roamed Nebetah's body, grasping and pinching at her flesh.

I hoped my new sister-wife would have the good grace not to conceive before I could consider how to prevent it without implicating myself.

The Duat
Gate 1
Part 2

I am greeted by a ba. She seems composed of mist. She wraps her arms around me, enveloping me in the scent of lilies. I do not recognize her, yet I know her.

"Mother?"

She pulls back and smooths my hair. She died of plague when I was very young, leaving behind only her absence. The hall is now filled with the dead. All faces I know: Tiye, Beketaten, Taheret. Nofret, glaring at me. So many.

I scan the crowd, searching in vain for my lost children. I ask, but the bas just shake their heads. The ceremonies were not performed. Those children will never join the blessed dead.

One I hoped never to see again catches my eye: Akhenaten. His glare accuses me. Let him. That I made it possible for him to join the blessed dead while my children are consigned to oblivion will forever be my greatest sorrow.

Sekhmet places a hand on my shoulder. "It is time to move on."

"Not yet. Please," I say.

She shakes her head, implacable.

I take my seat in the barque, watching as my mother and those I knew in life drift away. "I'll be back," I say and hope it's true.

Amenhotep IV, Year 4
(ca. 1350 BCE)

Shortly after the marriage feast, Amenhotep decided to celebrate his own reign. Still only four years in, it was early for a Sed Festival. Though he had been circumspect while making plans, I suspected he intended the festival to mark a change — further implementation of the plans he would not disclose.

In any event, it served to give notice to all of our vassal states and allies that the younger king was now in full power, and representatives from these lands now waited to present their gifts. I sat together with Amenhotep; a situation unprecedented. Nebetah, Tiye, and other family members sat behind us, including the children with their nurse.

A magnificent prince of Kush approached the dais. Above his multicolored kilt, the skin of his well-muscled torso shone with a dark luster, and golden bands circled his massive arms. I felt a heat that had nothing to do with the sun beating down on us.

The prince brought forward two animals on leashes — a baboon and a cheetah cub. Amenhotep accepted them and then passed the baboon to Nebetah and the cheetah to me. I took the cub onto my lap. When I scratched its chin, it rubbed its temples against me, exactly as Sekhmet had done years earlier. Nebetah beamed. Silly woman. She believed Amenhotep had shown her the greater favor with the gift of the baboon, the symbol of Djehuty, god of

93

wisdom. Only I knew the true contempt he had for the gods. The cheetah, with its tawny coat, symbolized the light of the Aten. For those who understood, the king had just shown his clear preference for me.

A Kinahhu nomad prince presented us with a matched pair of dwarves. Mutnedjmet squealed with delight when she saw their tumbling performance, and so Amenhotep gifted them to her. She responded by jumping up and down and clapping her hands. Amenhotep's eyes devoured her as she did so. She was a full woman now, prettily flushed with excitement and heat. It was past time to speak with Father about securing a husband for her.

A slight pounding in my head gave me pause. I looked to the children. They were drowsing against their nurses. The baby, Ankhesenpaaten, fed but without enthusiasm. Amenhotep had ordered removal of all sunshades so that we might bathe directly in the light of the Aten, but I worried for the little ones. When the baby stopped feeding, the nurses gathered all three together and formed a shade with their own robes. I relaxed a little.

Next in line, a Naharin prince approached. By his side was a pretty, young woman. The prince bowed to us. "As promised, King Tushratta of Naharin sends his virgin daughter for your bride."

I stiffened yet still managed to smile. The princess stepped forward. A veil covered her head, but underneath could be seen a golden diadem fitted with fluttering gold leaves topping her curly, dark hair. She wore heavy fringed robes and must surely have felt the heat. I could not tell if she was flushed or if her cheeks were artificially rouged. She lifted her eyes to meet Amenhotep's and then immediately dropped them. From the corner of my eye, I saw his hands clench the armrests of his throne.

"You are Kaluha ... Kahab ... Kiya?"

The prince opened his mouth to respond, but Amenhotep stopped him. "I asked her."

The princess curtsied. "Kelu-Heba, Highness."

Amenhotep laughed. "How can any civilized tongue be expected to pronounce such a monstrosity? *Kiya* will suffice."

"The remainder of the gifts have been delivered directly to your palace," said the prince. "A pair of horses and a golden chariot; a litter adorned with gold and jewels; cloth; garments; all manner of jewelry; a saddle; dresses of purple, green, and crimson; and a large chest to hold the items, as requested."

As requested? I had heard of neither a promise from King Tushratta nor a request from Amenhotep.

The prince continued. "In return, my father, the king, requests that Kelu — Kiya — be granted the title of Queen Consort."

My body jerked back, unbidden. No wonder I had not been made privy to this correspondence.

Amenhotep waved a hand. "That is out of the question, even more so now that I have seen her. She is but a girl and almost certainly untried in the bedchamber, as is your barbaric custom. My Great Royal Wife must be both learned and capable of shouldering much of the burden of rule."

"Kiya was born and raised in a royal household. She is no stranger to the running of one. Her education is the finest."

My paternal grandfather — Amenhotep's maternal grandfather — was born in Naharin. He was likely as aware as I that the finest education for Naharin girls consisted of spinning, weaving, cooking, ordering household supplies, and dealing with servants. She likely could not read even her own language, let alone ours — far from the duties Amenhotep expected of me.

"We shall see," said Amenhotep. "For now, she is a secondary wife. Should she prove herself an able scribe, fluent in multiple languages, well trained in animal husbandry and the arts of war, then perhaps there may be room for advancement."

The prince blanched. "Those are not suitable pursuits for a lady."

"Perhaps not in the backwaters of Naharin, but here in the civilized world, we hold to a higher standard."

I knew my education was well beyond what was expected of a Queen of Kemet but felt gratified that Amenhotep saw my skills as essential. My plan was working.

"But," continued Amenhotep, "there is one duty in which young Kiya may prove more capable than my current wives. I need an heir, and the wife to produce one will be certain of my greatest favor."

I would need to extend my plans for Nebetah to include Kiya.

Amenhotep drove his chariot out to the lake, one arm raised. I followed in my own chariot. The crowd pressed in on all sides, for this was a spectacle no one in memory had ever witnessed — the king and his Great Royal Wife driving their own chariots. Always, before, the king would release the Apis Bull and run alongside him, but Amenhotep preferred the chariot as a symbol of the Aten riding across the sky.

I pulled up next to Amenhotep and prepared to ride. Amenhotep signaled his horses to start, and I did the same. On the track, I deliberately fell a few paces behind Amenhotep. It would not do for the people to see any person as an equal to the king.

We started at a gentle pace, gradually increasing as we went, until we were all but flying. The faces of the spectators blurred into lines of color drawn across the facades of the palace and the temple of Amun. My weight shifted with the motion of the chariot, my hands controlling the reins as if of their own accord. I resisted the urge to throw back my head and laugh — it would not be dignified — but I felt it.

A collective gasp from the crowd shook me from my reverie. Just ahead and to my right, Amenhotep's chariot recovered from a near tumble. I scanned the ground, searching for imperfections, and determined to severely punish the worker who had not properly prepared the way. Then the cause of the trouble became apparent. Amenhotep lifted one arm in a victory gesture. Driving a chariot one-handed was difficult enough at slow speed. At full gallop, with a turn approaching, it was nothing short of reckless.

Amenhotep's chariot veered suddenly in front of mine. It tipped over, throwing him onto the ground, where he rolled several times before coming to a stop. His horses, tied together, fell in a tangled heap. I reined in and managed to turn my horses in time to avoid a collision. The crowd was silent as I leaped from the back of my chariot.

Before I could get to him, Amenhotep pushed himself to his knees. He stayed there for a moment, pressing a hand to his temple, before rising to his feet. He surveyed the crown, then raised both arms, and turned in a slow circle. The crowd roared. What might have been a complete disaster, Amenhotep turned into a show of his personal victory over chaos. It fit his plan so perfectly,

I briefly wondered if it had been staged. I doubted it, considering how unlike Amenhotep it was to risk his own person, yet could not rule it out entirely.

As stable hands arrived to slit the throats of the fallen horses and remove them from the arena, Amenhotep strode over to where Maya was sitting. "You have seen how the Aten has given me his protection."

"Truly, you are blessed by the gods," said Maya.

"You will concede, will you not," said Amenhotep, "that because I, Lord of the Two Lands, supreme over all the people of the earth, am favored by the Aten, that is evidence that the Aten is supreme over all the gods."

"I do not doubt the power of the Aten," said Maya, "but all the power of all the other gods is nothing next to that of Amun."

Amenhotep signaled to two soldiers. They reacted so swiftly; I knew it had been planned ahead of time. They grabbed Maya, tied his hands behind his back, and threw him into a chariot. Amenhotep mounted another and gestured for me to retrieve mine. Soldiers in chariots formed a ring around us. I noted my father among them. Other officials took their places with the soldiers in the chariots: the royal architect, his assistant Bek, the new vizier, and the master of horse.

"Where are we to go, and what, may I ask, are your plans for the priest?" I asked.

"He will not be harmed, simply re-educated."

Father took the reins of a chariot and joined our procession heading away from the river, out into the desert. I fell in beside him. "Did you know of this?"

Father shook his head. "I received a summons, just as the others did. I take it you did not know, either?"

"I did not."

"The public abduction of the highest priest in the land is an ill omen."

I shared his apprehension.

A hawk circled overhead, black against the blue of the sky. Finally, Amenhotep stopped, dismounted, and ordered the rest of us to do the same. He ordered Maya flung down onto the burning sand, and his bonds cut. When he tried to stand, Amenhotep shoved him back down. "On your knees." He held a horse whip in one hand and made a wide sweeping gesture with the other. "I have brought you here to show you the domain of the Aten."

Maya glowered but said nothing.

"The Aten shines down on all lands and all peoples. He is everywhere, always. But it is here, in the desert, where he is at his full power. Look around you. As far as the eye can see, there is nothing but desert. It stretches many miles in all directions, interrupted only by the narrow ribbon of the river valley. Even you cannot deny the Aten's power."

"I deny the power of no god," said Maya, "but neither will I deny the supremacy of Amun."

Amenhotep brought his whip down; Maya fell face first. All of the gathered officials looked to the ground. I touched Amenhotep's elbow, and whispered low so no one else could hear, "I beg you, stay your hand. The high priest of Amun is better as an ally than as an enemy."

Amenhotep lowered his voice as well. "He must learn obedience."

"Agreed," I said. "But it is easier to attract flies with honey than with sour wine."

"Easier still to attract flies with horse shit," he said. "He will not give up power easily."

"If he does not like it, he can be sent to a temple in Kush."

Amenhotep spoke through bared teeth. "That is your answer for everything — send them away."

He was referring to my handling of my serving girl, Aset. Before Amenhotep could bother her further, I found her and her husband both positions in a noble household in Mennefer. I suspected it was his thwarted desire that bothered him more than the loss of Aset, for he had found solace elsewhere in short order, with one of the myriad girls who were flattered by his attentions.

"I am simply concerned that the beating of the high priest of a much-loved god will win you no favors with your subjects."

Amenhotep nodded and then raised his voice to address Maya. "I have no wish to do you harm. I am simply following the directive of my god. The Aten wishes his supremacy to be known and acknowledged by all."

"It is my duty to ensure that Amun is given his due reverence, and thus keep the balance of Ma'at, even if that means denying the wishes of my king."

"I am king. It is my duty to keep the balance of Ma'at." Amenhotep's whip hand twitched. "It is your duty, and that of all other subjects," he pointed the whip at everyone in the crowd, myself included, "to carry out my orders." He circled Maya. "My consort, the great Nefertiti, wishes for me to show mercy. She advises me to use diplomacy to obtain my ends."

"The Great Royal Wife is wise."

Crack. The whip carved a path into the flesh of Maya's back. "The Great Royal Wife is a woman. She is soft-hearted." Crack. "I am not." Crack. "You will acknowledge the supremacy of the Aten."

"I will not."

Crack. "You say your duty is to maintain Ma'at. Think what would happen if the high priest of the former supreme god opposed the king. Kemet would be plunged into chaos. Is that your desire?"

"It is not I who flirt with chaos," said Maya.

Crack. "I grow tired of this game," said Amenhotep. "You will acknowledge the Aten, or I will have you put to death."

Maya met his eye. "Death is what it will take."

Crack. Amenhotep staggered, put one hand to his head. Crack. Crack.

If I had surmised his plans correctly, Amenhotep had just put himself in an impossible situation. He needed Maya to concede publicly. The threat of execution was an empty one, and Maya knew it.

The whipping continued. When Amenhotep was done, Maya lay prostrate in the sand, his back reduced to ground meat. In places, white bone glistened. I squeezed my eyes shut to stop the tears. When I opened them, Bek nodded to me.

"Say it," said Amenhotep.

Maya lifted his head, and shook it.

Amenhotep looked at one of the soldiers and opened his hand. The soldier handed him a small, wooden box. Amenhotep opened it, walked slowly over to where Maya lay, and emptied it. Granules cascaded from the box to Maya's back. Maya screamed. The granules scattered, running of their own accord across the ruined flesh. Ants.

I wanted to place my hands over my ears and run. Instead, I held a crooked finger to my mouth. Maya's howling sounded like a wounded jackal or an angry spirit — no longer a human thing.

Amenhotep bent to place his head next to Maya's mouth. "Did you say something?"

Maya's mouth moved, and though I could not hear the words, the smile on Amenhotep's face told me what they were. Amenhotep waved to his soldier, who handed him a wineskin. Amenhotep uncorked it, and poured the contents over Maya's back, provoking more shrieking. I caught the scent of lemon as the ants scattered and ran.

Bek had moved closer to me. "Are you well, Highness? Shall I request a litter for you?"

I snapped at him. "Certainly not. Do you take me for a child who must be coddled?"

I turned from him, mounted my chariot, and made ready to depart. Maya was given a robe to hide evidence of the beating and was allowed to stand in the chariot, accompanied by the driver. Military chariots were positioned to both sides, with Amenhotep out front. The ride home was silent, save for hoofbeats in the sand and the occasional whimper from Maya as he stood, rigid.

On our arrival back at the festival grounds, Amenhotep jumped from the back of his chariot with such enthusiasm that only I noticed the wince and the pause he gave before speaking. Perhaps his head pained him from his earlier mishap, yet he helped Maya dismount, giving every impression of great tenderness. Then he ascended the dais, Maya behind him, taking each step with care.

Amenhotep raised his hands for silence. "The high priest of Amun, and myself, the high priest of the Aten, have communed with each other and with the gods out in the red lands. It is now known that, above all other gods, the Aten reigns supreme." He gestured for Maya to come forward.

Maya came forward, glancing to the right and the left. A soldier caught his eye and raised a wooden box like the one that had carried the ants. Maya's shoulders slumped. "It is known," he said.

Chapter 18

The festivities continued well into the night. Though I tried to retire early, I was thwarted by the early desertion of the one whom the festival honored, he himself being anxious to become better acquainted with his new, young wife.

So, it was well into the seventh hour of the night when I entered the quarters given to Maya. He lay prostrate on his bed, his wounded back laid bare, and glistening with honey in the lamplight. His headrest had been removed, and he lay with his head hanging over the edge of the mattress, his forehead resting on the bed rail. He was so still I thought him asleep, or worse. I stayed long enough to discern the small, but regular, expansions of his torso. As I turned to go, I was surprised by the sound of his voice but could not understand his words.

He repeated himself. "Is this the Ma'at the king brings to us all? The humiliation of the priests, and through us, the gods themselves?"

I had asked myself this same question ever since the events of this afternoon. But I needed still more time to determine what I should do about it, if indeed I could do anything at all, so I answered with the only truth that mattered for the moment. "It is not for either of us to question the will of the king."

Maya turned his head to look at me. "You know. You are a seer."

I ignored the flickering of the lamp as the hand holding it trembled. "I am no such thing."

"I was watching you at the funeral of the Wesir-King, Amenhotep, the third of that name. Your eyes followed the gods as they entered the tomb. You cowered from their rage."

I hesitated, at a loss for how to convince him he had not seen what he so clearly had. I knew Tiye had also noticed my odd behavior that day. I wondered how many others had, and how many had come to the same conclusion as Maya.

I thought Maya laughed at that, though it came out as more of a snort. "The king does not know, does he?"

"He knows how I was chosen by Sekhmet."

"But he does not know you can see the gods, talk to them," said Maya.

"That is a private matter. It does not concern the king."

Maya emitted a gurgling sound I came to realize must be laughter. "I think it would concern him very much that his Great Royal Wife knows that his faith in the Aten is misplaced."

"I am done here." I spun around to leave.

"I also speak with the gods. They fear the coming destruction of Ma'at; they plead with me to restore it."

I hesitated a fraction of a second at the door. Long enough for him to notice.

"Ah. They plead with you also."

I turned to face him.

"Perhaps you listen a little too closely to their pleas," he said. "Your husband would be most interested to know you are working against him."

"He is not interested in anything you have to say."

"I needn't tell him. I only need tell someone he trusts. His mother, perhaps." He smiled. "You will see that I am reinstated and that all lands, assets, and powers are restored to the temple of Amun."

I laughed, to show him what I thought of his demand. "That is not in my power, and even if it were, I would not do it."

"It is common knowledge that you are the true power behind the throne. You can change his mind."

"Common knowledge is wrong. He trusts me with mundane details because he does not wish to be bothered by petitioners. Major decisions are made by the king alone, and he accepts neither input nor influence from me."

"For your sake, I hope that isn't true." He winced.

I moved to help him but then instantly regretted the reflex that made me do so. He deserved to suffer. I eyed the linens covering his lower half, noted his shallow breathing, and thought how easy it would be to end his threat forever. Then my mind turned to the two guards outside the door. If Maya should die, and I the last one with him, I would surely be caught and disgraced before facing my own execution. I left him.

Chapter 19

Rather than committing murder, I decided it would be better to breathe poison into Amenhotep's ear. If he believed Maya to be suffering from delirium, then his threats would hold no sway over me. It would not be difficult to convince him of this, but time was of the essence. I must get to him before Maya did, and especially before Maya could speak with Tiye.

I found Amenhotep's quarters empty. Given how much he valued his solitude, this was unexpected — he rarely spent an entire night with any woman, even me. Although I knew full well where he was, it would have been unseemly for me to barge in, so I sent Taheret to find him and report back to me. After a time, Taheret burst through the door to my chambers.

"Highness, you must come quick. The king is indeed with Kiya in her quarters, but his physician is there as well. His Highness has taken ill, and all of the women are waiting for word."

I raced down the pillared hall leading to the king's quarters and the women's quarters. I arrived at Kiya's quarters, seething. I found Amenhotep there, sitting up in her bed but seeming very weak, Kiya by his side. "Why did I hear of the king's illness from my serving woman?"

"It is nothing," said Amenhotep. "A bit of a headache. The physician has given me a draft of poppy."

Kiya bowed her head. "Apologies, Highness. I not know proper thing to do. I thought only of his Highness's health."

Amenhotep stroked her head. "The girl must be forgiven."

"She knows better now, and in the future, I expect to be informed immediately, should the king take ill."

"Yes, Highness, I promise," said Kiya.

"I will see to it," said Amenhotep.

"If you are recovered now, I shall take my leave," I said. "Shall I accompany you back to your quarters?"

He placed a hand on Kiya's. "That won't be necessary; I shall stay here a while longer."

On returning to my apartments, I wakened my sister, Mutnedjmet.

Her eyes flew open. "What is wrong?"

I motioned for her to accompany me to my study and handed her a box.

She opened the box and sniffed. She lowered her eyebrows. "What is it?"

"It is called silphium. I knew it from the apothecary at the temple of Sekhmet. It comes from the Ribu lands, and it has taken many months to secure a supply without being discovered."

"What does it do?"

I swallowed. "It prevents a woman from conceiving."

"But you haven't any sons yet. Why would you take this?" she said.

"It's not for me, you fool. If I were to make regular visits to the women's quarters, it would raise suspicions, but you are there every day with the royal children. You are in a position to slip this to two of the king's ladies: Kiya and Nebetah."

Mutnedjmet put a hand to her mouth. "I couldn't."

"To be effective, they must take it every day," I said, "but you won't need to always be stealthy about it as it is also useful for cough, sore throats, fevers, indigestion. And it is not well known in Kemet, so they will not suspect."

"Neffie, you can't do this."

"I have no choice. If either of those two gives the king a son before I do, I may lose my position as Great Royal Wife," I said. "What shall happen to our family then?"

"What if the king finds out?"

"You better see that he doesn't," I said. "Our entire family depends on this. It's up to you to preserve us all."

I sent her back to bed and made ready to retire, myself. However, the question of what to do about Maya kept me staring into the dark for hours. Given Amenhotep's reluctance to leave the arms of his new wife, I could hardly have broached the subject with him. I could not deliver what Maya demanded, and I did not know how much time I would have before he revealed my secret. There seemed only one prudent course of action, yet it was one I had no taste for. It was an easy thing to eliminate a rival before it was born but to kill one already alive? Did I dare? Did I dare not?

In the light of day, my decision made, I went to visit Maya to tell him I would do as he asked. Entering his room, I was met with the stink of decay. A physician was with him, though I did not need to hear his words to know the truth.

"Blood poisoning has set in," he said.

I crouched down next to Maya so he could see my face.

"Pray for me, Highness," he said.

I lowered my voice so that Maya could hear but the physician could not. "Best beseech your Amun. See if he deigns to help you."

I turned and left. Blood poisoning was always fatal. Perhaps the Aten truly was asserting his supremacy. Or perhaps it was my Sekhmet removing a problem for me so that I need not dirty my own hands.

Akhenaten, Year 5

(ca. 1349 BCE)

When the floods came, the royal family, and entourage, assembled on several boats, accompanied Amenhotep on a journey north to Mennefer to celebrate the Aten.

The trip afforded me a rare opportunity to enjoy my children. While living in the palace, affairs of state often kept me too busy to see them. Here, I was relieved of all duty and played with my daughters in the cabin, along with Mutnedjmet, Taheret, Tiye, and Father. Ankhesenpaaten was taking her first wobbly steps, helped by proud sister, Meritaten, and aunt, Beketaten. Meketaten sat in my lap, drowsing. With one hand, I arranged pillows so I could put her down to sleep.

Amenhotep burst into the cabin. "We are approaching a city now. We must make our appearance."

"Allow me to put Meketaten down. She needs to sleep."

"Certainly not. She must be with us."

"If I force her to go, she will be cranky," I said.

"The people must see all of us, and a unified whole. They must have confidence in our dynasty, our legacy."

Knowing he wasn't going to give in, I raised myself and picked up Meketaten. The motion woke her. She rubbed her eyes and began to whimper.

Amenhotep picked up Ankhesenpaaten and took Meritaten by the hand. When we moved from the dark cabin into the bright sunlight, Meketaten roused further and began to wail.

"Silence the child," said Amenhotep.

"I cannot. She needs sleep."

Amenhotep paused, weighing the benefit of a populace seeing us in disharmony versus seeing us minus one child. "Very well. Send her back to the cabin."

I rushed back and placed her in Mutnedjmet's arms. Meketaten was now in full wail. "Try to calm her to sleep," I said.

When I took my place beside Amenhotep, he handed me the baby. We stood a few steps back from the edge, visible to the multitudes onshore who had turned out to watch us pass. We waved to them and encouraged the children to wave as well. Meritaten waved and jumped with such enthusiasm, her father had to hold her by the waist to prevent her falling overboard. Ankhesenpaaten blinked and yawned. I prayed she wouldn't start bawling as well.

By the time the walls and the harbor of the city were behind us, Ankhesenpaaten was asleep on my shoulder. I returned to the cabin to put her to sleep. Amenhotep returned to the other side of the cabin, which he shared with Kiya.

At nightfall, the boats anchored. The crews went ashore, and their fires flickered in the blackness. On the far horizon, high cliffs blotted out the stars and I was reminded of getting lost in the desert on a night very much like this. I shivered.

Amenhotep joined me looking out at the riverbank. "Would you prefer to sleep ashore? I know it was a practice of your father's."

"No, thank you."

"The children are sleeping?"

I nodded. "Yes. Finally. I am just taking a few moments to enjoy the silence before retiring, myself."

"Same." Amenhotep closed his eyes and rubbed his temples.

"Your head still pains you?"

"At times. The physician is preparing poppy. I will be well again in no time."

The full moon and the stars outlined cliffs against the far horizon.

"This is a beautiful place," said Amenhotep. "Very peaceful."

"Yes," I said.

We stood a moment, and then Amenhotep said, "I must retire. The Aten will call us back to duty all too soon, I'm afraid."

We rose before dawn to greet the Aten, as was our custom. Amenhotep and I, with the girls, waited for him to make his first appearance over the horizon. Our entire family and entourage were spread across the deck of the ship. Tiye's scowl etched a little deeper at this hour of the morning. Others were rubbing their eyes, running hands through tousled hair, and stifling yawns. On our accompanying barges, everyone had turned out, presumably as bleary-eyed as we. I could see Father, having returned to his own barge, with Tey, both casting looks of disfavor our way. Even onshore, the figures of the crewmen were facing east. When the king issued an order, everybody followed, no matter their personal preference.

Presently, the Aten edged over the clifftop. I shook the sistrums, and Amenhotep started singing the hymn.

"Splendid you rise in heaven's lightland,

O living Aten, creator of life!"

I missed a beat. This was a hymn I had not heard before.

Amenhotep continued.

"When you have dawned in the eastern lightland,

You fill every land with your beauty."

Partway through, he paused. "Forgive me, Father," he said. "I am truly awed by your magnificence." He continued with the hymn, with a newly acquired, perfectly timed catch in his throat.

After the ceremony, Amenhotep remained staring at the horizon, lost in thought, for some while. Finally, I approached him.

"Did you like the new hymn?" he asked, without taking his eyes from the shore.

"Yes, very much."

"I wrote it last night. I was inspired by the Aten's beauty."

"Forgive me, but everyone is wondering when we are to up anchor. We have already lost more than an hour of daylight."

Amenhotep's eyes widened, as if he were surprised that I was there and could speak. "What is it you wish of me?"

"We are waiting for the order to move on."

"Yes, of course. Mustn't keep the gods of Kemet waiting." He sneered.

On the return journey, Amenhotep ordered the boats to stop in the same place, though it was yet several hours until nightfall. Next morning, during our sunrise ritual, instead of singing the hymn, he turned to us. "My glorious Father, the Aten, spoke to me in a dream last night. He told me it is here, this place."

We all waited for him to continue. When he did not, I asked, "What do you mean it is here?"

He smiled, having waited for someone to ask that very question. "Our new capital city. We will move here."

I looked at the bleak landscape. Red lands, with nothing more than a thin line of green against the desert gold. No city, not even a small village to break the monotony, because growing anything in this place would require hard labor.

People looked to each other, unsure of how to respond.

"There is nothing here," I said.

Amenhotep sighed. "That is why I am the visionary, and you deal with the mundane — you cannot see. Look at the Aten rising."

I looked to the Aten, now half-visible between two mountains, and I understood. It was the hieroglyph for "horizon."

"It is a sign of the Aten's favor," said Amenhotep. "We will build a city here; the grandest city Kemet has ever seen. It will last for millions and millions of years. We shall call it Akhetaten, and henceforth I shall be known as Akhenaten, the first of that name, for there shall be many others." He squeezed Kiya by the waist.

Kiya clapped her hands. "Shall be magnificent city. With palaces, and temples, and pools."

Her response ignited the crowd. Cries of, "blessings on your new city," and, "long life to King Akhenaten," echoed throughout.

Looking at our proposed new home, another, possibly more accurate, reason for Amenhotep's choice occurred to me. I leaned in close to him. "This seems a poor location for a city because of its barrenness, but that is what attracts you. This place does not belong to any god, unlike Mennefer does to Ptah, or Waset does to Amun."

Amenhotep — Akhenaten — shrugged. "Perhaps that is why the Aten chose it for himself."

Chapter 21

A feast celebrated our return to Waset. The hall was filled to capacity, and serving girls bustled from table to table, filling wine cups and replacing empty bowls with full ones. Perfumes mingled — cinnamon, myrrh, and geranium.

Akhenaten rose and gestured for the musicians to stop. He waited until all eyes were upon him. "You have doubtless heard the rumors by now. I have heard them myself."

Twittering from the crowd.

"I'm here to tell you they are true. The ones about our new city and my change of name, not the ones about the grand vizier's wife." He paused, open-mouthed. "On second thought, those might also be true."

The grand vizier scowled, but the rest of the crowd, including his wife, roared.

Akhenaten smiled, waiting for the commotion to settle. Once it had, he put a finger to his lips, and took a deep breath. "So that all may know of my devotion to the Aten, father to us all, I shall henceforth be known as Akhenaten. So, it shall be written from this day forward.

"As a sign of his love for me, the Aten has revealed to me his plan. He has shown me a place in the desert that shall be transformed into a great city. The city of Akhetaten. To the west, it is protected by the river. To the north, east, and south, it is protected by a sweep of cliffs. There, the Aten can shine down his life-giving rays to us for all eternity."

I watched for a reaction but saw none. By this time, the court had had sufficient opportunity to absorb news of a new city.

Akhenaten continued. "Not everyone will be moving along with the court."

This produced a response. People froze, waiting for the next words. Some, afraid they would not be allowed to accompany us; others, no doubt, afraid they would be required to.

"Staying with the court is a privilege," said Akhenaten. "Only those who have earned it may accompany the royal family to bathe in the glory of the Aten. Nor will I compel anyone to accompany us who does not wish it. It must be a mutual choice. All those who wish to stay are free to do so."

A general sigh of relief.

"Those who will be making the trip are the chosen of Aten; a special people, the ones who will build a new Kemet. It is only for those who are brave and daring, as this is virgin land, and we will be reclaiming it from the desert. We will be pioneers together in the name of the Aten." Akhenaten took his seat.

Thunderous applause.

Perhaps Akhenaten would allow me to remain behind. I knew it a vain hope but wished for it, nonetheless. The land was fit for very little, and I worried about how the children would fare in such a harsh landscape.

As the diners resumed their feasting and the music started up again, Father came to me. Seeing Akhenaten was preoccupied with his beer, and with Kiya, he squatted beside me.

"You do not remember that place, do you?" he said.

"What place?"

"It is to be expected — you were a mere child."

"Do you mean the site of Akhetaten?" I said.

He nodded. "It is where we camped that night, we nearly lost you. We found you as the sun was rising between the mountains."

I felt a sudden chill as the course of my life collided with that of my destiny. This would be the place where I would be called upon to restore Ma'at, just as Sekhmet had told me twice — once before my wedding and once on that long-ago night in the desert. Where the fate of Kemet and all those who dwelt within it would rest on me alone. I had known since childhood that this must happen, but always as some far distant happening. Now that it was upon me, I was not at all certain I could bear it.

Chapter 22

I held my arms straight to allow my servants to scrub me down with natron and to shave my body and scalp. The water rinse, while warm, left a slight chill in the morning air. As one servant toweled me dry, and another started with my makeup, I calculated the quantity of grain the treasury could afford to part with in order to please the delegation from Kush yet go unnoticed by Akhenaten. I slipped my arms into the pleated dress, waited while it was wrapped and tied, and slipped on my sandals.

I bent my head to accept the crown. It was of my own design — reminiscent of the king's blue war crown but with smoother, sleeker lines — and fashioned with a snug fit so as to obviate the need for a wig. I took a deep breath and passed through the women's quarters into the hall and mounted the few steps to the audience chamber. I took my place on the throne, situated at the top of the steps, surrounded by four columns. The fanbearers, now including my father, Ay, stood already waiting on either side. I nodded to the guards, who opened the doors.

The Kushite delegate entered at the head of the line. I watched as a man crossed the hallway, his feet falling on the floor tiles depicting those subjugated to Kemet, hands bound behind their backs. Each step symbolically crushed the Hatti, the Ribu, the Kush.

When the man reached the foot of the steps, he prostrated himself below me.

"Rise," I said.

He stood. Though he was a giant of a man, his position forced him to look up to me. "Lady of Grace, Great of Praises, Lady of the Two Lands," he said, "I come here as your servant, to beseech your help. Long have the mines in Kush served Kemet's mighty king, but now work has stalled. The slaves and prisoners have little to eat. Even the overseers grow lean. Hungry men cannot work." He clenched his jaw.

Akhenaten had instructed me to be stingy, to demand their gold without giving a fair price. Kush was a province of Kemet; we needn't negotiate. Slaves and prisoners were not worth consideration. But I understood what the delegate had left unsaid. Hungry men were dangerous, and a province full of dangerous men is a danger to the whole country.

"I shall grant you another sack of grain per day for every two hundred workers and for every one hundred overseers."

He bowed his head. "That is gracious of you, but I fear it is insufficient."

While I wished to please the workers to the extent that their discontent did not lead to revolt, I had no trust that the delegate's communication of the situation was entirely accurate.

"That is a near doubling of their current wages."

"Yes, Lady," he said.

"You are dismissed." I watched him turn and go, hoping my decision had been the correct one. Some way down the line of supplicants, I noted two familiar figures, and I sighed. I would have to bring those two to Akhenaten himself. I handled the intervening requests with as much haste as decorum permitted and beckoned forward chief architect Hatiay and his assistant Bek, husband to my Taheret.

After prostrating themselves, and offering the usual flowery introductions, Hatiay stated his business. "I have drawn up plans for the new city according to the king's request." He held up a roll of papyrus.

I gestured to the outer edge of the hall, behind the papyri-form columns. "Wait here. When the morning audience is complete, we shall bring them to him together."

Hatiay spread his papyrus plans across the table in the king's private quarters. "It is brilliant, Highness — a planned city, with wide, straight roads. None of the dark warrens that plague the old cities, lending space to criminals and ne'er-do-wells."

"There will be none of that in the Aten's city," said Akhenaten.

"It will be truly magnificent."

"It will."

Hatiay pointed out lists and calculations. "If we hire teams of stonecutters, stonemasons, builders, and artists, we can have it completed in ten years, eight if we rush."

"Eight years?" Akhenaten's face turned red. "Unacceptable. We move within the year."

Hatiay trembled. "A year is not possible. Eight will be pushing it."

"You will find a way, or I will find someone who will."

Hatiay stared at his plans. "I very much—"

Bek interrupted. "There is a way. If we use smaller blocks, construction will be faster. It takes far less time to fashion enough small blocks to fill the same volume as one of the large blocks than it takes to fashion one of the large blocks. Also, using sunken relief will be faster than bas-relief."

Akhenaten turned to Hatiay. "Is this true?"

"It is highly unusual," said Hatiay. "I've already told the boy—"

"You mean your assistant already spoke of this to you, and you did not see fit to tell me?"

"It's not how things are done." Hatiay bowed his head.

"Will the buildings still stand if they are made of smaller blocks?" said Akhenaten.

"The step pyramid of the great King Djoser, and its entire funerary complex, was built using smaller blocks," said Bek. "It is still standing after two thousand years. What's more, the sunken reliefs will last longer as they will not be blasted so much by wind and sand."

"Using the smaller blocks and sunken relief, can the city be built in a year?" said Akhenaten.

"Not the entire city, no," said Bek. "But the main temples, and palaces can be completed within a year. It will be ready for the royal family and the court to move in. Construction in the city itself will be ongoing for at least three years, perhaps four, depending on how many people wish to live there."

Akhenaten considered this. He pointed at Hatiay. "You are relieved of your post. Bek is now the chief architect."

Bek looked from one to the other. "I did not mean ... I am a sculptor at heart. My master is the great architect."

He stammered in such a way that I believed it had not been a power play. The poor man was frightened, as well he should be.

Akhenaten dismissed Hatiay with a wave. "I have no time for those who cannot see my vision." Turning to Bek, he said, "You will proceed with building, and if you need instruction, come to me. Henceforth, you shall be known as 'the apprentice whom his Majesty taught.'" He followed Hatiay out.

Bek stared at Akhenaten's retreating back and rolled the papyrus. "How much does the king know about architectural principles?"

"It is your job to see he does not need to know," I said. "Is it true? Can you get the better part of the city done as you said?"

He nodded without looking up. "Yes, Highness."

"For your sake, I hope you are right."

He took the papyrus under his arm. "I am always right in my calculations."

The Duat
Gate 2

The boat descends into the Duat and approaches a closed gateway, guarded by a serpent standing on its tail. Again, I must name the gatekeeper in order to pass. I am less nervous this time, as I have become accustomed to my perfect recall of the texts I just read.

"O Mistress of the Sky, Lady of the Two Lands, the mistress of mankind, the one who distinguishes everyone. The name of the gatekeeper is Child of the Fashioner."

Inside, there are three sections. The first is for the evil and the wicked. They are bent with care and dressed in rags. They wear no wigs at all, and if they have any hair of their own, it is patchy and fine. Many are covered in sores.

The next houses the blessed dead. They are all dressed in the finest linen, with glowing, sparkling jewelry. Their wigs are elaborately plaited and styled. Their faces beam with happiness.

Although it is not cold, I shiver. I know that, to join the blessed dead, it is necessary to follow the teachings of Ra during one's lifetime. For a time, I did not, though it was not of my own choice. Perhaps the gods will be forgiving.

Or perhaps they will not need to be. It could be reasoned that I never left the teachings of Ra, for the Aten is an aspect of Ra. The beginning of my life was spent in service to the gods, and the last years spent trying to return Kemet to a state of Ma'at. In between, I did what was necessary to survive, but in my heart, I never abandoned the gods. Never. This will surely be enough. It must be.

In the third section, the gods wait to greet me. As I disembark, they embrace me, one by one, except for Amun. He is not fond of me, and for that I cannot fault him, for I sought to return him to the status of the small, local god that he was before his priests became powerful.

At the end of the line, Ptah takes my hands. I find Sekhmet behind me; she had followed me from the boat.

"The path before you is a perilous one," says Ptah, "full of many obstacles you must overcome before you can join us and the blessed dead, in the Field of Reeds."

"The obstacles will be manifold, for you have committed grievous crimes against us."

I glance back at the multitudes of bas, content in their afterlife. Each and every one had to pass through the Duat first and defeat the obstacles I am about to encounter. I have a greater portion of both wit and strength than most, and if all of them could do it, so can I. So, what if I should have more to overcome than the rest? My entire life was composed of one hindrance after another, and I prevailed over every one, until the last, and that because I trusted when I knew better. It is a mistake I will not repeat.

"I am ready."

Akhenaten, Year 6

(ca. 1348 BCE)

Akhenaten walked with Kiya hanging off his arm. I trailed behind, cheetah on leash. With me walked our children, their nurses, and Mutnedjmet and her dwarves. True to his word, Bek's calculations were indeed correct, and the court moved into the new palaces a year later. As part of our welcome, Bek gave us a tour, pointing out all of the architectural and artistic highlights, of which there were many.

The king's house, where Akhenaten and I would be living with our children, lay to the east of the Royal Road. Small by comparison to our palace in Waset, still, it boasted a treed courtyard, a private lake, our own altar, and a nursery for our children with plenty of space for more. My apartments were grand, airy, and covered in delightful paintings of me with my daughters.

From the courtyard, we crossed the bridge over the road to the main palace. I stopped to look out from the Window of Appearances and noted the position from where I had looked back at this spot when Sekhmet had first shown me the city. I could just see the tops of the temple pylons, with their blue and red flags.

Akhenaten joined me at the window and held up Meketaten so she could see. Seeing us there, the people walking below stopped to stare at us.

"Hand me your bracelets," said Akhenaten, putting Meketaten down.

I stared at him. He held out a hand, so I pulled the pins, and opened the hinges. I replaced the pins carefully before handing them to him.

He pointed to a man and a woman in the crowd. They stepped forward, eyeing each other. "A small token of appreciation from your king and queen, for following us in our vision." He tossed my bracelets out the window.

Naturally, this attracted the attention of everybody who had been watching. Bodies pressed up close, hands waving in the air. Akhenaten pulled a couple of rings from his fingers and tossed them out. Then, he held up Meketaten again. I held up Ankhesenpaaten, and with Meritaten between us, we waved to the crowd below. Cheers rang from the street. Before the applause faded, Akhenaten herded us away to continue with our tour.

I did not begrudge the loss of my bracelets — I had many others — but I wondered if Akhenaten's intention was to bribe the populace into loving him.

The main palace was built around an enormous courtyard. The women's quarters flanked either side. Each side possessed its own sunken gardens and airy rooms decorated with paintings of lotus and papyrus. Surrounding these were the residences for the ladies. Nebetah, of course, was assigned her own apartment, which was the only wife's chamber ready for occupation. The rest consisted of single, small rooms in rows, suited only for concubines. Kiya did not have space in the women's quarters. I exulted. Perhaps she would be sent back to Naharin.

Yet, I continued to watch Akhenaten and Kiya as they walked. She grasped his arm. He bent to whisper in her ear, and she stifled a giggle. He was not giving her up. Where, then, would she be housed?

During a lull in the tour, I sidled over to Bek. "Why is it Kiya has no quarters in the palace?"

He blushed. "That is a matter for you to discuss with the king, Lady."

"What has he done?"

Bek looked at me with profound sympathy. "I am sorry."

"Whatever it is, it's not your doing."

On our first morning waking up in Akhetaten, we rose before dawn to ready ourselves for the sunrise ceremony. It was a grand spectacle, meant to rival all the rituals for all the other gods. Akhenaten and I each mounted a golden chariot, pulled by horses dusted with gold powder. As the sole intermediaries between the Aten and his people, the entire family was to participate. Meritaten, now five, rode with her father, while Meketaten and Ankhesenpaaten, three and two respectively, rode with me.

The Royal Road was designed for this very purpose — to allow two chariots to ride abreast, and so we started off together, with Akhenaten riding slightly ahead of me. In the rear, the extended family — Tey, and Mutnedjmet with Beketaten — followed so they could act as my priestess choir. The Aten himself had not yet made an appearance, though the blackness of night was giving way to a deep blue.

With it being so early, I did not expect many spectators, and so I was shocked to see the street lined with what must have been the entire population of Akhetaten at the time. People jostled to get a glimpse of us and met us with cheers. Children waved and laughed.

Though well practiced in the art of charioteering, I had never done it while attempting to simultaneously corral two young children. Meketaten clung to the sides of the chariot, surveying the crowd with big eyes. Ankhesenpaaten, however, jumped and bounced, and I feared to lose her. I positioned myself and planted a foot to limit her movement. This affected the speed at which I could drive the horses. Akhenaten had no such limitation, Meritaten being older. Nor did he appear to notice my difficulty, and so the gap between us grew until he was well ahead. He did not wait for me before veering off to the banks of the river.

By the time I reached them, Akhenaten and Meritaten had both bathed, and temple staff were scrubbing them down with natron. I joined them with the two younger girls, as did the rest of our group. Akhenaten left us to enter the temple precincts alone while we purified ourselves.

When we ourselves were ready to enter the temple, I expected to find Akhenaten in the robing room, but he was not there. We changed into the purified linens, picked up our instruments, and stepped out into clouds of incense. Still, I did not see Akhenaten.

The eastern sky was fading to a paler blue. Not wanting to miss the moment, I started shaking my sistrums. My ladies fell in behind me, following my rhythm. Offerings of meat, vegetables, and flowers had already been laid out on the altars. Priests ran around, placing cups of water, wine, and milk on the altars as well.

The temple musicians, the finest in all of Kemet, sang and played on the harp. I led the group toward the inner sanctum, but I alone could enter. As I passed through to the interior, a faint sliver of the Aten himself made its first appearance above the far cliffs. It crossed my mind that I could do nothing, merely pretend to carry through as Akhenaten himself had done at his Wesir-father's funeral. Yet, Akhenaten had chosen to build this temple roofless, and unlike Akhenaten, I would witness the god's displeasure at my rebellion. I fell to my knees and then touched my forehead to the flagstones. When I rose, I resumed shaking the sistrum rattles and sang praises to the Aten as he rose higher in the sky, until his entire disc shone down upon me.

I squinted up, searching for any sign as to whether the Aten was pleased or displeased with my performance. He reached his hands down toward me and said not a word.

"Come, sit."

Akhenaten sank onto the bed. I knelt behind him, kneading his shoulders. "It has been a long, arduous day," I said. Indeed, it had. After the sunrise ceremony, there were dedications, tours for the newly arrived nobility, and then a feast to celebrate our arrival.

Akhenaten's shoulders sagged and I could feel him relax under my fingers. "Send for the physician for some poppy," he said.

"Is your head paining you?"

"No, but I find it helps me to sleep."

I went to the door and asked one of the guards to fetch the physician.

"I missed you during the ceremony this morning," I said.

"You embarrassed me today."

I searched my memory and could not think what he meant. "How so?"

"You fell behind in the chariot procession. It is unlike you. You and I both know you can drive circles around me."

And here I had thought I was the one embarrassed by that incident. I took a breath. "Not while taking care of two little ones. Meketaten is fine, but Ankhesenpaaten is too young to know caution. I suggest she be excused from the ceremony for another year."

He waved a hand. "Impossible. We are the divine family. We must appear to the people."

I knelt behind him again and resumed the massage. "Very well. Might I propose a slight change then? You take Meketaten and I take the other two. Meritaten is old enough to ensure her younger sister does not jump out of the chariot while I am driving."

Akhenaten shook his head. "You will take Meritaten and Ankhesenpaaten. Send Meketaten with your sister. You shall be performing the ceremonies on your own."

I did not know how to respond. "Surely, I was not such an embarrassment that you no longer wish to be seen with me."

He waved a hand. "Of course not. That is not why I did not perform the ceremony this morning. I wished to see how you would handle it on your own, and you performed admirably. As I knew you would, being a trained priestess."

"I am confused. Why should you wish for me to perform the ceremony on my own?"

"I am the son of the Aten — such theatrics are beneath me. It is your duty from now on, and you must train the priests properly so that they can perform when you are unavailable."

"If you wish."

I poured oil onto my hands and rubbed it into his shoulders and back. He closed his eyes and moaned. I gave him a few moments before broaching the subject I had been agonizing over since the previous day. "I notice Kiya does not have quarters in the palace, yet it does not seem you are angry with her."

He turned his head and opened his eyes. "Kiya is not in the women's quarters because I have built her a palace of her own in the north of the city."

My hands stopped moving of their own accord. How could this have happened without my knowledge? I was consulted much on the building of the city, so the only way it could have been kept secret was by deliberate choice. To give myself time to formulate a calm, reasonable response, I wiped my hands on a cloth. "I was not aware she had grown so high in your favor."

He turned away from me. "Jealousy does not become you."

"I am not jealous." That was not strictly true — I was jealous, but not in the way he meant it. "I fear the people will see this as a developing rift between us and lose confidence in your vision before they have had the chance to truly see it blossom."

"Nonsense. Kiya has been moved out and away. You are still here with our daughters. The people will see us as a unit. Indivisible."

Perhaps he was right, and yet he was not sending away Nebetah or any of his concubines. "Kiya has been granted autonomy, authority. None of your other women have been granted such."

His eyes narrowed, and his mouth hardened. "I see. You are not jealous of me; you are concerned for your position."

I felt a flutter inside. He was right, of course, but again not for the reason he thought. I cared not for power, but I had no wish to languish, forgotten, in some back corner of the women's quarters. But I could not let him know this. I poured some fresh oil and let my hands move further down his back. As I worked, I whispered in his ear. "Naturally, I am on fire with jealousy. I want you all for myself — how could I not? But I am the Great Royal Wife, and as such I cannot think only of myself. I must think always of your best interests." I slipped my hands around his waist so as to massage his chest muscles and to allow full contact between my body and his. "It is maddening, when all I really want is you."

"My other wives are of no importance. I took Kiya only to avoid insulting a fellow king, and Nebetah was to please my mother." His voice quavered. He took my hands in his and pulled me over to his side. "The only sons that will matter are the ones you give me because it is only through our children — sons and daughters — that the true royal bloodline of the Aten will be established."

He put a hand to my face. "Mistress of sweetness, beloved one, you soothe my heart. To me, you are she for whom the Aten doth shine, Mistress of Upper and Lower Egypt, Great Lady whom I love for millions and millions of years." He kissed my fingers.

He used the same tone of voice as he had when announcing the Aten's revelation for the new city, for his declaration that the Aten had saved him after his chariot accident. Practiced, sure, overly expressive, designed to convince. I did not believe him, but I knew what he expected of me, and I responded by straddling his legs and pressing my mouth to his.

A knock interrupted us before we could start. I had forgotten the physician was on his way. I met him, took from him the bowl of poppy, and brought it to Akhenaten. He put it down on the table by the cot.

"You are not going to take it?"

"Not at present," he said. "It will put me to sleep. Right now, I have important work to do." He pulled me onto his lap. "I must start the next King of Kemet."

Chapter 24

Kiya accepted my request to meet with her at her palace. The only access was from the river. When I disembarked at the watersteps, a guard informed me the Lady Kiya would meet with me in her throne room. I gritted my teeth and thanked him. Under normal circumstances, I would never have accepted such an insult, but under normal circumstances I would not be deigning to visit her in her home.

My attendants and I passed through the first courtyard and on into a garden. A pond, ringed by papyrus and populated by ducks, ibis, and kingfishers, occupied the central portion. Surrounding the pond, terraces overflowed with sycamore, fig, and pomegranate trees. On the north side, according to the plans Bek had reluctantly shared with me, would be pens for animals, and beyond that, an aviary.

We skirted the pond and entered the hypostyle hall leading to Kiya's throne room. She sat, immobile, watching us approach. I noted that, in place of a queen's crown, she wore a simple diadem atop her voluminous wig.

Standing at the foot of the steps leading to her throne, I pulled myself up to my full height, though I still had to strain my neck to meet her eyes. "There is a matter I wish to discuss with you."

Kiya crossed her arms. "Cannot imagine what." Though her command of our language was improving, she would likely never lose her accent.

I switched to Naharin. "We can speak in your native tongue, if it is more comfortable for you."

"Prefer Kemetic. Your Naharin is so poor, I cannot understand."

I had learned Naharin as a small child and spoke it as well as she did. She had simply recognized my offer for what it was — a deliberate reminder of her foreign origins and my superior education. I shifted back to Kemetic. "Very well. I am here to offer you the services of my sister, the Lady Mutnedjmet, as lady-in-waiting."

As expected, Kiya laughed at the offer. "You send me your sister as spy?"

"Please," I said. "I already have so many spies watching you, I hardly have need of one more." A servant came in with some wine and offered me a cup, which I accepted. I inclined my head toward her as she left. That particular woman was not one of my spies, or I would never have pointed her out, but it was true I had them. "I have spies among the gardeners, the food tasters, the cooks." I smiled at Kiya's clenched teeth. "Do not fret. If you manage to ferret them out, they will be replaced."

"If not a spy, what? You do not giving me a gift out of kindness. She is how much incompetent?"

"Not at all. She is a fine lady-in-waiting," I said. "The finest. I have trained her exceedingly well. She does come with those two dwarves, though, and they can be trying at times." I took a sip of wine and placed one foot on the lower step. "As you well know, the king has an eye for pretty young ladies. I need to remove Mutnedjmet from my household because he has been eyeing her much, lately, and he will have what he wants. It is in both our interests to keep her out of sight."

Kiya nodded. "I understand. It is for best. Far easier for me to ... how you say? ... shine more than her than it is for you."

I did not respond to this. Better for her think me insecure than guess my true motive. With her moving into her own palace, she now had her own cooks. I needed Mutnedjmet with her to ensure she continued getting dosed with silphium. As there was no one else I could be sure to trust, I myself would take over inspection of the food for the women's quarters in order to continue supplying Nebetah. A significant duty for me, but one I felt I had no choice but to take on.

Kiya narrowed her eyes. "Your sister will not distract king from me." She waved an arm. "This palace proves his favor."

"You are the daughter of a king," I said. "You must surely know about the constancy of a king's favor."

Kiya blanched. "I know how to keep it. And how to advance."

I was about to respond that that must be why her father gave her away to a foreigner. Then it occurred to me that that probably was exactly why. She must be watched more closely.

"You have nowhere to advance," I said. "The position of Great Royal Wife will not be coming available."

Kiya laughed. "Keep failing in your duty; I not need to replace you to see my son on the throne."

I drained my cup and placed it at her feet. "No, but you must produce one first."

I left, beckoning my attendants as I went. From now on, I would no longer trust others to read Kiya's personal correspondence. I, myself, would read everything, especially that which she sent to her family. Kemet must not become a gift for Naharin.

Chapter 25

On returning to my chambers, I barred the door before opening the chest at the foot of my bed. Most days, I waited until past nightfall, when the household was asleep, before performing this ritual, but this day I truly needed solace. I removed the clothing, and dug down to the bottom, where I kept my statue of Sekhmet. I placed her in the corner and anointed her with cedar oil. I prostrated myself to her and prayed, begging her to keep me in Akhenaten's favor.

The hard floor disintegrated, and I found myself kneeling in the sand, the harsh rays of the sun searing my skin. I looked up to see Sekhmet, dressed in linen that glittered with gold flakes, everywhere gold — in her hair, dusting her skin. I bowed my head. "Lady."

Sekhmet's voice echoed. "In order to gain my protection, you must change the king's path away from his current one. You must stop his religious changes and restore Ma'at. The gods will not tolerate being denied. It is for this that I saved you."

I protested. "Akhenaten is not denying the gods. He is only worshipping his favorite, as kings, and indeed ordinary folk, have always done. The people of Kemet may worship as they please."

"Maya cannot. The high priest of Amun was publicly humiliated and granted a slow, painful death."

I shivered and dropped my gaze. "The priesthood of Amun was too powerful. It threatened the kingship itself. Though I did not agree with Akhenaten's methods in this case."

"Maya was not the only one forbidden from worshipping as he pleased," said Sekhmet. "You are no longer allowed to display my statue."

"Only because I am the Great Royal Wife, and we must appear to the people as a unified whole. The Aten requires this."

"You must do better."

I sat back, alarmed at the anger in her voice.

Sekhmet continued. "You must do more than merely appear to be a unified whole. If you should fall apart, you will no longer be in a position to influence him, and all will be lost."

My anger rose. "You will not help me keep Akhenaten's favor unless I change his current path, but I cannot do this unless I stay in Akhenaten's favor," I said. "Do you wish me to fail? Am I simply a pawn in some greater scheme of the gods?" Alarmed at my own outburst, I bowed my head, and opened my hands in supplication. "I am sorry, Great Lady of Ma'at. Please, what am I to do?"

She weighed her next words. "I concede your point. I will assist you so far as to keep you always fair to Akhenaten. However, I cannot help you restore Ma'at. That you must do yourself, for Akhenaten is blind and deaf to me and to all of the gods save the Aten."

I agreed. He was. "Yes, Lady."

Sekhmet waved her arm. Beside her, the air shimmered, and a window opened. Through it, I saw people who were starving. Their ribs and collarbones showing through their skin. Small children with yellowish hair and protruding bellies. The image shifted, and I saw people working, building, carrying bricks and stones, their backs bent from years of toil. The image shifted again. I recoiled. The faces were flushed, listless, the eyes vacant.

"No," I said. "I do not wish to see this."

"You must," said Sekhmet. "The Aten is powerless. This is what will come if you do not stop it."

I willed myself to look back and wished I hadn't. The face looking back at me was my own sweet Meritaten, my firstborn, her breath rasping in her throat. Dying of plague.

Akhenaten, Year 7

(ca. 1347 BCE)

Mutnedjmet and I played in the gardens with the children. Every so often, Mutnedjmet's dwarves would tumble past in front of them, at which the girls would clap their hands and giggle.

Mutnedjmet nudged me. "Leave the children with their nurses for a moment. I must speak with you."

I rose and took Mutnedjmet's hand. When we were out of earshot, she spoke. "It is increasingly difficult to deliver the silphium. Kiya favors her other ladies-in-waiting and grows weary of me."

"You must find a way," I said. "Our family's position depends on it."

"There is another option." Mutnedjmet grew quiet until I elbowed her. "Perhaps you are not the problem. Perhaps it is the king who is unable to conceive a male child."

I stopped walking and took a breath lest I answer in anger and arouse suspicion from the children's nurses. "Your other option is treason?"

"You should consider it," said Mutnedjmet.

"And face execution if caught?"

Mutnedjmet shrugged. "It is only a matter of time before one of the other wives gives him a son, and then you may be sent away."

"You underestimate the king's affection for me."

137

"Uh-huh," said Mutnedjmet.

I did not respond.

"Consider it," said Mutnedjmet. She called to her dwarves, and they followed her out of the courtyard.

Though I tried to ignore them, I kept hearing Mutnedjmet's words. Perhaps the fault was not mine. An image of Bek, his eyes searching for mine, leapt unbidden to my mind. I returned to my children. Ankhesenpaaten was chasing Meketaten in circles around their nurses. If not for them, I might dare. They would not be maltreated for my crimes, but I knew well the pain of growing up without a mother and would not wish it on my own daughters.

Akhenaten, Year 8

(ca. 1346 BCE)

When Akhenaten entered my chamber, he sent my attendants away. "And take the child with you."

The baby wailed as Taheret moved her away from my warmth.

"We must have the physician examine you," said Akhenaten. "Surely, there is more to be done."

I pulled myself to sit. "We have tried everything. I had been eating more meat, I have been spending more time in the sun to darken my complexion, you have tried entering me from behind. I've been dosed and poulticed."

"And yet, another girl."

"The gods must be displeased with us that they don't send us a son."

I didn't even see his hand before it connected with my face and sent me crashing into my cot.

He leaned in so close I could smell the wine on his breath. "There is only one god. Only the Aten. It is your lack of faith that is causing all these girls. You will pray, and pray hard, that Nebetah's child will be a boy."

I nodded.

Akhenaten rose to his full height. "Now. You will pray now."

I shifted myself on the bed.

"Properly."

I took a deep breath and lowered myself to the floor. My midsection and lower quarters protested. A sharp pain took me, but I nevertheless prostrated myself and prayed. "Blessed Aten, who watches over all the peoples in all the lands, beneficent ruler of the heavens, giver of life and happiness, please watch over this family now and bless this new child you have given us. And most especially, please watch over my sister-wife Nebetah and, in your infinite wisdom, grant her a son."

I deliberately did not ask that Nebetah be granted a healthy son.

Chapter 28

I settled on the cushions spread around the plank floor. The cabin protected us from the ferocity of the sun's heat, but the air quickly became stale. A warm bundle wriggled in my arms. Still less than a month old, Neferuaten was more alert than any of my other babies. Her dark eyes watched every move of mine. She wrinkled her nose and turned her head, rooting against my clothing. She was also greedier than my other babies, scarcely stopping between feedings. I handed her to a wet nurse.

"I was right, was I not?" said Nebetah, leaning back, and placing a hand on her swollen belly. "It is a lovely day for a ride on the water."

I nodded. "A shame we are not in the delta. We might hunt ducks in the marshes."

Nebetah wrinkled her nose. "I cannot stomach duck. It upsets my digestion, lately."

"It is not the eating of it, but the catching of it that relaxes me."

"You have never been the most feminine of ladies. I've never understood my brother's attraction to you," said Nebetah, reaching for the platter of olives.

"There is much you do not understand." I rose and went outside. Akhenaten was there with Kiya. His arm lay, protective, around her waist as he nuzzled her neck. Sighing, I crossed to the other side and leaned against the back wall of the cabin. A village on the shore lay glistening in the sun's rays. The fields were hidden underwater at this time. Irrigation channels directed the flood waters further inland, turning the homesteads into small islands. The waters were dotted with papyrus rafts.

The deck rattled, and a small figure hurtled itself into me. I looked down into the limpid eyes of my firstborn. "Halloo, Mother," said Meritaten.

I caressed her head and yanked on her sidelock.

Four more sets of small feet came pounding around from the stern and ran screaming at me, pulling Bek along in their wake.

Seeing me, he bowed. "Forgive me, your Highness. I sought to keep the children occupied. I had thought all of the ladies were in the great cabin." He disentangled his sons from my daughters, admonishing them for having touched me, and apologizing.

"No need for apologies. They are too young to be held responsible for their actions. Next time, they will know better."

"Very gracious of you, Highness," he said.

"Have you been demoted of late?"

His face went blank.

"Yesterday, you were chief architect and sculptor. Today you are royal child-minder."

He smiled. "Taheret and the nurses are hoping the baby will sleep. I am doing what I can to contribute to that end."

"She does not like to sleep much."

"That is because she knows much," said Bek. "She has a lively mind. When she is older, she will be a force to be reckoned with."

"You can tell that already?"

"Of course. She favors you greatly."

I shifted position, fearful that he had just made a declaration of some long-hidden feelings. Unaware of my discomfort, he lunged to grab a child who threatened to pitch himself overboard. The boy laughed, and so did Bek. I sighed in relief. Not a declaration, just a simple statement.

My girls gathered around me, and I hoisted Ankhesenpaaten up, she being still too small to be trusted to stay well back from the edge. Bek pointed out various features of the farms along the river.

"There is the shaduf," he said. "It is used to bring water from the river into the canal to irrigate the fields. Of course, it is not needed at this time of year." He pointed out to what appeared to be another expanse of dark water. "The field are under there. Once the river recedes, the oxen will help in the plowing."

"What are all the boats for, Father?"

"The farmers cannot work now, so they fish to feed their families," said Bek.

"You know a great deal about farming," I said.

He turned to me. "My father was a farmer."

I was confused. "I was told your father was Men, the royal sculptor."

Bek shook his head. "Men and his wife took me in after my parents died of plague. They were distant cousins, but as they had no children of their own, they raised me as their son."

"I did not know. I am sorry for your loss," I said. "My mother also died of plague when I was very young."

He nodded. "I know. I am sorry."

Of course, the past, mine or anyone else's, holds no secrets at court. As the boat rocked slightly, I noticed his arms flex as he held tighter to his son. His body looked almost to be chiseled from stone, so perfect were the lines of muscle. He was hard where Akhenaten was soft. I had to remind myself he'd acquired this hardness first through toiling in the fields and now through working with stone.

Soon, the children bored of this occupation and begged to go into their room in the cabin for some sweets.

"By your leave, Highness?" he said.

I nodded. "Of course. The sun is well into its downward journey. It is time they slept as well." I hugged my girls before they skipped away.

Before following them, Bek muttered something. So low was his voice, I was not sure I had heard it correctly. Though I would swear he had said, "The king is a fool."

It being indeed into afternoon, I decided sleep sounded like a fine idea. Returning to the cabin, I found the other ladies curled up amongst their cushions, drowsing if not yet in full sleep. I took my own space and settled. My mind, rebelling against my body, chose instead to replay the recent scene over and over again. Bek's last words haunted me.

In the end, the exhaustion of my body won out over the restlessness of my mind, and my consciousness slipped away.

I found myself back inside Sekhmet's temple. The stones on the floor cooled my feet. I ran down the hypostyle hall, past the towering columns toward the shrine, anxious to see her. She had promised to keep me in favor with Akhenaten, and I sorely needed her assurance now. She must have been as anxious to see me, for she was waiting outside the door of her shrine.

I bowed. "Great Lady. I—"

"I know why you are here, and I know the trouble you face. Come inside with me. You shall be pleased."

Together, we entered the shrine. Inside, Sekhmet's husband, Ptah, sat at a potter's wheel. He worked a lump of clay.

I whispered, not wanting to disturb the god at his work. "Who does Ptah fashion today? Is it another child of mine? A boy at last?"

Ptah glanced at me as he worked. "It is the next royal child to be born."

I grew silent and turned my head, fearing to see Nebetah's child, fearing she would be given what I had been denied.

Sekhmet cupped a hand under my chin and turned me back to the scene before us.

"How much better if you had simply allowed my efforts to work. The silphium should have prevented this."

"Our way is better," she said. "You will see."

The lump on the potter's wheel grew as it spun. It took on a bulbous shape, which Ptah pinched together at the bottom. Still, it grew, gaining shoulders, and a torso. I wished to look away again, but Sekhmet's arm on my shoulder prevented it. After the shoulders had risen from the mass, I noticed a slight wobble, as if the clay were off-center. From then, the shape grew crooked, twisted. It grew into a boy child, but one so twisted it could scarcely walk, let alone rule a kingdom.

My eyes flew open, and I found myself back amongst my cushions in the cabin of the barge. I smiled.

Chapter 29

"Highness, I never meant to steal. I simply need pasture for my cows. I did not know the land had been given to the temple," said the peasant cowering beneath my throne, not daring to look upon my face.

"Notices were called ..."

I put up a hand when I saw the herald enter the hall, and I motioned him to come to me ahead of the long line of supplicants. He leaned in, so as not to be heard by anyone save myself. "The time is near. Lady Nebetah's child will be here soon."

At once, the saga of the unfettered cow became strangely compelling. I longed to stay and hear more rather than face the possibility of my downfall. I chided myself, for Sekhmet had shown me this child would cause no competition for me, and came to a quick decision in the matter at hand.

"The owner of the cow shall give a measure of milk to the temple for the damage done to temple land. There will be no further petitioners this day." Both cow owner and temple priest eyed each other with loathing as I exited the hall.

When I arrived at Nebetah's apartments in the women's quarters, there was still no word. The groans of a woman bearing down could be heard from within her bedchamber, and I knew indeed it would not be long. Akhenaten leaned by the door, with Tiye by his side, one arm on his shoulder. She threw me a scowl as I entered.

"Are you sure you wish to be here?" said Tiye. "The birth of a legitimate heir would not bode well for you." A healthy boy for Nebetah, an heir born of two of her own children, would be her triumph as well. It had been her plan for her son ever since he became Crown Prince.

The gods had shown me this child would be no source of pride, yet still my innards fluttered. "I am here for my husband." I emphasized the last word.

Akhenaten turned to look at me. "The Great Royal Wife has been dutifully praying to the Aten that this child be a boy. She desires nothing but the glory of the king, the Aten, and Kemet."

His eyes challenged me to say differently, but I declined. I knew that all of his protests that only my children would matter would be true only so long as I had a son.

Silence fell, and we all looked toward the closed door. A small, weak cry followed. Akhenaten and Tiye burst into the chamber. I stood back at the doorway, watching. Ipu held up a red, wriggling form. "Your son, Highness." Nebetah relaxed and laughed at the announcement. Tiye turned and grinned at me, pure malice on her face.

Akhenaten took the child to his chest and turned to face his mother. "Behold — the Prince Tutankhaten." As he did so, I caught my first full view of the baby — the perfect curl of the newborn spine, the straightness of his limbs. Yet, there was something odd about his feet. The left one turned in at an odd angle.

"What is wrong with his foot?" I asked.

Tiye clucked. "Such spite does not become you. You have seen enough babies born to know that foot will uncurl as he grows."

Never had I seen a baby with just such a foot, but the only babies I had seen so young were my own. I glanced at Ipu, whose knowledge was infinitely more vast than my own. "Is this true?"

Ipu looked from me to Akhenaten to Tiye. "It is as the king's mother says."

I turned and walked out of the women's quarters, head high. Word was already flying that the king at last had a son. Everyone turned to watch me, conversation stopping as I passed. I looked straight ahead, feigning deafness. Once through, I picked up my pace, anxious to reach the privacy of my own apartments before the tears started. I turned onto the bridge above the Royal Road and kept to the far side while passing the Window of Appearances.

Alone at last, I flung myself onto my bed and gave in. I could not understand why Sekhmet would play false with me. Or rather, I did understand, but felt the unfairness of it. I was not in a position to do as she demanded.

After a time, the tears stopped. Drained and exhausted, I rolled over and lay staring at the Aten's rays painted on the ceiling. I still had options. Well, one option at least. I considered doing away with the new Crown Prince but quickly discarded that idea. He would be too well guarded, and with the most to lose by his presence, I would come under immediate suspicion should grievous harm come to him. I could hope that he would fail to thrive but knew I could not count on such favor from the gods. Even as I entertained these thoughts, I loathed myself for it. He was an innocent, just as my own children were, as I myself had been when Sekhmet took me in her cruel grip. His birth was not his fault, yet I hated him for driving me to consider infanticide.

No, I had but one remaining chance to remain Great Royal Wife that I could abide. That was to give birth to a son before this one grew into childhood. And if my husband could not provide, I knew one who could.

Chapter 30

"Here, beyond the storerooms, there is room for a garden or a pool, according to your desire." Bek pointed to a space in the new palace design with one sun-bronzed arm.

"A pool, I should think. I enjoy a swim in the mornings."

He rolled up one papyrus and unrolled another, offering it up for my inspection. "Are you quite sure we may discuss this without the king? He has requested personal approval of all temple projects."

"Long discussions of the whys and the wherefores bore him. He prefers for me to give him a condensed version."

"So, I will need to present this to him as well?"

"I'm afraid so," I said. "But the second presentation will be brief. He will approve it, and you can return to work. I will send a guard to summon him once we are done."

"Very well."

"Ascend. I must inspect the plans more closely."

He scaled the steps, and one of my fanbearers moved to the back of my throne to allow Bek the space next to me. My father, the other fanbearer, stood with his arms crossed.

While Bek recounted the difficulties of finishing the Small Aten Temple, I contemplated how best to broach the issue uppermost in my mind right now.

I believed he desired me, as I did him. Or so I hoped. I hoped I hadn't misinterpreted simple kindness.

As he spoke, I rested a hand on top on his wrist, and leaned in to scrutinize the papyrus. Bek swallowed hard, but made no other acknowledgement. When his speech was finished, he pulled his arm away, reluctantly I thought.

I gestured to Father. "Send for the king that he may approve the temple plans."

He glared at me but left. He would not question me in the audience chamber, in front of an underling. I sent the other fanbearer to announce to the few left in line that I would hear no more petitions this day.

Once they had gone, I spoke in a whisper, without turning my head toward Bek.

"In the west end of the city, past the Storehouses of the Aten, there is an unfinished villa. Do you know it?"

"Yes."

"I shall be there at the fourth hour of the night. If your desire is as mine, meet me there, but only if it is what you want." While I knew he would not refuse an order from his queen, I would not compel him against his wishes. Such an arrangement would be functional at best, and I reasoned that if I were about to risk my life, I might as well derive some pleasure from it. I had given little thought to what I should do if he refused.

So long was Bek silent that I thought he had not heard me. Then, "Yes, Highness." He descended the steps without looking back.

For the ruse, I borrowed Mutnedjmet back from Kiya's household and dismissed my other ladies. I feigned illness and insisted only my sister could comfort me. I knew the other women thought my sickness to be jealousy of Nebetah and the new prince, and that suited me fine. I left orders that I was not to be disturbed.

Mutnedjmet dressed in my clothes, while I took the clothes of a lowly servant, including a hooded cloak. I slipped out around the storerooms and exited the palace through the servants' entrance. I skirted the back of the Small Aten Temple and the Storehouses of the Aten. Once inside the residential area,

I became lost in the narrow streets. I knew where the villa was, and had arranged for the workmen to temporarily halt construction, but I had only ever seen it in on a papyrus drawing. Finding it in reality proved tricky.

By the time I arrived, it was well into the fourth hour, but the villa was dark. I entered through the garden and passed through the columned hall before reaching the master bedchamber. The basin of water and the cloths I had ordered stood on a table. It was deserted. I hoped Bek had not given up and left. Yet, the other possibility — that he had refused me — would be worse. "Yes, Highness," he had said, and I wondered now at the meaning of his words and the significance of his pause. Did he answer only to stop me from speaking further? Did he fear telling me he did not desire me? What I should do if he did not arrive, I did not know. I made mental note of all the other men of my acquaintance. While there were some I would not have minded taking for a tumble (one of our new, young stable hands came to mind), there were none other than Bek that I could trust to be discreet. Curse my vanity, and my need to be adored. I should have ordered Bek here and been done with it.

Soft footfalls crossed the tiled floors. I hid in the shadows and pulled my cloak closer around me so that I might observe without being seen. Lamplight flickered, illuminating a similarly cloaked figure. Its back was facing me, so I waited for it to turn. As it did, Bek's face appeared inside the hood. I stepped into the doorway and pushed back my hood.

Bek bowed. "Highness. I apologize for my lateness. I feared you had already been and gone."

"I only just arrived myself and feared the same about you." I unhooked my cloak, and let it fall to the floor. Bek stared, open-mouthed, at my rude attire. "I could hardly have slipped from the palace in my finery," I said.

Bek shook his head. "You are a vision, Highness, no matter what you wear."

"Considering the nature of our ... assignation ... do you think you might call me something other than 'Highness'?"

"No." Seeing my look, he scratched his neck and continued. "What I mean is, what I call you now is how I will always think of you. I've no wish to forget myself and call you 'beloved' when we are in chambers with your husband."

I smiled, for I knew I had chosen well. "Wise man. Likewise, I shall call you only by your name, so that I do not refer to you as 'heart of my heart' when I am in my apartments with your wife."

I beckoned him into the bedchamber. He followed, put down his lamp, and discarded his cloak. He came to me and enveloped me in his arms. I tilted my head back, anticipating his kiss.

He merely held me close, stroking my wig. "I do not know what gods are smiling upon me that I should have you in my arms right now."

Please, do not let the fool speak of love. Whatever we do together, it can never be about love. And, though I was using him, I had no wish to hurt him. To forestall any uncomfortable declarations, I pushed away from him and wriggled out of my tunic. He uttered a sharp intake of breath. The fabric of his kilt tented below his navel. I unknotted the kilt and drew him to the sleeping cot.

I spread my legs, expecting him to enter me right away. Instead, he nuzzled my neck, and massaged one breast. He pulled at my wig. I clasped at his hand to stop him.

"I wish to see you as you really are."

I removed my wig and tossed it to the floor.

Bek caressed my scalp. He traced a line of kisses down my neck, and still down, until he grasped my other nipple in his mouth and sucked. A jolt passed directly to my nether regions, causing my back to arch and a moan to escape my lips. Bek responded by releasing my nipple and continuing the line of kisses down to my navel.

My body craved the release he was withholding. "What are you doing?" It sounded harsher than I intended.

Bek look up at me and smiled. "I intend to give you something your husband does not."

"You presume to know what my husband gives me?"

"He does not seem to me to be the solicitous type." He placed his head between my legs and probed with his tongue.

"Sweet goddess ..." Waves of pleasure took me. "You are right — my husband does not do this for me."

Bek looked up at me and grinned.

"Well, don't stop now." Eagerly, he bent to his task. I clutched at the bedsheets and lifted my hips to him. He clasped my buttocks. The climax shook my whole body and left me panting.

Bek lay beside me, eyes squeezed shut. I placed a hand on his chest. He removed it. "Give me a moment, Highness. I must rest a while, or I may spend myself before I am of any further use to you."

I glanced down. He was beyond ready. I reached out a hand, but he grabbed my wrist and turned me over to face away from him. He slipped an arm around my waist. "Let us stay like this a while. Letting me hold back for a time will help me give you the son you need."

I turned to face him.

"I am no fool," he said. "Perhaps you desired me before now; perhaps you did not. In any event, you are not so besotted with love for me that you would risk your life for a few moments of pleasure."

I pulled away from him. "If you knew this, why did you meet me?"

"I almost did not. That is the reason I was late — I decided I would not be your plaything. I lay awake, thinking of you, naked and clinging to me, vowing I would have no part of it." He lay back and shrugged. "In the end, I was powerless to resist. I am the besotted one."

I turned away. "Do not say such things."

"Why not, because they are true? Ever since I first saw you, I cursed my common birth. Had I been born a noble, perhaps ..."

"Unless you had been born royal, and Crown Prince at that, you would still not have been acceptable to my father."

"Who you marry is your own choice; your father cannot force it."

I thought of my own choices surrounding my marriage to Akhenaten. "Under the law, that is true, but there are ways of convincing a person to do what you want regardless of what the law says."

He stroked my face.

I stifled an unexpected urge to cry. "If not for the machinations of my father, and the attentions of the Crown Prince, I would have happily stayed in the temple devoted to Sekhmet, and I would never have met you, noble or not."

Bek drew me close and kissed my forehead.

"In that case, I must give thanks to the gods for placing me in your service." He pressed his mouth against mine. His tongue flickered in and out, teasing.

I pushed away. "I can never love you. Love is a luxury I cannot afford."

Bek squeezed my waist and rubbed his nose against mine. "I know." He cupped my face in his hands and kissed me again. "If this night is all there ever is between us, the memory of it shall bring me happiness for the rest of my days."

I threw my arms around his neck, kissing him.

He shifted me onto my back. When he started to roll on top of me, I launched all of my weight at him. He landed squarely on his back, with me straddling his hips. His eyes widened.

I wriggled until he slipped inside me and leaned down to whisper in his ear. "There will be no holding back this time."

I adjusted my hips, moving backwards until I found just the right angle. I started with a slow thrust. Bek held my face in both hands, alternately kissing me and biting at my lip. It drove me so mad, my hips increased their tempo. Without releasing my mouth, Bek clasped my buttocks with one hand, driving me closer to him. I became frantic. My thrusting lost its tempo, becoming a chaotic jumble. The slowness of Bek's kisses only increased my frenzy.

I turned my head slightly. "Hold me tighter." I felt I might die if he did not. "Now!"

He grabbed my hips with both hands, crushing me against him. He thrust his own hips, trying to match my erratic rhythm. He looked into my eyes. His head rolled back, his body spasmed, and his hands released his hold on me. I increased my pace, truly deranged by now, desperate to continue while he was still hard. My own release came seconds later.

I collapsed on top of him. My cheek rested against his chest. I could feel his heart beating under his warm skin. He ran a hand over my scalp, kissed the top of my head, and lay back, panting.

When the glow had worn down to a small ember, I rose and brought the water and cloths over to Bek. I wrung out a cloth and applied it between his legs. He tensed.

"It is cold?"

"Not unpleasantly so." He looked at me, grinned, and then looked away again. The corners of his mouth kept trying to turn up.

"What is it?" I asked.

He shook his head, so I poked him.

"Well," he said, "it's just that hauling all that dirt in the fields as a boy, I never once thought that one day, the most powerful woman in the world would be scrubbing my balls."

I dropped the cloth and looked away.

"There." Bek pointed to me. "You almost laughed."

I turned back to him, and to my task. "I can honestly say it was not in my life plan, either."

"It seems you have done many things that were not in your life plan."

I plopped the damp cloth onto his chest. "You finish. And be thorough. It wouldn't do for us to return to the palace stinking of sex." I took another cloth to tend to myself.

"You leave first, Highness," said Bek when we were once again dressed. "Then I can follow at a distance to make sure you are not bothered by anyone."

As I stepped outside, I felt a tug on my cloak. Bek pulled me back inside, and into his arms. "I am sorry," he said. "I did not mean to upset you. I don't want any of our short time together to be spent fighting." He kissed the top of my head.

I drew him down and kissed his lips. "You did not upset me, merely reminded me of where my responsibilities lie."

"Will we meet again?"

"Two nights from now, if you are free."

"I am now," he said.

I pulled away from him and slipped out into the night. For the first time in my adult life, I prayed that I would be slow to conceive.

Chapter 31

"Unacceptable," said Father. "The king's horses must be housed better. We need stables to extend all along here." He moved a finger across the papyrus, indicating a whole sweep behind the temple. "The stalls must be bigger and grander." He had warmed quickly to his new duties as Master of all the Horses of His Majesty.

"Not possible," said Bek. "We must build the stables small for now. They can be expanded later, if necessary."

"Nonsense," said Father. "The entire complex must be grand from the outset."

"The king wishes for the temple to be completed post-haste. We cannot waste time on stables."

"It is the king's wish that the temple be a testament to the glory of the Aten, and that includes the stables, the cookhouse, the granary, and all other accompanying buildings."

"If that is the case," said Bek, "the king may tell me so himself."

I put up a hand. "Enough." Bek was coming dangerously close to impudence that would be cause for eyebrow-raising, should I allow it to continue. "Bek, you will build the stables according to Ay's specifications."

Bek glowered at me, and for a moment I feared he would contradict me. But, he simply clenched his teeth, glanced sideways at Ay, nodded, and left the courtyard.

I massaged the back of my neck.

"You need to be more careful," said Ay.

I looked at him.

"My request was outrageous. I expected, as always, you would be open to negotiation. You'd tell Bek to build the stables as he had planned, and appease me with, say, improved armories at a later date. One might think you were trying too hard not to grant favors to your young architect."

I froze for a moment and then turned my head, as if I had simply been contemplating the ripples on the pond. "One may think what one likes," I said. "I am tired, nothing more."

"That comes of too many late nights." He eyed me up and down. "And of the results of those nights."

"I'm in no mood for your riddles," I said.

"I am not criticizing you. I am gratified that you have finally taken matters into your own hands, even if you did delay too long. Even though Nebetah had the first Prince, one born to you will be the legitimate heir."

I turned away as I spoke. "I have no idea what you are speaking of."

Though there was no one else present, he leaned in to whisper. "Did you really suppose Mutnedjmet, the silly girl, figured out on her own that the king may be the reason you have not birthed a boy?"

I stared at him, open-mouthed.

"Somebody had to ensure our family's continued good fortune," he said. "You seemed unconcerned about it. I had thought you too spineless to take up the suggestion, until my spies noticed you creeping in and out of the palace at regular intervals lately. I knew you were meeting Bek."

My mind raced. Father would not betray me, for our interests aligned in this matter. Still, if there came a time when our interests did not align, would he use this knowledge as leverage?

He continued. "And, either you have grown recently fond of sweetmeats and hostile toward exercise, or your nightly exertions have already borne fruit."

Though my courses were not yet due, I feared Sekhmet had once again failed to heed my prayers. The night before, my breasts had pained while Bek suckled, and they still pained now. Faint cramps flitted in and out of my belly. I must act fast. Akhenaten had seen me with child four times before — he must not see it now until he had reason to believe he was the father.

Chapter 32

I chose a red dress embroidered with gold. Akhenaten had told me once he liked those colors on me. The pleated linen hugged my shape, still slim for the most part. My breasts strained at the fabric a little, though not nearly as much as they would weeks from now. Instead of my usual short wig, I opted for one with long, elaborate plaits, so tightly styled it would stay in place all evening. I also requested light makeup, with just a dusting of gold, so that it would not crack and run with sweat. My usual perfume was exchanged for a lily scent, which I knew to be Akhenaten's favorite. When Kiya was well into her cups, I would remain as I was now — the perfect image of a goddess.

The second part of my strategy also went according to plan. I arrived at the banquet late and had my presence announced. Every head turned to look at me as I passed through the outer columns into the main space. Many a male jaw dropped. Akhenaten ceased his banter with Kiya to see what had caused the sudden silence. When he saw me, he dropped the joint of meat that had been halfway to his mouth. He recovered himself in a moment, rose to meet me, and sat me down at my place beside him. To his other side, Kiya scowled.

"How go the plans for the new temple?" he asked.

"Well, indeed," I said. I thought it best not to mention my concession to Father, which would delay completion. I would have to fix that later.

Akhenaten spoke to Kiya but kept one hand on mine, gently squeezing. Bek, seated nearby, rested his eyes on our joined hands only momentarily and then resumed his conversation with Taheret. I felt a stab of envy for my lady-in-waiting. She would be the one in Bek's bed tonight, and from now on. I consoled myself with the thought that I had finally secured my future.

Within moments of taking my seat, servants appeared with plates of wine and food. The fatty scent of roast duck made the bile rise in my throat, obliterating what lingering doubt I still had regarding my condition. I pressed a crooked finger to my mouth and swallowed. I forced myself to eat, though I took only small bites and paused between. I must be seen to be eating.

Akhenaten leaned in. "You are especially beautiful tonight." His hand slipped behind my back, and he caressed my buttocks.

"Thank you," I said. "And you are especially handsome." I took a bite of lentils and pushed away the figs.

Akhenaten called a servant over and thrust the plate of figs at her. "Take these away. You know the Great Royal Wife abhors figs." He turned back to me. "Is there anything else, love?" The hand on my buttocks squeezed.

I shook my head and let my plaits fall to cover the side of my face. Experience had taught me that the best way to get Akhenaten into bed was to pretend you were not thinking of it yourself.

He pushed my hair back behind my shoulder. At that moment, Kiya tugged on his kilt, and whispered something in his ear. He laughed and grasped her waist. He did not acknowledge me again. I caught Bek's eye once — it held a mixture of sympathy and triumph.

As the final course was cleared and the dancing girls were regrouping, I excused myself and stood up. I was tired and must be fresh for the sunrise ceremony in the morning, or so I said. In reality, the combination of heavy perfume, sweat, and rich food unsettled my stomach. As I walked out, I affected a sway to my hips I did not normally possess. Once clear of the banquet room, I headed for the nearest courtyard for a few moments of fresh air before turning to the bridge to our private palace.

With my recent meal no longer in danger of being ejected, I paced my rooms. Would my brief appearance at the banquet be enough to turn Akhenaten away from Kiya for the night? If not, I would have to work all the harder the next day. I would tend to his bodily care, his cosmetics, as I had done in the early years of our marriage. My hands could still make him believe a passion I did not feel. If even that should fail ... such a waste to cast out a child I had risked so much to conceive. And the casting out would prove riskier than the conception, for it would be difficult to hide from my ladies.

My head jerked up at the sound of footsteps at my threshold. The door swung open, framing Akhenaten's swaying form. His mouth formed a lop-sided grin.

"I'm glad to see you are still awake. Saves me the trouble of rousing you."

Chapter 33

Under cover of darkness, I pushed aside the reed matting covering the doorway and slipped into the empty villa. After passing through the columned hall, I heard what sounded like footsteps coming from the master bedchamber. I froze, fearful I had been caught. All was silent again but not dark. A lamp burned in the bedchamber, casting a thin wedge of light toward me. I thought of running, but I knew I would be caught before I'd made it through the door. I placed my lamp on the floor, picked up a length of wood — the only available weapon — and flattened myself against the wall of the chamber, holding the wood high.

The shadow of a man flickered against the far wall. It grew smaller as he approached. I lunged out, brandishing my makeshift club. It connected, and the intruder fell backwards onto the floor. I pressed my advantage and raised my hand high.

The figure raised his arms above his head. "Highness, it's me."

I dropped the wood. "Bek?" I dropped to my knees beside him. "Are you hurt?"

"No, Highness."

"How did you know I would be here?"

"I didn't," he said.

I rose and offered him a hand up.

"I come here sometimes, when I wish to be alone."

"Why?"

He looked at me. "For the same reason you're here now."

"I am here to inspect the place. The owners will be arriving soon."

"Of course. This inspection couldn't be trusted to someone else? During daylight hours?" he said.

I turned away from him. "I should not have sided with Ay against you."

"I was angry at the time, but I understand why you did it. You were greatly concerned with other matters at the time." He reached a hand from behind me and stroked my swollen belly. He whispered in my ear. "Is it mine?"

"Any child I birth belongs to the king."

He grasped my shoulders and turned me around. "That is not what I asked."

I did not answer.

"We are alone, Highness, and I will not speak of it to anyone. If you do not trust in my loyalty, remember that I am as guilty of treason as you are."

"I am never alone. My father knows about us."

Bek let go of me. "Can you trust him?"

"My downfall would be his as well."

Bek touched my cheek. "You are wrong. You are always alone."

I blinked hard to clear my vision, which had suddenly grown blurry. Bek pulled me to him and wrapped his arms around me. I clung to him and sobbed into his neck while he stroked my hair. After a few moments, I pushed away.

"You don't need to hold back for me," he said. "Let it out."

I shook my head. "If my eyes are red and puffy in the morning, I shall have to explain why."

Bek dried my tears with his thumbs and then traced their path with his lips. My breath caught in my throat. He nuzzled my neck. I pulled him over to the bed and untied his kilt. Our lovemaking was slow, and gentle. Neither of us wished for it to be over.

Afterwards, we lay curled together, his cheek resting on my belly, one hand gently stroking it. I felt the first flutterings inside.

"Did you feel that?" I said.

Bek raised his head. "What?"

"The child moved. It is perhaps a little early for you to feel it from the outside. In a few more weeks ..." I remembered that there would be no few weeks for us.

He patted my backside, sat up, and reached for his kilt. "It is fine. I have felt the movement before. When Taheret was with child."

I, too, sat up and gathered my clothes. As I was about to go, Bek grabbed my arm. "Before you leave, I want to tell you that the gift of holding you in the darkness has been the greatest honor I could ever receive."

I brushed away his tear and kissed his cheek before heading out into the night. I navigated the twists and turns of alleys, now imprinted in my mind, without conscious direction. The moon was high and full, casting empty shadows across the earthen pathways. The emptiness and the silence echoed the desolation of my ba. At times, I thought I heard footsteps, but registered this only in the back of my mind. If I thought about them at all, I assumed they were Bek's, for he often followed me back to the palace, at a distance.

It was thus that I was surprised. When the footsteps were very close behind me, I spun around, expecting to confront Bek.

The brute facing me leered. "Well, you're not half as old as I expected. You shouldn't be out on your own at night." He reached out an arm and slammed me back against a wall. "It's not safe." His breath stank of onions and stale beer.

I ducked my head. I made frequent outings in front of the people of Akhetaten, and my face was well known. Though it might grant me safe passage, it would not do for this lout to know it was his queen he attacked. I looked around frantically, but there was no convenient weapon at hand this time.

When he pressed himself against me, I tried to maneuver one leg to fall between his, so that I might bring up a knee forcefully.

He outweighed me by a good measure and had little difficulty forcing my legs apart. He hoisted me up against the wall, but he needed both arms to hold me there. I brought down both of my hands against his ears. He let me slide down and raised his hand to hit me. I rolled away before he made contact. He grabbed me from behind and held me fast to him. I felt his hardness against me. He struggled to lift my robes. I stomped on the instep of his foot, and he lost his hold on me. When I swung around, I landed a firm kick to the side of his head.

At that moment, another figure crashed into my attacker, sending him flying into the dust of the alley. He brought a rock down on the man's head and stood up, wiping his mouth.

"Are you harmed, Highness?" said Bek.

I shook my head. "Is he dead?"

Bek knelt to feel for a pulse. "Not yet." He raised the rock again.

I grasped his wrist. "No."

Bek rose again. "You are more merciful than I."

"Not at all. Killing him will raise questions we do not wish to answer. Instead, send him to the gold mines in Nubia. He will pray for the release of death."

"Perhaps not merciful, but certainly wise," said Bek. "I will walk with you until we are in sight of the palace."

"You will do no such thing," I said. "Follow unseen, at a distance, as you have always done." I drew him down for one last kiss and left him there.

The Duat
Gate 3

Entering the third gate, we are faced with two fire-breathing serpents. One is just inside the gate, facing away from us; the other is at the opposite end, facing toward us. Believing these the first obstacle to overcome, I stand, head raised, proud and defiant, daring them to challenge me. But they barely notice me. They just blow fire above our heads as we pass below them.

Inside, there is a lake of fire. Surrounding the lake are twelve reanimating mummies. They tear at their linen bandages so that their dead, cracked flesh is exposed. Some of it flakes off and is consumed by the fire. Their faces are fixed in permanent rictus, as if silently screaming. These unfortunates are mired between the living and the dead. They have not yet earned their place among the blessed dead, but neither have they been condemned to dwell among the wicked. There is still great danger for them, and for me, for in order to reach the Field of Reeds, they must feed off a living ba, a thing I still possessed. Yet, they and the lake of fire could do harm to me only if I were truly wicked.

I hold myself strong and push my doubts aside. As we pass, the mummies stop their rending and tearing. They stare at the passing barque and at me. I keep my gaze fixed straight ahead. In the periphery, I see their shapes twisting, dark against the burning lake. I hear their garbled cries, and I am aware they follow the barque. I will myself not to tremble. One of the shapes hurls itself at me. The distance is too great; it falls into the lake. Desiccated flesh and old linen crackle, and flames erupt, crackling and hissing.

Once past the lake, I see a writhing shape in the distance. It gradually resolves itself into Apep, Ra's great enemy. His serpentine body is held by Atum and his nine followers, their arms barely encompassing his girth. They are all that prevent him from striking. When he sees our barque, Apep lunges. Two of the gods lose their grip, but Atum and the rest hold firm. Apep shakes his head in rage, his tongue flicking in and out between enormous fangs.

Again, I stare straight ahead as if I cannot see the danger before me. As we pass, Apep jerks his midsection in one direction, his lower portion in another. He makes of himself a spear and launches at me. Reflexively, I turn my head and find myself staring straight into his maw.

Akhenaten, Year 9

(ca. 1345 BCE)

"At long last, our city, the sacred city of the Aten, is dedicated to him, as am I," said Akhenaten. "I swear an oath to the Aten, and to all of my people, that I will never leave this city, nor will I ever stop serving him."

I shifted my bulk to relieve the pressure on my back. Still weeks away from the birth, I was already larger in girth than I had been with any of my girls. Though I was reluctant to fully believe it, this pregnancy had been so different from my previous ones that I had hope that Bek had succeeded where Akhenaten had failed. It was not only my size that was different. I had managed to control my early sickness only a few short weeks (long enough to allay suspicion, though just) before it exploded, leaving me exhausted and weak for months. When the sickness left, my hunger returned with a vengeance, and in particular my craving for animal flesh.

The difference was marked enough for Akhenaten to be confident I carried a boy. This day, we sat on a dais in front of the pylons of the inner courtyard of the main palace. I held the place of honor to his right, and our daughters were seated between us. Meritaten held onto Neferuaten, who kept squirming, wanting to try out her new, tentative steps. Nebetah and the young Tutankhaten, wriggling in his nurse's arms, were relegated to the rear. Kiya kept her place to Akhenaten's side. Of course.

In spite of my apparent good fortune, I was uneasy. The babe's size presaged a difficult birth — dangerous, even, if he kept growing. Even more than the specter of death in childbed, I was haunted by the image of a twisted, malformed boy child. If the presaged misshapen child was not Nebetah's son, would it be mine?

I became aware of Akhenaten's attention on me. He was leaning down, attempting to speak quietly with me. I had not heard a single word.

"Are you even listening?" His face was turning red.

I snapped to attention. "My apologies. The heat has me feeling a little faint."

"Send for poppy now. My head pains me."

I thought that if only he would relent and allow us some shade from his precious Aten, then his head would not pain so, but I did not say it. Instead, I took Neferuaten onto my lap and whispered to Meritaten to fetch the physician. As she left, she turned enough for me to see her face in profile. I was struck by how mature she looked. At eight years old, her face had slimmed and I could already see on it the image of the woman she would become. Gone was the childish pudginess evident in Sekhmet's vision. In fact, she now bore little resemblance to the plague-stricken child of my nightmares. Not only did she did not fall prey to it, there had been no outbreak of plague in all of Kemet. Sekhmet had been playing me false. I did not understand why, nor did I much care at that moment. What mattered was that Meritaten was no longer in danger. And if she was not to die of plague, perhaps I would not give birth to a monster.

With some reluctance, I turned my attention back to Akhenaten's speech, lest I be caught not paying heed again. He droned on about his devotion to the Aten. When Meritaten returned with the poppy, he took the bowl and drained it and then handed it back without looking at her.

The foreign ambassadors and representatives of vassal kings stood in line to pay homage to us. One by one, they presented gifts and declared their loyalty to Akhenaten. He greeted each one warmly.

"I must speak with you," Mutnedjmet's voice whispered from behind.

"Must it be now?"

"Kiya grows suspicious. She will no longer take food or drink from my hand. She insists a different servant serve her."

I glanced at Kiya, now embracing the Naharin ambassador, a cousin on her mother's side. "I will think on another way to deliver the silphium to her. But, perhaps," I said, rubbing my belly, "it no longer matters."

When the line at last drew to an end. Akhenaten stood at his place once again. "The Aten watches over all people, in all lands: Naharin, Babylon, Kush, the Hatti lands. He is the father of all people. He is not only the supreme god, he is the only god." He signaled with an arm.

I sat straighter. This was the first I had heard of such a declaration and did not know where it was leading.

Several men entered the courtyard, carrying a statue of Amun on a litter. He was resplendent in his finest robes and garlanded with wreaths of flowers. They placed it in front of the dais. Akhenaten descended and accepted a hammer from one of the men. "The Aten requires no images, nor will he tolerate pretenders."

He raised his arm and brought down the hammer on the face of Amun. A tiny chip of stone broke loose. Not enough for Akhenaten, he screamed and brought the hammer down again. Amun's nose broke off. The third blow severed the false beard. Akhenaten rained blows down upon Kemet's former chief god. When he finally drew back, panting and clutching at his head, Amun's face had been completely obliterated. Akhenaten handed the hammer back to its original owner.

"Finish the job," he said.

Several men attacked Amun with hammers, feet, and bare hands. Shouts of encouragement and cheers echoed as the god's garlands and clothing tore to bits, and he lost hands, and arms, and feet. In the end, Amun was reduced to a mound of pebbles and linen shreds. A rain of petals drifted and fell upon the ruined mess.

Not everybody cheered. Many stayed silent, and even among those who did cheer, many did so half-heartedly, out of duty rather than conviction. This was what I was meant to prevent, though how I could have done so without prior knowledge of Akhenaten's intent, I did not know. What I did know was that it wasn't only the gods who would be undone by this pronouncement. What of the people whose lives centered on their gods? What solace would they find in a god that spoke only to their king? To whom would they turn to make their fields fertile, or themselves? What hope of an afterlife?

Akhenaten leaped back onto the dais. "You see now that Amun is nothing. The Aten is everything. Henceforth, all temples shall be closed, save those dedicated to the Aten. All lands formerly belonging to the temples revert to the crown, to be used in the glory of the Aten."

It was my turn for a pounding head. All of the priests and temple employees — they would be seeking me out on the morrow, asking what they should do for a living now. I must somehow see that they were taken care of without angering Akhenaten. The sickness I felt in that moment had nothing to do with either the baby or the heat.

Chapter 35

I could hear the din from the robing room. Voices talked over each other, getting louder, trying to be heard. They pounded in my head like waves battering the shore. I took a deep breath and entered the audience chamber. Father stood to one side, and my step faltered when I saw Bek standing in for my usual fanbearer. My appearance caused such an uproar, I was certain no one noticed my misstep. I used one hand to lower myself into the throne as gracefully as was possible under the circumstances.

"What about the bakers? We have worked hard for the king. He cannot close the temples..."

"Not as hard as the butchers. We must be heard ..."

My back ached.

"How are we to live if the temples close?"

The chatter echoed inside my head.

Bracing myself with one hand on the arm of the throne, and leaning hard to leverage myself, I rose as fast as I was able. I grasped my scepter below its stylized god's head and crashed its forked end into the floor.

Silence.

"His Highness has already spoken on this matter. There is nothing more to be done for it. You will cease operations immediately."

The protests grew louder again. A second crash of the scepter brought them all to attention. "If you wish to speak, you must choose one among you to speak for all."

I waited for their choice. In truth, I had given this much thought in the past several hours and had already devised a solution. But if they believed their pleas could sway me, I would gain their confidence.

An older man with the shaved head and plain, white kilt of a priest came forward, half-stepping and half-shoved. He bowed before speaking. "Highness. All of the considerable temple assets — land, ships, grain — are now being absorbed by the royal coffers."

"Careful," I said. "You tread dangerously close to treason."

He bowed again. "My apologies, Highness. I meant no harm, only that we are all now without work and without means of feeding our families."

I took a moment to appear to be considering his words. "That, we must remedy. Those of you with military training must join the army. We always have need of soldiers. For those who are qualified, we have need of scribes. The temples of the Aten will be expanding and increasing, so we will have continued need for butchers, weavers, priests, bakers, and other workers."

I called to my scribe. "You will see that lists are made of those who are left without work, and what work needs to be done. No one shall starve in the Aten's kingdom."

Back in my own chambers, I collapsed onto a chair. Taheret came running to massage my feet.

"How are you feeling, Highness?"

"Miserable," I said. "These next few weeks cannot pass fast enough."

Voices came from the other side of my door. "See who it is, and send him away. I will see no one."

Taheret left and returned shortly, followed by my father.

"I apologize, Father, but I have no patience for visitors right now. Taheret was supposed to turn you away."

"Do not be angry with her. She tried, but I refused."

"Have your say then, and be gone so I might rest a while."

"I come to congratulate you on how you handled the displaced priests and temple workers. You have become quite skilled at statecraft."

I leaned my head back and closed my eyes.

Father sent Taheret from the room. "It is a shame you cannot handle your husband so well," he said. "This road he is on is complete folly. If it is not reversed soon, he will do irreparable damage to Ma'at, and all of Kemet will suffer for it."

I kept my eyes closed and spoke as if none of it concerned me. "As king, he is divine. It is not for us to question him." Father was right of course, but I would not be trapped into a treason not of my own design, if entrapment were his goal.

"He listens to you. He trusts you," said Father. "You are in a position to persuade him back to the path of Ma'at."

I opened my eyes. To my complete bewilderment, people and gods always seemed to think this of me. "He trusts me to handle the day-to-day tedium he has no taste for himself. I have no influence in matters of religion. That is his domain."

"His religion is a pretence. It is nothing more than an attempt to take all the power of the nation for himself."

Right again. "He is king. All the power of the nation is already his."

"He is no ruler," said Father.

"Enough," I said. "I will not tolerate this kind of talk. Not in my chambers and not anywhere else."

"What will you do? Report me?" He stood facing me, arms crossed, daring me to defy him.

I met his stare. "I will not report you for idle talk. But neither will I protect you should your views become public knowledge."

At that moment, the doors to my chambers swung open, and Akhenaten thundered across the threshold.

A sudden tightening of my abdomen caused me to grip the armrests of my chair.

Akhenaten turned to Ay. "Get out." Once Ay was gone, he continued. "I understand you rewarded the priests of false gods today."

I sighed in relief as the contraction passed. "I did not reward them. I placated them."

"It amounts to the same thing. They deserve no mercy from us."

"I did not do it for them," I said. "I did it for us. If you count all of the workers — not just the priests, but the cooks, masters of horse, scribes, and the rest — in all of the temples in Kemet, they number in the thousands. They are more than the population of our great city, respectable though that is. I have done what is necessary to turn them from enemies to allies."

"They would not dare disobey their king."

"Hungry people are dangerous people," I said. "Instead of handouts, I have given jobs. They can now feed themselves and their families, but they must work to do so. With full bellies, they will happily do anything their king asks of them, especially if they owe their full bellies to the king's good grace."

Akhenaten took a step back and was silent a moment. He smiled. "You are very wise, my dear. The Aten was correct to guide me to place the people in your hands."

"Was it also the Aten who guided you to deny all other gods? To close their temples?"

"The Aten guides me in all things. I am merely his instrument."

"I have heard vague rumors of discontent." I paused, but when Akhenaten did not react, I continued. "There are those who believe you take this step only to increase your own power." At his look of fury, I hasten to add, "It is nonsense, of course — as king, your power is without limits, but such is the talk."

Akhenaten's jaw clenched. "If that is how some wish to perceive it, it cannot be helped. But should you hear anyone say such, you shall report it directly to me."

I intended to tell him — yes, of course — but an intense pain ripped through my body. I doubled over, clutching my belly. Such was the pressure, I had to fight not to push, to try and keep my son inside me.

Akhenaten was with me. "What is it my love? Is our son anxious to be born?"

I gritted my teeth until the pain subsided. "It cannot be. It is too soon." It was more a cry of despair than a denial of what was happening, for by now I had no doubt.

"You are wrong, love. You are already far bigger than you were with any of the girls. You will soon be delivered of a strapping, healthy boy. Shall I send for Ipu?"

I nodded. "Send her here."

He spoke with the guards and returned to me.

I began to shiver. Akhenaten was right — the child was bigger than any of my others. And what if it was the misshapen monster shown to me by Ptah? Sekhmet had shown me false about Meritaten, but that did not mean Ptah had done the same. I feared, truly, that this would be my last child. My last day. With the next pain, I bore down. I could not help it. I knelt in front of my throne, clutching the armrests for support.

Akhenaten tried to make me rise. "Come, I will help you to the birthing pavilion."

"It is too late for that," I said. I reached for his hand, some little bit of comfort while I labored, but my hand met only empty air. I turned to see he had gone. I looked around frantically. Unless Ipu arrived within moments, I would have no help. I unknotted my sash, slipped out of my outer robe, and bunched it up between my knees.

A commotion behind me accompanied Ipu's arrival. She breezed through the door, having gathered my women in her wake. I let out a breath I had not been aware I was holding.

Reaching from behind, Ipu placed one hand on my belly and probed inside with the other. "This one is well on the way."

"It is much too soon."

Her eyes roved over my belly. "Are you certain there was not an error in the dates?"

Heat rushed to my cheeks. "Quite." Even counting the real date of conception, it was still a full month too soon.

"Hmmm." She turned me around and ordered Mutnedjmet to sit in the chair and support me under the arms while I leaned back against her. "There's no time to worry about it now."

I leaned back while my body squeezed the child from me. Ipu barely had time to catch.

"You have another fine daughter."

"No. Look again."

"This child will not sprout a manhood no matter how many times I look," said Ipu.

I looked myself. All of my subterfuge, the risks I had taken were for nothing. I rubbed at my eyes. I would not cry.

A hand grabbed my belly, kneading the tender flesh. "Is there anything you notice about your new daughter apart from her not being a boy?" said Ipu.

Taheret had the baby now. Her tiny red face screwed up and she let out a yell. "She is very small." This confused me, for I had expected a large baby.

"Exactly," said Ipu, still working my midsection. "Given your size, I feared your ability to survive the birth." She grabbed on to something, and it wriggled inside me.

"There is another?" I said.

"There is. This is why I found it difficult to tell where your baby was sitting." She pushed and pulled. "This one is backside first; I am trying to convince it to move."

A pain drew me upright. "I don't think he's listening."

She inserted her hand. "Indeed, not."

When the pain started, I took deep breaths to keep from pushing. "Is it dangerous for him to be born this way?"

"It is not preferable," said Ipu, "but it can be done. Especially when it is the second of two, and the way is already open." She took my hands, helped me to my knees, and gestured to Mutnedjmet. "Around this way." The legs of the chair scraped across the tiles as she pushed it out of the way so she could take her position behind me. "With the next pain, I want you push gently. I'll have to guide the baby out."

The next one eased out by degrees, with the gentle hand of Ipu ensuring no limbs were caught on the way out. When all but the head had emerged, Ipu placed a hand on my back. "Lean forward, as if you are prostrating yourself in front of your god."

Mutnedjmet helped me down, and Ipu helped the child the rest of the way. When I heard the thin cry, I tensed for the announcement. None was forthcoming.

"Is it a boy?"

No response.

I repeated myself, louder. "Is it a boy?"

"No, Highness," said Ipu.

I collapsed onto the cold tiles and sobbed. But Ipu would not let me wallow for long. There was still work to do. Once it was over, and I had properly bathed, I retired to my bed. Taheret sent for the wet nurse and started a search for a second.

I lay facing the wall. Mutnedjmet and Taheret sat by me, trying to comfort me. I wished they would leave so I could plan, but I did not have the energy to order them gone. Kiya was no longer taking the silphium, and Nebetah conceived even while taking it. If I did not find another way, another prince would be born to one of them soon enough. My one consolation was that I now had reason to seek out Bek again, but I knew it a dangerous option. Father knew of our trysts, and if he could discover us, others could as well. Every time we met, it increased the risk. And, yet ...

"After a few days, you'll get over the disappointment and love them, just as you do all the others," said Mutnedjmet.

A hand rubbed my back.

"It's funny," said Taheret. "I know they all look alike when they're brand new, but these babies remind me very much of my own when they were born."

I froze. Bad enough they were girls, but if they should look like Bek, it would be noticed. I should have to find him a posting elsewhere. Though his proximity would doubtless tempt me into taking further risks, the thought of never seeing him again was like a spear to the heart.

"Don't listen to her," said Mutnedjmet. "They are both the image of you."

I turned over, about to demand to see the babies. I hoped Mutnedjmet was being truthful, but she knew of my late-night meetings with Bek. She may simply have been trying to allay my fears.

Just then, the door to my chamber swung open, and Akhenaten stormed in. "Leave," he said to my ladies. "You, too." This to the wet nurse, who removed herself with both infants, the one wailing for having been removed from the breast.

I raised myself to a sitting position as he towered over me.

"As my wife, you had one job to do, and you have failed."

I looked him in the eye. "With respect, as your wife, I do a great many jobs, and excel at most."

He put his face a hand span from mine and roared. "Except one."

I flinched and hated myself for it.

He straightened up. "You will keep your duties in the audience chamber. You will keep your title. For now. But I will no longer waste my seed on a woman who can produce only girls." He turned and strode out the door without a backward glance.

After he left, I started shaking. Tears left wet patches on the bed linens. I would have no sons.

Chapter 36

In spite of giving birth to two babies, I did not take the usual fourteen days of rest I had with all of my other births. If I was never to have a son, the only hope I had of remaining Great Royal Wife lay in the value of my work.

I avoided Bek as long as I could. When he came into the audience chamber, I would not look at him. When he requested a meeting, I delayed. I could not delay indefinitely, however, for we did have legitimate business that needed to be addressed. I opted to have the meeting in the courtyard. There, we would be seen but not overheard. I arranged for a table to be set up under a canopy. A mild desert breeze wafted in, curling the edges of the papyrus as we studied plans for a city zoo.

"Neferure and Setepenre," I said.

"I beg your pardon?"

"Their names. The announcement will be made tomorrow evening, but it is fitting that you should know first."

Bek nodded. "Thank you."

"You should not have taken the place of my fanbearer," I said.

His gaze did not move from the papyrus. "I knew it would be a difficult day for you."

"It was an unnecessary risk."

He took a deep breath. "I am sorry you did not get the son you desired."

I made a pretence of studying the papyrus. "It was a need, not a desire."

"Then I am doubly sorry."

"I will not be trying again, if that is the reason you inquire."

He did not speak for some moments. "It pains me that you think such. I am concerned for you."

I never thought otherwise and accusing him of feigning his feelings for me pained me more than it did him.

"I heard he is angry that they are girls."

"He is. But they are still his daughters, and they will not be harmed."

In my peripheral vision, I saw the tension drain from Bek's body. I wanted to give him something. "Living in the palace, and working closely with their father and myself, you will be able to watch them as they grow."

He snatched the papyrus away and rolled it up. "That is all?"

"What did you expect?"

"About the girls? Exactly this."

He paused, and for the first time in this conversation, I turned to look at him. The vulnerability in his eyes produced a catch in my throat. I looked around to see who might be watching.

"I thought that we ... I'm not a fool, but I hoped you might at least feel some affection for me."

"I wanted but one thing from you, and that, you could not deliver. You are as useless as my husband in that regard."

Bek closed his eyes for a moment and then nodded and left.

I walked the other way, toward the pond, so I would not be facing any of the windows, nor any of the others in the courtyard. It was better this way. Better for Bek to think me unfeeling, even cruel, than to know the truth. Now that I could never be with any man, his knowing how I longed for him would be torture for him. For both of us. It would only be a matter of time before one of us made a fatal blunder. I clenched my jaw and squeezed my eyes shut. I must not cry.

Akhenaten, Year 10

(ca. 1344 BCE)

The moment I stepped into the robing room, I heard the commotion from the audience chamber.

"You cannot do this," came the voice of the priest of the Aten.

"Do not presume to tell me what I can and cannot do," said Akhenaten.

I hastily donned my crown. Akhenaten had not shown himself in the throne room since we moved to our new city, and indeed for some time before that. That he would choose to hold audience there knowing I would not yet be there could not but bode ill. I stepped into the room. A team of sculptors, hammers and chisels in hand, Bek at their head, stood assembled in the hall. They squirmed but did not protest. Bek gazed at the bound captives painted on the floor tiles, refusing to meet my eyes. I wondered what threats Akhenaten had made. Or, perhaps, he did not need threats — common people could be intimidated by the mere presence of their divine king. He was, after all, near to a god himself.

I touched Akhenaten's arm. "May I ask what the trouble is?"

He turned to face me, eyes wide as if he were surprised to find me in the very place I worked for him nearly every day. Tiye stood beside him.

"The names of all gods save the Aten are to be destroyed wherever they appear," he said, "be it on temples, on tombs, or in private homes. I must not allow a lack of faith to destroy what I have built."

I withdrew my hand and took a deep breath. This must not happen, but it would. Akhenaten had already assembled his enforcers. "Of course, you may do as you wish," I said. "However, I do hope you will consider carefully the consequences of such a course of action."

"The consequences will be that the Aten will have his due place as the one and only god."

"The people love their gods," I said, thinking of my own complicated relationship with Sekhmet. "It will take time for them to make such a big change."

"Time?" said Akhenaten. "They don't need time; they need leadership. Someone to tell them what is right."

"The Aten does not need to destroy in order to prove himself superior," said the priest.

"The Aten speaks to me," screamed Akhenaten. "No one else. Me! Only I know what he wants, and he wants all other gods to be gone. Obliterated. Known for the lies they are."

"I understand," I said. "But, perhaps you would consider a less complete destruction. You speak of desecrating the dead, of doing great dishonor to your own father and ancestors."

Tiye put her arm around her son's shoulders. "If the king wishes it to be done, it is to be done." She glared at me. "You would do well to remember your correct role as wife."

"As you remember yours?" I said. "You support your son as he robs your deceased husband of his name."

"Enough," said Akhenaten. "This is not a negotiation. The Aten is the one and only god of all the lands. And you shall lead by example."

I stared at him, not understanding.

"Do not think I don't know that you still keep your statue of Sekhmet."

I swallowed. Akhenaten crossed his arms, daring me to defy him in front of the priest, his mother, the sculptors, and scribes. Tiye clung to his arm, gloating.

I nodded.

Akhenaten swept past me and stopped in front of Bek. He took the hammer and chisel from his hands and stepped aside. He gestured for me to go ahead of him. "You shall collect Sekhmet and bring her to the Window of Appearances." He gestured to a herald. "You shall spread the word that the king and the Great Royal Wife will be speaking momentarily."

Numb, I started walking. As I passed onto the bridge over the Royal Road, I heard many footsteps behind me. I entered my bedchamber alone, removed Sekhmet from her hiding place in the chest beneath my linens, and carried her to my outer chamber.

"Your jewelry," said Akhenaten.

"I beg your pardon?" I said.

"You have jewelry, amulets, containing the names and images of gods. Bring them as well."

I placed the statue down on my table and emptied my jewelry box. I picked out a few rings, some armbands, and a necklace — I had little that did not contain the image of the Aten. Akhenaten did his own search and picked out several more objectionable items. He put the discarded pieces back in the box and gave it to one of the sculptors to carry. The rest he left strewn across my desk. He took Sekhmet and held her upside down against his hip.

I looked to the entourage of sculptors currently blocking the doorway of the chamber. Perhaps, with enough of a run, combined with the shock of it, I could break through them and flee down the corridor. I quickly dismissed this idea, for they were all thick, strong men, devoted to their king. Not even Bek would support me after my cruel treatment of him. And if I should escape, where would I go?

Akhenaten noticed my hesitation. "It is time," he said.

An idea occurred to me. "No."

Akhenaten drew himself up and glared at me. "You dare defy me?"

I met his stare. "I do not. I simply ..." I had been about to suggest that a public ceremony would give the people warning. They would have time to hide their own statues and amulets. Then, I decided that was as it should be. I would sacrifice my Sekhmet to save others. I hoped she would approve. "... Sekhmet is mine. I shall carry her."

Akhenaten looked down as if surprised to see her there. He handed her to me. I held her gently.

I brushed past Tiye on my way out. We wound our way through the palace to the Window of Appearances above the grand avenue. Akhenaten gestured for the jewelry box to be placed on the ledge. The crowd below cheered, expecting, as usual, that we would be throwing gifts down below. When neither Akhenaten nor I did anything, the cheering died down, and people started looking around, wondering what was happening. Usually, when we gave out gifts, it was in honor of a special event, and there was none that day.

Slowly, Akhenaten took the lid off the box. He pulled out the first piece, an intricate necklace of gold and lapis, featuring a goddess wearing a throne-shaped headdress, extending her wings. "Aset," he said, curling his lip in disgust." He pulled out another. This goddess wore a house-and-basket headdress and held her wings in front of her body. "Nebthet." One by one, he removed my treasures and laid them on the ledge, showing them to the audience first, and naming the offending gods. A golden pillar: "Wesir." Falcon earrings with feathers of precious stones: "Heru." An armband with a row of smiling, golden baboons. "Djehuty. Pretenders, all. False gods. Each one is an insult to the Aten. Every time you worship one of them, that is devotion stolen from the Aten. It pains him, your lack of faith. No more."

I willed myself to watch as he raised his hammer and brought it down on the first piece. Bits of metal and precious stone sprayed into the air. Some of the shards landed on the avenue below. Nobody moved to pick them up. He repeated the action until all of my jewelry lay in pieces. Conscious of Tiye's eyes on me, I kept my gaze forward and clenched my jaw to keep it from trembling. Akhenaten brushed the bits off the ledge, down into the street. People eyed them and then each other.

I moved into my place beside Akhenaten and placed Sekhmet on the ledge. "It shall be done with all images of the old gods. You will turn over your jewelry, amulets, and statues. They will suffer the same fate as my own, freeing you to devote yourselves entirely to the Aten and only the Aten."

I took the hammer and chisel from Akhenaten and lay Sekhmet down on her back. The chisel trembled as I held it against her throat. I raised the hammer and it hesitated for an instant at the top of its arc before I drove it down. The edge of the chisel bit through the gilt, and deep into her wooden neck, angled up toward her head. For a brief moment, I entertained the idea of casting her into the crowd, hoping someone would rescue her and keep her safe. Instead, I again raised the hammer. When I brought it back down, I did so with such force the chisel connected with the stone beneath her, clanging noisily and rattling my arm. Sekhmet's lion head fell to the ground and bounced a few times, before rolling. It came to rest face up, its eyes accusing me.

Sculptors and scribes were sent to all the nomes of Egypt and Kush to erase the names of the gods wherever they appeared. In our own Akhetaten, there was no need for destruction, for never were the names of any god but Aten carved into our walls. There remained only the house-to-house inspections. Though I had no taste for it, I accompanied the military on their rounds to ensure there would be no overstepping.

"You ought not to have come," said Father. "Bek and I can handle this."

"If I did not think so, I would not have appointed you."

"The people will blame you for the loss of their gods instead of the one responsible."

"What makes you think I am not responsible?" I said.

"I know how devoted you were to Sekhmet for all the years you studied at her temple."

"People change," I said.

Bek made a noise that might have been a suppressed exclamation or might have been a clearing of the throat.

Father leaned closer to me and lowered his voice. "I know what the destruction of Sekhmet cost you."

I searched his eyes but, finding only sincerity, I nodded.

"Normally, you attempt to mitigate your husband's folly to increase your own favor. Today, you seem to be doing the opposite. I cannot help but think you must have some plan in mind."

And there it was. "People will resist. I wish only to ensure that no one is harmed in the enforcing of the king's orders."

Father looked at me, agape. "You think Bek will treat the population harshly?"

I elbowed him. "It is not Bek that concerns me, nor you, and well you know it."

Our military escort was comprised of very large, very experienced Ribu and Kushite troops carrying axes and clubs in addition to bows. They were much accustomed to using force.

"I am insulted you think I cannot control my men," said Father. "I assure you, any infractions will be severely punished."

"Punishment can only come after the damage is done," I said. "In the presence of their queen, they will behave with more decorum.

Father nodded. "You may be right at that."

We set out from behind the Small Aten Temple and passed the Storehouse of the Service of the Aten and onto the packed dirt pathway into the residential section of the city. We passed the large villas of the nobles and wealthy merchants. Those would be left until last. I could not resist a glance down the alley leading to the villa Bek and I had used, and I wondered if he thought of it with longing or bitterness.

We came to a stop at the edge of the settlement, where the homes were single rooms, with sparse furnishings, and the owners held few possessions. House by house, we searched. What families willingly gave up, we collected in an ox-drawn cart. Once we'd finished the first street, we parked the cart, and a search was conducted of the entire street. Anything found hidden would be taken. I entered the first home with the soldiers. They overturned the one table and opened boxes. I helped and, to my relief, found nothing.

At the next house, I opened a box and removed the linen stored inside. The owners — a middle-aged woman with her teenage son and daughter, stared at me fearfully. They kept staring at the box. I found nothing contraband inside but noticed my hand hit the bottom before it should have. On inspection, I found a slight nick in the wood. A false bottom had been installed. I smiled, replaced the family linen and continued helping with the search.

Before leaving that place, I heard screams from outside. Emerging, I saw a father and three young children had barred the doorway of their home. The father held a hand to his nose, and red seeped out. A little girl cried. A woman was kneeling in the street, begging the soldiers not to hurt her children.

I strode over. "I made it clear that no one was to be hurt."

The soldiers stepped aside. "This man refuses to let us pass," said one.

"Please," said the woman. "Don't hurt him anymore."

I offered the man a hand and helped him up. When he saw my face, he pulled away, bowing as he went.

"Back inside," I said to the family.

The parents looked to each other and then backed into the home, leaving the doorway clear. I crossed the threshold first. The man looked away from me, but the woman's gaze kept flickering to a spot in the corner. There, a patch of the earth floor of the home had been recently disturbed. I strode over and stood on the darker ground, ensuring that my long dress covered it completely. I turned, and my eyes met Bek's. I had not known he was so close behind me.

"Bid the soldiers enter," I said.

Once the home had been searched in vain, I made certain to be the last to leave. As I passed the couple, the man seemed about to say something. I held up a finger and shook my head.

Bek did not acknowledge what he had seen, but the rest of the day he encouraged my participation in the exercise.

The searches took many days, and I accompanied the soldiers as much as I was able. When at last it was done, I took some time with my masseuse. We had hardly begun when a herald announced the presence of the king. I sat and tied the sheet around me. The masseuse left at my command.

Akhenaten stormed in and stood over me with arms crossed. "I have just seen the results of your collections."

I was in no mood for recriminations. "And?"

"And there should have been more — far more."

"I assure you, your soldiers were very thorough." In fact, they had brought back wagons full of statuettes, amulets, and jewelry. All had been handed over for destruction save one wooden statue of Sekhmet, a poor substitute for the one I had lost, but the best I could do.

"There are tens of thousands of people in Akhetaten. There should have been three times that amount."

"Don't forget that most of the citizens are poor and can afford little." I rose and offered him the massage table. When he lay down, I began to gently work his neck and shoulders. "Is it any surprise your people should have so few images of gods?"

"How do you mean?"

My fingers kneaded his flesh, working out the tension in his muscles. "The ones you chose to accompany us here, the ones who wished to come, are loyal to you. Worship of the Aten, through you, has long since replaced the old gods in their hearts. What remained was but a token. A habit."

He flipped onto his back. "You are certain?"

"Of course. Your people love you."

He grunted. "That doesn't help our coffers, does it? A city is expensive to build."

Stripping the citizenry to chase his fantasies. The destruction of my own jewelry had been only for show, of course. Of the pieces seized from the city, any precious stones would be removed, and the gold melted down. "The royal coffers are in fine shape," I said. Those coffers had been laid bare in the building of Akhetaten, but the recent influx of income from seized temple goods and land had replenished them to a large degree.

He grabbed my wrists and moved my hands to his chest. As I massaged, his eyes closed in pleasure. A bulge grew under his kilt. He fumbled with the knot on my sheet. It fell to the floor.

I toyed with the knot on his kilt, easing it. He pushed my hands away, tore the fabric, and grabbed my waist. I assisted by climbing onto the table of my own accord. In spite of his declaration that he would waste no more seed on me, he was a hedonist at heart. When the urge came upon him, he would not be denied.

I rocked my hips against his and closed my eyes. Images of the dark villa flashed before me — painted papyrus murals flickering in the rushlight, the full moon shining through the window. I could feel the hardness of Bek's body, the softness of his lips on mine. I snapped my eyes open, fearful lest I call out for Bek. Though the sight of Akhenaten huffing and grunting dampened my enthusiasm, I did not slacken my pace. Nor did I stop the cries of pleasure he would not know were false.

When I tired of it, and he seemed no closer to the end, I leaned over for a kiss and instead bit his lip — not hard enough to hurt, just hard enough to excite. He responded by clamping an arm around my backside and grinding his hips into mine. I cried out and shuddered, as if the climax were upon me. That accomplished the feat, and he soon lay exhausted and panting beneath me.

He held me close to him. "In my heart, I have not entirely given up hope that you might yet have a son."

I lay silent. I had given up hope and did not dare to rekindle it. "Even should I not, you already have a son."

"Not all sons are fit to rule."

I looked at him.

"Tutankhaten is a cripple. Despite Ipu's assurances, his foot has not straightened out. And he's dimwitted besides. Well past a year and still he does not even try to babble."

I had noticed the child's foot but was not aware of his otherwise slow growth. Though it was still far too soon to know how he would develop. "Do not fret. Children grow at their own pace."

He stroked my back. "Kiya is with child."

I moved aside far enough to see his face. The news was not a surprise, but his knowledge of it was. I had noticed her looking more rounded of late and looking pale in the presence of food. One of my more mature ladies, who already had five children near full grown, had found herself expecting once again. In helping her to obtain herbs to solve the problem, I managed to secrete some for Kiya as well. It would be considerably more difficult if Akhenaten already knew of her condition.

"You are certain?"

"She was examined by Ipu a few hours ago."

So, it was public knowledge, then, or would be before morning, and she was likely further along than I had realized. She had been wise to conceal it.

"Please pass along my most sincere good wishes."

"Why don't you do so yourself, at dinner tonight."

I had no appetite. "I would, but after days of walking the city, I am exhausted."

He pulled me back down beside him. "You need to learn to let officials do their jobs."

"Without proper oversight, it is not possible to know that those you appoint are doing the job you intend."

Chapter 38

I sat in the women's quarters gardens, anxious for it to be over. Since Kiya had birthed her child some weeks ago, she had kept the court waiting. She had kept the child hidden, claiming she wished to keep her from illness. As if there had been any illness in the court of late. Even now, when she had insisted we all gather for the official presentation, still she kept us waiting.

Nebetah alternately paced and stood within sight of the entrance, waiting for the commotion that would herald the arrival of the new princess.

"You needn't fuss so," I said. "It's just another girl, no competitor to bump your son from the line of succession."

She glared at me, white faced. "Even if it were a boy, my son would still be the first-born son, still the one with the superior blood claim."

I glanced to where Tutankhaten played with his nannies by the fish pool. He crawled now, but awkwardly. I rose and walked over for a better look. The boy's foot still curled up. He seemed to feel my scrutiny and turned his head to look up at me. The effort so unbalanced him that he nearly flopped over, but the smile on his pudgy face was so infectious, I found myself smiling in return. He quickly turned; his attention caught by movement in the reeds.

I knelt by him. "Hello, young prince," I said.

The child did not acknowledge me.

"Tutankhaten," I said. Still, he did not respond. I turned my head to look at Nebetah. "Does he not even know his own name?"

She bit her lip and failed to meet my eye. "He has been unwell lately. He is unwell frequently, but he is smart, and he is kind. He will grow to be a fine king."

If he is kind, I thought, he will not survive to be king. Not that he would even be considered should he prove to be the simpleton he promised thus far. Was he, perhaps, the monster Ptah had shown me, after all — his deformity being of the mind more so than the body? This thought confused me. How could that vision be correct, if Sekhmet's were not? And hers was certainly not, for Meritaten was near a young woman now, long past the chubby faced child I saw dying of plague.

Some of the younger ladies came running to announce the imminent arrival of the king, Kiya, and their new child. Mutnedjmet and Meritaten rose from their seats on the floor to stand beside me as Akhenaten entered first, followed by Kiya, who held the new princess in her arms. She pushed back the swaddling so we could see her face. Scrawny and red cheeked, with tufts of black hair. She bore little resemblance to my own pudgy babies.

"May I present the Princess Meritaten-the-Younger," said Akhenaten.

Beside me, Meritaten stiffened. "Did he name the new princess for me?" she whispered in my ear.

"It seems so."

Kiya flushed, and I notice her jaw tense. It was not her choice, then. The younger children clapped and rushed to see the baby. Kiya knelt, seemingly relieved at the distraction.

I glanced at Akhenaten and tilted my head. He came to me, and we moved away from the crowd.

"I wonder at her name," I said. "Would it not be more fitting for her to have her own name?"

Akhenaten shrugged and turned his back to Kiya. "Your daughters are the only ones who are important. They are the only ones who can continue the royal line. This one is no use to me."

While my first instinct was to gloat, I reminded myself that I had never produced a boy, and still he had not cast me aside. He would not do so with Kiya, either.

Akhenaten, Year 11

(ca. 1343 BCE)

The chariot approached the pass, and I notched another arrow. I waited until I had the copper target in clear sight, quickly accounted for the speed of the chariot, the direction of the wind, and let loose. The arrow glanced the side of the target, knocking it over but causing no real damage.

"Impressive, Highness," said the Master at Arms as my driver slowed the chariot.

"An impressive *miss*." He would have castigated one of his men for such an attempt. "Again."

He ran to right the target. "Are you certain, Highness? You have been practising long, today; surely you must be getting tired." He wiped the sweat from his eyes.

Ah, so his concern was not for me. In truth, I was tired, and my accuracy was waning as a result. "Once more."

I sent my driver on another circuit behind the military barracks and took aim. As the arrow whizzed harmlessly past its objective, I noticed several chariots in my peripheral vision, approaching from the desert. A familiar figure dismounted and approached. For the first time, I was aware of how the slump in his shoulders, and the paunch over his kilt, had increased in recent years.

I nodded to the Master at Arms. "One last time, and I will quit for the day."

The horses' hooves kicked up a cloud of sand as they took off. I tracked the motion of the target relative to my position and extrapolated, anticipating where it would be. This time, the arrow found its mark, penetrating through the target to the other side. I leaped off the back of the chariot, still holding my bow.

"I see your skills have only improved with the years," said Akhenaten. "Perhaps I should put you in charge of training the army."

I wished he were not jesting. Spending my days outside, in the company of army men — men without guile or pretension — seemed an attractive prospect. "If you were to do that, you should have to take over the audience chamber yourself." I dismissed the Master at Arms.

Akhenaten wrinkled his nose. "That would not do at all; I'm afraid you're stuck where you are."

Stuck indeed. "May I ask why you have sought me out?"

"I did not. I came out to the desert to meditate and happened to see you out here."

"I am glad you did. I have a matter I wish to discuss with you in private."

"On the way back."

We gave orders for the horses to be stabled and the chariots dismantled and stored. Then we began the walk back to our private palace, surrounded at a distance by Akhenaten's guard.

"You have a nephew living in Shedet, I believe," I said.

"Yes. What of it?"

"I think it would be best if we brought him here to Akhetaten and schooled him with the royal children."

"Whatever for?"

"He is twelve, now, and well on in his studies, if my sources do not mislead me. He seems an intelligent, capable lad."

Akhenaten nodded. "It is what I hear of him as well."

"I was thinking it might be prudent to betroth him to Meritaten."

Akhenaten looked at me. "That would never do. She is the eldest. She must become Great Royal Wife to the next king."

"If that is so, this is the only way to accomplish it. Meritaten is nine years old already, and still there is no heir fit to wear the mantle of kingship. Should she marry a man not yet born? By the time he is capable of siring heirs of his own, she may be past childbearing."

"My nephew is not of my seed."

"No, but he is of your blood, and that of your illustrious father. He will be acceptable to the people."

Akhenaten grunted. "He is not acceptable to me. My successor must be of my direct line."

"I am thinking only of your future, your vision. Should the Aten call you home before a healthy son is born to you, what should happen to your vision?" To our right, the enclosure walls of the Great Temple of the Aten gleamed white. "What should happen to your beautiful city?"

Akhenaten grew silent.

"There must be a clear line of succession. It must be known and uncontested. Otherwise, should some mishap befall you, Kemet will descend into chaos, and all your work will be undone."

"The Aten will provide the heir in his own time. We must be patient. The Aten has revealed his plan and is simply waiting for the right time to bring it to fruition."

I wanted to tell him that the best candidate for kingship may not be in the direct line but decided against it. Anything that implied he himself may not have been the best choice for king would not help my case.

"The appointment will not affect the Aten's plans, but it will serve to stave off those who think the kingship is vulnerable. It will project stability and order."

Akhenaten laughed. "With the Aten behind me, the kingship is anything but vulnerable. But, you are not wrong. A public display of continuity will bolster the confidence of my people. Just not a betrothal."

We walked for a bit in silence. Suddenly, Akhenaten stopped. "I've got it," he said. "I know how we shall secure the succession."

"How?"

"Ah, now for that we will need a lengthy discussion about how it shall work. You may have some ideas regarding how to sell it to the people.

"I have some time free tomorrow in the morning."

"No, now. At once upon our return."

I scowled. "I suppose I can reschedule the Kushite ambassador."

"Excellent," he said.

I was unsurprised that he did not catch the sarcasm in my voice. "Very well."

He reached over to squeeze my shoulder. "What a great day it was for Kemet when the Aten placed you in my path."

The Duat
Gate 4

Apep's head jerks back, his body writhing. Atum and his gods have subdued him. I am so shaken as we pass to the next gate, I fumble over my words, but in the end, name the gatekeeper as "Long-Horned Bull."

Here, there are three levels, and we enter at the top. The Lake of Uraei is guarded by the Uraei serpents, the Lake of Life by twelve jackal gods. Past these lakes are twenty-four beings — twelve gods and their doubles. I must pick out the true gods, without error. I inspect each and every one and worry so hard over the question that, were I still alive, sweat would be streaming down my face.

One of the gods meets my scrutiny, and I notice a flaw in his left eye. It bears a slight cast and wanders a little. It should be his right eye. I search for his twin and, sure enough, the twin has the fault in the right eye. I point to him as the true god. The false one disappears. More confident now, I search for tiny faults, eliminating the pretenders until I have successfully completed the task and earn entrance into the middle level.

Here, there are shrines dedicated to the nine followers of Wesir. It is my duty to perform the opening of the eyes and mouth, to resurrect them. As I work my way down the line, I purify each in turn with natron and incense and touch their mouths. To each, I offer the heart of a bull and the foreleg of a calf.

At the end of the shrines, the serpent Hereret greets me. She coils herself around me. Her tongue, flicking against my skin, disorients me. I see myself all at once as a child lost in the desert, a young bride, and a middle-aged monarch. The threads of time tangle and become confused. When she releases me, I am left panting and shaking on the cold stone floor.

Akhenaten, Year 12

(ca. 1342 BCE)

In Year 12 of the reign of Akhenaten, the first of that name, I lost the title of Great Royal Wife, but not in a manner I would ever have foreseen.

Meritaten and I turned slowly for Akhenaten.

He whistled low. "You are both so lovely." He slipped an arm around my waist and jiggled Meritaten's wig. All three of us were dressed in identical white robes with long, red sashes. Even our jewelry matched. Akhenaten and I wore our blue crowns, while Meritaten wore a golden diadem fronted by a cobra.

This was his alternative to a betrothal for Meritaten. In any other reign, it would have been shocking, but given the complete upheaval of custom already accomplished, taking a woman as coruler hardly caused a ripple. Besides, it was merely a formalizing of the role I had been playing for many years.

A king requires a Great Royal Wife, but instead of choosing from amongst his other wives, Akhenaten insisted on keeping the titles within the family. Meritaten would fill the role for both of us, the title indicative only of her ceremonial function. She would not, of course, be expected to fulfill other wifely duties. A king may take to wife his sister and produce children, as did the gods, but not a daughter. Never a daughter.

"It is a steppingstone for her," he had said.

"What do you mean?"

"As it was for you." He had placed a hand on each of my shoulders, and waited until I met his eye. "You began as Great Royal Wife and will become my coregent. Meritaten begins as Great Royal Wife and one day shall become king, as you do now."

I momentarily lost the power of speech. "You wish to make Meritaten your successor?"

"Why not? The Aten requires both a man and a woman to rule his earthly kingdom."

The implication dawned on me. Naming Meritaten heir to the throne meant I was mother to the heir. So long as this situation endured, my position would be secure, even without the title of coregent. But there remained one problem. "She will still need a man to rule with her."

"Yes. We shall find one for her," he said. "Perhaps my nephew, perhaps another royal child. Perhaps even a foreign prince."

The wind blew hot, driving whirlwinds of sand before it that stung my eyes and scraped my skin. Akhenaten and I took our place in the state palanquin, the great golden chair, protected by lion and cobra figures. Fifteen bearers hoisted us up, and we swayed with their motion as they marched in step with each other toward the desert parade grounds. The blazing sun stung my eyes, the kohl offering little protection when staring directly into it.

Both Meritaten and Meketaten followed closely behind us, as did my ladies, the younger girls with their nurses, and our bodyguards.

The crowds gathered to watch, as always. They prostrated themselves as we passed, as always, and cheered. Delegations had arrived from all over the empire and beyond. As we passed, we heard shouts in many different languages. One might have been forgiven for thinking that the citizenry had regained their former enthusiasm for our divine presence, but I was not fooled. I knew most of them were happy because they knew they would be fed. And the now ubiquitous soldiers, standing every few arm-spans among the people, belied the relaxed atmosphere. Asiatics, Ribu, Kushite. Not an Egyptian among them.

Our bearers set us down in front of the canopied pavilion. As we dismounted, a disturbance erupted in the crowd, and an old woman burst through the line, so startling the soldiers that they hesitated before responding.

She was dressed in tattered, hooded robes. She extended a hand, scabbed and filthy, and grabbed my arm. I could feel the burn of her flesh and I cried out involuntarily. One word entered my mind: plague. I drew my arm back in disgust. Before I could utter a word, a soldier grabbed her.

"Sorry, Highness. It will not happen again."

"No, it will not," said Akhenaten. "See that the men who let her through are arrested."

"Of course, Highness."

As the soldier dragged her back, the top of her hood slipped back, and I glimpsed her face: golden fur, sharp teeth, and leonine eyes throwing accusations.

I fell back against the palanquin. A gasp from the crowd brought me to myself, and I straightened.

Setepenre ran to me, arms open. I swept her up, causing Neferure to start crying. I started to walk off. Neferure's wailing grew louder. Akhenaten stamped his feet impatiently. I decided he would rather wait than listen to that yelling through the whole ceremony. I bent down and gathered her up in my other arm.

The tears stopped, and Neferure leaned against my shoulder, gazing up at me. The thoughtful look on her face gave me a start. She very much resembled Meritaten, a fact I had given nothing more than a passing thought to before. A chill sucked all the heat out of the air.

Akhenaten put a hand on my arm. He smiled at the attendees and dug his nails into my flesh. "It was an old, demented woman. Calm yourself." Yet, his voice wavered and he himself trembled as he pulled me along.

I plastered a smile on my face and mounted the steps to the dais. Akhenaten and I took our thrones, with Meritaten seated between us. The other girls sat around us, with a bowl of fruit and some toys to occupy them. An attendant handed a bowl to Akhenaten. He took it and gulped a deep draft. I could smell the sour scent of poppy.

"Does your head pain you much today?"

Akhenaten closed his eyes, savoring the brew. "Not at all. It simply brings me closer to the Aten." He continued drinking slowly. By the time he emptied the bowl, he appeared calmer. His hands had stopped shaking, and his face relaxed.

When people stopped flowing into the temple courtyard, Akhenaten stood. He waited until the crowd hushed. He began. "This, Year 12 of the reign of Akhenaten, the first of that name, has now become Year 1 of the Aten. For I have now become the Aten's earthly body. Every thought, every action of mine is now the Aten acting through me." He paused for the audience to understand the weight of his words. "Because of this transformation, I am no longer able to shoulder the burden of kingship alone. So, as the Aten, I have chosen a coregent — one who exemplifies the teachings of the Aten while balancing out the maleness of his chosen vessel. I present to you now, Ankheprure Neferneferuaten."

I stood. An attendant came forward with a crook and flail, wrapped in white linen. Akhenaten unwrapped these and gave them to me. I held them crossed, against my chest.

A disturbance arose to one side of the dais. We all turned to see what had happened. Kiya lay on the sand, her ladies-in-waiting fanning her. While we were watching, Kiya blinked her eyes, looked directly into mine, raised herself to a sitting position, and allowed her attendants to lift her back to standing. Someone brought her a stool.

"My apologies. It must be the heat." She accepted a drink of wine and sat back down.

It was not the heat. I knew it, she knew it, and she knew that I knew it. She had chosen her time carefully to ensure I knew she was once again with child. I pitied her, for I understood her desperation. The end of my insecurities meant an increase in hers.

With Kiya back amongst her women, Akhenaten gestured for Meritaten to join us.

"A king needs a Great Royal Wife, and young Meritaten is ours. Welcome to your new queen."

Cheers from the assembled guests. I waited for Akhenaten to continue with his speech. Instead, he bade us all sit down to receive the visiting dignitaries. He did not announce Meritaten as heir. He did not. Why did he not? Had he simply forgotten, or did he mean to give himself an easy way to renege on his promise should his whim change? Did he never intend to keep the promise at all?

Foreign dignitaries made their way to the front of the dais, bowing and presenting gifts. Black and red pottery from Keftiu, in the middle of the Great Sea; copper and bronze ingots, slaves, olive oil, and cattle from Kinahhu; ivory, gold, ebony, and slaves from Kush. I acknowledged them.

If Meritaten was not the heir, then my position had never been safe. It would be highly irregular to depose your own coregent, but what about Akhenaten's reign had ever been regular? I cursed myself for a fool. In my arrogance, I had ceased to monitor Kiya altogether. Late last year, she had birthed another girl, Ankhesenpaaten the younger, and now there would be another. Her fertility rivaled mine. If I did not stop it permanently, she would one day give Akhenaten a son.

A prince of Naharin bowed to us. He praised us and gifted us with horses, chariots, and woolen textiles. His face was flushed with heat, his eyes unfocused. If Akhenaten insisted on drawing out the ceremony through the hottest part of the day, the Naharin prince would only be the first to succumb.

How would I do it? I quickly dismissed the idea of having her killed. Akhenaten loved her, and if she were taken from him, she would remain forever young and beautiful. If however, she were to be publicly disgraced ... perhaps, with another lover. In the meantime, something must be done about the child.

Chapter 41

I handed the box to one of Mutnedjmet's dwarves. "You understand what you are to do?"

"I am small, not simple. Mix it with some of her food."

"You will be well rewarded if you succeed."

"And take the blame if I fail." He looked up at me with his piggy eyes.

"All the more motivation to succeed."

He nodded and slipped out of the courtyard. After a suitable delay, I did the same and met up with my guards before seeking out Meritaten's new apartments in the women's quarters. For all of her new titles, she was still just a girl. Her sidelock had been cut only days earlier. This would be her first night away from her sisters and her nannies.

When I reached her rooms, I was stopped by the presence of Akhenaten's guards. "My apologies, Highness. We cannot allow you to pass. King's orders."

"I am also your king. Let me pass."

The two looked at each other. "That's as may be, but His Highness is also the god, and we cannot let you in."

And there it was. He would always outrank me. My own soldiers looked to me for instructions. There were three of us and only two of them, but I was unarmed and hindered by my ceremonial robes.

As I was contemplating my next move, a voice carried from inside the living area. "Let her in."

Akhenaten staggered a little, drunk from too much wine and the poppy. My eyes fell to the floor. A single tile was cracked and broken, the corner gone, leaving a small, dark hole. Meritaten's table sat in one corner, covered in the contents of her jewel box. One tiny, perfect lapis scarab — one I had given her for protection — lay upturned on the floor, legs in the air. Lamplight fought against the blackness of night, and the oil added its scent to the sickening mixture of flowery perfume, male sweat, and sex. Akhenaten's eyes appeared as dark hollows, the surrounding kohl smudged. His lip rouge was smeared all around his mouth. He had discarded his robes and wore only a linen sheet, knotted around the waist. He could not have done this, I told myself. Even he could not be so monstrous. But even as I tried to dissuade myself, I knew it was true.

"What have you done?"

"Nothing that is not my right. My duty," said Akhenaten. "The Aten must have a direct heir."

"She is a child. And she is your daughter."

"She is no longer a child. She reached womanhood some months ago."

"This was ..." I lowered my voice. "You planned this all along. You did not tell me because you knew I would not agree."

"I am the Aten now," he said. "I do not need your agreement."

Sobbing drifted from inside the bedroom. I pushed past Akhenaten, and he staggered. Meritaten lay curled up on her sleeping cot, covered in a blood-spotted sheet. I called out to my guards, asking for a bowl of water and clean cloths. Akhenaten was stumbling out into the corridor.

This was my fault. If I had not wasted time on Kiya's child, I could have been here sooner. I could have stopped him before he started. Offered myself or one of my ladies. No. It would have made no difference. If only I had given him a son. Then he would not need to use our daughter now. I sat beside her and pulled back the sheets. Her slight form shivered, and my breath caught in my throat. I looked away so that she would not see my tears. She must see me strong.

When the water arrived, I bathed her and held her as if she were still a small child. I stroked her head, now stubbly with new growth. "I am sorry. I cannot ..." the words could not escape through the lump. I swallowed. "I cannot stop him." I bit my lip. I was coregent of Kemet, charged with protecting the land and its people, and I could not even protect my own child. "I cannot stop him, but I can keep you from bearing a child until you are old enough to do so without harm to yourself."

Meritaten looked up at me, eyes wide. "You have this power?"

I nodded. "In the morning, I will bring you some herbs. You must make a tea every day. As long as you do not forget to do this, you will not have a child." I hoped it were true. Silphium was not a perfect contraceptive. Nebetah had conceived while taking it, but such was rare.

She was silent so long I thought she had not heard me or did not understand. "I will never forget." She was not referring only to the herbs.

Chapter 42

"Your information is reliable?" I asked.

Father glared at me. "Completely. The revolt in Kush is escalating. It must be put down immediately before our gold supplies are interrupted."

"Why bother me with this?" asked Akhenaten. "It is a matter for my coregent. I have more important things to attend to."

I sat on the edge of Akhenaten's desk. Ay and Bek stood to either side.

"Because, as king, you must be the one to put down the rebellion," I said. A show of strength from you will ensure obedience for years to come." It took supreme effort to even look at him, and more so to do it with an expression of calm.

Akhenaten scanned the three of us. "So, the three of you decided to unite to try and convince me to lead an army."

"We were hoping you would see the need, Highness," said Bek.

Akhenaten waved his arm in my direction. "Nefertiti is king as well as I. She may go."

I cannot deny I felt a thrill of excitement. To leave this city at the head of an army and lead my people into battle. It would be glorious. I sighed.

"Surely, you don't intend to send a woman at the head of the army," said Father.

"Why not? She is king, and you have trained her well, have you not? I recall her skill with a throwing stick very well.

"Begging your pardon, Highness, but hunting ducks is a long way from killing enemies in war," I said. "I was never trained for such."

"I have no doubt you would perform admirably," said Bek.

I froze. Bek had seen me fight in a way neither my husband nor father had. In a real life situation, not an exercise. Akhenaten looked to him and studied his face.

Bek held Akhenaten's gaze. "I've seen her on the training grounds. She wins more often than not."

Akhenaten laughed. It started small and then turned into a full belly laugh. "It is obvious you are not a military man," Akhenaten said after he had calmed down. "She wins because the soldiers dare not harm their king."

That was certainly why he always won on the training ground. Or at least used to, when he'd still trained.

Father grunted, insulted at the slight to his training. "Her Highness's fighting skills aside, if she were to head the army, the enemy would see it as weakness."

Akhenaten waved a hand. "They are Kushites. They allow their women to do all manner of unseemly things. Including war, if I'm not mistaken."

"You are not," I said, "but not only must we give a show of strength, we must also set an example of civilization."

Akhenaten sighed. "The Aten is neither male nor female. Such differences matter little to him — to me. When we moved the court to Akhetaten, I vowed I would never leave here, that I would stay and serve the Aten for all time. Surely, you do not expect me to break an oath to my god?"

He would not. No matter how vital the journey, nor how persuasive our arguments, he would not leave. And I could not. There was no one I could trust to take the reins of government for the months such a campaign would take. No one to see to Meritaten, or to Meketaten, now nearing womanhood herself. "Neither will I leave. My place is here beside you."

The tension in Bek's jaw relaxed.

"You are not going to defend the empire?" said Ay.

"Of course, we are," I said. "We will send you, Father, with the army to the viceroy in Kush to quell the rebellion. We will also search out alternative sources of gold and do so openly."

"If you do that, the Kushites will believe we are afraid they may succeed in breaking away from the empire," said Bek.

"On the contrary," I said. "They will know they are expendable, and they will fall in line lest they lose our protection."

Akhenaten clapped his hands. "Once again, a brilliant solution. Whoever wields the weapons, it is you who shall beat down the Kushites, my dear." He turned and left.

Ay turned to Bek. "That is all."

Bek glared and turned to me. "If you have no further need of me, Highness."

No further need? Well, none I was able to indulge. I took a deep breath before answering, hoping Ay and Bek would both take it for a thoughtful pause. "You may go."

The moment Bek was gone, Father started. "What is the matter with you? You cannot leave a campaign of this significance to an underling."

"Do not tell me you have no wish to go," I said. "I know you relish it."

"You know me well. But I am thinking of the empire — the Kushites will interpret the king's absence as weakness."

"How do you suggest I force Akhenaten to go?"

Father grumbled but did not have a response. "You noticed Kiya's performance at the ceremony, I am sure."

"Of course."

"She and that child must be removed."

"That child is the child of the god," I said. "There is nothing we can do." I dared not tell him of the steps I had already taken.

"You will lose your crown," Father said. "It is only a matter of time before another woman gives his Highness a healthy son. Then you will be out, and you will have brought it upon yourself by your own weakness."

As Ay made to leave, he nearly collided with Bek returning. Bek was out of breath and sweating. Behind him, in the same state, was the royal physician.

"Highness. It's the plague."

"I've just come from the camps of the Naharin," said the physician. "The plague is raging. They must have brought it in with them."

I felt the color drain from my face. The bulk of the visitors stayed in camps on the outskirts of the city, well away from the population, but high-level dignitaries stayed within the palace itself. I remembered the Naharin prince and his reddened face. If it were plague and not simply excess heat as I had thought ... "Send them out," I said. "They must leave Kemet immediately."

"It may be too late. There are signs in some of the other camps as well."

"Father, you will gather the army and eject all foreigners immediately."

Ay bowed and went to fulfil his duty.

"Highness, what of the children?" asked Bek. "They must be taken out of the city."

"You may send your boys away, but the king will never agree for his children to leave."

"Do not ask his permission."

"I don't recommend it, Highness," said the physician. "After the festival, any one of us could already be carrying plague. By traveling, we could be spreading it all over Kemet."

I saw again Neferure's face flushed and listless and thought again of Meketaten's impending womanhood. "Do it. Meritaten cannot leave, but the younger girls shall go with your boys. It will be some time before the king notices their absence."

Bek's body lost a little of his tension, and I cursed the fate that gave me to Akhenaten instead of this man, who would fight to protect his children even when he could not acknowledge them.

"My relatives in Iunu will be happy to take them in," he said.

"Let them know they will be well compensated. Send Taheret as well, and the children's nannies."

"You should consider moving the court to Waset."

"Not recommended, Highness," said the physician.

"No. I must stay, and so must you. We must show we are not afraid."

Chapter 43

"Highness, come quick." Taheret shook me awake.

"What is it?"

"Trouble at Kiya's palace. She is ill."

"Send for the physician, and trouble me about it no more." The dwarves had done their work. She would soon lose the child, if she hadn't done so already, and that would be that.

Taheret sat back on her heels. "The physician has asked for you. He said for you to be discreet."

I dressed quickly, and in Taheret's clothes, and ordered the bargeman to take me there. A lump sat in my belly, growing heavier with each dip of the oars. Could the physician tell what had really happened? Worse — were the dwarves caught at their work, and had they named me? I did not think so, for if I were under suspicion, I would have been wakened by soldiers, not my lady-in-waiting.

It was still full dark when I entered Kiya's palace through the courtyard and skirted the pond to reach her private rooms. The physician was pacing by the door to her sleeping chamber. Her ladies were huddled in a corner, weeping.

"I have been informed that the lady Kiya is unwell."

The physician stammered, and I noticed his grey pallor.

"What has happened?" I said.

He stepped aside and bade me enter her room. Kiya lay sprawled half off her bed, head to the side, vomit pooling on the floor below. The smell of it permeated the close air. "When did this happen?"

"She started convulsing in the night, and her ladies sent for me. She was gone before I arrived, and I sent for you immediately."

The dwarves must have given her too much of the herbs. I cursed them for being fools and myself for trusting them with such a delicate mission. I would have to have them removed, lest they implicate me.

The physician edged closer to me. "I had hoped you would be the one to inform His Highness."

Ah, so that was the reason for the summons. I could not blame the little man for his fear — Akhenaten was not known for taking bad news well. "Of course. He has lost his favorite wife and a child at once. Better he learn it from me."

"You hadn't heard then, Highness?"

"Heard what?"

"Lady Kiya lost her child some days ago. It was a boy. His Highness was quite ... incensed."

How had I not heard about this? I had been preoccupied with foreign wars and plague, yet still I should have heard whispers. Unless Akhenaten did not want it spoken of. Did not want her spoken of. "He blamed her. He shunned her."

The physician looked at me meaningfully before nodding. It was no secret Akhenaten had once turned away from me for failing to produce a boy, so it surely did not surprise him that I guessed correctly what Akhenaten's reaction would be to birthing a dead boy.

"She poisoned herself?" I asked.

"I would say so, yes," said the physician.

"Clean her up," I said to her ladies. I cursed myself even more now. I needed rid of the child, but Meritaten needed Kiya to live. Now there would be none to distract him from her. I staggered against the wall.

The physician reached out for me. "Are you ill, Highness?"

I shook my head and righted myself. "Delaying the inevitable will not help matters. I must go." I took my leave before the physician could respond further.

As I boarded the boat back to the main palace, the black sky was turning indigo. Once the boat landed, I made my way over the bridge to our private palace to speak with Akhenaten.

I found him in his sleeping quarters, curled around a concubine. The girl awoke when I entered, blinking in the lamplight.

"Wake him," I said.

She nudged him, but he did not rouse. She tapped again, but he did not respond. I sat down on the bed, edging her out of the way, and shoved Akhenaten. He moaned softly but did not stir. I lifted one arm and dropped it. It fell limp. I noticed a cup sitting on the table, drained but coated in dregs. I lifted it to my face and sniffed. The bitter aura of poppy was stronger than usual.

"How much did he drink?"

"One cup, no more."

"Earlier in the day?"

She lowered her eyes.

"I thought as much." I placed a hand on his chest, and an ear by his mouth. His heart beat against my fingers, and his breath tickled my face. "Well, there is nothing for it but to wait until he rouses on his own." I left instructions with the guard to send for me the moment he woke, and under no circumstances to allow him more poppy, and returned to Kiya's palace.

The physician leapt up when he saw me and drooped again when he saw I was alone. "The king is indisposed," I said. "She must be sent for embalming."

His eyes flickered to the other room, where the corpse lay waiting. "If you think it best, Highness."

"We can hardly leave her here. Have her removed to the House of Purification. Order them to prepare her so far as they can without cutting her open, until his Highness can see her."

The physician nodded.

As we left, a runner arrived with a summons for the physician. "It's the vizier, Nakhtpaaten."

"What is it?"

The runner looked from me to the physician and back again.

"Out with it," said the physician.

"It's plague, sir."

Chapter 44

"Are your children ready?"

"They can leave any time," said Bek. He handed me the vial I had requested.

I nodded thanks. "The ship sails in two hours. Nebetah has agreed to let the Crown Prince go as well."

"So soon?" Bek moved closer than was wise. "What are you not telling me?"

I leaned against my desk. "The vizier has plague. It has come to court."

Bek paced.

"Also, the king will be distracted for now." I told him of Kiya's death.

He nodded. "You are right to act now. I will see Taheret and the children are waiting."

As he left, he nearly collided with a runner.

I stood. "Has his Highness awoken?"

"Yes. And I am told to tell you he is in a foul mood."

When I arrived at his quarters, Akhenaten was seated on the bed, clutching his head in his hands. The bedside table was overturned, and broken glass littered the floor. I ordered the concubine out of the room.

He looked up at me with bloodshot eyes. "More poppy."

I pulled the stopper from the vial I had brought with me and offered it to him.

He drained it in one swallow and grimaced. "That was not poppy."

"It was mandrake. It will ease your pain." I sat beside him and placed a hand on his back. When he didn't pull away, I began massaging his shoulders and then his neck. The base of the skull and up around his ears. I felt him relax as the headache lost its grip. He slipped his arms around my waist and leaned his head on my breast. I kissed his scalp, dreading the moment when I would have to speak.

His body started to shake. At first, I thought he was convulsing, but the choking sounds from his throat told me he was crying. I patted his back, as I would one of our children.

"They're trying to destroy me."

"Who is?"

"Pretenders to the throne. They want me to fail."

I rocked him back and forth. "The people love you. No one wants you to fail."

He pulled away from me. "Then why have I no healthy sons? Someone has been interfering with my women."

I froze, afraid to speak. Had my deceptions with the silphium been discovered? Was it only a matter time until my hand in Kiya's miscarriage was discovered?

He continued. "They are turning away from the Aten. I want the palaces searched for idols and amulets."

I relaxed. "It shall be done. But first, we must speak of Kiya."

Akhenaten pushed away from me and strode across the small room. He hit a hand against the wall, cracking the plaster. "You shall not utter her name."

I kept my voice even and low. "I know of the death of your son."

He spun around. "How do you know this? I have spoken of it to no one."

"Kiya was in much despair both at the loss of your son and the loss of your favor. She loved you greatly."

He moaned at the sound of her name but did not catch the significance of the past tense.

I stood and placed a hand on his shoulder. "She is dead. By her own hand."

He looked at me, his eyes puffy and bloodshot, surrounded by smudged remnants of kohl. "You lie. You say this to drive a wedge between me and my beloved. You are jealous."

"It is true I have no love for Kiya," I said, "but I would not make such a cruel jest. She is in the temple. The embalmers wait only your word to begin their grim task."

"No." He pushed past me and out the door of the chamber. The concubine, no doubt listening, flattened herself against the wall to avoid a collision.

I followed him out of the nearest palace door. He turned toward the Royal Road and, once reaching it, swung to the left to the small Aten Temple. I ran to follow, the guards trailing in my wake. Seeing their king approach both half-dressed and half-deranged, the temple guards opened the door. Akhenaten crossed the first courtyard into the second. He brushed aside the reed matting at the door and entered the tent that constituted the House of Purification. The embalmers came out. Knowing he would wish to be alone with her, I waited by the door flap.

First came the sounds of something heavy smashing on the floor. The embalmers, waiting nearby, looked alarmed. More crashing indicated many items being thrown or tossed over. The embalmers moved to re-enter the tent but stopped at a look from me. Instead, they stared helplessly at the canvas as the tools of their trade were laid waste.

"Whatever is destroyed shall be replaced immediately," I said.

They nodded but did not appear comforted.

The destruction ceased and I waited. As I wondered whether I should go in, I heard a new sound. It started as sobbing and then raised in pitch. The keening grew in intensity. In every wail was the sound of a heart breaking. He had lost his love.

When at last he grew silent, I peered into the room. Jars of honey, frankincense, and myrrh lay shattered, their contents coagulating into a sticky mass. Fragments of obsidian blades and alabaster jars littered the stone floor. Akhenaten sat slumped against the leg of the table where Kiya lay. I glanced at her as I neared. She was covered with a sheet, but even so, I could see that one side of her face and most of her front had turned purple. The scent of death hung about her.

I crouched by Akhenaten and reached out a hand. He turned away from me and sobbed louder. When I patted his back, he recoiled from my touch.

Chapter 45

Initially, the plague worked in my favor. During preparations for Kiya's funeral, all of her belongings were taken from her palace and moved to the Royal Tomb in the eastern cliffs. That left her palace empty, and the plague offered the perfect excuse.

Akhenaten began spending even more time in his private chapel in our palace, praying to the Aten. Though he preferred not to be disturbed, there was little recourse for one wishing to speak with him in those days. And *one* meant me, for no one else dared enter his grief for fear of provoking a rage such as he had visited upon the House of Purification.

I entered and knelt behind him, off to the side so he could see me. Eventually, he motioned me forward.

"I apologize for interrupting your prayers."

He shook his head.

Taking that as a dismissal of my apology, not of me, I continued. "There is an urgent matter we must discuss." I moved forward and knelt beside him.

He turned to face me. His expression was blank, but there was a hollowness in his eyes. He seemed barely there. "Nothing will ever be urgent again."

A thrill of alarm raced through me. Did he mean to follow Kiya into the afterlife? The thought came, unbidden, that his death would solve many problems. Kemet could be returned to the gods. To Ma'at. And I would be released from my debt to Sekhmet. Meritaten would be safe. I suppressed the thought immediately, but still it hung between us like a veil.

"The plague," I said, remembering my reason for being there, "is raging mainly in the south of the city. The north is, thus far, untouched."

"I was not aware it had blossomed so." He was aware of very little outside his own self at that moment.

"I propose we move Meritaten, and the entire women's quarters, into the north palace and isolate them there. If we control who enters and leaves, we can perhaps keep them safe."

He nodded. "Agreed. But not Meritaten, nor our other daughters. We must present a united front to the people. We have nothing to fear. The Aten will protect us."

"Our younger daughters, and the Crown Prince, have already been evacuated to the countryside." They had been gone some weeks, and he had not noticed their absence.

He closed his eyes. I braced myself for his rage, but it did not come.

"That should not have been done without my approval."

"They are Kemet's greatest asset. The future of our dynasty. As is Meritaten. If you wish for her to birth a new Crown Prince, she must live through this."

He opened his eyes. "You had the plague as a child, did you not? And yet, here you are. The Aten showed you his favor, even then. He will do so again."

My survival had nothing to do with the Aten. Plague was Sekhmet's domain, and it was she who had spared me then. I had no doubt she would do so again, for she was not finished with me, but nor was she pleased with me. I could not trust that she would not use my children to punish me for my lack of progress.

"I was blessed, indeed," I said, "but my mother was not. Nor were my older siblings. The Aten did not favor them, nor did he favor Kiya. He does not tell even you all of his plans. How are we to know which of your other ladies, or children, shall fall?"

"If the Aten wishes to take them, nothing we do can stop him. He is all powerful."

"True. But we need not place them in harm's way. Losing children to the Aten may be unavoidable, but to lose them to our own folly is unthinkable."

He nodded slowly. "So be it. Do as you wish."

Chapter 46

The journey into the eastern desert was a paltry reflection of the one we had undertaken years earlier into the west. This time, there was no pretense that it would be a traditional burial. Akhenaten and I walked in the priests' position behind the wailing women who followed the ox sledge with the coffin. The number of followers was greatly diminished — though the plague had, for the most part, receded with the annual flood waters, some families were diminished in size, and those who had survived were much weakened and unable to make the trek.

Though I was obliged to maintain dignity, I kept a discreet look out for the gods. Heru, who should have been circling above us, was absent. Nor were there flashes of tawny fur in my peripheral vision, nor green-skinned mummies following the coffin into the tomb. Perhaps they were there, and I had finally succeeded in banishing them from my sight. Though the possibility that they had abandoned us unsettled me, I did not regret that I no longer heard their wailing.

When we reached the cliff face, workers drove the ox pulling the coffin up the narrow ramp in the middle of the steep staircase. I chanted hymns to the Aten to distract myself and Akhenaten from the pebbles rolling down. The occasional cart wheel stuck on a step. So much as I was able, without raising my head, I watched the lurching of the cart and prayed the coffin itself would not come rolling backwards and crush us. Yet both ox and cargo managed the incline and disappeared into the open maw of the tomb.

Once the business of delivering and placing the coffin into the sarcophagus and sealing it had been accomplished, and the ox and drivers had returned, Akhenaten and I started up the steps, leaving the rest of the procession behind in the sands. Though he was not obligated to officiate at the death of anyone save another monarch, Akhenaten insisted he do so for Kiya. He also insisted that, as coregent, I join him.

The stairs were difficult to navigate, and I was glad of the slow pace required by the occasion. To preserve dignity, I had to stare straight ahead and feel with my feet for the edges of the steps. In an effort to avoid landing on my face or tumbling backwards, my toes scraped against the risers more than once. Akhenaten walked a few steps above me, appearing to have no such awareness of our peril. His feet fell heavily, thudding on the stone. I watched him for signs of unsteadiness, but he moved unerringly forward.

The inside of the tomb was lit by a series of rushlights. The main corridor led down into the heart of the cliff. A series of holes marked the walls, where more chambers would be cut for our children, when their time came to journey to the Blessed West. I sighed. If Akhenaten's folly were permitted to continue, there would be no journey to the West for any of us.

Just before the steps leading to the main burial chamber, the one reserved for Akhenaten himself, a doorway to the right opened on a brand new chamber, where the sarcophagus lay with its grisly contents. Reliefs of foreigners, soldiers, and the royal family with arms raised in adoration of the Aten covered the surrounding walls. Akhenaten, the girls, and I were depicted worshipping in a temple, with the Aten rising overhead. Outside the temple, birds and animals rejoiced at the sight of the Aten. I realized Akhenaten had given Kiya a visual representation of his own Hymn to the Aten, the one he had written himself, to guard over her in her eternal sleep.

Akhenaten raised his arms, and began to sing:

"Splendid you rise in heaven's lightland,

O living Aten, creator of li—"

His voice broke, and he looked about to weep. The sight moved me, so I took his hand, and joined my voice to his.

"When you have dawned in eastern lightland,

You fill every land with your beauty.

You are beauteous, great, radiant,"

"Betrayer."

The word was so low, I thought at first I had only imagined it. Then a flash of white streaked by.

"When you set in western lightland,

Earth is in darkness as if in death;"

The face of Ma'at appeared over the sarcophagus. "You betray me."

Other shapes coalesced out of the shadows. A jackal, an ibis, a hippopotamus, a hawk. Several human forms, some of them mummified. A lion. They howled, growled, roared, and screamed. The noise filled the small chamber and rang in my ears. Through it all, voices cried.

"Betrayer."

"Imposter."

"Failure."

"You will pay."

I wanted to block it out but dared not let on it was happening.

"Birds fly from their nests,

Their wings greeting your—"

Without my support, Akhenaten could not continue. He looked to me, his pained eyes begging for my help. I started to tremble, as if cold. My teeth chattered, and I collapsed on the floor.

Akhenaten knelt by me. "I did not know you loved Kiya so well."

I looked to him. That he could think such amazed me, but I did not dissuade him. "Your pain is my pain, my love."

He helped me rise. Seeing my weakness gave him strength, and he was able to finish the hymn. The cacophony of voices blended into a single shrill buzz. I planted my feet and wrapped my arms around my body to keep myself from bolting from the chamber before he uttered the final words, altered for the occasion.

"The Son of Re who lives by Ma'at, the Lord of crowns,
Akhenaten, great in his lifetime;
And the great Lady whom he loves, the Greatly Beloved,
Kelu-Heba, Kiya, living forever."

He touched his fingers to his lips and then pressed them to the sarcophagus. I looked toward the corridor, beyond which lay the open air. My feet turned before he had finished, and I walked as close behind him as I could on our way out.

When at last Akhenaten broke forth into sunlight, he stopped to greet the mourning party below. I followed immediately, and the voices ceased. I wanted to fall to the ground in gratitude but settled for gulping in the fresh breeze. The sudden clearing of my head combined with the influx of clean air made me lightheaded, and I lurched forward. My sandals slid on some loose pebbles, and I saw the stone steps drop away beneath me.

Akhenaten turned and held out an arm to prevent me from falling. "Do not let your grief blind you to your surroundings. I cannot bury you as well."

Breathing heavily, I peered down at the ground. Faces stared up, startled. I drew myself up to my full height and raised an arm. I allowed Akhenaten to go ahead, and we started our journey back down. Once back on solid ground, I vowed to avoid any such responsibility in the future. And to have my own tomb built at Waset. Deep in the ground.

Midway through the procession back, a voice in my ear made me jump. "Highness."

I turned to see my father's face and relaxed. He motioned me to the side, out of earshot of the rest of the column.

He slipped an arm around my shoulders, giving the appearance of a loving father. "You seemed quite moved by Kiya's death," he said, voice lowered.

"It has been a tiring day; that is all." We walked apace with the rest of the mourners as we talked.

He nodded. "That it has, but that is not the reason you nearly fell down a staircase. Are you with child again?"

I shook my head.

"Pity," he said. "If not that, then what? Guilt?"

"Guilt?"

He lowered his arm and shrugged. "Your rival was young, healthy, and carrying the king's child. There are some who find it suspicious that she should die of such a silly accident. They think it more likely she was poisoned."

The official story was that she had fallen down some steps and hit her head. Akhenaten did not want it known how he had rejected her and what she had done because of it. But that Ay had uncovered a portion of the truth was no surprise.

I resisted the urge to snap my head around. "I had no hand in her death, if that is what you imply."

"I know you did not," he said. "I am simply telling you how it appears to some. Whatever the reason for your lapse today, you'd best suppress it lest suspicion falls on you."

"There is no reason for suspicion to fall on anyone," I said. "Kiya miscarried a boy child some days before her death. The king rejected her and wanted her spoken of no more. She was desolate. I am surprised your spies did not discover this."

Father faltered in his steps but quickly recovered. "As am I. I had no idea she had lost the child." He thought for a few moments. "It is good news. There will be no investigation."

We walked some way in silence. "If you thought Kiya had been murdered, why were you so certain I had not done it?"

"You haven't the stomach for it," he said.

He was possibly right about that, but I did not think that was the reason. I thought back to the sight of Kiya in her chamber, face down on her cot. I scanned my memory. There had been no tableware in the room. No empty cups or bowls. If she had killed herself, how had she administered the poison if not by drinking it? And how had she removed the cup and returned to her bed before death took her? She might have had a servant clear it away, but I did not think so.

"And you do," I said.

"I did what needed to be done. I could not allow your weakness to jeopardize our position." He dropped back and returned to the main column.

The Duat

Gate 5

Part 1

Though shaken by the serpent Hereret's attention, I stand proud at the head of the barque. I survived the trials so far. I feel strong and, ironically, physically powerful, as I have not felt in the last few years among the living. Life has trained me well for adversity — death can do no worse.

When we reach the Arit gate, the jackal gods Aau and Tekmi let us through, revealing nine more gods within, and the serpent Teka-hra, who leads us to the magnificent judgment hall. Forty-two gods await, and all I need do is declare the prescribed sins I did not commit.

I approach the first god. "Hail, Usekh-nemmt, who comest forth from Anu — I have not committed sin."

To the second: "Hail, Hept-khet, who comest forth from Kher-aha — I have not committed robbery with violence."

And down the list. "... I have not stolen ... I have not slain men and women ..." I stop at this phrase. Well, I have not slain men and women in the plural.

"... I have not stolen grain ... I have not purloined offerings ... I have not stolen the property of a god ..." have I? I failed to stop Akhenaten when he did; will the gods think it the same thing?

"... I have not uttered lies ..." but I have. Every time I declared my love for Akhenaten, every time I stroked his ego and told him I acted only for him, it was a lie.

"... I have not carried away food ... I have not uttered curses ..." I have to suppress a smile. Surely, everyone who utters this confession is less than honest, and surely it is no great transgression.

". . I have not ... " I stop, sure that Qerti, who I am presently addressing, can see the truth I have long tried to hide. He will cast me out now, toss me into the ranks of the evil and wicked should I let the lie cross my lips. Yet, if I admit my guilt, the result will be the same. I take a mouthful of air, having not yet broken the habit of breathing, and look Qerti in the eye. "I have not committed adultery. I have not lain with women."

Her-f-ha-f is next in line. "Hail, Her-f-ha-f, who comest forth from thy cavern — I have made none to weep." I see Bek's face in the dim lamplight, drying his tears that last time before our twins were born. Meketaten's face when she realized I had known what her father would do, and I did not stop it.

"Hail, Basti, who comest forth from Bast — I have not ..." my voice catches, "... eaten the heart." How could I not be consumed by anguish? All of my children, save one, dead. Bek, pushed aside for so many years. That day hunting ducks in the marshes — I might have let Akhenaten win. How different my life could have been had I acted differently.

I continue. I must. "... I have not attacked any one ... I am not a woman of deceit ... I have not been angry without just cause ..." I must declare — twice — that I have not been debauched by any woman's husband.

The confessions start to blend one with another. "I have not shut my ears to the words of the truth ... I have not blasphemed ... I have not acted with undue haste ... I have done no evil."

"... I have not worked witchcraft against the king."

"... I have not cursed any god."

"... I have not acted with arrogance."

"... nor treated with contempt the god of my city."

"... have not slain the cattle belonging to the god."

I collapse, spent.

Akhenaten, Year 13
(ca. 1341 BCE)

"She is only ten. She is too young."

"Young she may be, but Meketaten is now a woman," said the nurse. "It is time she left the nursery."

"You will conceal this," I said.

The woman looked away. "Not so easily done."

"Of course it is. You hide the evidence; claim it was you or one of the other nurses."

She bowed her head and spoke so low I could not make out the words.

"I beg your pardon?" I said.

She raised her voice only a little, but it was enough. "It is already known in the women's quarters."

I glared at her. "I beg your pardon?"

"I said—"

"I heard you. What I want to know is why this news wasn't brought to me first."

She fidgeted. "There was no reason to, Highness. We thought it was good news."

Of course, for most girls, it would be. The nurse would not have known, but that did not ease my anger. I stood and pointed a finger in her face. "If that child comes to any harm, it will be on your head."

"What harm could possibly—"

"Get out."

She bowed and left. Once she had gone, I sat down at my desk and placed my head in my hands. It was too soon. I had counted on more time before facing Meketaten's womanhood. Time to prepare a deception, to at least delay the inevitable until it would no longer place her in peril. I wiped my tears with the back of my hand. The most powerful woman in the world, and I could not protect my own child. I went to my bedchamber, opened my trunk, and found my personal store of silphium in the bottom, under my fine linens. I took some with me, enough for a few weeks, and placed it in a small wooden box. It was all I could do for her.

I found the north palace in a bit of an uproar. The plague had abated for the most part, but we had not yet moved the women back into the main palace. I had thought to do so within days but decided now to postpone it a while longer.

Someone had located a new room for Meketaten, around behind the pool, in part of Kiya's old apartments. Right next to Meritaten. When I entered, she was sitting cross-legged on her bed, dressed in white linen. Though she still had the body of a girl, her figure was beginning to round out. She jumped up when she saw me and ran to embrace me.

"Mother, have you heard?"

I stroked the stubble on her head. Her hair would be allowed to grow now, and her sidelock cut. "I have."

She looked up at me, smiling, her front teeth crooked. "I am a woman now."

I clenched my teeth and blinked to hold back tears. She would not have a happy womanhood, but I would see it was at least not cut short. "Come, sit with me." I sat on her bed, and she sat beside me.

I pulled out the box with the silphium and gave it to her.

Her eyes sparkled, and she opened the lid. Her face froze and then sagged into a frown. She was, perhaps, expecting jewels, but she was a polite girl.

"Thank you, Mother," she said.

"You must take this every day. Mix some with your food, or take it as a tea, however you like."

She nodded.

I crooked a finger under her chin and raised her face to meet mine. "It is important. You must never forget."

She nodded. "What is it for?"

I opened my mouth to tell her the truth but thought better of it. It might be weeks, or months, before her father decided to pay a visit. Perhaps he would not. Telling her would not change things; it would only frighten her, perhaps needlessly. "It will make you grow beautiful and strong and help you to live a long life." That was mostly true — the herb would keep her alive long enough to grow into her beauty.

She smiled again and kissed my cheek. "Thank you, Mother."

"But you must tell nobody about it," I said. "Find a safe place nobody will ever look."

She frowned. "Why can't I tell anyone about it?"

I leaned in close to her. "Because the other women will be jealous and may take it from you. You are special because you are the daughter of two kings, and they are nobody, and they know it."

She trembled. "I want to go back to the nursery."

I stroked her head. "If only you could, but you are a woman now. I would not trust a child with a secret so important as this herb, but I know you are not a child anymore."

She puffed up. "You can trust me, Mother."

I did not know if I could trust her, she still being so young, but I knew for sure I could not trust her father, and I would not let him hurt her. I would send her away. Where, I was not certain. For obvious reasons, Akhenaten's relatives in Shedet would not do. Perhaps Bek's adoptive family in Iunu? Or, perhaps, there was a way to send her to a peasant family. Akhenaten would never find her there.

Though I had insisted the women stay at the north palace well after the plague had subsided completely, I could not do so indefinitely. I managed to secure the palace for Meritaten. She would stay there with her retinue, while the others returned to the main palace. Akhenaten was not pleased but eventually agreed when I mentioned Meritaten would need the space for all of the children she would give him. The words tasted vile, but they worked. He gave her ownership of the palace, but under no circumstances would he allow her younger sister to stay on with her as a lady-in-waiting. Meketaten must return.

The first night back, I asked Mutnedjmet to come fetch me if his Highness should enter the women's quarters to visit with his daughter. I did not retire that night. I did not even disrobe. Instead, I paced my chambers, waiting. Finally, I unrolled some papyrus scrolls. Boring missives about grain supplies. The hieroglyphs swam before my eyes, and my head fell forward.

No runner came that night, nor the next. The third night, exhausted from my previous vigils, and now doubtful Akhenaten planned to visit Meketaten at all, I retired to my bed and fell into a deep sleep.

Hands shook me awake. I opened my eyes to see Mutnedjmet holding a lamp. "You asked for word if his Highness should visit Meketaten."

I flew across the bridge, into the main palace, and from there to the women's quarters. As I neared Meketaten's room, her screams filled the air. I ran to her door and pushed it open. Meketaten knelt on the floor, her torso on the bed. Akhenaten was behind her, thrusting. He leaned on her back and pressed her into the bed so she could not move. As I approached, his body shuddered, and he let out a low moan.

I grabbed his shoulder and spun him around. His eyes widened in shock when he saw me. He thrust a fist toward my abdomen, but I dodged in time. While I was in motion, he swept a leg around, knocking both of mine out from under me. I went down, landing first on my posterior before my head hit the tile floor.

He rose and grabbed his clothing. "This is your fault," he said, knotting his kilt. "If you had given me sons, I would not need to do this."

My head swam, but I fought myself up to a sitting position.

He backhanded me across the face. "You are not indispensable. Should you ever attack me again, I shall prove it." He turned and left.

Meketaten lay on her bed, whimpering. I moved to her and touched her back. She retreated from my touch.

"It's me," I said. "Mother. He's gone now."

She turned over. I sat beside her and allowed her onto my lap. When her sobbing slowed down enough for her to talk, I brushed her tears away. "You must take that herb in the morning, and every morning from now on."

She rolled her eyes.

I turned her head to look at me. Now that it had happened as I had feared, she needed to know the truth. "It's more important now. It will stop you from having a child while you are still too young for it."

She pushed away from me. "You knew?"

"Meke—"

"You knew he would do this to me and you didn't stop him?"

I closed my eyes. "I could not."

"You are king, too. You can do whatever you wish."

"Would that it were so, but it is not."

"You can stop him; you just won't."

"It is more complicated than that," I said. "You are too young to understand."

She turned away to face the wall again. "Has he done this with Meritaten?"

"Yes." It came out as a whisper.

"You all knew. Everybody knew, and nobody told me."

"I hoped he would not bother you."

She turned back, a puzzled look on her face. "That is why you moved Meritaten to the North Palace. To get her away from him."

I said nothing.

"But you left me here."

"I tried, Meketaten. I tried to assign you to Meritaten as a lady-in-waiting. Your father wouldn't have it."

"I hate you."

I touched her knee. "You don't mean that. You're just upset."

"I hate you! Get out."

"Excuse me?"

"You heard me," she said.

"I will leave, but I will be back when you are feeling better. You will need me then."

She did not respond.

I turned to leave.

"I will never need you again," she called out to my back.

I knew it was her pain talking. I hoped it was. In the morning, she would want her mother. I made sure she had other ladies with her through the night. I hoped she would take the silphium as I told her.

Chapter 48

Meketaten did not want me the next morning, nor the next, nor the next. My plans to have her brought out of the city came to nought when she ran away from Mutnedjmet and threatened to tell her father. Every day for nearly a month, I visited the women's quarters, so I would be available should she need me. Every day I returned to my own palace, my arms and heart empty. Finally, I could bear it no longer, and quit going altogether.

It wasn't until some months later that I saw her, arm in arm with her father. I was out with the twins, Meritaten, and Mutnedjmet, enjoying the spring weather and hunting for frogs in the pond. When Meketaten saw me, she pulled on Akhenaten's arm, but he refused to turn away and instead headed straight for me.

I came out of the pond, knowing I presented quite a sight with my mud-blackened feet and the hem of my dress tucked into my sash.

Akhenaten seemed not to notice my state of disarray. "This feud between you two is silly." He turned first to me. "As you can see, the girl is happy as my wife." And then to Meketaten, he said, "And your mother wants only to serve the Aten. You two will come to an understanding. I cannot have this discord amongst my women."

I had to bite my lip to keep from laughing. He had no idea of the discord amongst his women.

"Do not return until you are on good terms again." He strode away, leaving Meketaten alone with me.

Once he was gone, Meritaten climbed out of the pond to join us.

Meketaten stared at us both but refused to speak. I noted that in the months since I had last seen her up close, she had grown into womanhood. Her hair had grown out, and she wore extensions woven in, threaded with delicate silver bells. Her ears, arms, and fingers were draped in gold and jewels. Even her figure had filled out some, and I believed she was at least two finger-widths taller. She looked years older than her actual age.

"Is it true? Are you happy as your father's wife?"

She nodded.

"I am glad you are happy."

"But you still don't like it," she said.

"Of course not. Even if it were not such an unnatural thing, you are far too young."

She lifted her chin. "Father doesn't think I'm too young."

"Indeed not. That is the problem."

"You are jealous."

This time, I nearly did laugh. "You are no threat to me."

"I'm Father's favorite now. He has given me apartments of my own."

"And I am his coregent. The one who does the tedious business of running the empire. You have not replaced *me*; you have replaced Kiya. And I warn you — you cannot compete with a ghost."

She crossed her arms. "I can give him that which neither you nor Kiya ever did."

I sucked in my breath. "Tell me you have been taking the silphium I have been giving you."

"Why should I wish to do that? Father says when I birth the new Crown Prince, he will make me Great Royal Wife and move me into the North Palace." She looked at her sister. "Meritaten will be my servant."

Meritaten narrowed her eyes and opened her mouth to respond, but I silenced her.

I moved closer to Meketaten and dropped my voice. "Heed my advice. If you wish to survive to my age and beyond, you will not tell others what your plans are, not even me. And you will use strategy. If you are to be mother to the Crown Prince, wait a few years until you are strong enough to withstand the birth and wise enough in the workings of the women's quarters to protect his interests." When I straightened, I saw Akhenaten returning.

A smile spread across Meketaten's face. "That is what you are doing, aren't you?" she said to Meritaten. "Using strategy. Then I need not fret about you beating me." She inclined her head toward me. "Thank you, Mother, for relieving me of that worry."

Meritaten grabbed her hand and spoke, quickly and low. "He doesn't care about you. About any of us. He only wants a son."

Meketaten pulled her hand away.

Akhenaten arrived and slipped a hand around Meketaten's waist. "I see you three are conspiring. "Anything I should be worried about?"

Meketaten shook her head, causing the bells in her hair to tinkle. "Mother and Meritaten were just telling me how to best please you."

Akhenaten's eyes widened. "Were they, now? I look forward to sampling the results of that conversation."

Meritaten looked away and clenched her jaw. I felt I was about to be sick. Then my eye was drawn to Akhenaten's hand as he squeezed Meketaten's waist. I realized her new womanly curves were not due so much to the bones widening, but to the flesh rounding. I snapped my eyes back to her face. She gave a half-smile and cocked an eyebrow before they walked away.

Akhenaten, Year 14

(ca. 1340 BCE)

At banquets, Meketaten now occupied the place Kiya once had on the right side of her father. Still with the sensibilities of a child, she would jump up and clap whenever an acrobat or dancer did something she liked. And Akhenaten doted on her, more so as her belly grew rounder. She herself seemed to pay little heed to the burden she carried, having neither the experience nor the wit to understand her own peril.

The night celebrating the river flood was different. Meketaten picked at her food and ignored her father's affections. I wondered if he had hurt her.

Dancing girls approached our tables. They bent over backwards, fairly tying themselves in knots. Normally, this would have Meketaten smiling at the very least, but I noticed a tear streaking down her cheek.

I leaned in to Akhenaten. "What ails Meketaten?"

He shrugged. "She said something about pains in her back earlier. She seems better now."

"Did you send for Ipu?"

"Of course not."

By my calculations, Meketaten had a good two months remaining, an assessment Ipu agreed with. But with her being so slight, perhaps the child had nowhere left to go but out. "She needs to see Ipu."

243

"She's fine."

She hadn't been fine since he'd spread her legs too soon after she became a woman, but I chose not to respond. Instead, I watched her every move from the corner of my eye.

Midway through the singer, Meketaten clutched her belly and let out a cry.

"Shush," said Akhenaten.

I went to her, squatted behind her, and put an arm around her.

She clutched at me, burying her face in my shoulder. "It hurts," she said after it had passed.

"I know, my sweet." I rubbed her lower back. I did not know whether this was cause for alarm or not. It was not uncommon for women to start feeling spasms weeks before the birth.

She pushed away from me, a look of horror dawning on her face. She rose, and I saw the spreading wetness on the back of her dress. She trembled. "I'm sorry." Tears flowed freely now. "I didn't mean to."

I steered her toward the edge of the hall. "It is nothing to be ashamed of. Your waters have ruptured, that is all."

Akhenaten rose. "Bring her back here this instant."

"Unless you want her giving birth right here in front of all the court, you'd best let us go." I pointed to the puddle under Meketaten's chair and the trail following her.

"It is too soon for the child to be born."

I wanted to yell back that that was what you got when you conceived a child on a child but decided it was not worth the time. On our way out of the banquet hall, I sent a runner for Ipu and asked him to send her to the birthing pavilion.

When the pain started again, she crumpled, unable to walk. I scooped her up and carried her. I staggered but kept going, determined. She was slight in build but had added some weight. The guards saw my struggle, but they were not permitted to touch either one of us.

"Highness."

I put Meketaten down gently and turned. Bek was jogging to meet us. My breath caught at the sight of him.

"Your abrupt departure caused quite the stir," he said.

Meketaten doubled over. Bek picked her up and carried her through to the women's quarters, out into the central courtyard. Seeing him risk a beating for touching a royal simply because she needed him — because I needed him — I felt a pang at the remembrance of how cruel I had been to him. It had been the right choice, but still it pained me.

When we reached the pavilion in the back corner, Bek lay Meketaten down on the mattress as tenderly as if she were one of his own. Ipu and her assistant arrived just after we did and shooed us out so she could examine Meketaten.

Alone outside the pavilion, Bek whispered in my ear. "If he ever touches Neferure or Setepenre, I will kill him."

"If he touches another one of my daughters, you will not have to."

He held my gaze and nodded.

Just then, I saw Meritaten headed our way. Bek and I stepped apart, but she seemed not to have noticed.

"You should not be here," I said.

She wrung her hands. "How can I not be? She is my sister."

Meritaten had always taken care of her younger sisters. I understood her desire to stay but feared the result should it not go well for Meketaten.

"Your mother is right," said Bek. "This is no place for you."

"I promised her," said Meritaten. "She is afraid. The other women all talk about how she is too young, that she will die." Her voice caught. "I promised her that she would not die alone."

I put a hand over my mouth. I had thought her too naive to understand, but she did. Not in the beginning, or she would have heeded my warning and taken the silphium. But she had known for a long time, and she was terrified.

"Meketaten is not going to die," said Bek.

"Do not lie to me," said Meritaten.

I fought the urge to cry. Both my girls needed me to stay strong. "She is in great danger, but she may live," I said. "The child is very early and therefore very small. She has a chance."

Ipu appeared at the entrance to the pavilion. "It will not be easy, true, but her death is not a foregone conclusion."

Hearing it spoken aloud by the expert, I released my breath and leaned against a pillar.

Bek nodded. "Please send word to let me know of the princess's condition." He nearly collided with Akhenaten on the way back to the palace entrance. Bek sidestepped to avoid contact with him, somehow managing a bow at the same time.

Akhenaten snapped his fingers at Ipu. "If the child is born now, will he live?"

"I have seen babies born this early survive, but it is rare."

"Then you must stop it."

"Can't be done," said Ipu. "Once the waters have ruptured, the baby must come out, or mother and child will both die of blood poisoning."

"If my son dies, it is on your head," said Akhenaten.

"If either of them dies, it is on your head," said Ipu. "Children are not meant to have babies."

Akhenaten lunged at her. I stepped between them and deflected his blow. "Ipu is the only person who can save your son. And your daughter. You will not harm her."

He stood, panting, and for a moment I thought he would strike me. But he simply nodded. Before leaving, he said to Ipu, "If you must choose between them, save my son."

Meritaten started crying. "No."

Ipu patted her shoulder. "Don't fret, child. Never once have I sacrificed a woman to save a baby, and I'm not about to start now."

"Thank you," I whispered. "And you need not fear the king. Should it not go the way he hopes, I will see you safely away from Akhetaten."

"That's the advantage of my profession. No matter where I go, women are having babies," she said. "But I will do my best to see you do not need to go to the trouble of hiding me."

Nebetah asked permission to enter. "I would like to help, if you'll allow it."

"Nebetah has been a great friend to Meketaten," said Meritaten.

I nodded, and we went into the pavilion. Meketaten was sitting up on the mattress. When her face screwed up and she grabbed at her belly, Ipu eased her down to the floor on hands and knees.

"Stay in this position when the pains come. It will encourage your baby to turn, so he can be born," said Ipu.

"The child is facing out?" I remembered my own first labor with Meritaten and knew Ipu's "not easy" was an understatement if such was the case now.

Ipu shook her head. "He is presenting a shoulder."

Then he had quite a way to turn. I shuddered. It would be more difficult than Meritaten's birth.

"What of the amulet to Bes?" I said and then stopped at Ipu's expression. "Of course." All such amulets had been destroyed. Meketaten would have no protection from Bes or from Het-Heru. My child must suffer from the loss of Ma'at that I had failed to prevent.

"Your Aten is all the protection she needs, or so the king believes."

I nodded. "Of course." I could not voice my doubts, but I had little confidence in a god that stayed so far away, watching from such a distance. He seemed to care very little for the troubles of his people, even those who were supposed to be his favorites.

Still, ladies came in, carrying bunches of papyrus and lotus. Meketaten should derive some small protection from those.

Nebetah and I stationed ourselves to either side of Meketaten and massaged her lower back. Meritaten sat on the floor in front of her, so Meketaten could see her, and touched her hand.

Each time the pain subsided, Meketaten relaxed and collapsed against Nebetah, who stroked her head and whispered in her ear. Each time, my heart broke, but I said nothing. Meketaten's comfort was more important than my own. After she got through this, I would work on repairing our relationship.

"If you stop fighting the pain, it will be easier to endure," I said.

"Easy for you to say," said Meketaten. "You never feel anything."

I was taken aback but chose not to be offended. It was the pain talking. Or did I really appear that way to her?

"Your mother is right," said Nebetah. "When the next pain comes, instead of screaming, try taking a deep breath, and relaxing your midsection."

Meketaten still looked doubtful.

"It will help your baby turn, and then it will be over faster," said Ipu.

When it started again, Meketaten screamed again.

"Deep breath," said Nebetah.

Meritaten squatted in front of her. "Breathe," she said and demonstrated by taking in a deep breath through her nose, letting it out slowly through her mouth.

Meketaten tried it. She breathed in and out, and her screams were reduced to low moans.

"There," said Meritaten. "Did it hurt less?"

"No," said Meketaten, "but I minded a little less."

"That's something," said Ipu. "Keep it up."

And keep it up she did, for longer than I thought she could have. Early sunlight filtered through the vines surrounding the pavilion, and the shadows shortened to near midday. And still, the child was no nearer being born.

Meketaten flopped down onto the floor. "I can't do this anymore." She sobbed.

"I'm afraid you'll have to, but you can take a little break for now," said Ipu. "Take a draught of this." She had had the foresight to send her assistant for some poppy some hours ago.

Meketaten drank it, and we helped her onto the mattress. She would sleep a little now and regain some of her strength. The rest of us arranged sleeping places on the floor. We would also need our strength.

"She threw it out," said Nebetah. "The herb you gave her. Scattered it in one of the courtyard ponds."

It did not surprise me. "Why would she do such a thing?"

"Because she is young and does not know who to trust and who not. She believed her father's words about training her to take over your position."

I raised my head. "He promised her that?"

"He promised her the moon itself if she should give him an heir." She paused. "One that is not deformed."

I lay back and looked at the vines above. Enough light filtered through for me to make out individual leaves.

"Once it was certain she was with child, the women started talking about how she was going to die in childbirth. At first, she thought they were jealous of her, but after a time she began to realize there was truth in their words. She started begging all of us to help her be rid of it."

I rolled over to face her. "And no one would help her?"

"No one dared. She carried the child of the god, and well he knew it. The punishment would have been dire, should the perpetrator have been caught."

"I would have done it," I said.

Nebetah sniffed. "You did not stop him from taking her in the first place."

"No one stops Akhenaten from satisfying his lust. You know it as well as I."

She nodded. "I do know it. Truth be told, I would have helped her, had she asked sooner, but she had already felt the child move. Ipu advised me Meketaten would be in danger either way by that time."

I sighed. "Perhaps it is best. If she had succeeded in ridding herself of it, and had it been a boy, the king's anger might have made her despondent enough to do herself harm." The sudden withdrawal of her father's favor after having built up her expectations and trust for months would have been a real blow to her. She might have really ended her own life, as it appeared Kiya had.

"I thought of that as well."

I was silent a few moments. "Thank you," I said. "Thank you for taking care of her when I could not."

"I trust you would do the same with my son."

Ah. So that was her motivation. No matter, she was good to Meketaten when it was needed.

"He is a sweet boy, and despite appearances to the contrary, he is quick of mind," she said. "Though he will never be king, he may do well in some advisory position."

"Tutankhaten is the king's son, and brother to my daughters. I will see that he wants for nothing as long as I shall live."

"Thank you."

The exhaustion of my body won out over the turmoil inside my head. It seemed no time at all until I was woken by Meketaten's moans, but outside, the sun hung low in the west.

Ipu was examining Meketaten. One hand palpated her abdomen; the other probed inside. She withdrew her hand as Meketaten bore down. "Stop. Do not push."

Meketaten pulled her knees to her chest and pushed harder. "I ... can't ... stop."

Ipu placed her hands on Meketaten's knees. "Look at me. Now, breathe. Relax."

Meketaten looked at her and took a tentative breath. She relaxed her legs, and took another breath, and another.

"Very good. Until I tell you otherwise, whenever you feel the urge to push, do exactly this. Do you understand me?"

Meketaten nodded.

"The child hasn't turned?" I asked.

"Oh, he's turned, all right." She wiped her hands on a clean piece of linen. "He's now presenting a hip instead of a shoulder. I'm going to have to be a little more persuasive." She pointed to me. "You, get behind her and hold her arms and shoulders," and to Nebetah, "You hold her legs down."

We took our positions, and Meritaten stood to the side, where her sister could see her. Ipu's hands pushed and prodded. She leaned into the job, applying pressure between pains. Meketaten whimpered and cried out. It took effort for Nebetah and me to hold her still. After what seemed an eternity, Ipu stood back and wiped her brow. "It is done. The child is in position."

We all smiled, including Meketaten. Nebetah released her hold. Her smile evaporated. The sheets below Meketaten were soaked in bright red.

"Move her up, and support her under her arms," Ipu said to me.

I did as told. Meritaten sat beside us, holding her sister's hand.

"Prepare the herbs and the linens," said Ipu to her assistant. To the rest of us, "We have to get the baby out before we can stop the bleeding."

I wanted to ask if it could be stopped even then, but was afraid I already knew the answer.

Ipu planted herself at the end of the mattress and placed a hand on Meketaten's knee. "Now, when the next pain comes, you push. Slowly."

Meketaten tensed.

"Gently, now," said Ipu. "You have to ease that baby out so you don't start bleeding any worse. Do you understand me?"

Meketaten nodded. She gripped Meritaten's hand and pushed.

"That's it," said Ipu. "Just a little more. Excellent. I can see the baby's head now."

Nebetah, Meritaten, and I all relaxed a little. I nuzzled my cheek against the top of Meketaten's head.

After a few more pushes, Meketaten broke down. "I can't do it." Her body shook.

"Yes, you can," I said. "This is the worst part, but you're almost finished. Soon you'll be holding your own baby in your arms, and you'll forget all about the pain he caused you." I tried not to think of the other pain she would feel when he died, as he almost surely would.

"I can't do it. It's stuck."

"Your baby is not stuck," said Ipu. "It just resting partway."

Meketaten shook harder. "I'm so cold."

Ipu and I looked at each other over Meketaten's head. It was close inside the pavilion. Everyone else was cloaked in a sheen of sweat, hair plastered to their heads. Even naked as she was, Meketaten should not have felt cold.

"Get her some sheets," said Ipu to her assistant, who promptly draped three layers of linen over Meketaten's upper half.

Meritaten looked to me. She knew something was wrong by our reaction. "But, Mother ..."

I shook my head.

"I want you to start pushing now," said Ipu. "Do not stop."

Meketaten bent her head with the effort.

"Harder," said Ipu.

Meketaten sobbed. "Get it out. Please."

"Keep pushing just a little longer." Ipu reached her hands up. "Come on, almost there." A weak cry sounded.

"Is it out?" said Meketaten.

"We've got a head." Ipu worked with her fingers. "Okay, one more little push will do it."

Meketaten smiled. "One more, then."

Ipu caught the child, a boy, and we all smiled. I saw the look of horror on the faces of the assistant and Nebetah before I saw the blood. So very much, more than I would have thought Meketaten's slight frame could hold.

"Mother, I'm cold."

Ipu pulled the sheets down over her legs.

I held on to her. "I'll warm you up, my sweet." I kept holding her as the light in her eyes dimmed and then went dark. When her muscles slackened and went limp, I clutched her to me and rocked her, as I had when she was a babe. Her hair smelled of sweat and lotus, the perfume she'd worn to the banquet. I heard the keening, but it was some moments before I realized it issued from my own throat. I felt my heart had been scooped from my body.

Chapter 50

Too soon, I found myself back at the bottom of a cliff, staring up at the opening to the Royal Tomb. I had not thought to be back here again for many years yet. I started up the steep steps behind Akhenaten. With each footfall, I was conscious of the great drop behind me. It would be so easy to trip. After Kiya's funeral, it would surprise no one. They would merely think me oafish.

Inside, the rushlights were set up to light the way to the chambers behind Kiya's, where Meketaten lay. I could barely bring myself to look at the reliefs showing Meketaten on her deathbed and the family, including me, wailing in mourning.

Her sarcophagus dominated the room, but it was what lay on top of it that drew the eye. A tiny little coffin, too small for even a house cat but large enough to hold the thing that killed her. No. I pushed that thought from my mind. The child was an innocent, as she was. It was its father that had killed her, and I had allowed it. I may as well have taken a knife to her throat — it would have been kinder.

Akhenaten raised his hands, and he began his hymn to the Aten. He did not falter as he had when he had sung it for Kiya. His own child. Two of his own children, and he could not muster a single tear.

I closed my eyes and wished I could close my ears as well, for I did not wish to encounter the gods on this day. I knew myself to be a failure and a betrayer; I did not need to hear them say it. As the hymn droned on without any disturbance, I opened one eye and then the other. The tomb was empty, save for the four of us.

Akhenaten turned to me, and I began to accompany him, looking around to see if I would be beset. Nothing, save the sound of my own voice, echoed off the walls. Where were the gods? They should be here. Meketaten needed them to take her to the Blessed West. She was just a child — she would not find her way on her own.

My voice faltered as the truth dawned. There would be no afterlife for Meketaten. We had turned away from the gods, and now they had turned away from us.

Akhenaten motioned for me to go on, but I could not. "This is wrong," I said. "We killed her, and now we deny her an afterlife."

"What insanity do you speak? The Aten chose to take her; it was not our doing. And the afterlife is a lie. You know this."

"It's not a lie. The Field of Reeds exists. Your forebears are there, as are mine. But not Kiya, and now not our Meketaten." I collapsed on the floor and sobbed.

"I am losing patience with this. If there were an afterlife, do you not think I'd be sending my daughter and my son there now? Do you not think I would have sent my beloved Kiya there?"

I thought that to make himself a god, he would not consider it too great a price to sacrifice the afterlife for everybody but himself. "You are wrong."

Akhenaten prodded me with his foot. "Get up." When I didn't move, he kicked me in the ribs. "I said, get up, woman."

I glared up at him. Through my tears, his face appeared twisted and purpled. I thought how unfortunate it was that all the court had accompanied us on this journey. The steps into the tomb were narrow and steep, and had there been no witnesses, an accident would not have been questioned.

I rose slowly. "Never strike me again."

He took a step back. "You cannot appear to the people like this. Your eyes are red, and your cosmetics are running."

"They will see a grieving mother."

"They will see their monarch questioning the will of the Aten, and it will undermine their confidence."

I snorted. "You proclaimed yourself to be the Aten, and yet when you bedded your own daughter, she died. Either you are not the Aten, nor are you blessed by him, or you killed her deliberately. That is the conclusion you fear will be drawn."

Akhenaten swung his arm at my face. I grabbed his wrist and twisted his arm just enough for him to wince. "You will not strike me again." I released his arm.

"And you will not undermine me in any way," he said. "In the eyes of the people, and the army, I am the Aten, and you are not indispensable."

I longed to punch his pompous face. In our youth, I would have been hard pressed to win in hand-to-hand combat with him, but in the intervening years, he had dropped his rigorous training schedule, while I had not. I would relish the feel of my fist connecting with his soft belly, of the sound of crunching facial bones. I might face execution, or I might escape punishment by flinging myself down the stairs. I could choose the avenue by which I joined Meketaten in oblivion. My hands twitched in anticipation. Yet I still had five daughters living, and without me, they would be completely at his mercy. A poor shield I had been thus far, yet I vowed to do better.

When he winced slightly, and clenched his facial muscles as if in pain, I knew the means by which I could control him. The poppy. All I need do is indulge his need for it, and he would be incapable of harming our remaining daughters. With any luck, it might even kill him eventually.

I lowered my head. "My humble apologies. It was my grief talking. I have not ever, nor shall I ever, speak poorly of you to anyone. I have not ever, nor shall I ever, present anything other than our complete unity." The words burned my throat as they rose to my tongue.

He nodded. "I know you to be a good and faithful wife and coregent. I forgive your womanly weakness."

I was forgiven, but he would never be.

Chapter 51

Bek and I watched the boat pull out from shore, carrying the hope of our dynasty away from the plague. For near two years, it had disappeared, and just as we began to believe it gone forever, it returned with a vengeance. Taheret, her boys, and my girls waved from the deck. A military boat pulled out from the reeds and blocked their path. Another one came up alongside. Together, they forced our families back to shore.

A soldier jumped from one of the military boats — a general, carrying a staff. "No one is to leave Akhetaten."

I stepped forward. "I give the orders. You are to allow this boat to pass."

"Apologies, your Highness. Our orders come from higher up and apply most especially to the royal family."

As the children began to disembark, Bek put a fist into the wall, cracking the plaster. "He would risk his own children."

"He does not acknowledge the risk," I said. "He believes us to be under divine protection."

"I fear he is in for a rude surprise," said Bek.

"I hope you are wrong."

"As do I."

"I shall try to prevail upon him," I said.

I searched the temple first, expecting to find Akhenaten praying. When he was not there, I returned to our private palace and to his rooms. He was sitting at his desk, holding a reed stylus, and seeming to write on a soft clay tablet.

"My apologies. I did not mean to interrupt," I said.

He put the reed and tablet aside. "Nonsense. I am simply catching up on some international correspondence."

"What correspondence?" It came out more harshly than intended. "I mean, is this something I should be aware of?" So far as I knew, Akhenaten had not participated in foreign affairs in many years. He preferred to leave that to me.

"It is nothing. Just some foreign king complaining that I do not send him enough golden statues." He leaned back in his chair. "I might, perhaps, promise him some if he agrees to send more glassware."

I controlled the urge to spit in his face. Plague was raging once again, and he was worried about table settings. "I understand you have given orders that no one shall leave Akhetaten," I said. "Including our children."

He folded his hands over his ample belly. "If you had not already spirited them away without my knowledge during the last bout of plague, while I was grieving for my beloved Kiya, I would not have thought to give orders without your knowledge. It seems I was right to do so."

"If you would allow me to remove them to safety, I would not need to act without your knowledge," I said. "By keeping them here, you may be signing their death warrants. Along with those of anyone else who might wish to leave."

"We are, all of us, the chosen of the Aten, living in his great city. We will be safe."

"We are already not safe," I said. "The plague is here. There have been deaths, and there will be more. Many more."

"We must not interfere with the Aten's will."

I took a deep breath and unclenched my fists. "At least allow the children to leave. They are the future of our dynasty."

"I get so tired of repeating this," he said. "We are a family unit and must be seen as such. If the people know we are afraid, they will also be afraid. They will lose confidence in us, in our dynasty, and in the Aten."

The people had not had confidence in us in a very long time, if indeed they ever did outside of our own little enclave. "We will at least remove them to the north palace, along with the entire women's quarters, as we did last time."

He opened his mouth, presumably to object.

"We can call it a holiday, if you prefer, but we must take some precautions," I said. "How much confidence would the people have in us if we started dying one by one?"

"Very well, if it will stop your harping," he said. "The children and the women's quarters move to the north palace with Meritaten. But you and I continue our daily appearances."

"Of course."

"Why has Beketaten not been invited to join the holiday at the north palace?" said Tiye.

"You know as well as I that it is no holiday," I said.

"You do not care to protect your husband's sister from the plague?"

I looked to Beketaten, sitting on her bed. She was slightly droopy, her eyes hooded and unfocused, her face flushed. "I can see from here that she burns with fever."

"It is not the plague," said Tiye.

Perhaps it was not. It might have been a simple passing illness. "It is a chance we cannot afford to take. If her illness passes, Beketaten may join the women's quarters at the north palace."

"If it passes?" said Beketaten. Her eyes were wide with fear.

Tiye sat beside her and patted her head. "Do not fret. Of course, it will pass." She turned abruptly; her body wracked with coughing. When she pulled her hand away from her mouth, a trickle of blood rolled down her palm. She tried to hide it by wiping her hand on the bed sheet.

I stared at the thin red smear on the white linen. Tiye pushed the sheet behind her, but she knew that I knew the truth. She was as much afraid for herself as for her daughter. Already weakened by illness, were she to catch the plague, she most certainly would not survive it. My heart constricted.

"The children are the future of the dynasty. They must be protected at all costs. I am truly sorry." I turned to leave.

"This is your doing," said Tiye, rising to her feet and following me. "You think I don't see how you undermine my son, your king? You destroy Ma'at and bring chaos upon us. The Aten is angry. He will destroy us because of you."

I spun around and raised a hand to strike her. She stared defiantly back at me, yet she trembled. The skin under her eyes puffed out, and her jowls drooped. Her face was criss-crossed by tiny lines. She was just an old woman. Old, and for possibly the first time in her life, afraid. I lowered my hand. I would not abase myself by beating an old, fearful woman.

I chose my words carefully, for I knew anything I said would be embellished and repeated to Akhenaten. "Whensoever and howsoever you meet death, may you do so with full understanding of the true meaning of Ma'at."

Chapter 52

From the courtyard at the north palace, I watched a vulture loop around over the northern suburb of the city. Once, twice. Another joined, at first in a lopsided, elliptical pattern as if drunk, but gradually tightening until the two shapes circled together, black against the white hot sky.

White linen clung to my skin, pasted there by a thin sheen of sweat. I turned from the sight of the scavengers and shivered. More of the city's poor. Or the rich. Not a household had escaped untouched, anywhere in the city. Including our own. Beketaten had succumbed early, followed in quick succession by Tiye herself.

I turned to go inside and clapped my hands together. "Gather the children," I said to Taheret, "it is time to go."

Taheret bowed her head and spoke in a low voice. "Highness, it would be best if the children could be spared such a trek out into the brutal desert ..."

I turned on her. "Bring them at once."

Taheret trembled, but she left to fulfill her duty.

Once she was gone, I collapsed on a chair. Secretly, I wished it could be so. The children did not need to be dragged into yet another funeral procession. Yet, Tiye had been their grandmother, and it would be unseemly for them not to attend. In this instance, I agreed with Akhenaten.

Presently, Taheret reappeared with the three youngest girls, all dressed in their finest linen. Neferure and Setepenre stood quietly, large eyes staring up at me. But Neferuaten clung to Taheret, her head drooping. I knelt down for a better look. The child's eyes were unfocused. I touched the small forehead and drew my hand back almost immediately. I picked up the little girl, holding her close. Neferuaten's head lolled to one side, and I could feel the burning through two layers of clothing.

So, this had been the reason for Taheret's fear. She did not wish to tell me the plague had stricken one of my own. "I shall take her back to her bed myself."

Akhenaten entered with Meritaten and Ankhesenpaaten as I was leaving. "The boat is ready to leave for the temple."

"Neferuaten is unwell. I shall return her to the nursery, and then we shall leave."

Akhenaten's eyes widened as he took in the flushed skin and the feverish eyes. He took two steps backwards. "Today we entomb her grandmother and her aunt. She will go."

Had my arms not been full, I might have slapped him. "She cannot endure a full day out in the sun."

"Nonsense," said Akhenaten. "The healing rays of the Aten will restore her to health."

I moved as close to him as he would allow and whispered through clenched teeth, "You will not kill another one of my daughters."

He half-raised a fist, and then his eyes flickered from my face to Neferuaten's and back. He didn't dare risk the plague himself. "And you shall not deprive my daughter of the healing of the Aten."

"She cannot walk."

"Then your servant shall carry her." He waved an arm in Taheret's direction. "At some distance from me." He turned to go. "I shall expect you momentarily."

Meritaten and Ankhesenpaaten moved to come closer. "Go with your father," I said. When they hesitated, I roared, "Go. Now." It was too late for all of us in the room — we had already been exposed — they did not need to be. But I did not wish to frighten them by letting them know the extent of the peril.

I turned to Taheret. "I will carry Neferuaten until we get to the grounds. Unfortunately, I will not be able to do so during the procession."

Taheret nodded and trembled.

"Carrying her now will not place you in any more peril than you are already in."

A tear dripped down her cheek, but she remained silent.

"When was the last time you saw your boys?" Bek had taken some rooms on the outskirts of the city to wait out the plague in what he hoped to be safety.

"Several days ago."

I sighed. "Very well. They may yet be safe. Do not approach Bek today, and do not allow him to approach you. He will respect your wishes if it means keeping your sons alive. Take Mutnedjmet with you — she has already been around the children — and keep them as far away as is possible from anyone else."

Taheret nodded. "I—." Her voice caught. "I understand."

In spite of Akhenaten's certainty that the Aten would heal Neferuaten, she languished after her time out in the sun. She became even more listless and would take neither food nor drink. Within days, she was joined by Setepenre and Neferure, and I was sitting by their bedside, praying for a miracle.

The physician came but could do nothing. He gave them carnelian carved with hands to drive out the disease demon. He challenged the demon directly. "Come out, you visitor from the darkness, who crawls along." He poulticed them with garlic and honey, meant to repel the demon. None of it worked.

I sent Taheret and Mutnedjmet away so I might speak with him alone. "You must call on the gods. Djehuty, Heru. Sekhmet. Draw their pictures on the children's bodies. Surely this will save my daughters."

He harumphed. "It might, if I were able to do it without facing death myself."

"No one outside of these doors will know of it," I said. "You have my word."

"The gods would know," he said. "When I reach the judgment hall, how would it go if I had denied their existence to the common people yet begged their help when it suited those who had banished them?"

"You do not serve the common people; you serve the nobility, and I doubt very much that you deny the existence of the gods to them," I said. "You think I don't know about hidden statues and amulets, and secret prayers, but I am neither blind nor deaf." It was a guess, but an accurate one, judging by the look on his face.

"I am sorry," he said. "My hands are tied, and your Highnesses are the ones who tied them. If you were to loosen the bonds, however ..."

I rose and felt the anger burn. "You dare to use my children as blackmail?"

"Mama," said a small voice behind me. I felt a tugging at my skirt.

I took a few steps toward the physician. The hand clutching at my clothing loosed and let go. "I make the laws in Kemet. You will obey me, without expectation of reward, or you shall be punished."

The physician laughed. "Your threats are meaningless. I already have the fever. It is a matter of days, weeks at most."

For the first time, I registered the slickness of his skin, the glazed look in his eyes.

He leaned in closer to me. "The plague is the great equalizer. It takes peasant, nobles, and kings." He looked into my eyes. "You have spent so much time in the sickroom, you will be as dead as the rest of us inside of a month." He turned and left.

Shaking, I sat down again. Neferuaten lay motionless on the cot, head to one side, one arm dangling over the edge, where it had dropped when she let go of my skirt. Her eyes stared at the bright birds and marshes painted on the wall.

"No." I knelt beside her and placed a hand on her chest. No regular rise and fall. No heart beating. I gathered her in my arms and rocked back and forth.

I jumped at a hand on my shoulder.

"Let me take her," said Mutnedjmet.

I shook my head. I had turned away from her as she lay dying. I would not turn from her now.

"You have two others who still need you," said Mutnedjmet.

The twins lay coughing and rasping on the cot, oblivious to their sister's death. I looked to Neferuaten's face, serene in death. Her suffering was over, and Mutnedjmet was right. The twins still needed me. "Let Taheret take her," I said.

Mutnedjmet squatted beside me. "Taheret has taken to her own bed. She has been working through her own sickness, uncomplaining, for the last two days."

"That is not true. I would have noticed if she were ill."

Mutnedjmet nodded at the bed. "You have noticed little beyond this bed since this started."

I handed Neferuaten to her. "You and I have been here since the beginning. How is it we have not been felled?"

She nestled Neferuaten close to her chest. "It is said that those who have survived plague once seldom get struck with it a second time."

"But what about you?" I helped her rise to her feet.

"Perhaps I will yet be stricken."

"You could die caring for someone else's children, without having had a chance to have your own. This doesn't frighten you?"

Mutnedjmet shrugged. "Who says I ever wanted children?" She looked away and sighed. "There is no point in fearing that which you cannot control."

I nodded. "See that Neferuaten is properly cared for." Most embalmers refused to touch plague victims, fearing they should become ill themselves.

"Do not fret," she said. "Somewhere in this city there remains an embalmer who can be persuaded. Or coerced."

After she left, I knelt on the floor beside the twins and closed my eyes. "Sekhmet," I said. "Sekhmet, I need you." I stopped, aware of how hypocritical I sounded. I had failed her repeatedly, and yet here I was on my knees, begging her help. "I would not ask for myself, for I know I do not deserve it. Please, if you ever loved me, please spare my children. Take away their sickness, and if you must still take someone, take me in their place."

I opened my eyes, and there in the room sat a stately, golden lioness. Her fur and eyes glowed from within. She licked a paw.

I prostrated myself in front of her. "Great One. I know this is my doing. I have not fulfilled my promise to you. I can do better. I will do better. I will see that the gods are reinstated — that their temples are restored. I will go even further and see you are elevated to the highest among goddesses."

The lioness stopped her grooming and twitched her tail. "Would that I could believe you." She pushed herself up onto her feet and walked through the wall.

I chased after her and pounded on the wall. "I speak the truth. I speak the truth." I sank to the floor, sobbing.

A thin cry brought me to my senses. Setepenre thrashed, tangling the sheets, and disturbing her sister. They favored me. I had so feared they would look like their father and lay bare my act of treason for the whole court, and Akhenaten, to see. And yet, every time I looked at them, I saw Bek and loved them all the more for it. And Sekhmet knew it. She would punish me for my inaction by taking the ones I loved best. I lay down with them and held them both close. Perhaps I could yet catch their plague and go with them. They were too little to navigate the Duat alone.

Akhenaten, Year 15
(ca. 1339 BCE)

A shadow fell across me as I sat under a canopy by the pond in the courtyard. The twins and Neferuaten had loved to play here, catching frogs, and getting covered in mud. As had Meritaten at one time. Meritaten, who I had believed to be safe, succumbed soon after her younger lookalike. I looked up to see Bek standing there. I glanced to the side, checking to see if my guards were still at their posts. Their eyes were trained on us.

"You are needed in the audience chamber," said Bek.

"I have spent more than ten years listening to complaints. It is Akhenaten's turn."

"You know as well as I that the empire will disintegrate entirely before his Highness enters that chamber."

"Perhaps that would not be such a bad thing," I said.

Bek moved a foot toward me and then checked the guards. He remained where he was. "You do not mean that."

"I cannot bring myself to care what happens with the empire." Or with anything else, I thought.

"Do you think you are the only one who has lost? Look around you. There isn't a family that has remained untouched in the whole of Akhetaten."

"Knowing that does not make my suffering any less. I have lost five children within a year."

"At least you have the luxury of mourning them," he said.

I looked up at him. I had not considered that he, too, would feel the loss of our children. I longed to take his hand. I slid a glance at the guards, and whispered, "I know you loved them, too."

His eyes glistened.

I raised my voice again. "You should go."

He shook his head. "I can't do that. Not until you return to work. Kemet needs you."

I turned away. "They were not even buried properly. The embalmer Mutnedjmet found for Neferuaten died before the job could be done. None could be found for the twins, or for Meritaten, later. Their bodies were dumped in a mass grave with those of peasants and farmers and artisans."

"Same with Taheret."

"They will not have an afterlife."

"According to your husband, they would not have one anyway."

"Do you believe that?" I asked.

"When my life is at stake, I believe what I am told."

I smiled. "Good answer."

"There," he said. "I knew you had not forgotten how to smile."

I did not respond but simply stared at the pond.

"The court is in tatters. All of Kemet is in tatters. Confidence in your Highness's reign, and in the Aten himself, has been shaken to the core. A show of strength is desperately needed."

I sighed. "Why must it be me? Why must it always be me? I am tired."

"Because you are the only one capable of it." He sighed as well. "I know this is not the life you wished for, but it is the one you were given. You can rise to the challenge, or you can cower in the corner like some scared little girl."

For a brief moment, I felt like striking him, though I recognized the ruse. "You hope that if you insult me, I will respond by proving you wrong."

"You always enjoyed the work."

Something inside me squirmed. True, the challenges of diplomacy had brought me a degree of satisfaction amidst all the frustration. But I had never confided this to Bek, nor to anyone else; instead, I had consciously projected the image of taking it on as an unwanted duty. It unnerved me to find I was so transparent. "I wouldn't use the word 'enjoy.'"

"At the very least, you will find it a distraction," said Bek. "While you are immersed in work, you will forget, for minutes at a time, that ache deep inside."

"Truly?"

"Truly."

"I suppose you won't stop pestering me until I give in," I said.

"No, Highness."

"Very well," I said. "You may announce that I will be present in the audience chamber momentarily, on one condition. You must accept the appointment of chief advisor."

He raised both eyebrows.

"The court has been all but stripped bare. Several positions need to be filled. I need someone who is not scheming on his own behalf. That is all." It was not all. His presence brought me comfort.

He bowed. "I am honored, Highness."

I watched Bek as he walked away. His shoulders were still strong, but there was a slump to them that had not been there mere months ago. The guards as well — they were new; I did not even know their names — stood with a droopiness that was uncharacteristic of military men. Perhaps they were not. Perhaps they were the best of what remained. And who had hired them? Not Akhenaten, surely. My father? Bek?

More than Bek's admonitions, it was the realization that I had slipped so far as to leave my personal safety to others that moved me from that seat. The fear that ripped through me told me I was still alive, and I wished to stay that way.

I found my statue of Sekhmet where I had hidden her, at the bottom my trunk, wrapped in some old clothing. I used the linen to polish the wood and placed over her head a tiny wreath of flowers I had woven earlier. Then I placed her in the corner and knelt before her. I hoped the words I had rehearsed would not leave me now.

"Sekhmet, Great One, she who grasps every impious man to annihilate him utterly, she who is the pupil in the eye of Heru. I failed to stop the destruction of Ma'at, and I have thus failed you. You, who have thrice delivered me from certain death: first from the plague that killed my mother, then as a child lost in the desert, and again from plague. I blamed you wrongly. I thought you took my children and left me to live as a punishment, but now I understand it was all my doing." A tear rolled down my cheek. "I did not keep my end of the bargain, and so ..." a lump formed in my throat, and I had to swallow hard before I could continue. "... and so, I had no right to expect you to keep yours.

"I understand now what I must do." I thought for a moment. "No, that's wrong. I always understood; I was simply afraid to do it. Afraid of Akhenaten, afraid for my own worthless life. I am not afraid anymore because I have seen the consequences of my inaction. Perhaps, in your wisdom, that was your plan. It will not happen instantaneously, but it will start now. I will do what is right, even though I am afraid. I will restore to Kemet the Ma'at I helped destroy." I kissed her feet. "Please tell me it is not too late. Tell me there is still time to repair the damage done."

The door opened in my outer chamber, and I turned my head to the noise. As I did so, I could swear Sekhmet shook her head. I looked back at the statue, but it was maddeningly still.

"Nefertiti, sweet." Akhenaten's voice sounded in my rooms.

In haste, I rewrapped the statue, and shoved it back into the bottom of my trunk. The minute the task was completed, I knew the hypocrisy of it. I had acted out of instinct, but perhaps it was the correct action. A lack of circumspection could result in sanction, even demotion, and I would need my current rank to do this duty. "It starts now," I whispered as Akhenaten staggered into my bedchamber.

A smile oozed across his porcine face. "Ah. Here you are."

His words were slightly slurred, and he staggered a little. As he approached, I caught the scent of poppy on his breath. Formerly, even a little poppy would put him to sleep. Of late, I'd needed to order more and more to get the same effect. Of all the people spared by the plague, why did he have to be one? I suppressed the traitorous thought that Sekhmet could have at least made my task easier by striking down the one person who stood in my way.

Akhenaten put an arm around my waist, drew me close, and nuzzled my neck.

I pushed him away. "What are you doing?"

"Do you refuse me?" He clenched his jaw, and his fists.

He had finally slipped over into madness if he thought himself a physical threat to me. Yet I could not refuse him outright, not if I wanted to succeed. "It has been long since you have taken me to bed. I was not expecting it and have not prepared myself adequately."

"Nonsense," he said, slipping both arms around me. "You are as beautiful as the day you bested me at duck hunting."

Meaning that his women's quarters was as depleted as every other sector of the court, and he was in need of an outlet. "I have sent scouts up and down the river, seeking the most beautiful young women for you. Your women's quarters shall be as robust as ever, soon enough."

"You are a good wife," he said.

I steeled myself not to recoil from his kiss. His hands cupped my buttocks and held my hips firmly against his erection. Starved for pleasure for far too long, my body responded involuntarily. I let my eyes drift closed. Perhaps if I pretended he were Bek, or the new master of horse, I could achieve some much needed release myself. I could use him as he meant to use me. I pulled him to my bed, unknotted his kilt, and helped him raise my dress.

He grabbed my face and shook my head gently. "Open your eyes."

He would not even allow me my fantasy. I did as he asked, but the sight of him already red-faced and sweating, though he had yet to exert himself, instantly killed my passion. I pushed myself backwards, so I was no longer directly underneath him. He sat back, his member flagging. He stroked himself, attempting to make himself ready again. Without much success.

So, the poppy was having the desired effect.

"Remove your clothing," he said.

"My apologies. It has been too long," I said.

He slumped and, to my great surprise, began to cry. "It is falling apart," he said.

I suppressed the urge to laugh, deciding it best to assume he was not referring to his member. "It is the way of things that people lose faith in their god after a great tragedy," I said.

He stopped his sobbing. "You are much mistaken. The people's faith is as strong as ever."

I could not deny the truth in that statement.

"It is our dynasty that is falling apart." He wiped at his eyes. "Five of our daughters are dead ..."

Five of my daughters, I thought; only three of yours.

"... the Crown Prince is a simpleton, you're past childbearing ..."

If that were true, my husband, I'd be summoning our new master of horse to my bedchamber the moment you leave it. An idea struck me — as coregent, I shared equal ownership of the women's quarters. As I was already seeking new recruits, I could, perhaps, seek out one or two for myself.

"... Meritaten is dead, and Ankhesenpaaten still too young."

You will not be forcing yourself on my remaining daughter ever, if it is in my power to stop you.

I moved behind him and started kneading his shoulders. My fingers sank into the soft flesh. "You worry needlessly," I said, deciding now was the time to give voice to the plan I had been devising. "The solution is simple."

He half-turned his head. "It is?"

"Of course." I moved my hands up to his neck. "You choose an heir from among the nobility and betroth him to Ankhesenpaaten."

"Can't be done," he said. "A commoner cannot be king."

"I am king, yet I am a commoner," I said. "Your own mother, the great Lady Tiye, was a commoner. The last two generations have made it a habit to marry outside the royal line. If we choose, we can make it tradition."

"You are coregent, not the primary king and not the head priest."

"Of course, those titles must only go to royalty. Grant them to Ankhesenpaaten. Her husband would be coregent; she would be primary ruler and high priest." Such would also be an affront to Ma'at, as the reign of Akhenaten's ancestor, Hatshepsut, had proven. Her kingship was bought at the expense of granting excessive powers to the priesthood of Amun, the situation that had led to the need for reform, started by Akhenaten's father, and taken to extremes by Akhenaten himself. But giving him an option would relieve his obsessive need to produce more heirs and would buy me time to come up with a better solution.

"Don't stop," said Akhenaten.

"I shall return." I asked the guard to send for more poppy. Given his emotional state, I hoped it would not take much more to put him out completely. "It will soothe you and allow you some much needed rest."

I returned to the bed and to his massage.

"There is merit in what you say," he said. "I will think on it."

"Do not think too long. An heir must be chosen while you are still ..." the words caught in my throat "... young and vigorous, if the succession is to go smoothly."

He nodded.

When the draught arrived, he drank deeply, and was sleeping within minutes.

Akhenaten, Year 16

(ca. 1338 BCE)

The sun was past the zenith, the heat of the day eased only a little by the slight breeze in the courtyard. I walked past the line of new prospects for the women's quarters. There were six girls from the far provinces of Kemet, including one from as far away as Kush, for me to inspect. The scouts had done their job well. All six were beauties, full of figure, and young — all six, silly enough to think life as the king's plaything was something to be desired. Five stood, heads bowed, staring fixedly at the grass. One stood straight, casting occasional shy glances at me. Her eyes were a startling green, giving her an exotic look Akhenaten would surely favor.

"What do you think?" I asked.

Nebetah spoke low so the girls would not hear. "My brother would certainly prefer the green-eyed beauty." She frowned.

"You do not?"

"She would be trouble in the women's quarters," she said.

"Agreed." The girl's demure nature had a practiced look. Such dissemblance invariably hid an ambitious nature.

"You," I said. "What is your name?"

"Nofret, Highness."

"You may report to my chambers. I have need of a body servant."

273

Her face crumpled.

"Have you a complaint, Nofret?"

"No, Highness. It's just ... my apologies." She bowed her head. "It is not for me to question your divine person."

"You may speak freely," I said.

"I thought I was here to serve our great king," she said.

"Kemet has two kings," I said. "You would do well to remember that."

She blushed. "Of course. I only meant that ... well, I was told there were certain needs of the king that I would be tending to, which of course ..."

I caressed her cheek. "What did you think I meant by 'body servant'?"

Her mouth fell open.

I took a couple of paces back. "You are dismissed." I ordered one of the servants to show her an empty room in the servants' quarters of our private palace and instructed her to be waiting in my apartments. The rest, I sent with another servant to be assigned rooms in the women's quarters.

Watching her leave, Nebetah bit her lip to avoid laughing. "You are awful. Teasing the poor girl like that."

I raised an eyebrow.

"You don't mean you really intend to ..."

"She is not the first, but she will be the finest thus far. Did you not notice the sway of her hips?" I sighed. "I may have to suspend my duties for this afternoon so that I have ample opportunity to sample her endowments."

Nebetah said nothing.

"You may stop feigning shock," I said. "For years you have lived with women, married to a man who visits you seldom, if at all anymore. Do not tell me you have not given in to temptation."

"Yes, but that is me," said Nebetah. "I always thought you above such hedonisms."

"I have all the desires of a woman and the same limited choice of outlets as you." We stared at each other in the sudden realization that we were far more alike than unlike. For the first time, I wondered how she felt about her life as a secondary wife. Did she once have other ambitions, as I had? Had she, perhaps, been pleased when Akhenaten made me Great Royal Wife in her place, thinking herself free of the confines of tradition? Or, having been raised to it, did she simply not know any other way to live?

Before I had the chance to ask her, a group of children ran through the courtyard, laughing and playing. A lifetime ago, Nebetah and I had been among them. I smiled at the memory and opened my mouth to speak of my nostalgia. Nebetah, however, was looking beyond the little group to a lone straggler, limping with one foot curled under, and carrying something under his arm.

"Tutankhaten is, what, seven now?"

"Yes."

"How does he fare?"

"You see it yourself," said Nebetah. "He is always on the outside."

"Is it a senet board he carries?"

Nebetah nodded. "He carries it everywhere. If he cannot find someone to play with him, he will play by himself."

I approached him and squatted down so my face was level with his. "How are you on this fine day?"

"Quite well, thank you. How are you on this fine day?" He spoke as if he had to concentrate on each word, but I could detect no other trace of impediment. His tone was very adult. I supposed that came from too little contact with other children.

"I understand you like to play senet."

His face brightened. "Do you like to play?"

"Her Highness has important duties to attend to," said Nebetah.

Tutankhaten's head bowed. "I understand."

"Nonsense," I said. "My 'duties' will be waiting on me whenever I return. Shall we play?"

He nodded.

I led him to a table under a sunshade and helped him set up the board. "Please go easy on me. It has been many years since I played senet, and I may be a little out of practice."

Tutankhaten shook his head. "I grant no mercy, and I take none. Whichever one of us wins must do so fairly."

I smiled. "Spoken like a true prince."

I had spoken in jest but found myself very much in need of mercy. The boy had an innate sense of strategy, honed by many hours of practice. During the game, I took the opportunity to assess the state of his education. He spoke at length of the history of Kemetian kings. When I spoke to him in Naharin, or Hatti, he answered in kind without hesitation. He was a very long way from the simpleton we had all supposed him to be.

When the last of Tutankhaten's game pieces entered the afterlife before mine, I shook his hand. "It was an honor to lose to such a worthy opponent."

His eyes lit up. "Do you want to play again?" He gathered the pieces and started setting them up.

"I would love to. Alas, duty calls." I stood up.

His whole body sagged.

"Are you free tomorrow at midday?"

He straightened up. "I believe so." He glanced at his mother, who nodded.

"I shall see you then." I gestured for Nebetah to follow me.

"Thank you, Highness," she said. "He is very lonely."

"He is thoroughly enjoyable," I said.

Nebetah puffed up. "I always thought so, though few take the time to see it."

"That is truly a shame," I said. "For not only is he well mannered, he is exceptionally quick of mind. How many languages does he speak?"

"Four, perhaps five," she said. "He picks them up from the ladies in the women's quarters. He can write some of them as well."

Without any formal instruction. "From now on, I shall oversee his education. Perhaps bring in better tutors, see that he is challenged."

"May I ask why, Highness?" Nebetah appeared to be holding her breath.

"I do not wish to give false hope," I said. "I shall begin his education in earnest, and we shall see the result." His physical deformity would be easy enough to hide from the masses, and should he prove adept enough, the inner circle might be persuaded to look past it, especially in the absence of any other full-blooded male royal heirs. If Akhenaten could be persuaded, this would end his obsessive need to produce more heirs and keep him from our sole remaining daughter.

The Duat
Gate 5
Part 2

As I lie trembling on the floor, Anpu approaches. He stands over me, hands on hips. I know what he wants, what must happen now. I struggle to my knees, open my arms wide, and close my eyes. The sensation of his hand plunging into my chest is curious. It isn't painful, but I feel stifled, unable to breathe. And though I know breath is no longer necessary, I struggle against it all the same.

When Anpu's fist withdraws, it is holding something slick and shiny. He places my heart on the scale, to be weighed against the feather of Ma'at. Ammit sits beneath the scales, his crocodile jaws snapping at the heart, just beyond his reach. Djehuty stands nearby, his stylus poised above a sheet of papyrus, ready to record the result.

I glance from one god to another. If any of them has prescience, or even a preference, of which way the test will go, none gives any sign. Save possibly Sekhmet, who gazes at the scales with a look of intensity. Have my recent actions returned me to her favor? If my heart weighs heavier than the feather, will she intervene and prevent me from being devoured by the beast? Will she allow me to dwell for eternity in the Field of Reeds?

At first, for the space of seconds, the scale remains motionless. Then, as if a breath of air wafts through the chamber, the feather flutters, and the plates of the scale tremble. My eyes fix on my feather, willing it to sink. Instead, it rises.

The heart dips below level. Ammit lunges, jaws agape. My heart is obscured in darkness.

Akhenaten, Year 17

(ca. 1337 BCE)

Tutankhaten's tutors gathered in chambers in our private palace to present their report to my top officials. Ay was present, of course, and Bek, in his capacity of chief advisor to the kings, was also in attendance. When the tutors had finished, they left us alone to discuss the future of Kemet.

"What say you?" I asked.

"The boy is exceptional," said Bek.

"So it would seem," said Ay, "but it will be difficult to make him acceptable as king. People will see only his deformity and think him a monster."

"That is why we must start now," I said. "If we subtly spread the word that his body is twisted because the gods have endowed him with cunning and insight beyond that of a mere mortal, he will be well accepted by the time Kemet is in need of an heir."

"You speak of gods in the plural," said Ay.

"This chamber is secure," I said. "Between the three of us, we must acknowledge that Akhenaten's revolution will not outlast him. Not if Kemet is to survive as a nation."

Ay grinned and leaned back. Bek shifted nervously in his chair.

"Tutankhaten was born the Crown Prince," said Bek. "It is no treason to support him as heir."

"It is if the king does not support him," said Ay.

"He will," I said. "I shall see to it. But even the king's support will not guarantee a smooth succession. After Akhenaten's death, Tutankhaten will need the support of the army and of court officials. That is why I am appealing to you today."

A knock sounded on the door. Nofret entered with a fresh jug of wine. When she placed it on the table, I squeezed her hand. Such a public declaration of possession was uncharacteristic, and I immediately felt self-conscious. I glanced up to see Bek looking in my direction. I raised an eyebrow at him. He looked away.

"I cannot promise wholehearted support at this time," said Ay after Nofret left, "but I will take a more active interest in the boy. Form my own opinion about what sort of king he would be."

"As will I," said Bek.

"I was hoping you would join the ranks of his tutors," I said. "You have great skill with mathematics.

Bek inclined his head. "It would be a great honor."

Once Ay had left, Bek hung back. "I can't help but notice that, of late, all the prettiest girls bound for the women's quarters end up in your employ."

"Jealous?"

"Of course," said Bek.

My heart fluttered.

"Why should you keep all the pretty girls to yourself? Send me one or two."

I laughed and punched him in the shoulder. He feigned hurt. I slipped a hand behind his head, and pulled him in for a kiss. He pulled me close, squeezing my buttocks.

The last time Bek had held me like this, our tiny babies had moved between us. I clung to him and cried. He stroked my hair and kissed the top of my head.

"I miss them, too. Every day."

When I did not stop crying, he sat me down in a chair and crouched in front of me, holding my hands.

"It is all my doing," I said.

"No, it isn't," he said. "There is nothing you could have done to prevent their deaths."

This only made me cry harder, for I knew it was not true. He put his arms around me and held me close. When the tears stopped, I pushed myself away. I don't know why I started talking. Perhaps, in the moment, the need to unburden myself outweighed my need for his good opinion. Or, perhaps, my intent was to sabotage our union once and for all because I did not feel I deserved him. In any event, once I started talking, I could not stop, though I knew every word would be turning his heart away from me forever.

I started with getting lost in the desert as a child. I told him of the promise Sekhmet extracted from me, and the demands she made through the years. I admitted how I had failed her, failed to stop Akhenaten, and how our children had paid the price.

When I was done, Bek looked thoughtful.

"You think me mad."

"On the contrary, I believe every word," he said. "I have seen you react at times to that which no one else can see or hear. I always thought you bore a great burden, but now I understand it was far greater than I imagined."

I stood and walked away from him. "Do not absolve me."

"There is nothing to absolve," he said. "You have been badly used by the gods."

"I made a promise I did not fulfill."

"A promise made by a lost, scared child with no understanding of what it meant."

"I did not even try. Not really," I said.

"Your husband does what he wants," said Bek. "This I have experienced for myself. You never had the power of stopping him."

"Until now," I said.

He sucked in his breath. "Do not put yourself in danger."

"Have you not been listening? I have been in danger my entire life."

"I think you should consider the possibility that the plagues, the famines, the loss of your children were not punishments. Perhaps all of this was the gods' plan to force you to act so that the king's revolution does not survive him, as you said earlier. I believe the gods are acting in their own self-interest, not Kemet's, and certainly not yours."

"Everybody acts in their own self-interest," I said. "But without the gods, Kemet would no longer be Kemet. My own interests are irrelevant."

"Not to me." He rose and took my hands in his. "You have my support. I pledge myself to you. I am yours." He kissed my cheek. "But for now, I must go before anyone notices how long I've been here."

I watched his retreating back and made a decision. Akhenaten had had Kiya to bring him comfort. Why should I not have Bek?

I called out to him. "If you wish, you may come to my private apartments tonight," I said.

He turned and walked back to me. "You are certain it is what you want?"

In that moment, I was certain I had never wanted anything so very much. I nodded. "Wear women's clothing."

His eyes widened. "Have your tastes changed so much?"

"So the guards will take you for a body servant. It is not unusual for one of them to spend the night."

"Now I truly am jealous."

"Then take their place."

He touched my cheek. "I'd like nothing better. But if your husband should find out ..."

"We need not worry about him. These days, he notices only that which is brought before him." Indeed, I thought, he was so often insensate from the poppy that at times he barely took note of that which was brought before him. "So long as we are discreet enough to escape notice, we have nothing to fear." I spoke with confidence, though we both knew it would be no easy feat, and the consequences dire should we be discovered.

He touched his forehead to mine. "Until tonight, my love."

Chapter 56

I turned over slowly and rose with caution, lest my belly spill its contents. At first, I thought it an overabundance of rich food combined with my advancing age, but with the fourth consecutive morning, along the increasing tenderness of my breasts and the delay of my courses, I was forced to admit the truth — my prodigious fertility had conquered all efforts to quash it. This left me with two options: seduce Akhenaten so he might think the child his, or cast it out before it became obvious. I hadn't the stomach for the former.

A spasm sent me racing for the bathroom. When Nofret came in, she wrinkled her nose.

"Too much wine last night," I said.

"Overindulging can be bad for your health, Highness." Her eyes bored into mine.

I froze. "You are right, of course. I shall be more prudent in the future."

After she turned, I let out the breath I had been holding. It must be done quickly, before her suspicions were confirmed. I stood on the stone slab, allowing Nofret and the other servants to scrub me down with natron. While the rinse water chilled my skin, and hands toweled me dry, I pondered how to do it. It was still early enough that it could be accomplished easily. Birthwort would be the obvious choice, which was precisely why I could not use it — everyone knew its purpose. A large dose of aloe would have the same effect. It would be more troublesome for me, but that could not be helped. Aloe had the advantage of having a multitude of uses, so it would not be unusual for me to request some. Indeed, I need not bother the physician at all — the kitchens kept a store of aloe to use against burns.

As I left my chambers, I nearly collided with Ay.

"I am glad to find you home," he said. "I need to speak with you."

"Not now, Father," I said. "I have urgent business to attend to."

"Not so urgent as this," he said.

"Later, Father." I pushed past him and set out toward the kitchen.

He called after me. "This concerns the fate of the empire."

I stopped. I supposed a few more hours would make no difference to the ultimate solution of my little problem. I beckoned him back into my chambers.

"Not here," he said. "Follow me."

He led me into the courtyard, past the sycamores and date palms, and through the gate. He turned right, compelling the guards following us to quicken their pace. He stopped at the House of Correspondence, a little way behind our palace. "Have you ever visited here?"

"I have no reason to," I said. "What I haven't written or dictated myself, I have read."

"Are you certain of that?"

With a shudder, I remembered finding Akhenaten busy with correspondence. "May I ask what brought you here?"

"Word came through military channels that there is big trouble in the provinces." He led me to a desk strewn with clay tablets, themselves covered in Asiatic script.

I sat and began to read. The first was a dispatch from the mayor of Qatna in Naharin, pleading for archers. The Hatti were attacking, everything was in flames. I glanced at some of the other tablets. Several tablets were from Rib-Hadda of Byblos begging for our armies. His own wife wanted him to go over to the enemy to save themselves.

From Urusalim: "As the king has placed his name in Urusalim forever, he cannot abandon it!" Then, later: "Lost are the lands of the king."

The Hatti had already overrun Naharin and were well into Kinahhu. Kemet itself was in great jeopardy.

I put down the tablet I was reading and gripped the edge of the desk. "Has Naharin fallen?" I asked without looking at Ay.

When Ay did not respond, I turned to face him. He nodded.

I grabbed the closest tablet, threw it against the wall, and yelled. Bits of clay exploded out, littering the floor. His own grandfather's countrymen, and he did nothing. Nothing but ask for gifts.

"Why was I told none of this? These messages should have been brought directly to me."

"He must have hidden it from you deliberately. Perhaps he thought you would cajole him into doing something, as you did with the revolt in Kush."

"The empire is disintegrating all around us," I said.

"And it will continue to do so, so long as nothing is done about it."

I looked at him. "You will round up all of those responsible for dealing with foreign messengers and see that they are beaten. That will persuade them to send all such correspondence to me, regardless of any instructions to the contrary."

"If that is all you are capable of doing, then Kemet is doomed."

He was right, of course. Kemet would not survive as a nation, let alone an empire, if Akhenaten were not removed. Perhaps I had been encouraging his poppy habit too effectively and had inadvertently contributed to the problem. If he had been more clear-headed, he might have seen the danger and at the very least brought it to my attention. If, however, the dose were increased, it would kill him, and probably sooner rather than later. His habit was well known at court — his death would not be questioned. It would be no great difficulty to obtain poppy for myself and give it to him instead.

But I could not confide my plans in Ay, nor could I allow him to openly ensnare me in such a course of action. "If there is any more talk of treason, you shall see what I am capable of."

"It is more treasonous to continue on as you are doing." He turned and left.

He would have to be watched more closely, though I would have to tread delicately, for he had the support of the army.

On returning to my chambers with a stoppered jar of aloe, I found Nofret with my herbal chest open on my bed. My linen chest lay open on the floor, linens strewn about. My secret Sekhmet rested on top.

"What is the meaning of this?"

She smiled at me and took a pinch of silphium in her fingers. "It took some while to discover the purpose of this particular herb. I think the king would like to know that his wife needs to prevent conception, though she has not lain with him in ..." she paused, "... at least in all the time I've been here."

I put the aloe down on a table. "You need better informants. Silphium is used for fevers and indigestion."

"Too bad it didn't work," she said. "What would the king do, I wonder, if he knew you were carrying the child of a rough serving man?" She cocked her head. "Is it the Master of Horse? I have seen you eyeing him whenever you take out a horse or chariot."

"You are mistaken." At least she had not guessed the identity of the child's father.

"I don't think so," she said. "You never overindulge in wine or anything else. Except the pleasures of the bedchamber. If you are as insatiable with the Master of Horse as you used to be with me, it is little wonder you find yourself in this predicament." She cast a glance at Sekhmet. "I suspect the king would also like to know about that."

I considered how to deal with this. If Nofret had wanted to destroy me, she would simply have gone to Akhenaten with her story and have done with it. She told me because she wanted something from me. The problem was that once she got it, she would not be satisfied long.

She tilted her head toward the jug on the table. "Birthwort, no doubt. It works but is decidedly unpleasant. Or so I have been told. But you needn't worry — I shall help you. I shall see that you are not bothered while you are indisposed, and I shall see that the evidence is burned."

"And what is the price of your 'help'?"

She brightened. "Not much, really. I want chambers of my own. I am tired of sharing with your other girls. I also want finer linens and more gold jewelry."

"That is all?"

She tossed the herbal chest aside and stood to face me. "One more thing. You will make me your chief consort."

I gasped.

"Do not flatter yourself," she said. "It is the title I want, not you. It is what you robbed me of by taking me from the king when I first arrived here. You may continue taking lovers as you choose, and I will do the same."

I considered several approaches and settled on the one most likely to catch her off guard. "I have a different solution. One you will not like so much." I drew back a fist, and planted it in her gut, just below her rib cage. When she doubled over, I shoved her onto the floor, picked up Sekhmet, and raised her high above my head.

Nofret lay whimpering on the floor. A flash of pity stayed my hand. But if I did not follow through, she would destroy me utterly — whether by exposure or by a slow bleed, the result would be the same. I brought the base of the goddess down on her head.

Not hard enough. She turned her face to me, her eyes pleading. When I raised my hand again, she used hers to cover her face. I hammered her head. Once. Twice. Three times. When I had finished, she lay still, her skull caved in.

I fell to the floor, shaking, while her sightless eyes accused me. My belly heaved, and I scarcely had time to turn away to avoid retching all over her. I had no choice. Had I allowed her to live, it would have meant my death. And Bek's. Telling myself this, true as it was, failed to comfort me.

I pulled the linens from my bed and draped them over Nofret so I would not have to look at her anymore. I wiped at my eyes with my fist. I had to act quickly, before she was missed. Or I was. I picked up Sekhmet and wiped the blood and hair off on the bed linens. I repacked the herbal chest and my linens and then put the chest back in its place under my bed.

I would need help disposing of Nofret. I did not fear punishment. She was a serving girl, nothing more, and I had the power of life and death over her. What I feared was discovery of the reason why I had killed her. I was not prone to violent rages, quite the opposite, and such a sudden change in character would provoke intense interest.

My first thought was of Bek, but I knew this would forever change me in his eyes, and that I could not stand. There remained only one person who would neither think less of me for this act, nor expose me. I could trust my father completely to act in his own interest and keeping me in power was in his own interest, and so I sent for him.

I paced the outer chamber until he arrived.

When the guard finally admitted him, I sighed heavily. He stopped in his tracks and bore a look of apprehension.

"I have done something." I took him by the hand and led him to my bedchamber.

He eyed the bundle on the floor before moving to it and lifting the linen. "A serving girl? You killed a serving girl?" He exhaled sharply. "What did she know?"

"She discovered certain activities of mine and attempted extortion in exchange for her silence."

He stood to face me. "I sincerely hope the activities you refer to are a plot against his Highness."

I did not flinch from his gaze but said nothing.

"Do not dare tell me you would risk everything for the sake of a good tumble."

"It is more than that."

"I always believed you smarter than that," he said. "Yet, perhaps I should not question why you have done this but rather celebrate that you at last are showing potential to become the ruler Kemet needs."

"I take no pleasure in this," I said.

"Do not fret," he said. "After the first time, it gets easier."

I shuddered with the realization that Kiya had likely been neither his first nor his last. "There will not be a second time." I could not even think of the slow death I had planned for Akhenaten without retching.

"To be a strong ruler you must show no mercy."

"I have no wish to rule. I never did."

"So, what's your alternative?" he said. "Run away with Bek and spend the rest of your life farming onions in the delta?"

I opened my mouth to respond, but no words came.

"I thought as much," he said. "Help me roll her up better."

We bent to our task, and once completed, I had the idea that if I hefted the corpse myself, it might solve my other difficulty as well, with less trouble than the aloe. I bent to allow my legs to take the weight and staggered as I rose. Nofret was deceptively heavy.

Ay took her from me and slung her over a shoulder. "I should think it would cause considerable talk if the King of Kemet were seen removing her own dirty linens."

As there would be if the head of the army were seen doing so. But, I reasoned the talk would be less, and should it be noticed that the strange sight coincided with the disappearance of a favored body servant, better that he should be associated with it than me.

"Drive her out into the desert and leave her for the vultures and the hyenas."

He nodded. "I'll do that. And you keep your knees together from now on."

As I watched him go, I could not help but think he was right. If I wished to step aside from the kingship, there was only one way out for me, and I had little taste for it.

Chapter 57

Seized with cramps, I rushed to my private toilets. Both ends evacuated profusely, and at times simultaneously. When it subsided, I staggered back to my bedchamber and lay down. My skin was slick with sweat, so I lay on top of the linens and attempted to doze off before the next attack.

When physical exertion had not done the trick, I was left with no choice but to take the aloe. Because I did not want the reason for my indisposition to be known, I refused all offers of aid and ordered my servants not to send for the physician.

After several hours spent between cramping, violent purging, and fitful dozing, at last it seemed my body had emptied all of its contents — all but the one I most needed to expel. At that point, the fluids shooting forth appeared as water, and then they stopped, to be replaced by dry heaving.

Somewhere between the toilet and my bedchamber, I fell to the floor and lay there, my limbs useless. I had taken too much aloe. I was going to die, and I thought that death was not such a bad prospect. My eyes drifted closed, and then a thought struck. If I were to die, the embalmers would remove my womb and know of the child. They would tell Akhenaten. I raised one leaden arm, pulled myself forward a couple of paces, and collapsed again, but this time I smiled. I decided it was an appropriate revenge. Akhenaten would know I had betrayed him this time, and he could spend the rest of his miserable life wondering how many other times, and in how many other ways.

At some point, I felt hands moving me and a male voice whispering, though I could not make out the words. I saw a face — Bek's? Everything went black.

When I woke again, I was in my own bed. My mouth was dry, but the cramps had ceased. A servant girl was there. Thuy. "Wine."

Thuy poured a glass from the jug on my table and handed it to me. I drank.

"Slowly, Highness," she said. "Lest you make yourself sick again."

"How long was I asleep?" I asked.

"A day, and a night, and some of the next day," she said.

"Did I ...?" I could not ask her that which I needed to know. If the child lived, it was still a secret and must remain so. "Help me dress." I swung my legs to the floor. The room spun, and I nearly fell back down. I gritted my teeth to make the dizziness go away.

Thuy looked down. "Are you sure you wouldn't rather rest, Highness?"

"From the sounds of it, I have been resting far too long."

She helped me wash and dress. As she was starting with my makeup, a knock sounded on my door. The guard announced Bek. I dismissed Thuy and let him in.

"I am surprised to see you looking so well."

"Not nearly as surprised as I am."

"I imagine so." He let out a long, slow breath. He put the back of a hand to his mouth, and tears glistened in the corners of his eyes. "I feared I had lost you." He cupped my cheek in his hand.

I kissed his hand. "You shall be burdened with me for years to come."

"I hope so." He touched his forehead to mine and sighed.

"What is it?" I said. "Has something happened?"

"I don't wish to trouble you." He released me. "But you need to know. His Highness is planning a marriage feast for himself and Ankhesenpaaten."

I felt like the wind had been knocked out of me. "When is this feast to take place?"

"Tonight."

"No," I said. "Cancel all plans. I shall deal with Akhenaten."

I found him in his own chambers, trying on jewelry. "Which do you prefer — the sun disk pectoral or the eagle?"

I wanted to rage at him, but I knew it would have no effect. I took a deep breath. "The sun disk, of course. It glows like the Aten himself." I helped fasten it around his neck.

He admired himself in the mirror. "You do have fine taste, my love."

"There is time before the feast. Come, let's sit."

He cocked an eyebrow. "No need for jealousy. If you want me, all you need do is ask. But right now, I must get ready."

I bit back a retort that if that were what I wanted, scarcely any time at all would be needed for the act itself. But it occurred to me that I could solve both problems at once. And if I played it well, I could convince him we had lain together without actually sullying myself.

"It is an important day," I said. "I only wish to help you relax." I turned him around and began massaging his shoulders.

"Yes." He leaned into me. "I must be in top form tonight."

"She is young and inexperienced," I said. "Perhaps it would be better if you spent some of your ardor beforehand, so as not to frighten her." My belly spasmed, and for a moment I thought I might retch again. I moved my hands down his spine.

He grasped me by the waist and pulled me to his bed. I straddled his hips and massaged his chest. "You are very tense," I said. "Is your head paining you?"

"You know me too well, my sweet."

"Perhaps some poppy would help. Not enough to dampen your passion, just your pain."

He looked doubtful.

"You know your needs. You know to take just the right amount." I ordered the poppy and kept him busy while waiting for it.

When it arrived, he gulped it.

"Take care," I said, taking the cup from him.

He snatched it back. "I will say how much I need."

While he drained the cup, I ordered a second, and asked for it to be stronger.

He drew me down to the bed and lay on top of me. He covered my mouth with his and grabbed at my breasts. I stroked his erection but shifted my legs to make access difficult. He pushed my hand away and forced my thighs apart. I moved up to stay out of his reach. He grabbed my hips and pulled me back.

Just then, a knock sounded in the outer chamber, and the guard announced a messenger.

I took advantage of Akhenaten's momentary lapse of attention and went to retrieve the cup. "I ordered a second draught of poppy, in case the first was not sufficient." I placed it on the table by the bed and sat down next to him.

He resumed kissing me, but when he tried to grab a breast, he missed and got my shoulder instead. He looked to his hand, as if he did not recognize it, and tried again. He sat back, his eyes unfocused. Unfocused until they lit upon the poppy. He reached for it, but I grabbed it first, lest he miss and spill it on the floor.

I held it to his lips and helped him drink. Once it was gone, he lay back. I straddled him and nuzzled his neck, moving slowly down his body. At the sound of his snoring, I stopped. I arranged a seat by his bed. When he showed signs of waking, I would nestle down with him, and he would think we had lain together, and that the child was his. If indeed there still was a child.

My belly ached, and I feared a repeat of the previous night. When I visited the toilet, however, I found I had begun bleeding and knew it would increase greatly before it subsided. I could not risk Akhenaten waking and finding me so. I threw on one of his robes to hide the damage already done to my dress and returned to my own apartments.

I told Thuy I was still unwell and asked her to send fresh linens. I lay down and wadded up some of those linens between my thighs.

The pains started slowly and lasted several hours, leaving me exhausted. In the end, I balled up the bloody linens under my bed to be burned later and fell into a deep sleep. By the time I woke, the sky outside was black. I hastily cleaned myself, dressed, and went to Akhenaten. He was gone, and I feared I knew where.

I woke the guard at the women's quarters and asked him to direct me to Ankhesenpaaten's new quarters.

"You cannot go in there," he said. "The king is with her."

I grabbed him by the throat and pressed him against the wall. "You will tell me where they are and allow me entry, or you will find yourself working a mine in Mafkat." I released him.

He swallowed and rubbed his neck. "The same quarters given to her older sister."

I found Ankhesenpaaten on the floor in the corners, tears streaking down her cheeks, vomit staining her shift. Akhenaten sprawled face down on her bed.

I knelt by Ankhesenpaaten, and examined her. Bruises were forming on her upper arms, but I could find no other obvious damage. "Are you hurt?"

She shook her head. "He tried, but he fell asleep before he could."

"You will spend the night in my apartments, with me." I led her to the door. "Ask Thuy to bring you water and clean linens, and help you wash up."

When she was gone, I checked Akhenaten. He seemed completely still. I placed a hand on his back. His skin was clammy. His rib cage expanded and contracted, curse him. I braced myself against the bed, slipped both arms underneath him, and flipped him over. I eased him up so I could slip the linen bedcovers out from underneath him without waking him. Out of six children I had borne, only one was left to me. He would not kill her as he had done the others.

I rolled the linens into a ball, used it to cover his mouth and nose, and pressed down hard.

Akhenaten's eyelids flew open, and he clutched at my hands. I leaned my whole body across him. In recent years, he had degenerated to such an extent that he would have had difficulty removing me even without the influence of the poppy. But, in his current condition, it was impossible.

His body convulsed, and he retched. I leaned more heavily against him, fixing the linen in place, hoping he would choke on his own vomit. His fists beat against me.

All the while, I maintained eye contact. I watched as the light in his eyes dimmed and went dark. After his struggles ceased, I stayed in position until my own muscles ached with the strain, and still I did not move. I could not now afford for him to live and to recall this encounter.

When I could no longer hold the position, I drew back. I held my breath and waited to see if he would rise. The whites of his eyes were streaked with red, and his skin was darkened into bruises around his mouth and nose. I checked for breathing and for a pulse. Finding none, I rose, intending to leave. But seeing his face in what appeared to be no more than peaceful sleep, my mind whirled with images. His face when I beat him at duck hunting. Our wedding night. His joy when Meritaten was born.

I took a moment to stifle the unexpected, unwanted tears and left before I forgot the monster he had become. The one who forced his own daughter to bear a child too young. The one who forbade his small children to escape the plague. I remembered the twisted, broken kitten. The circumstances of his father's death. The circumstances of our marriage, and the choice he'd given me that was not a choice. He had always been a monster, and he did not deserve my tears.

I flipped him over onto his belly again, and stuffed linens under his face so that the bruising would appear self-inflicted.

On my way out, I stopped for a word with the guard. "The king is quite ill. He is sleeping now, but you may wish to call for the physician in the morning."

He nodded. "Yes, Highness."

Ankhesenpaaten lay curled up on my bed, sleeping in spite of her fear, in the way only the young can manage. I washed to rid myself of Akhenaten's stench and lay down beside her, one arm around her. Thus, I lay through the night, listening to her breathe, and watching the progress of the stars through the window.

When at last the sun's rays streamed into the room, I roused Ankhesenpaaten and called for Thuy to help her dress for the day. When they were gone, I retrieved the linen bloodied from my miscarriage of the day before and secreted it inside my trunk. My breath caught in my throat as I realized I had rid myself of the child for nothing. There were now none left alive to know that Akhenaten had not been its father, save for Ay, Bek, and myself, and none of us would ever have spoken of it. Had it been a boy, I might even have promoted a rumor that it was a Heru-child — conceived after the death of his father. He might have been the king Kemet needed.

I squeezed my eyes shut and swallowed hard. I must not be seen to be crying before receiving news of the king's death. I shoved the trunk back into place and left to submit myself to the usual morning routine of cleansing and massage.

I had just finished a natron scrub when running footfalls sounded on the tile floors. A messenger stopped briefly to speak with the guards and then entered the room, breathless, and bowed to me. "You are needed, Highness. It's the king."

Chapter 58

While assembling for the procession into the desert, everyone jostled to get a look at the coffin. It lacked any references to Aten whatsoever. More, the crossed arms were covered in feather decorations — a clear reference to the god Wesir. Whispers speculated about the meaning of it, about whether the body was wrapped with amulets of the gods (it was), and about the presence of priests of Amun with their sacrificial bull and calf, walking ahead of young Tutankhaten and me. The mood was cautiously hopeful.

In lieu of a formal announcement, I decided it would be best to start as I intended to continue. The fact that Akhenaten would have hated it only made it sweeter. The one concession I did make to his wishes was to have him buried in the family tomb in the cliffs east of Akhetaten. He vowed he would never leave his city, and so I ensured he could not follow us when we did.

In front of the steps into the tomb, the coffin was propped upright and facing south, on a mound of clean sand. I walked with Tutankhaten to ensure his awkward gait did not send him sprawling in front of the assembled guests but withdrew so that he might perform the Opening of the Mouth without my assistance. I watched as he poured the water, purified with incense, and offered the bull's heart. I felt a great wind brush past me, and thought I heard the low murmur of voices. I looked around, expecting to see the gods in attendance, but saw only Tutankhaten and the priests. I glanced to the crowd gathered behind me. Perhaps the wind had simply carried the sound of their voices up to me, for surely the gods would be granting him no afterlife. Or, perhaps, the gods wished to ensure he was really dead, and it was I who had lost the power of seeing them. No matter.

On the walk back into the city, Ay left Tey with the women and took me a little aside, just far enough so we would not be heard over the wailing women.

"It was not a clever move, but it is not irreversible," he said. "You are coregent and have been for many years. The normal course of events would be for you to rule."

I sighed. "I was Akhenaten's Great Royal Wife, mother to his children, coregent, and apologist. I am not what they want now."

"It is up to you to show them otherwise," he said. "You have the support of the army."

"When Hatshepsut ruled alone as king, she did so by currying favor with the priesthood of Amun. She set in motion a chain of events that led to forever increasing powers for the priesthood and decreasing powers for the king until we must guard ourselves against usurpation by the priests. Shall I do the same with the army?"

He grunted. "You make excuses for your own lack of ambition."

"As you fail to excuse your excess of it," I said.

He clenched his jaw but did not reply.

"My duties have not changed. I am still regent for the king."

"Your title has changed greatly," he said. "You are king no longer, merely a glorified helper. And you will lose even that when the king reaches maturity."

That was, of course, part of the attraction. I could set things to right, and then leave court life for good. Perhaps return to the temple of Sekhmet. Or to an estate in Shedet. "Retirement does not sound like such a bad thing."

"Not to you, perhaps."

I chuckled. "You needn't worry. Your granddaughter sits on the throne. Our family's position is secure, as is yours, so long as you want it."

"So long as that remains true, you have nothing to fear from me." He melted back into the crowd before I could respond.

To underestimate him would be perilous, and I must think carefully before implementing changes. For the moment, the army had much work to do in reclaiming our lost empire, and Ay would be too busy abroad to concern himself about affairs at court.

Turning my head as I reclaimed my own place in the procession, I caught sight of Bek. Yes, a great many things would change now that I was free to choose.

Tutankhaten, Year 2

(ca. 1335 BCE)

In the delta, the water lay on the fields and sparkled in the sunlight. What was dry land for most of the year had been transformed into a warren of tributaries and islands. Even in the heart of Mennefer, canals threatened to overflow.

A flock of ducks startled at something moving in the reeds — a hippopotamus, perhaps, or a crocodile. I watched them flapping overhead, squawking their displeasure.

Bek squeezed my hand. "There will be time later, my love."

"It has been too long," I said. "I only hope I have not lost my skill with the throwing stick."

"I shouldn't worry about that. What you should worry about is the fact that I am considerably more difficult to beat than some soft princeling."

I suppressed a laugh. "So, you say."

"To be sure, I am clumsy with a throwing stick," he said, "but my slingshot is deadly. How do you think young peasant boys pass the time?"

"It is my understanding you spent much of your childhood in school."

Bek nodded. "Teaching the noble boys how to use a slingshot."

I laughed.

The boat turned into the temple waterway. Ahead of us, the divine barque had been tied, and priests were carrying out Ptah and Sekhmet. When our boat docked at the watersteps, I disembarked first, allowing Bek to fall in with the other officials, Ay among them, with Tey. Ankhesenpaaten followed me. Together, we aided Tutankhaten. When he was on solid ground, he linked arms with Ankhesenpaaten.

I whispered in his ear. "Just as you practiced."

He nodded, his grey eyes wide. They set off slowly.

He had left his walking stick behind. It was vital that the people see their king as strong. Invincible. For this reason, I had kept Tutankhaten's public appearances both brief and rare. In two years of kingship, this was his longest public outing, and he would be under much scrutiny.

I followed several paces behind, studying the effect. Tutankhaten leaned on Ankhesenpaaten. When he started to stumble, she put an arm around his waist to steady him. They handled it well. Their physical closeness should be taken as simple affection between young lovers, and it seemed to be. The crowds lining the procession way jostled for a glimpse and fairly jumped to touch their foreheads to the ground as the royal couple passed. It was as the early days in Akhetaten had been for me.

After the gods had been returned to their sanctuary, the priests turned to carrying litter chairs for the king and queen. As the temple lacked a Window of Appearances such as we had used in Akhetaten, we positioned ourselves at the entrance. In keeping with the spirit of the Opet Festival, instead of gold and jewels, we distributed thousands and thousands of loaves of bread and jugs of beer. The peasants received their gifts with laughter and blessings.

I turned my head. Bek was bent to his task, hefting jugs of beer and passing them down the line. I scanned the crowd but did not see Ay. I caught Bek's eye and tried to ask him where Ay had gone. I mouthed the words and gestured. When he understood my meaning, he looked around, and shrugged. When the man next in line jostled him, he resumed passing the jugs.

A little girl held her arms out to me. She had the long hair of the peasant class, decorated with petals, berries, and small clay fish ornaments. Her bare feet were filthy, but her eyes were bright, and she smiled at me. I handed her a loaf and chucked her under her chin. "What a pretty young lady."

An older woman, a grandmother perhaps, came up behind her and stopped short when she saw me. She stared a moment before yanking the bread out of the girl's hand and tossing it back to me. Then she led the girl into the crowd to await bread and beer from the king and queen.

I sighed. Those far removed from our former court at Akhetaten still believed me to have been a party to Akhenaten's "reforms.". I prayed that Tutankhaten would never cause Ankhesenpaaten to be hated so.

After the long trip down the river back to Waset, I stood to address the assembled nobles, officials, and members of the court. I signaled for the music to stop, and I waited for conversation and the sounds of clinking plates to die down.

"There has been much talk about what the plans are for the future. When the court left Akhetaten, certain assumptions were made about the course of Kemet, assumptions that have been challenged by my decision to hold the annual Opet Festival in Mennefer, in honor of Ptah and Sekhmet instead of Amun. It is time now to set those assumptions right."

I scanned the crowd. Ay sat to the left, with Tey to his right. Three priests of Amun were seated to his left. I swallowed. "The court shall move to Mennefer on a permanent basis. As well, the ruling couple shall change their names to Tutankhptah and Ankhesenptah in order to remove the honor given to that god favored by the heretic."

All eyes were now on me. Not a hair stirred in the dense air. "This marks a new beginning for Kemet. Or, rather, an old beginning, for in former times, Ptah was honored by the king when Amun was still an obscure regional god, dreaming of someday being recognized outside of his own backward little nome. Ptah represents Kemet's purest state, one we return to now. Ptah will erase the heresy. Sekhmet will erase all memory of plague and protect us. Ma'at shall reign for millions and millions of years."

Cheers sounded from those assembled. While none wished to continue Akhenaten's folly, most did not wish to return to the days when the priesthood of Amun held sway. Most, but not all. Ay and his priests glowered at me and left the banquet hall.

Chapter 60

Having made my announcement, I settled in to enjoy the rest of the banquet. I ate sparingly but savored every morsel. The music coursed through me, my heart beating in time to the sistrums and cymbals. The dancing girls writhed, hips and breasts swaying. I ordered more wine.

"It does not worry you to see your father cozying up to the priests of Amun?" said Bek.

"It does not worry me tonight. I shall concern myself with it tomorrow." I took a deep draught of the wine and relished the way my head began to swim. I put the glass down. "Tonight, I have had enough of crowds. Shall we retire to a more private location?"

"You go ahead," he said. "First, I want to find out where Ay went with those priests."

"If you must, but do not take too long." I walked away, hips swaying to the music in what I hoped was an alluring fashion.

On the way to my quarters, I felt lighter than I had in many years. Perhaps ever. And it was not the wine. Within a few short years, Tutankhptah would take his place as king in deed, instead of just name, and I would be free. I could return to the Temple of Sekhmet. I could retire to an estate in Shedet. I could even remain with the court and become the terrifying dowager, as Tiye had done. So very many possibilities.

At the door to my apartments, the guard bowed his head. "Highness." He shifted his gaze so as not to meet mine.

I entered to find Ay seated on the corner of my desk. I moved to call my guard, but the door closed.

"You seem alarmed to see me," said Ay.

"You should not be here," I said. "My guards have orders not to let anybody in."

He stood. "The priests of Amun have considerable backing. Undermining them was a mistake."

"It pains me to see you throw your lot in with them, Father. You know how they undermine the role of the king. And you do not need their support."

"It is you I do not need. You said it yourself — my granddaughter is on the throne; my position is secure." He grinned. "You have made yourself obsolete."

The lightness I had felt only moments earlier left me. It felt as though a stone had lodged itself in my belly. I clutched at my dress to keep my hands from shaking. "Once again, you speak of treason. A crime punishable by death."

Ay took a step toward me, fists clenched, every muscle in his chest and arms taut. I resisted the urge of my child-self to flinch under his scrutiny, and instead held myself firm.

"Ah, Neferneferuaten." My once-held coronation name oozed from his lips. "You are no longer the reigning monarch. You could have been, but you prefer the power behind the throne. Neither are you popular with certain factions. You will not be missed."

Before I could even grasp the true meaning of his words, well-honed instincts took over. I feinted left, and when Ay followed, I spun around, gathering up the skirt of my dress and tucking it into my sash.

With my movement now unrestricted, I picked up a chair and swung it at him. He moved, and so avoided the full impact, but it did put him momentarily off-balance.

I ran to the door of my chamber, slamming right into the doors and getting bounced back. I pushed on them. Barred from the outside.

An arm closed around my neck and raised me off the floor. I grabbed at the arm, trying to dislodge it, but though advanced in years, Ay was still a powerful man.

My vision darkened. Desperate, I clawed and scratched.

Ay lowered me until my feet touched the floor. He loosened his hold but did not let go. I gasped for breath, and still he held firm. In that moment, I knew he could not kill me. Not even he could go so far. Even so, I knew I would never forget.

His free hand stroked my wig. "Nefertiti, my pet," he whispered. "You were the best of my children. The smartest, the strongest. I always loved you best."

"I know, Father," I said, and stroked the arm still resting against my breast. Perhaps, I thought, he would accept a governorship in Kush. He would see that as an honor, not a demotion, and would not fight me on it.

The hand stroking my hair cupped an ear. The other hand cupped the other. Too late, I knew I had erred. One quick twist, a sound like the snapping of wood, and blackness ...

Field of Reeds

Ma'at herself stays the beast. She holds on until I can see what she must have known. The scales have not yet struck a balance. For now, my heart rises until it is level with the feather, and still it rises.

When the heart sinks again, I do not move a single muscle. At last, the scales come to rest, and it appears the heart and the feather are level.

There is a commotion amongst the gods.

"It cannot be," says Anpu. "I have followed her actions. Her heart must surely be heavier than the feather."

The gods gather around, crowding me out so I can no longer see.

"The heart is heavier," says Wesir.

"You are mistaken; it is lighter," says Aset.

I am now shaking. I will not be allowed to continue the journey. I will cease to exist.

"Throw the heart to Ammit," says Anpu.

More discussion and arguing.

"That is not the way it is done," says Nut. "When there is disagreement, the ka is allowed to continue, given a chance to redeem itself."

"An exception must be made for this one," says Heru. "By her actions, we were banished from all the land and made to wither."

"She must pay," says Anpu.

Enough. I can endure it no longer. My entire life was spent in adversity. Every time I dared raise my hopes, they were dashed. If the afterlife is to be more of the same, I want no part of it. I rise and approach the gods. "Anpu is right. Throw my heart to Ammit and let me die forever. It is no more than I deserve."

"That is truly your wish?" says Aset.

I bow my head. "I failed my children. I failed Kemet, and I failed the gods. I am not worthy of eternal life."

"She will move on," says a voice I recognize.

I look up to find Sekhmet looking at me. "I claimed her ka when she was but a child. The decision is mine. She must still pass through seven more gates. She will show us her true worth."

I spent a lifetime trying to run from her dictates, and now at the end, she would deny me my last wish? I open my mouth, but Sekhmet cuts me off.

"No, I do not grant you this wish, for you know not what you are asking," she says. "You spent the few paltry years of your life evading your responsibilities and think you would be better off dead for eternity. Did I choose a witless idiot after all?"

I am confused. "I failed you most of all."

Sekhmet shook her head. "You chose the longer, more difficult road, but you eventually fulfilled your promise."

"But, I did not elevate you to most high."

"I did not ask you to. I only asked you to restore Ma'at." She took my hands. "The time of Ptah and Sekhmet is long past. Now is the time for Amun and Mut. Ma'at is merely balance; balance does not mean nothing ever changes."

I stare at her.

"Well? Get back in the boat lest I change my mind." She leans closer to whisper in my ear. "Do not fret. You have already passed the greatest challenges. The rest of the way is easy by comparison.

I nod, and she follows me back onto the barque.

I step out of the barque, into the sunlight. After so much time in darkness, I have to shield my eyes. As far as I can see, reeds dance in the wind. They must be cut with channels of water, for here and there, ducks rise and flap away into the distance.

A figure, black against the light, approaches. I freeze, not knowing who it is. As the figure nears, his head blocks out the sun, and I can see his face. I run to him and touch his cheek. "I did not expect to find you here."

"I went to your quarters, as planned. I found Ay with your corpse. He could not allow me to live."

"Oh, Bek." Yet another death I am responsible for. "I am so sorry."

He smiles. "I am not." He takes a hand. "Come, let me show you this new land."

I pull him close for a kiss.

Historical Notes

Ancient Egypt was the longest continuous cosmopolitan culture the world has ever seen, lasting from Narmer who first united Egypt into a single kingdom in approximately 3100BCE until Cleopatra VII's defeat by Rome in 30BCE. To give you an idea of the scale of this time period, the pyramids at Giza, built around 2500BCE, were more ancient to Cleopatra than she is to us. To Nefertiti, who lived in the fourteenth century BCE, the pyramids were as Charlemagne is to us, and Cleopatra was still more than a thousand years in the future.

Ancient Egypt was also the most conservative culture the world has ever seen. Look at a temple, a statue, a painting, or a hieroglyphic text from any point on that entire timeline, and it is recognizably Egyptian, even to the layperson. The Egyptian ideal was for everything to remain the same forever – this was part of their concept of cosmic balance, or Ma'at. In three thousand years, art, religion, and the role of the Pharaoh never changed, except for one brief period lasting less than twenty years. It was during this period that Nefertiti lived.

The ideal historical fiction narrative tells a compelling story without sacrificing historical accuracy. This ideal is not easy to achieve. The advantage of writing about such a distant time period is that there is much that we don't know for certain, which left me a great deal of leeway when crafting this novel. While I tried as much as possible to stick with valid theories held by

Egyptologists, there are a few times where I deliberately strayed from solidly known facts for the sake of the story. Here is where I separate facts from guesses from fabrication.

A Note on Terminology

Egypt's final royal dynasty, the Ptolemies (which culminated in Cleopatra VII) was actually Greek. While Egyptian culture continued undisturbed, the Greek rulers established sizable Greek populations within Egypt, most notably at Alexandria. This resulted in Hellenized names for many Egyptian gods and cities. Later Arab invasions further changed some of the geographical terms. It is largely these Greek and Arabic names that we are familiar with today.

For the sake of authenticity, I chose to use the Egyptian words for all proper nouns. In the accompanying maps and list of gods, I have given both the Egyptian name and the more familiar name.

Status of Women

While Ancient Egyptian women did not enjoy gender equality as we understand it today, they came much closer than in any other contemporaneous culture. Indeed, Egyptian culture granted women a degree of freedom and equality seen in very few cultures up until the twentieth century.

Women could marry as they chose, they could own property, and they retained their property after a divorce. It was unusual for a woman to work in a paid profession, but if she did, she was paid the same as a man doing the same work – something our own culture has yet to achieve.

Both sons and daughters were equally valued for who they were, not for the work they could contribute to the family. Children were usually educated in the profession of their parents. Boys would be trained in a trade, while girls were taught how to run a household. Boys might go to a temple school where they learned reading, writing, math, history, and other subjects. Theoretically, these schools were open to all boys, but in reality, only wealthy families could afford it. Noble girls may be given an education similar to that of their brothers, but this would most often be accomplished with tutors coming into the home.

A possible exception may have been those specifically training for the priesthood. The type of well-rounded education I gave to Nefertiti would certainly have been highly unusual, but I believe it to be within the realm of possibility, especially given the predominance of strong, intelligent women in the royal family of the period.

Marriage

There is no evidence of any kind of marriage ceremony from Ancient Egypt. Instead, both parties signed a contract, much like a modern prenuptial agreement, and the couple moved in together. The wife likely negotiated and signed on her own behalf. There are some examples where this is not the case, but they have to do with a slave who had not yet been freed, and an underage girl, and in both these cases one would expect that permission would be needed.

Judging by the large volume of love poetry surviving from the period, love was considered an important ingredient of marriage, even if it were not the driving factor in choosing a partner (and maybe it was, we don't know).

With royalty, however, marriage was more of a political necessity than a romantic endeavor. Therefore, it is possible, perhaps likely, that royal women were left out of negotiations.

Sexuality

Egyptians had few inhibitions about sex. They did not consider female virginity to be a requirement for marriage, and indeed did not seem to even have a concept of virginity. Unmarried people – both men and women – were free to take partners as they chose.

While fleshing out this novel, I came to the logical conclusion that with this outlook, experience would be appreciated. So, when I gave Akhenaten this preference, I was not intending to make him seem enlightened, but merely the product of a society that placed no value on virginity.

Adultery was a punishable offense and was considered a worse offense for women. The usual punishment was divorce, and that was the worst a man could expect. A woman could conceivably be killed for it, though this seems to have been rare. Presumably, there would be some degree of latitude if the man were the King, and the woman had no choice. Notably, if a man committed adultery, it was considered a worse offense if the woman was also married than if she were single.

Egyptians used both abortion and contraception. Various recipes survive for contraceptive suppositories. Some are questionable, containing ingredients such as crocodile dung (perhaps more of a repellent than a true contraceptive?). One used a mix of acacia and honey, and this may have been reasonably effective as acacia is now known to have spermicidal properties. For the purposes of my story, however, I needed a contraceptive that could be administered without the woman knowing about it. Silphium is a plant that is generally believed to be extinct (but has possibly recently been discovered still growing in Turkey); however, it was well known in the ancient Mediterranean. It became so popular in Egypt that they Egyptians developed a unique hieroglyph for it. It was used as a contraceptive, but as I indicate in the narrative, it was also useful for digestive ailments, as well as colds, sore throats, fevers, and a number of other ailments. Unfortunately, the first written reference of silphium's use in Egypt dates to a few hundred years after Nefertiti. It is possible, though, that its use was known by at least a few in Egypt before it came into widespread use, and if that were the case, the ones who would know would have been the priesthood of Sekhmet, the healer.

Both birthwort and aloe were likely used by the Egyptians to induce abortions. However, as depicted in the novel, using aloe for this purpose is quite dangerous, possibly even fatal. Do not try it. Herbs in general can be dangerous when misused. Always seek professional advice when using herbal remedies for any issue.

Medicine

Egyptians had some knowledge of anatomical structures. However, they lacked knowledge of how the internal organs worked. There are a few surviving medical texts, which contain a combination of surgical procedures, herbal remedies, amulets, chants and prayers. That is not to say their medical practices were primitive – in fact, some of their procedures would not be surpassed until modern times. One of those was their insistence on cleanliness.

Poppy was one of the herbs used in Egyptian medicine, and there is evidence that it was well known during the time of Nefertiti.

Physicians were almost always men, but there were likely a handful of women who worked in the profession as well. Sekhmet was the goddess of healing, and her priests were frequently trained as physicians, so it was not a big leap to assume some of her priestesses may have also been. While physicians performed all manner of procedures, what they did not do was manage childbirth. As midwifery was not an acknowledged profession, this duty fell to village women, in the case of peasants, or to household servants, in the case of the nobility. These women trained as apprentices and were highly skilled. Wealthy households would keep at least one woman trained in childbirth specifically for this purpose, though she may have performed other duties as well.

Plague

It is likely that plague did rage through Egypt during the reign of Akhenaten, as many members of the royal family, including several of the young princesses disappeared from public record. Given that Akhenaten's father seemed anxious to pacify Sekhmet, goddess of plague (he ordered the construction of 600 statues of her), it is possible that Egypt suffered from plague periodically at this time. There are medical records referring to plague, and it did come from the east, as it was referred to as the Asiatic illness.

It's not known what exactly what this plague was. It is speculated that it may have been bubonic plague, or it might have been the first instance of influenza transferring from animals to people. As people had never encountered influenza before, it would have been far more deadly than it is today, perhaps even more so than in 1918. I needed an illness that would confer at least some immunity after having had it once. Both bubonic plague and influenza fit that bill, but I also needed an illness that wouldn't leave the country completely paralyzed. Bubonic plague isn't contagious enough to spread the way I needed it to (given Egypt's relative cleanliness in comparison to Medieval Europe) unless it transforms into pneumonic plague, in which case it would have killed too many. So, I went with influenza.

The Afterlife

Most people today have at least heard of the Egyptian Book of the Dead (or the *Book of Coming Forth by Day*, as the Egyptians called it). The origins of this book date back to the time of the pyramids, and by the time of Nefertiti it was often written onto scrolls and buried with the dead. Royalty, however, tended to prefer a different book, the Amduat (called the *Book of the Hidden Chamber* by the Egyptians).

The descriptions of the Duat in the novel are a blend of those in the above two books, as well as the *Book of Gates*. This third book became popular among the royalty during the Nineteenth Dynasty, but its first appearance was in the tomb of the Horemheb, the last King of the Eighteenth Dynasty. Horemheb ascended to the throne about fifteen years after the death of Akhenaten, and his Great Royal Wife was a woman named Mutnedjmet, who may have been Nefertiti's younger sister. It is a reasonable conclusion that this book reflected beliefs about the afterlife held by Egyptians during Nefertiti's lifetime.

Nefertiti

We do not know for sure who Nefertiti was, or where she came from. There is a theory that she was a foreign princess given in marriage to Akhenaten, or even to his father originally. Evidence supporting this is found in her name, which means "the beautiful one has arrived". Kings of Egypt frequently added foreigners to their harems, but to make one the Great Royal Wife would have been unorthodox to say the least. Then again, Akhenaten was hardly a model of conventional behavior.

Evidence that argues against this identification is the fact that Ay's wife Tey held the title of Nefertiti's nurse. Had Nefertiti arrived in Egypt as an adult, she would hardly have needed a nurse. Sometimes this title was used to indicate a stepmother relationship, which may make Nefertiti the daughter of Ay by a previous wife.

Nothing is known of Nefertiti's childhood. However, if she were the daughter of Ay, entering the priesthood would have been in keeping with the Egyptian custom of training children in the professions of their parents as Ay's mother was a well- respected priestess.

Nefertiti did have six daughters, and no sons that we know of. There is no evidence that she ever committed adultery, or that any of the children were fathered by anybody other than Akhenaten. Also, the younger two girls were not twins, and I have no reason for making them twins other than expediency. Frankly, it got tedious having to write in yet another pregnancy every year or two. There's a reason why fictional characters seldom have large families.

When Nefertiti died is a matter of debate. It used to be thought she died, or was sent away, in about year twelve of Akhenaten's reign because she disappeared from inscriptions. That is now known not to be the case and it is believed that Kiya was the one who disappeared. At that time, Akhenaten crowned a co-regent, who was possibly Neferneferuaten, who used the feminine epithet, "effective for her husband," or may have been Smenkhkare (more on this individual later). In any event, there is a reference to Nefertiti firmly dated to the very end of Akhenaten's reign, and there is at least one representation of her as a mature woman, suggesting that she likely outlived her husband.

Nefertiti is generally thought to have been a firm supporter of Akhenaten's reforms because she is always depicted as such. Indeed, she is often depicted as an active participant. Keeping in mind that Egyptian art was highly stylized, and that what was carved onto temple walls was more propaganda than truth, I asked the question – what if she wasn't?

There is a mummy tentatively identified as Akhenaten. The coffin was almost certainly built for him, though whether or not the mummy inside is the coffin's original owner is up for debate. It was found in tomb KV55, which contained other artifacts from Akhenaten's family. As well, DNA analysis shows the mummy to be the child of Amenhotep III and Queen Tiye, so if he is not Akhenaten, he must be a brother (assuming the DNA analysis is accurate, and this is not universally accepted). The names on the coffin were hacked out in antiquity. Egyptians believed that speaking the name of the dead caused him to live again, so the removal of the name suggests this was someone hated, someone the populace did not want to live again. Akhenaten would fit this description.

Whether or not the mummy inside the coffin is Akhenaten, if the coffin was his it is interesting in that it indicates a traditional Egyptian burial, not an Atenist burial. Barring the possibility that he reverted back to worshipping the old gods near the end of his life, and I know of no evidence that he did, someone must of have arranged this traditional burial for him. If Nefertiti was his co-regent, and if she survived him, it would have been her. I know, that's a lot of ifs, but that's why I write fiction and not history textbooks.

Nefertiti's tomb has never been found, and her mummy has never been positively identified.

Akhenaten

Surprisingly little is known of Akhenaten's childhood. He had an older brother who was supposed to inherit the throne but died before he could.

There have long been theories that Akhenaten had some kind of physical ailment that resulted in his bizarre appearance. Froelich's syndrome has been suggested, but the problem with that theory is that Froelich's leaves its sufferers infertile. While we might allow that Nefertiti could have managed one or two children with another man, the idea that she pulled it off six times is difficult to accept. Marfan's is the current favorite, and it has the advantage of not resulting in infertility. However, the theory I subscribe to is that the strange appearance of Akhenaten and the royal family was nothing more than an artistic style. Egyptian art was highly stylized in order to convey ideas as well as images. I believe Akhenaten deliberately chose to exaggerate certain of his physical features in order to put him above the common people, and he chose an androgynous appearance to reflect the androgenous nature of the Aten. Earlier depictions of Akhenaten did not have these strange features, but whether that means earlier artists were downplaying his deformities or later artists were inventing them, we'll probably never know.

In the popular imagination, Akhenaten is often seen as a religious visionary who was centuries ahead of his time, a dreamer who was so wrapped up in devotion to his one god that he neglected his kingly duties and the empire collapsed around him. In reality, Akhenaten's religious revolution may have been less motivated by genuine belief than by self-preservation, and self-aggrandizement.

During the reign of Akhenaten's father, Amenhotep III, the priesthood of Amun was very powerful. Amenhotep feared that they may one day try to usurp the throne. This fear was not unfounded, for they did exactly that about three hundred years later, and it's possible they may have done so sooner had Amenhotep III and Akhenaten not taken steps to curb their power. As I indicated in the novel, the great power of the priests of Amun may have been partly attributable to the female King, Hatshepsut, who curried their favor in order to stay on the throne.

Amenhotep III made small changes by promoting the worship of the Aten and slowly lessening the influence of the Amun priesthood. Instead of continuing his father's subtle reforms, Akhenaten chose to disenfranchise Amun and his priests all at once and elevate the Aten to supreme god. It used to be believed he elevated Aten to the position of sole god; however, this is no longer universally accepted.

The Aten was unique among Egyptian gods because he was the god for all people, everywhere. The Hymn to the Aten, purportedly written by Akhenaten himself, resembles Psalm 104 closely enough to suggest that there was some influence back and forth between Akhenaten and the Hebrews, but in which direction is difficult to say. However, Akhenaten's monotheism did not resemble that of Abraham in any way. The Aten could only be worshipped by Akhenaten and members of his immediate family, which would include Nefertiti, and their daughters. Everybody else worshipped the royal family, and noble homes of the period included altars to Akhenaten and Nefertiti. In year twelve, Akhenaten went even further by declaring himself to be the Aten.

We know Akhenaten died in year seventeen of his reign, but we do not know how. Given the unpopularity of his rule, murder is not out of the question. He was originally buried in the royal tomb at Akhetaten and is believed to have been moved to the Valley of the Kings later.

Bek

A Bek really existed. He was the chief sculptor during the reign of Akhenaten, and his father was Men, the previous chief sculptor. His wife's name was Taheret. He was also given the title of architect and was known as "the apprentice whom his Majesty has taught". This suggests he was instructed by Akhenaten in the new artistic style.

There is no evidence that the historical Bek was Men's son by adoption, or that he had been born a farmer. There is no evidence that he ever had a sexual relationship with Nefertiti, or fathered children with her, and I have no idea how he would feel about the suggestion. Though, he may be pleased at the physical attributes I gave him – statues show him to have been a rather portly gentleman.

Tiye

Unlike Nefertiti, we know exactly who Tiye's parents were. Her mother, Tjuyu, was a priestess. Her father, Yuya, was a courtier. Tiye was a commoner, and it was a break with tradition for Amenhotep III to elevate a commoner to Great Royal wife, but it did set a precedent for his son to do the same.

Ay

As I have already mentioned, it is not known for certain that Ay was Nefertiti's father, but it is a reasonable choice. Ay was as ambitious as I have portrayed him. After the death of Tutankhamun, he married the widow Ankhesenamun, possibly his own granddaughter, in order to claim the title of King. Given his advanced age at that time, he ruled for only about four years. After his death, the kingship passed to the general Horemheb, who consolidated his claim by (possibly) marrying Ay's (supposed) younger daughter, Mutnedjmet.

Kiya

Like Nefertiti, we don't know who Kiya was or where she came from, but she was Akhenaten's secondary wife, and for a brief period, was his favorite.

Some scholars think she may have been the Naharin princess Tadukhepa, who was given in marriage to Akhenaten's father, and later inherited by Akhenaten. Alternatively, she may have been Egyptian. I chose to create another Naharin princess sent directly to Akhenaten. Some of the letters I include were actual letters that went back and forth between Amenhotep III and the Naharin king.

Kiya was almost certainly a nickname, because it means "monkey," and there is no record of her real name. She did have one, or possibly two, daughters, and maybe a son, or maybe not. She disappeared from the public record in about year twelve of Akhenaten's reign, indicating she either fell out of favor, or died. I decided it would be both.

Smenkhkare

For those readers who are aficionados of Akhenaten, Smenkhkare is the character who is conspicuous by his absence. Smenkhkare was either Akhenaten's coregent in years 12-13, or his immediate successor, ruling for only about a year prior to the accession of Tutankhaten to the throne. His Great Royal Wife was Nefertiti's oldest daughter, Meritaten.

Smenkhkare is another mysterious personage. He may have been a son, or a brother, of Akhenaten. He may have been Tutankhaten's father. He may even have been a foreign prince. Some think "he" was actually Nefertiti. The all-male epithets of Smenkhkare argue against this identification; however, the female ruler Hatshepsut used male terminology. It's possible Nefertiti did, too, and it's even possible she evolved her public persona over time from the male Smenkhkare to the female Neferneferuaten, or vice versa.

Smenkhkare is the other strong possibility for the mummy tentatively identified as Akhenaten. If so, as a child of Amenhotep III and Tiye, he would have been Akhenaten's full brother.

I chose to go with the idea that Nefertiti and Smenkhkare were the same person, and chose to eliminate the name Smenkhkare altogether, largely for the sake of simplicity.

Meritaten

The oldest daughter of Nefertiti, and Akhenaten, Meritaten ruled with Smenkhkare either during her father's reign or after her father's death.

Meritaten seems to have been named Great Royal Wife in year twelve, either to Smenkhkare or jointly to both her parents. If the latter is true, there is no evidence that Akhenaten considered it a real marriage, or that he ever had a sexual relationship with her.

Meketaten

Meketaten, the second daughter, died during year fourteen. She would have been between the ages of ten and twelve.

A scene in the family tomb at Akhetaten shows Nefertiti and Akhenaten mourning their daughter, while a servant holds a royal infant. This has led to speculation that the child was Meketaten's, and that she died in childbirth attempting to give her father the son he so desperately needed. However, nothing in the scene indicates that Meketaten was the mother of the child. The child may have been Tutankhaten, who was probably either her full- or half-brother. Or, has recently been suggested, the infant may symbolize Meketaten herself. Meketaten may have fallen victim to plagues that were ravaging the country. Or, she may indeed have died in childbirth.

Ankhesenpaaten

The third daughter was the one who survived longest. After her father's death, she married Tutankhaten (probably her full- or half-brother) and ruled as Great Royal Wife for about ten years. Early on, they restored Egypt's traditional religion, and she changed her name to Akhesenamun. After her first husband died, she married Ay (probably her grandfather). She most likely died some time during his brief reign, as no further records of her have ever been found.

Tutankhaten

In case you haven't sussed it out already, yes, Tutankhaten is King Tut. When he reversed Akhenaten's religious reforms, he changed his name to Tutankhamun.

It is not known for certain who Tutankhaten's parents were. The possible mummy of Akhenaten has been shown to be Tutankhaten's father through DNA analysis. DNA analysis also showed that his mother was the "younger lady" found in KV35 alongside Queen Tiye, and that she was his father's full sister. There are issues with the DNA analysis, among them the fact that this apparent brother-sister relationship could also be produced by three consecutive generations of first-cousin marriage, which in this family is a quite possible. This interpretation would make Nefertiti a candidate for Tutankhaten's mother. However, I chose to take the analysis at face value and decided Tutankhaten's parents were full siblings.

Amenhotep III and Queen Tiye had five daughters together (or maybe four as it's possible Nebetah and Beketaten were the same person – untangling family relationships 3,000 years on can be quite a challenge!), and it is not known which one was Tutankhaten's mother. There is no record of Akhenaten marrying one of his sisters, though this would have been a normal course of events for the King. Since we don't know Kiya's parentage, it's possible that she was the sister (Kiya was probably a nickname, remember). Since we can't say for certain who Nefertiti's parents were, it's possible she was the sister. And all of this is assuming that Tut's father is indeed Akhenaten, and not a different son of Amenhotep III and Tiye, in which case both Kiya and Nefertiti can be eliminated as candidates for his mother. I opted for Akhenaten as Tut's father, and the second youngest sister, Nebetah, as the mother, because at least two of the older sisters had been married to their father, and the youngest was still too young (assuming Nebetah and Beketaten were two different people).

CT scans of Tut's mummy reveal that he had a clubfoot, on the left. He would have always walked on the side of that foot. One hundred and thirty walking staffs were discovered in his tomb, most of which show signs of wear. As well, he had a partially cleft palate. This would have affected his speech development in early childhood. It would also have left him vulnerable to ear infections as an infant and toddler, which would have temporarily affected his hearing, and further delayed his speech. While this was something he could have overcome with time, given that even today deaf people can be mistaken for the developmentally disabled, it is possible that he was considered to be incapable of ruling, especially in early childhood. There is no evidence that he possessed exceptionally high intelligence, but also no evidence that he didn't.

Were Akhenaten and his Family Black?

At the time of writing, this question generates a great deal of controversy on the internet. Debates get quite heated. I am going to present the evidence we have available at this time. I am not responsible for the evidence, I am only reporting it, so please don't send me nasty e-mails.

I'm going to start with the more basic question – Were the ancient Egyptians black? First, it's important to recognize that the question is anachronistic. The ancient Egyptians were certainly xenophobic – anyone who wasn't Egyptian was inferior – but there is no evidence that they categorized people based on skin color, or that they held any kind of prejudice in this regard. Indeed, there are multiple examples of people of foreign origin (with, presumably, varying skin colors) assimilating into Egyptian culture and achieving high rank in society. But, looking through a modern lens, the answer to the question of whether or not ancient Egyptians were black is yes … and, also no.

Modern Egyptians display an incredible variety of skin tones, and it's likely most of this diversity was present in ancient times. The same Sinai Peninsula that gave the earliest human migrants a land route out of Africa also gave easy entry to later populations migrating back in. Prior to the desertification of the Sahara, Northern Africa was a most desirable place to be for paleolithic hunters, so there were multitudes returning. As a result, by the time Narmer united Egypt in around 3100BCE, thereby beginning Pharaonic history, the continent had already been blending together many cultures over many thousands of years. In addition, as an ancient superpower, Egypt incorporated communities of foreigners who assimilated into the local culture, but originated in countries now called Jordan, Syria, Iraq, Sudan, Libya, Greece, and possibly more.

So, the population was diverse, but what about Akhenaten's family? There is a strong belief that his mother, Queen Tiye, was black. This belief probably stems from the appearance of her famous bust, now in the Neues Museum in Berlin. It's carved from a dark-colored wood, giving the impression that she was dark-complexioned. The bust also appears to have an afro. I say "appears" because it is actually a headdress. Her hair is not shown at all.

It happens that we know quite a bit about Tiye's origins. She comes from a town in the south of Egypt known to be home to populations from Kush, in modern-day Sudan. We have a mummy that has been identified as Tiye with a high degree of certainty and we also have the mummies of both of her parents, Yuya and Tjuyu. While mummies don't preserve skin color, we can still get quite a bit of information.

Yuya, Tiye's father, has a large, hooked nose more characteristic of people of the Near East than Africa. In addition, he has a beard, which was highly unusual for an Egyptian, but was fashionable for people in the Levant area during this period. This was my basis for giving Ay, Tiye and Nefertiti a Naharin origin. That, and the fact that the name Yuya had multiple spellings, rare for an Egyptian name, but in keeping with a foreign name that Egyptian scribes were trying to transliterate into hieroglyphs.

Tiye still boasts a luxuriant head of hair. This hair is curly but is not an afro. She and her mother, Tjuyu, both have narrow, yet prominent noses. So, they are not likely 100% black. However, both of these mummies share another feature: the jaw is more prominent than the forehead. This is common in sub-Saharan African people, but uncommon elsewhere.

On the balance of evidence, Tiye, Great Royal Wife of Amenhotep III, and her relatives and descendants, including Akhenaten and Nefertiti, Tutankhamun, Ankhesenamun and Ay, seem to have been mixed race, as we would define the term today. It is possible that her bust is an accurate portrayal of her skin color, but we have no way of knowing that for sure.

As a side note, Egypt was invaded and defeated by Kush, and was ruled by sub-Saharan African kings for almost a hundred years in the eighth and seventh centuries BCE, about seven hundred years after Tiye's time.

Epilogue

During his reign, Horemheb (I know all the names are confusing, but he's the one who married Nefertiti's sister) nearly obliterated the names of everyone associated with the heretic Akhenaten, including Nefertiti and Tutankhamun. It's not known whether he did this out of anger or hate, or whether it was a more calculated decision to establish himself as a legitimate king and the restorer of Ma'at.

If it was his intention to erase the memory of Akhenaten and Nefertiti, Horemheb made one serious error. In dismantling the temples, he reused their blocks as filler in some of his own constructions, leaving them for archaeologists to discover. He also either failed or decided not to completely eradicate the failed city of Akhetaten. Beginning in the eighteenth century, fortune hunters and archaeologists began to uncover tombs, temples, and artifacts, slowly putting together the story of the heretic king and his queen. In the early 1900s, the now iconic bust was discovered in a sculptor's workshop (not Bek's, unfortunately), turning the name Nefertiti into a household word.

Ironically, it was this obliteration that led the ancients themselves to forget the existence of King Tut, especially after one of the region's rare flash floods covered all trace of Tut's tomb, allowing it alone of all the tombs in the Valley of the Kings (at least, of those so far), to remain undisturbed for three thousand years. The discovery of Tut's tomb by Howard Carter in 1922 unleashed on the world a madness for all things Egyptian that, for some of us at least, is not one bit diminished a century later.

If the Ancient Egyptians were right, and to speak the name of the dead is to cause them to live again, then Nefertiti is with us still.

Kemet (Egypt)

Ribu (Libya)
Iunu (Heliopolis)
Shedet (Fayoum)
Mennefer (Memphis)
Mafkat (Sinai)
Akhetaten (Amarna)
The River (Nile)
Waset (Thebes)
Kush (Nubia)

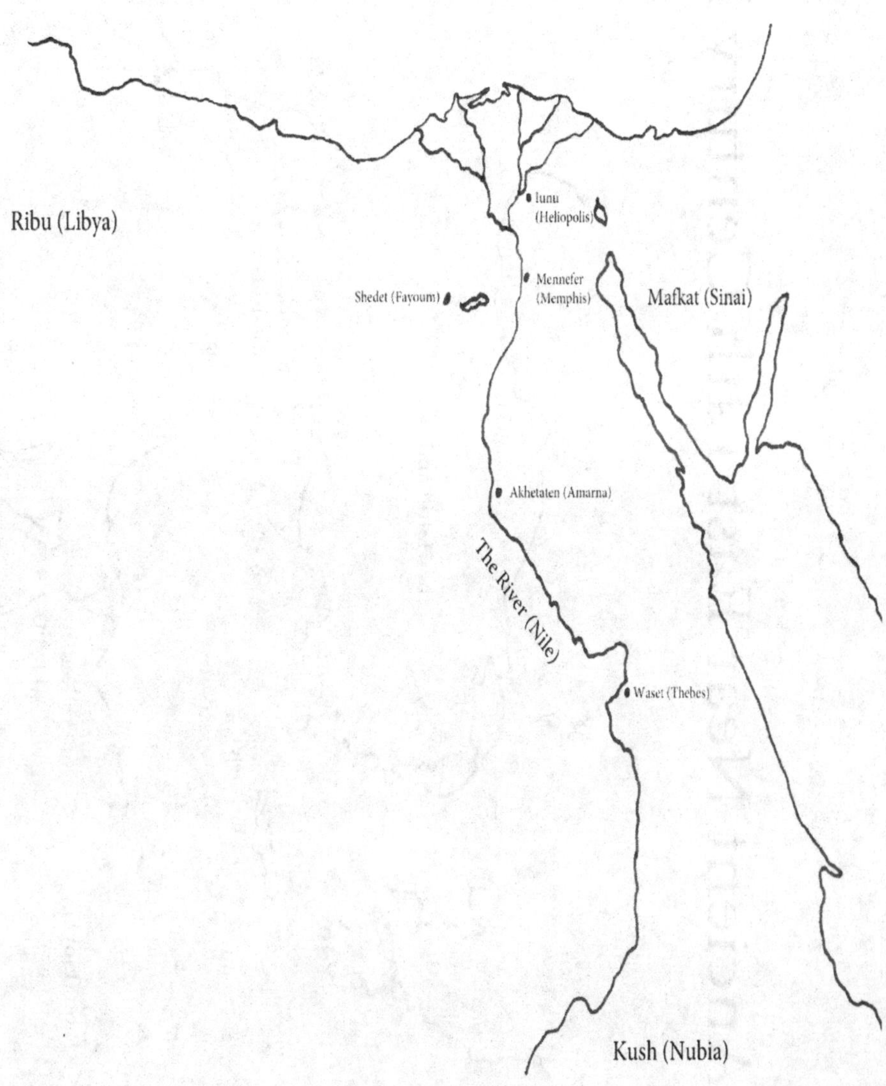

Ancient Near East 14th Century BCE

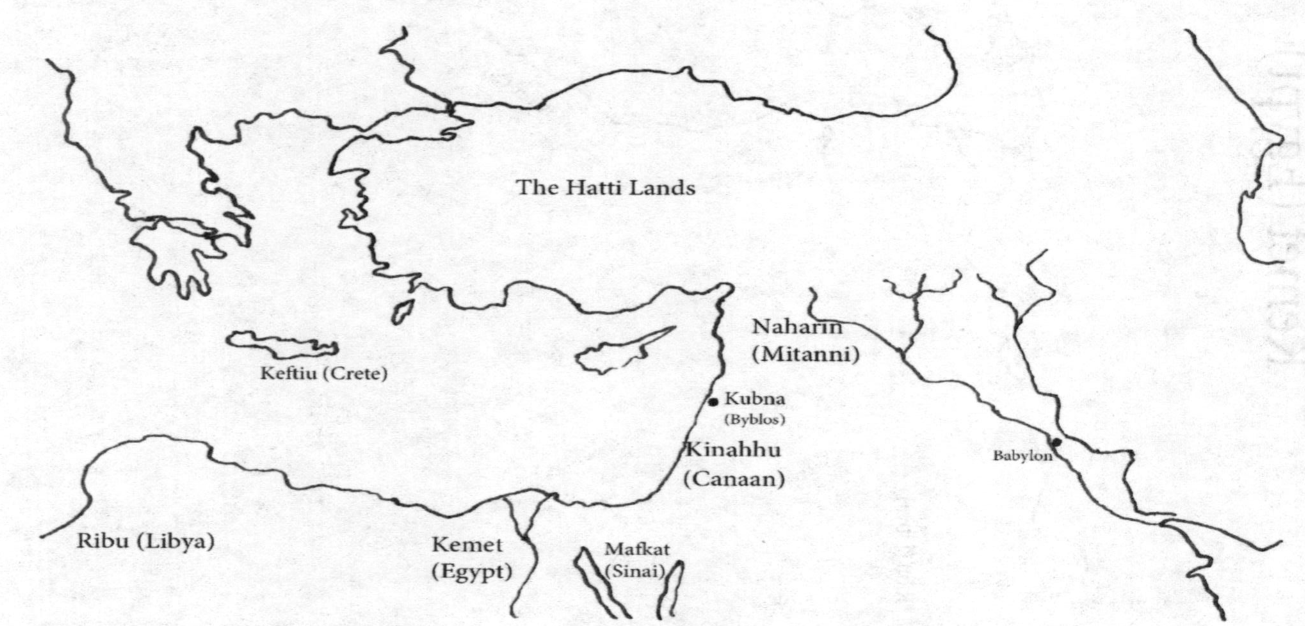

Acknowledgments

The term "writer" tends to evoke images of toiling in solitude and darkness, the only illumination coming from the computer screen. As accurate as this may be during parts of the process, a book doesn't happen without the help of other people.

Many thanks to my early readers – Laury Hickling, Carol Drewell, Jayne Richards, Kelly Brooks, and Mel Cober. Your insights were invaluable for crafting a rough draft into a solid manuscript.

To Sue Reynolds and James Dewar – your many writing classes and workshops, complete with deadlines, kept me on track. Your consistent, and gentle, feedback always let me know what was working and what wasn't. Your support of my work made me think that maybe, just perhaps, my writing didn't suck quite as badly as I thought. My heartfelt thanks.

Thanks also to Sherry Hinman, the first editor who took on my manuscript. Your comments were both constructive and thorough, and without your input my book would not have been ready to pitch to agents and publishers.

All my love to my children – Willow, Lorelei, Riley, Ayesha, and Earle – who always have to share me with "the book" and who often make every effort (at times even successfully) to keep the noise down so I can write.

Last, but definitely not least, to all the staff at Liminal Books for seeing something special in my manuscript, for taking a chance on a novice, and for putting so much time and effort into turning my idea into an actual book. Abby Macenka, cofounder, Siân Hyleg, author services coordinator, Penny Dowden, editor, Cherie Fox, graphic designer. THANK YOU!!

Lisa Llamrei was born and raised in the Toronto area. She studied languages at York University. At various times, she has been an actor, professional belly dancer, holistic nutritionist and entrepreneur. She currently lives north of Toronto with her family.